Praise for
Hope's Enduring

"Honor, love, and duty collide with a young man's passion to pursue God's unique calling on his life. Love and sacrifice conflict with a young woman's desire for friendship and normalcy. Kim Vogel Sawyer paints a vivid picture of the struggle between chasing the dreams God plants in our hearts and our desire to please and honor those we love. She reveals the beauty of God's prevenient grace and provision in ways we could never orchestrate—and the ultimate weaving of exquisite tapestries in surrendered lives. *Hope's Enduring Echo* is a novel rich in friendship, faith, love, and the resiliency of hope. A story to lift your heart and warm your soul."

—CATHY GOHLKE, Christy Award Hall of Fame, author of
Ladies of the Lake and *This Promised Land*

"*Hope's Enduring Echo* is a beautifully written story about finding hope in a dark and shattered place. As a former Coloradoan, I loved reading the unique history that Kim Vogel Sawyer discovered in Cañon City and her poignant reminder about the miraculous ways God rescues and restores His children."

—MELANIE DOBSON, award-winning author of
Catching the Wind and the Legacy of Love series

Praise for
The Songbird of Hope Hill

"In *The Songbird of Hope Hill,* Kim Sawyer has penned an unforgettable story of God's grace and redemption. Birdie's and Ephraim's love story is a parable for the love God has for us. You'll be thinking of these characters long after you've turned the last page. I know I still am."

—KATHLEEN Y'BARBO, *Publishers Weekly* bestselling author of
The Black Midnight and *The Bayou Nouvelle Brides*

"Kim Vogel Sawyer blends affecting atmosphere, complex circumstances, challenging conflicts, and rewarding resolution in her historical novel *The Songbird of Hope Hill*. In Birdie Clarkson, Sawyer has created that character we all yearn to comfort—the sinner who desperately craves love for her broken, humbled heart. One can't help but cheer for Birdie in her brave willingness to step forward into peace and freedom. This book satisfies our longing to experience again the kind of forgiveness and divine justice that only Jesus can grant."

—TRISH PERRY, author of *The Guy I'm Not Dating*

"What a precious story of God's grace and redemption! Kim Vogel Sawyer writes with poignant precision, weaving stories with depth that draw in her readers. *The Songbird of Hope Hill* had my full attention from its absorbing start to its tender finish, leaving me teary-eyed—and longing for a sequel. Splendid!"

—SHARLENE MACLAREN, author of twenty-three novels

"*The Songbird of Hope Hill* held my heart from the first page. Set in Texas in 1895, this touching story is about Birdie Clarkson, a good girl who was forced to make bad decisions, and Ephraim Overly, the son of a minister and his wife who want to save fallen women. That task proves to be a tough one, and secrets from the past haunt these characters like an ever-blowing prairie wind. Fans of Francine Rivers's *Redeeming Love* should enjoy this story of redemption and one young woman's need to find grace and forgiveness."

—LENORA WORTH, author of *Disappearance in Pinecraft*

"Kim Vogel Sawyer's *The Songbird of Hope Hill* illustrates that no matter how often or how far we fall, God is always there to help us back up. Truly nothing—nothing—can separate us from the love of God."

—JULIANNA DEERING, author of
the Drew Farthering Mystery series

Praise for
The Tapestry of Grace

"In this heartwarming story, Kim Vogel Sawyer reminds us that family doesn't always mean people who are related by blood. With tender care, Sawyer has created characters with struggles, pain, and dreams that readers will recognize in their own lives. Through these fictional friends, we see how God's unending love and grace can mend and restore what was once lost or broken. The pages of *The Tapestry of Grace* are filled with the kind of hope every one of us yearns for."

—MICHELLE SHOCKLEE, *Christianity Today* Book Award– winning author of *Count the Nights by Stars*

"*The Tapestry of Grace* is yet another story that shows Kim Vogel Sawyer's amazing ability to take readers to a different era. Her research and authenticity are wonderful. Augusta and Konrad had me reading well past my bedtime. Told with a steady pace and wonderful details, this is a story that will hold your heart until the last page. I felt as if I lived in this small Kansas town, and frankly, I didn't want to leave!"

—LENORA WORTH, author of *The Christmas Quilt*

"Just like dipping your spoon into a delicious meal, the first taste of *The Tapestry of Grace* rewards the reader with strong characters and the tease of an intriguing plot. From the very first page and running through every chapter, the story de-livers the tantaliz- ing spice of complicated motives in main and minor characters. My heart warmed as I became invested in the lives of these ap- pealing people. Kim Sawyer must be congratulated for deliver- ing a savory story that nourishes the soul of the reader."

—DONITA K. PAUL, award-winning author of the DragonKeeper Chronicles

Other Novels by Kim Vogel Sawyer

Hope's Enduring Echo

Hope's Enduring Echo

A Novel

KIM VOGEL SAWYER

WATERBROOK

A WaterBrook Trade Paperback Original

Copyright © 2025 by Kim Vogel Sawyer

Title page art: ssmalomuzh, stock.adobe.com

LIBRARY OF CONGRESS CATALOGING-IN-PUBLICATION DATA
Names: Sawyer, Kim Vogel, author.
Title: Hope's enduring echo : a novel / Kim Vogel Sawyer.
Description: Colorado Springs : WaterBrook, 2025.
Identifiers: LCCN 2024034763 | ISBN 9780593600832 (trade paperback ;
acid-free paper) | ISBN 9780593600849 (ebook)
Subjects: LCGFT: Christian fiction. | Romance fiction. | Novels.
Classification: LCC PS3619.A97 H68 2025 | DDC 813/.6—dc23/eng/20240802
LC record available at https://lccn.loc.gov/2024034763

Printed in the United States of America on acid-free paper

waterbrookmultnomah.com

1st Printing

Book design by Virginia Norey

For my grandson Ethan, who aspires to uncover evidence of life from long ago. My prayers go with you as you forge a God-honoring path. I love you muchly!

I waited patiently for the LORD;
and he inclined unto me, and heard my cry.
—Psalm 40:1

Hope's Enduring Echo

Chapter One

1915
Near Cañon City, Colorado
Jennie Ward

Arms outstretched like a tightrope walker, Jennie placed one foot in front of the other and kept a slow yet steady pace on top of the wooden pipeline running along the edge of the Arkansas River. The wind, moist from swooshing into the ravine and over the surging water, flattened Daddy's cast-off cotton shirt against her front and tore at her braid. Little strands of hair worked loose and danced on her cheeks, tickling, but she paid them no heed. She kept moving, moving, her unwavering gaze fixed on the large round pipe beneath her battered boots.

She'd told Mama during her short lunch break that she was so familiar with this route she could probably walk it with her eyes closed and never fall into the water below. Mama advised her not to test her theory. If she closed her eyes, she might miss a leak between the redwood staves. A leak could lead to a break. And a break would be disastrous for Cañon City residents, who relied on the pipeline to deliver water to their homes and businesses. Jennie'd only been teasing Mama, but after five hours of inspecting, she was tempted to give it a try. A few seconds of walking with her eyes closed would relieve the monotony of the task. But then, of course, she'd have to backtrack and walk it again in case she missed something. She better keep her eyes open.

Pausing for a moment, she rotated her shoulders and squinted at the cloud-dotted sky. The sun beat directly down, making exposed rocks on the hillsides glow and the ever-flowing river sparkle like diamonds. For only a short time each day could she enjoy full sunshine. The mountain ranges rising on both sides of the river cast shade the majority of the time. During the late fall and winter months, due to soupy cloud cover, the sun didn't reach their valley for even a minute. Even though many more miles of pipe awaited examination, she squandered a few seconds, enjoying the sunlight. Daddy'd done the same thing midday. If he'd done it, Jennie could, too.

As always happened when thoughts of Daddy intruded, a tumble of emotions rolled through her chest. How could resentment and worry and sorrow and sympathy all reside in her at once? Mama said seventeen was a tumultuous age, so all those different feelings shouldn't make her fret. Jennie remembered her mother's assuring smile when she'd said, *"You'll get them sorted out in time if you ask the Lord to help you."* Mama brought the Lord into nearly every conversation. Sometimes Jennie found the practice comforting. Other times, annoying. But those opposite reactions were probably also part of her tumultuous age.

With a sigh, she returned her focus to the pipeline. The toe of her boot pointed to a rusting bolt connecting two reinforcing rods. Something about the bolt didn't look quite right. Was it loosening? The bands of steel held the thin staves tightly together. Daddy'd told her that if a bolt worked loose, the pipe would weaken. Jennie leaned over and poked the bolt with her finger. It wiggled like a baby tooth starting to be pushed out of the way. She was supposed to make note of any changes in the pipeline's appearance.

She straddled the pipe, hooking her heels the way she'd held her seat during a pony ride at the circus when she was six. She pinched out the little pad of paper and pencil stub she carried in her shirt pocket and opened it to a clean page. Poking her tongue from the corner of her mouth in concentration, she made a sketch of the bars and the slightly askew bolt.

She couldn't resist smiling as the picture emerged. Mama's sister, Delia, had told her she should sign up for art class at the high school in Cañon City. But that was back when everybody thought she'd be moving in with Aunt Delia and Uncle Prime and going to high school. Before Daddy fell and broke his leg. Before Jennie took over walking this line. Before she entered the tumultuous age. She was probably too old to start high school now even if Daddy suddenly got out of his chair and said he'd be the linewalker again, so no sense in thinking about it. At least walking this line gave her opportunities to draw.

She sent a lingering look over her shoulder, then gave her forward view the same attention, getting her bearings. With a nod of satisfaction, she pressed the pencil tip to the page and wrote, "Section 6, roughly 1/3 in from the west, June 4, 1915." She reviewed the note, then snorted in aggravation. Why couldn't she ever remember the way the waterway men wanted the date recorded? In her mind, it didn't seem natural writing, "4 June 1915." Nobody else she knew put the day before the month. Neither Mama nor Daddy could explain it, but that's the way the waterway men wanted it, so that's the way Jennie was supposed to write it.

"Well, I can't fix it now," she muttered, jamming the pad into her pocket. When she returned to the house this evening, she'd rub out the date with the eraser from the tin case of artist supplies her aunt and uncle had given her for her fourteenth birthday and rewrite it. If she remembered.

She braced her hands on the pipe, preparing to push herself upright, but a pale stick of some sort propped against the rocky ledge at the base of the ravine caught her eye. She squinted at the object, trying to recall where she'd seen it before. Remembrance dawned. It was the bone that Daddy's old shepherd dog, Rex, had dragged home close to three years back. For a while, Daddy carried it with him. "To warn off critters," he'd said with a wink, waving the chunky length of bone like a baseball bat. He must have tossed it aside on one of his treks.

She slid from the pipe on the upward slope side of the ravine, climbed the rocky rise to the bone, and picked it up. She ran her finger along its edge. Warm from the sun and smooth, almost like polished wood. Such a funny bone, unlike anything she or her parents had seen before. Daddy had decided it was from a bear's leg. Jennie wasn't so sure. But maybe if she showed it to him, it'd remind him of old Rex. Maybe bring a smile. Sadness pricked. She missed Daddy's smile.

Carrying the bone with her, she returned to the pipeline. She laid it up on top of the pipe and then pulled herself up. So awkward, getting herself onto the pipe—first flopping on her belly, then swinging her legs around and sitting up, and finally standing. It'd been a lot easier when Daddy grabbed her hand and pulled her up behind him. She'd taken a few falls back when she was learning to get herself up there. But after all these many months of walking the route alone, she'd mastered mounting the pipe. Within seconds, she started off again, the bone propped on her shoulder like a fishing pole.

As she moved steadily forward, she reminded herself to change the way she'd written the date on the note she'd made. If Mama sent the weekly report in on the train with the date written wrong, the waterway men might figure out somebody other than Claude Ward was making the reports. Her family couldn't risk any of those men snooping around and discovering the truth—that the linewalker's daughter was doing the job instead. For twenty-two months already, her family had kept the secret. They couldn't let it slip now.

If the men found out Daddy wasn't walking the line, they'd fire him. If they fired him, she, Mama, and Daddy would have to leave their little house perched on a pie slice–shaped plateau above the pipeline and move to town. Her feet slowed to a stop, her thoughts racing. If they lived in town, it wouldn't just be once-a-month visits to Aunt Delia and Uncle Prime—she'd be able to see them every day if she chose. No more isolation—she could make friends and be carefree like other girls her age. No more walking the seven miles of pipe from one end to the other every day no matter the weather.

Her heart gave a hopeful flutter.

What was she thinking? Daddy didn't dare lose this job. Who else would hire a man who sat in his chair all day and stared morosely out the window? Where would she and her parents live if they got kicked out of the house the waterway men provided as part of Daddy's pay? Aunt Delia and Uncle Prime couldn't take all of them in, and her folks didn't have money to rent a house. But maybe Mama could— No, Mama couldn't get a job and support the family, because then who would take care of Daddy?

They needed the money from the waterway men. She shouldn't entertain what-ifs about living in town, going to school, having a normal life. Not until Daddy was well again. But would Daddy ever *be* well again? Mama prayed for it every day. She told Jennie to pray, too, and Jennie had. For a full year. But not lately. If God hadn't answered by now, He wasn't going to. Mama could waste her time imploring Him, but Jennie was done.

The pipe began to vibrate beneath her soles. She stopped and shifted, looking toward the curve where the train that ran between Salida and Pueblo would appear. How many people behind the windows would wave at her today? The vibration increased, and the squeaks and rumbling noises of wheels on track reached her ears. First a whisper, then growing increasingly louder, until the train rounded the bend and almost seemed to bear straight at her.

She curled her toes inside her boots and held her position, waiting until the engine passed before waving the bone back and forth like a flag, smiling at every person who lifted a hand in response to her wild greeting. Too quickly, she was watching the tail end of the caboose chug up the rails. Only five cars—the engine, three passenger cars, and a caboose—didn't take much time to go by. But its appearance always gave her a lift. Her only contact, however insignificant, with people other than Mama and Daddy.

Aiming a narrow-eyed glance upward, she said, "I sure would like to have a friend, God. If You're gonna keep me here, walking this line for Daddy, could You at least send me a friend?"

She heard the hint of sarcasm in her voice. Mama would be disappointed by it. Jennie'd been taught to be respectful to her parents, to other people, and most especially to the almighty God. But her tumultuous age sometimes got the better of her. If God was as forgiving as Mama said, He'd understand her momentary lapse into bitterness.

She waited until the pipeline stopped its gentle shudders, and then she set her feet in motion again. She'd taken perhaps a dozen shuffling steps when splashing brought her up short. Something was in the water. Animals didn't usually prowl at midday. Had a two-legged varmint showed up out here?

She gripped the bone in both hands and searched the river, first behind and then in front, her flesh prickling. "Who's out there?" she barked in her deepest, sharpest tone.

A young fellow wearing a brown felt bowler and a brown pin-striped suit, its pant legs water-soaked, stepped from behind a cluster of boulders. He stuck his hands straight up, the way criminals surrendered to law enforcement. "Just me. I don't mean you any harm. May I talk to you?"

Leo Day

The girl, leggy as a young colt and scowling as fiercely as a lioness protecting its young, held the bone like a club. Leo didn't want to give her a reason to swing. If the bone shattered, he'd never know if it was what he suspected—a leg bone from a young allosaurus.

With his hands still in the air, he took a hesitant forward step, his wet trouser legs riding up on his shins. "My name's Leo. What's yours?"

Her fine eyebrows tipped together, more in puzzlement now than fear. "What're you doing out here?" Her brown eyes skimmed his length. "You're not dressed for a hike, so don't try to tell me you got lost hiking."

He hid a smile. She was dressed like a ragamuffin—wearing a man's baggy shirt tucked into patched britches, the pant legs tucked into boots that had seen better days—but her chocolate-colored eyes glinted with intelligence. As well as distrust. "I was on the train. I saw you waving, so I jumped off."

Now her eyebrows shot up and her mouth went slack. "Why?"

"So I could talk to you."

She angled her head, her grip on the bone relaxing a bit. "Why?"

He wriggled his fingers, wincing. "May I put my arms down? I promise I won't make any sudden moves. But my hands are starting to tingle. Reduced blood supply, you know."

After a moment's pause, she gave a brusque nod.

Blowing out a breath of relief, Leo lowered his arms and flicked his wrists several times. "Thank you."

"You're welcome." Her tone still held apprehension, but she brought the bone down and rested it against her shoulder. "Why did you want to talk to me?"

Did he detect a hint of longing in her voice? He slid his hands into his jacket pockets, partly to present a nonthreatening pose but mostly to keep from reaching for the precious piece of history she held. "I'm a paleontology student from the university in Denver. When I saw the bone you were waving, I was curious about it. I hoped for a better look. Would you mind letting me examine it?"

Her shoulders slumped. She turned aside, giving him a view of her profile. Was her chin quivering? Such an odd reaction to his query. Unless she had some kind of attachment to the bone and didn't want to part with it. Maybe he should explain the deeper reason he wanted to see it. She might be sympathetic to his cause. He cleared his throat, readying his request, and she abruptly faced him.

"Here." She braced one hand on her knee and leaned forward, offering the bone.

The pipeline was roughly three feet in diameter. On the river side of the steep rise, the bottom of the pipe was as high as the top of his head—a good six feet above the ground. He had to stand on tiptoe to grasp the knobby end. Despite his eagerness, he took it gingerly lest he accidentally pull her from the pipe.

While he turned the bone this way and that, she sat and strad-dled the pipe. He sensed her gaze resting heavily on him. What might she be thinking as she observed his scrutiny of the old bone? Was she secretly laughing at him? He'd suffered ridicule more times than he could count over his interest in things from long ago. Nobody cared about old dried-out bones, his schoolmates taunted. Father didn't ridicule, but his disapproval was palpable. Leo had grown accustomed to people's negative reactions, but that didn't mean he'd welcome more of the same.

He risked a glance at her and found her face reflecting curiosity rather than disdain. His lips formed a small smile of their own volition, and he couldn't resist sharing, "This is a fine specimen. I'm fairly certain it's the scapula of an allosaurus. See the bulge here on this end?" He tapped the knob-like protrusion. "This is where the humerus, like our upper arm bone, connected. Of course, the soft tissue is long gone. No surprise, considering how many thousands of years ago this creature walked the earth." Thousands, not millions, as some of his college professors taught. How he hoped to one day prove his theory.

Shivers traveled up and down his spine. When he'd decided to spend his summer months exploring the areas where renowned paleontologist Charles Walcott uncovered the first known findings of two new species of fish, he hadn't expected to locate such an amazing piece of history on his very first day in Cañon City. Surely, his decision to come here was Spirit-inspired.

Hugging the bone to his chest, he turned to Jennie. "Where did you find this?"

"I didn't. My daddy's dog carried it home one day."

His elation plummeted.

"But my daddy might have some idea where it came from." A hint of sadness shadowed her eyes, but then she blinked and the expression cleared. "He and Rex—that's the dog—used to walk all over the hills around here."

Excitement stirred anew. "Do you suppose he'd show me?"

She looked aside. "No, he wouldn't show you." She faced him again, shrugging. "But if he describes the area, I could probably find it."

Was she offering to help him? He leaned forward slightly. "I would appreciate that very much."

She stared at him for several seconds, uncertainty warring with some other emotion he couldn't define in her expression. She brought up her feet and stood in a smooth motion, as graceful as a ballerina. Balanced on top of the pipe, she gazed down at him. "But I can't take you to talk to my daddy until I finish my route."

He had no idea what route she meant, but he would wait no matter how long it took. "I'll go with you." He swallowed. "That is, if you don't mind."

For the first time, a hint of a smile appeared on her heart-shaped face. "I don't mind." Then teasing danced in her eyes. "Try to keep up, college boy."

Chapter Two

Jennie

Jennie peeked over her shoulder. Although the base of the ravine now rested in full shadow, she spotted the college boy
trailing her. Pretty far behind, but within sight. She wouldn't crit-
icize him for it, though. He was walking on the sloped, slippery,
rocky bank of the river. It was easier going for her on top of the
pipe, and his arms were full with the old bone. Funny how he carried it. The way mamas cradled their sleeping babies. He'd probably slip less if he put it over his shoulder because he'd be better
able to see his feet. She'd suggested as much a half mile back, but
he shook his head and insisted he was fine. She reckoned a college
boy had enough sense to choose for himself, so she'd shrugged
and kept going.

Although they hadn't done much talking, it was nice to have
company. When he'd appeared in front of her, she thought maybe
God heard and answered her prayer for a friend. But he hadn't
hopped off that train for her—he only wanted to know about the
bone. She snorted under her breath. Since when did God answer
her prayers? She should've known better. Shouldn't have gotten
her hopes up even for a few seconds. But at least today she wasn't
all alone on her route.

She looked back again. He'd fallen even farther behind. His
pants were crumpled from mid-thigh to mid-calf where they'd
dried, but the bottom six inches of his pant legs were soaked and
sticking to his ankles. His foot slid from the rock and went into

the water. When he pulled it out, mud clung to the sole. He shook his foot, but only a few chunks dropped off. Jennie *tsk-tsk*ed, staring in dismay at his feet. He might never get all the muck off his once shiny patent-leather lace-up boots. He really needed to walk on the pipe instead.

Although she was already behind schedule and Mama would worry if she didn't get home at her usual time, she sat and waited for him to catch up. When he was close enough to hear her voice above the river's raucous song, she cupped her hands beside her mouth and hollered, "Climb up here on the pipe. You'll stay dry that way."

He staggered up the steep embankment and squinted at her. "Um, no, thank you. You might be half mountain goat, but I'm not."

His sour expression tickled her. She couldn't hold back a laugh. "Clearly not, considering how wobbly you are on the rocks." She stuck out her hand. "Give me the bone. Then duck under the pipe. It's a shorter reach from the other side since the ground slopes up. Trust me, you'll be able to walk easier on the pipe."

He seemed to measure the distance from the ground to her perch, his face set in a doubtful scowl. "Are you sure it'll hold my weight? I've never seen a pipe made from wood before. If there are rotten places, it could collapse and send both of us into the river."

Was he really concerned about her getting hurt? The thought warmed her more than the sun's rays had at noontime. "It won't collapse. My daddy walked it every day for years, and he's heavier than you. Besides, this pipe's made from redwood." She gave it several pats. "Redwood doesn't rot, swell, or shrink." That's what one of the waterway men had told her family, as prideful as if he'd been the one to create the trees himself. "It's safer up here than it is down on those rocks. So come on up." She bobbed her hand, inviting him to give her the bone.

His gaze skimmed the pipeline, then the rocky shoreline, and finally settled on her. He sighed. "Very well." He handed up the bone and followed her other directions. She tried not to snicker as he flung his foot up and over and pulled with his heel. He'd been right about not being much of a mountain goat. But he managed to straddle the pipe, then carefully moved to his hands and knees before standing upright. For a moment, he teetered, his mud-caked soles slipping. He caught his balance, straightened his jacket, and blew out a noisy breath.

"All right, I'll take the bone now."

She tucked it against her chest like a shield. "Are you sure you don't want me to carry it? At least until you get your footing?"

He shook his head. "No. I'm fine." His eyes shifted briefly to the river, and he made a face. "Well, as long as I don't look down, I'm fine."

She laughed again and gave him the bone. Extending her arms for balance, she turned a half circle and set off. She wanted to peek back and see how he was doing. The noise of the rushing water covered the sound of footsteps. Maybe he hadn't budged and was just standing there, hugging the bone. But she needed to stay focused on the pipe. She had a job to do.

There was a way to know if he was following her, though. Her gaze on the pipe, she called, "There's only about a mile and a half of pipe left this direction. Then we'll turn around and go back."

"How far back?"

His voice sounded close, right behind her. She grinned to herself. He was keeping up. "My family lives near the midpoint of the pipeline. It's a little over seven miles long altogether. You do the math, college boy."

She scanned the pipe below her feet and waited for his reply.

"So . . . approximately three and a half miles back?"

She nodded.

"How often do you walk this thing?"

As much as she'd longed for company, conversation could distract her. She needed to finish examining the pipe before she let herself get lost in talk. Reluctantly, she paused and peered over her shoulder. "I don't just walk it. I look for damage—cracks, holes, tiny leaks, rusting places in the iron bar . . ." He seemed to study her face as she spoke. "I have to report any damage to the waterway men so they can send someone to repair it before there's a bad break in the line."

"Is that your polite way of telling me to be quiet?" Although his words were teasing, his intense attention while she spoke made her feel as if he was truly interested in what she said.

She squelched a smile. "For now." Then she pointed at him. "But on the way back, you can ask me whatever you want to and I'll answer." Oh, it would be so nice to talk with someone.

"You've got a deal." He pointed with his chin in the direction of the end of the pipeline. "Lead on, mountain goat."

She choked out a laugh. "Mountain goat?"

He grinned. "You call me 'college boy.' I have to call you something."

Did he mean the term as a compliment just as she did with *college boy,* albeit with a hint of envy? Maybe, but she'd rather not be compared to the shaggy, curly-horned, stubborn critters that lived on the rocky crags. "How about you just call me Jennie."

"Fine, and you call me Leo."

Like friends. A delightful shiver rattled her frame. She should say no. After all, he was interested in only the dinosaur bone, not her. After today, she'd probably never see him again. Even Aunt Delia, who was ten years younger and a lot less strict than Mama, would warn her to be careful. But Jennie said, "Leo it is."

His smile rewarded her. Maybe a little too much. She cleared her throat. "Leo?"

"Yes, Jennie?"

She liked the way her name sounded in his warm baritone voice. This suggestion was going to be harder than she realized.

"Why don't you stay here while I finish the route? There's really no sense in you following me. Or . . ." She gulped. "If you want to, you could walk the pipeline the opposite way. You'll see my family's cabin on a rise to your right of the pipe. Nobody else lives out here, so you can't mistake it. That way you can talk to my daddy about the bone and be on your way faster."

He angled his head, his dark-blue eyes narrowing slightly. "Are you trying to get rid of me?"

"No!" The word burst out more forcefully than she'd intended. She swallowed hard and forced a shrug. "Not at all. I just don't want you to feel like you're wasting your time. You probably have to get back to the college pretty soon. Don't you?"

He bent over and laid the bone on the pipe with as much care as Mama used when putting her wedding china in the cupboard. Then he sat, dangling his feet on the river side of the pipe and placing his hand over the bone. "I'll be in Cañon City all summer, so I have some time to spend." He playfully shooed her with a swish of his fingers. "Finish your duty. I'll wait here and make a list of things to ask you when you get back."

That teasing tone of his would undo her if she wasn't careful. She returned to work, certain he'd grow weary of waiting for her and head for her family's cabin. But when she returned to the spot after finishing her inspection, Leo was still sitting there, one hand resting protectively on the bone and the other clamping his hat on his knee. The sight of his thick, wavy dark brown hair tousled by the breeze drew her up short for a moment. Such a contrast to the formality of his buttoned shirt, bow tie, and jacket, yet somehow perfect. She stared, wishing she could sketch him the way he looked at that moment, relaxed and carefree and approachable.

Suddenly he angled his head. His gaze met hers and he smiled. "There you are. All done?"

She might have been gone only a few minutes instead of an

hour and a half, so easily he greeted her. For some reason, his kind patience brought the urge to cry. She managed a little nod.

He settled the hat on his head, stood, and scooped up the bone, this time placing it against his shoulder instead of cradling it. "I guess I have to lead the way." He chuckled. "There's not space for you to step past me."

His easy smile and teasing nature reminded her of Daddy before he got hurt. Thinking about how Daddy used to be increased her desire to cry. She rubbed her nose. "You're right, so just follow the pipeline." Shame washed over her at her gruff tone, but she didn't know how else to hide her turbulent emotions. "I'll be right behind you."

"Answering my questions?"

A laugh sneaked past her tight throat. "Yes."

He moved forward, and she fell in step a few feet behind him. "All right, then, Jennie, let's start with the question you didn't answer earlier. How often do you walk, er, examine this pipeline?"

He asked question after question about the pipeline, her family's responsibilities, and the challenges she faced in being held accountable for its condition. She'd expected him to ask about dinosaur bones, a subject about which she knew very little. But she could respond from six years of experience as the linewalker's daughter. Leo made her feel smart and important, a unique feeling considering her shortened education and simple existence here away from town.

He switched the bone to his other shoulder, his steps slowing a bit. "When I saw you from the train window, I thought you were just a kid playing around on the pipe."

Her heart gave a little leap. That's what she and her mother hoped people would think when they saw her waving at the passersby. Leo's comment eased her mind but also left her feeling a little guilty.

"But you've really walked this pipeline five days a week, every week of the year, for the past six years?" A touch of wonder colored his tone, and even though she couldn't see his face, she imagined admiration in his expression.

She swung her arms, reining in a rush of pride. "Pretty much."

"That's amazing. How old are you, Jennie?"

The question was more personal than the others, but she answered without hesitating. "I turned seventeen in January."

He shot a startled glance over his shoulder. "You were only eleven when you took on this job?"

Apparently, she hadn't made things clear. "I was eleven when my daddy got hired as the linewalker. But I liked to be with him, so I went along most days. I . . ." A knot filled her throat. "I guess you could say I was a daddy's girl back then."

"Only back then?"

Now he was getting too personal. She didn't want to explore the honest answer to that question. Jennie swallowed. "I've been doing it by myself for—" She clapped her hand over her mouth. She wasn't supposed to tell anyone Daddy wasn't the one walking the line. "I mean . . . I . . . Daddy . . ." How to fix it? She didn't want to lie, but the truth could cause so much trouble. She blurted, "I'm only doing it to help. Daddy's been sick lately, but he's the real linewalker, not me."

Leo nodded, seemingly unconcerned. "When you said there wasn't anyone out here except your family, I thought you might be exaggerating. But you were absolutely right. No houses, businesses, or even a school. Do you take the train into Cañon City for school?"

"I finished grade five before we moved out here." How she missed those schoolgirl days. "But Mama's been instructing me since then. She was a teacher in Salida before she married Daddy. I study every evening."

"I can tell." He shifted the bone to his other shoulder. "You're very articulate—more so than a lot of young people who attend public schools. Your mother must be a good teacher, but you're also a good learner."

Jennie's chest went tight at his praise. "Well, I probably won't earn a high school diploma, like the kids who attend school in town, but Mama says a good education isn't defined by a piece of sheepskin."

"I agree. I—" He stopped and sniffed the air. "From where is that enticing aroma coming?"

The scent of roasting meat combined with cinnamon and apples reached Jennie's nose. She grinned. "Mama's cookstove. She's not only a good teacher—she's a good cook. And since it's coming up on suppertime, she'll tell you to take a chair and join us. I hope you like roasted pork and apple pie."

The smile he sent over his shoulder was sweeter than apple pie. "How much farther?"

She pointed up the hill. "A hop, skip, and jump."

He laughed. "Spoken like a true mountain goat. I'll let you lead the way."

Chapter Three

Etta Ward

E tta pushed a few straggling strands of hair from her forehead and looked at the little mantel clock counting its steady *tick-tock* on the shelf. Almost six. A good half hour past Jennie's usual return time. Where was that girl? She picked up the wooden spoon from the edge of the stove and gave the fried potatoes another stir. Claude liked his taters all the way done, but the slices might be as dried out as boot leather if she didn't serve them soon. Maybe she should fill a plate for him. Accustomed to eating at five-thirty, he was probably ravenous by now.

She laid the spoon on the edge of the cast-iron frying pan and turned. "Claude, would—"

From his chair in front of the window, her husband sat up and pointed. "Here comes Jennie. And she's got somebody with her." He leaned forward, and Etta could sense him bristling. "A fancy fellow from the looks of it."

Etta hurried to the window and peered out, her hand braced on Claude's bony shoulder. "My, he is dressed like a gentleman, isn't he?" Worry pricked. "You don't suppose the city council sent an official out to check the waterway and found Jennie walking it, do you?"

Claude shifted in the chair, dislodging Etta's hand. "He looks a little young to be an official. Besides, the only time they send someone out is when we report a problem somewhere on the line. That ain't been the case since last winter."

Etta leaned closer to the window. Claude was right. The man was dressed as fine as a big-city lawyer, but his face was youthful. And he was almost as handsome as Claude had been when she first laid eyes on him twenty-five years ago. She set her gaze on Claude's profile, seeing not his frown, thinning gray hair, and puckered brow but instead the smiling young man he'd once been. Love swelled up inside her, strong as ever, the one thing that hadn't changed since his accident. Her hand moved to his shoulder again as if it had a will of its own. She rubbed a gentle circle, her eyes sliding closed and a prayer forming in the center of her heart.

Restore him, Lord. Please restore him.

"What's that he's toting?"

Claude's gruff query drew Etta from her reverie. She looked out the window. Jennie and the young man were only yards from the cabin now, and she easily recognized the object in the man's hands. "Well, now, it seems he's got an old dried-up bone." She crinkled her nose. "I hope he doesn't think he's bringing it inside."

She hurried across the creaky wood planked floor to the open doorway and stepped out on the flat stone serving as a stoop. "Jennie, you're late."

Jennie jogged the final distance, remorse pinching her face. "I know. I'm sorry."

Etta smiled and lightly tugged Jennie's ragged brownish-blond braid. "No harm done." She shifted her smile to the young man, who stopped a few feet away as if uncertain of his welcome. "And who do we have here?"

Jennie waved him closer. "This is Leo Day, Mama. He's a paleontology student from the college in Denver, but he's spending his summer in Cañon City."

Suddenly Etta understood why he was holding on to that bone like it was a jeweled crown. She also understood Jennie's delay. Her daughter must've gotten caught up chatting with this visitor.

Good for her. Jennie needed, even deserved, those kinds of youthful interactions. "Is that so?" She extended her hand to the college student. "I'm Etta Ward, Jennie's mama. It's nice to meet you, Mr. Day."

The young man swept off his hat, anchored the bone beneath his elbow, then gave her a brief, firm handshake. "Thank you, ma'am, but please call me Leo."

"Leo"—she took a step backward—"come on in and meet Jennie's daddy." He and Jennie moved forward in tandem. Etta gestured to the bone. "You can leave that here at the stoop. Nobody will bother it." The young man surrendered the bone, and then he and Jennie followed her in. Jennie moved to the washstand, but Leo trailed Etta to Claude. "Claude, this is Leo Day. Leo, my husband, Mr. Ward."

The two shook hands, and Etta couldn't help but notice how frail Claude's once strong hand looked next to Leo's. *Restore him, Lord.* The prayer had almost become a mantra. When would God finally grant her plea? She shoved the errant thought aside and feigned a cheerful tone. "Leo is studying paleontology at the university. Isn't that interesting?"

Claude squinted one eye at the college student as if taking aim. "Studying old bones, huh?"

"Yes, sir. That's why your daughter"—Jennie ambled near, and Leo bounced an appreciative grin at her—"thought I should talk to you."

"Me?" Claude snorted. "I don't know anything about paleontology."

Jennie wrung her hands. "But haven't you seen the place where Rex found some bones, Daddy? I thought maybe you could—"

Claude thrust his palm into the air. "I can't go traipsing over the hills, Jennie, so get that thought out of your head."

Jennie bit her lower lip and turned aside, causing Etta's heart to roll over. There was a time Claude never interrupted anything his daughter said—when he listened closely and answered kindly whatever questions she asked. Claude's impatience wasn't with Jennie—it was with himself. But the wedge between them was fast growing into a chasm, and if something didn't change, they might never be able to bridge it.

Etta put her arm around Jennie's shoulders. "Supper's getting cold. All of us . . . let's sit around the table and eat. Leo, please tell us about your studies while we're eating. That will give Claude time to recall where that bone might've come from." She gave Jennie a little pat. "Set another plate at the table, honey, while I help your daddy."

Claude clamped the arms of the chair and pushed himself to his feet, grunting. "I can get myself to the table. Just see to the food."

His tone chastened her. And embarrassed her. What must this visiting college student think? But she gave her husband's arm a gentle pat. "Of course, Claude." She scurried to the stove.

Leo

"My father is the minister at a Presbyterian church in Denver." Leo answered Etta Ward's questions between bites of roasted salt pork, fried potatoes, and apple pie. He hadn't packed a lunch before boarding the train that morning because he hadn't planned on hopping off. He was hungry after his hike on the pipeline with Jennie. Though simple fare, the food was tasty, and the Wards were kind. Well, the Ward women were kind. Jennie didn't say much, but she listened with rapt attention to everything he said, often nodding and smiling at his replies to Mrs. Ward's friendly inquiries. The women put him very much at ease. Mr. Ward? The man was more taciturn than anyone else he'd ever met.

He tamped the remaining piecrust crumbs with the tines of his fork. "Actually, I come from a long line of preachers. My father, grandfather, and great-grandfather all led congregations. Great-grandfather Day served in England, though."

"My, you should be proud of your family's faithful heritage." Mrs. Ward's eyes shone with admiration. Would she change her opinion if she knew how badly he'd disappointed his father by choosing a vocation other than ministry?

Leo wiped his mouth with the square of cotton he'd been given to use as a napkin and laid the cloth aside. "Yes, ma'am. I'm grateful for the foundation of faith I was given by my parents." He valued it. He clung to it. He only wished he could make Father understand that he could share his faith while working as a paleontologist, too.

"I'm glad to hear it." Mrs. Ward stood, crossed to the stove, and retrieved the tall blue-speckled coffeepot. She poured richly scented brew into Mr. Ward's cup and then her own before placing the pot in the middle of the table. "Do you have siblings?"

"Yes, ma'am, two younger sisters. Daisy is almost ten, and Myrtle is twelve. They're pests." He laughed. "Or so I thought before I left home for college. Now I kind of miss them."

"Our Jennie's an only child."

Leo nodded, uncertain what to say. Clearly, this family was eager for company. He'd been welcomed to their table and plied with questions from the moment he sat down. But he couldn't stay much longer. The train to Cañon City would depart Salida at six o'clock according to the schedule he'd been given at the depot that morning. Somehow he had to get himself on board when it went past the Wards' cabin. Before he did so, he had questions of his own to ask. Questions Jennie said her daddy could answer. If he'd be neighborly enough to do so.

Sucking in a breath of fortification, he turned to the man who sat sipping his coffee. "Sir, may I talk to you about the bone your dog found?"

Mr. Ward didn't angle his head in Leo's direction, but his eyes shifted and met Leo's. They were as deeply brown as his daughter's but not nearly as warm. "Go ahead."

Not the friendliest tone he'd ever heard, but at least he seemed willing to listen. "Thank you. Do you happen to know where it was located? I believe it's part of the skeleton of an allosaurus. If I could find more of its remains, I'd have a better idea if my supposition is correct."

Mr. Ward set the cup on the table and cradled it between his palms. "I can't say for sure. But if I was to venture a guess, I'd say probably from one of the ridges south and west o' here. Rex did a lot of exploring up there."

Leo waited for further information, but Mr. Ward went back to sipping his coffee.

Jennie cleared her throat. "Daddy, are you talking about behind our cabin, or the rise on the other side of the river, behind the train?"

"Behind the cabin," he said in a way that intimated Jennie should have already known the location.

A flush brightened her cheeks, and she ducked her head for a moment. Then she looked at Leo. "I think I could point you in the general direction."

"But not tonight yet." Mrs. Ward shook her head. "It'll have to wait for another day."

Although eager to explore, Leo agreed. Heavy shadows encompassed the valley. When night crept in and full dark fell, nocturnal creatures would start prowling. He wanted to find remnants of a creature from long ago, not a live one with claws and teeth. "Of course. Besides, I need to find a curve where the train will slow enough for me to get on board when it comes by."

Mrs. Ward's eyes widened. "Oh my, I was enjoying our visit so much I forgot you need a way back to Cañon City. Of course, we should send you out right away. And you go ahead and take that bone with you if it will help you in your studies."

The woman endeared herself to him forever with her offer. He beamed at her. "Thank you, ma'am."

She stood. "Jennie, light the lantern and walk Leo to our usual jumping-on spot."

Leo jolted in surprise. Why would she send Jennie? Wouldn't it be better, given the hour, for Mr. Ward to escort him?

Jennie rose and headed toward a beadboard cupboard in the corner.

"Get the pistol, too," Mrs. Ward said.

"Yes, Mama."

Alarm propelled Leo from his chair. "I don't want to put Jennie in danger. I'm sure I can find a curve and get on without her help." He couldn't help gawking at Mr. Ward, sitting unconcerned and stoic, his focus on his cup of coffee.

Mrs. Ward chuckled softly. "Now, Leo, Jennie's familiar with this ridge, and our getting-on spot isn't far at all. It's only a safeguard to have the pistol. In all our years of living here, we've never had to fire it in defense."

Her calm statement relieved Leo, but he still didn't understand why the parents left this responsibility to their daughter. His father would never send Myrtle or Daisy out with a stranger as night was falling.

Jennie returned to the table, a pistol tucked in the waistband of her britches and a lighted lantern hanging from her hand. "Where are you staying in Cañon City?" She'd been so quiet during the meal, it almost startled him to hear her musical voice.

"The St. Cloud Hotel." The desk clerk had told Leo that the lobby doors locked at nine o'clock. If he didn't make it back before then, he'd need a key to get in. He reached into his trouser pocket, ascertaining he hadn't misplaced his key when he leaped from the train and then splashed across the river. To his relief, the leather tab and key were safe inside.

Jennie's face lit brighter than the match she'd struck to light the lantern. "You are? My aunt and uncle manage the St. Cloud. Maybe you've met them—Prime and Delia Flankston?"

Leo shook his head. "I'm sorry, I don't recall meeting them."

Mrs. Ward was beaming as if he'd given them a gift by registering at the two-story brick hotel in the center of downtown. "Oh, you surely will eventually. Delia's my little sister. I thought her a pest when I was growing up, the same way you do with your sisters. But now I'm so grateful for her. She's my best friend." Mrs. Ward caught hold of his elbow and walked him to the door, Jennie close behind them. "When you do meet them, be sure and tell them hello from Mr. Ward, Jennie, and me, will you?"

"Yes, ma'am, I will." Leo stepped outside and reached for the bone. Then he thought better of it. "May I leave this here for now? I might drop it when I get on the train. I don't want to damage it." He gazed at the bone glowing white under the lantern's soft beam. Would he find the entire skeleton? Would his name show up in a journal somewhere as the one who made a new discovery? If so, would Father be proud of him?

"Of course you may, young man." Mrs. Ward spoke so kindly it made his chest ache in a strange way. "I'll even bring it inside so it'll be sure and be here when you return." She picked it up, grimacing a bit, and set it just inside the cabin. She touched Jennie's back. "Hurry, now, honey. We don't want Leo to miss the return train."

Jennie nodded and hopped from the stoop. The lantern swayed, making the circle of light dance. "C'mon, Leo. It's not far." She took off at a half trot.

"Good evening, ma'am." Leo walked backward, waving to the smiling woman framed in the cabin doorway. "Thank you for the fine supper."

She waved in return. "You're welcome. We'll see you again soon."

He spun forward and caught up to Jennie, warmth flooding his chest despite the cool evening air. He hoped he'd see them again. He liked Mrs. Ward. And he liked Jennie. But Mr. Ward? He wasn't so sure about him.

Chapter Four

Jennie

"**B**ut, Mama, I've never done the shopping all by myself." Jennie gripped the paper torn from Mama's notepad and stared at the list of items written in her mother's neat script. Her mind reeled. "How will I carry it all?"

Mama chuckled softly. "Now, you know Uncle Prime will help you load everything on the train. Mr. Rawling will stop at our curve, as he always does when we've been to town, and you can ask Mr. Jenkins to help you carry the crates from the car. I'll make sure the hand wagon is waiting for you by the bridge."

After years of monthly rides back and forth from Cañon City, Jennie knew the train's engineer and conductor nearly as well as she knew her aunt and uncle, but she'd never asked either man for a favor. Mr. Jenkins, who rode in the caboose, always offered to help Mama because he was a gentleman and she was a lady. Did Jennie's tumultuous age classify her as a lady?

"But don't you want to go?" Jennie beseeched her mother with her eyes. She looked forward to their monthly outing. Going to town was fun, but best—she cringed even as she considered it— was a break from Daddy's woebegone attitude. Surely, Mama needed relief from his constant glumness, too. "Aunt Delia will be so sad if she doesn't get to see you. And what about church tomorrow? Maybe I shouldn't spend the night with Aunt Delia and Uncle Prime. I'll come home with our supplies right away."

"No, no." Mama escorted Jennie to the front door. "Stay the

night the way we've always done. Go to church with your aunt and uncle. They'll be disappointed if you don't. I'd rather you not make the trek from the rails to our cabin in the evening. Midday is better. Now go." Mama gave her a playful nudge, winking. "Have fun, but behave yourself even though I'm not with you."

Jennie'd been taught Someone was always with her. Always watching. The knowledge had curtailed yielding to many temptations over the years. But since God had stopped answering her prayers, she pondered whether He was paying attention to her at all. If not, did it matter how she behaved? Then she sighed. She wouldn't deliberately get up to mischief, whether God was watching or not. She didn't want to hurt Mama. Mama'd suffered enough.

She gave her mother a quick hug and then trotted down the rise to the footbridge. Daddy had built it the spring her family moved to the cabin so she and Mama could easily access the train tracks. She crossed the bridge, watching her feet. Some of the warped, weathered planks were four or five inches apart. A misstep could cause a fall. She enjoyed a dip in the river on hot days, but she preferred to get wet on her own terms, not because she lost her footing.

On the opposite side of the rapidly moving river, she stepped over the lines of track and leaned against the sheer rock wall stretching almost straight-up. She kept her gaze locked on the bend for the coming locomotive, but she felt the vibrations caused by the mighty engine even before she saw it. When the train entered the straightaway, she raised her hands over her head and waved. At once, brakes squealed, and the dust-covered engine puffed to a stop only a few yards from her waiting spot.

Sending a grateful smile to the engineer, Mr. Rawling, who tipped his cap as she passed, she eased along the wall to the landing on the first passenger car and climbed aboard. She settled on an empty bench at the rear of the car, and slowly the train chugged into motion again. She stared out the window at the river below, her heart heavy. She missed Mama's company. Her chin began to quiver. She set her teeth together and stopped the trembling.

"Well, hello there, Miss Jennie."

Jennie jerked her attention to the aisle. Mr. Jenkins, his cap set at a jaunty angle over his lank brown hair, smiled down at her. "Hello, sir. It's good to see you." She was especially grateful for the distraction from her lonely thoughts.

"Right back atcha." He glanced up and down the aisle, his brow furrowing. "Didn't your mama come with you? She ain't ailin', is she?"

"No, sir." Jennie held up the list of supplies Mama had given her. "She said I could do the shopping on my own this month." But why? Not once since they'd moved out to the cabin had Mama sent her to town alone. Even after Daddy got hurt, Mama went in for the monthly shopping and to attend worship service with Uncle Prime and Aunt Delia. Why hadn't she come this time?

The man gave her an awkward pat on her shoulder. "Well, now, I'd say that means you're growin' up. If you need help with your crates an' such, you be sure an' give me a holler. Be glad to lend a hand."

Maybe she was growing up if the conductor made such a gentlemanly offer to her. She sat up a little straighter. "Thank you, sir."

"No problem at all. Enjoy your day, now." He ambled up the aisle, his gait swaying with the car's rocking on the track.

Her brief exchange with the conductor lifted her spirits more than she could understand. When the train heaved to a stop at the Cañon City station, she hopped down from the little platform, unburdened in every sense of the word. She wove her way between waiting passengers and their stacks of luggage the way a field mouse skittered between grass-blades. She wouldn't be able to move so freely after she finished shopping.

Going to town was much simpler than coming back. She didn't even carry an overnight bag since she kept church clothes and toiletries in the closet of her aunt and uncle's guest bedroom. Why would she need all that frippery at the cabin? Even though Mama wore a work dress every day, she approved trousers and button-up shirts for Jennie out there. But Mama would be appalled if Jennie showed up in downtown Cañon City in Daddy's hand-me-down clothes.

Taking alleys and side streets, she hurried to Uncle Prime and Aunt Delia's Victorian in one of the city's nicer districts. Her aunt and uncle were at work, but Aunt Delia always left a key under a flowerpot on the back stoop. Jennie retrieved it, unlocked the back door, then slid the key under the pot again. The house was quiet and shadowy with its occupants gone and the electric lights off. She'd never been there all by herself, and it seemed strangely spooky. A shiver climbed her spine as she made her way through the silent hallway to the staircase leading to the upstairs bedrooms.

She pushed the light button at the base of the stairs, then darted up, taking two risers at a time under the glow of the wall sconces. Upstairs, she passed Uncle Prime and Aunt Delia's bedroom and entered the room she and Mama shared when they visited town. As quickly as possible, she changed from her britches, shirt, and boots into a pale-rose linen blouse, a straight brown skirt, stockings, and the pair of pointy-toed lace-up shoes Aunt Delia had given her for her most recent birthday. The black kidskin boots were grown-up, very ladylike shoes, and Jennie hated the way they pinched her feet, but she wore them because she loved Aunt Delia.

The tall oval mirror attached to the dressing table gave her a full view of her reflection from the opposite side of the room. She skimmed her hands down her hips, satisfied with the fit of the blouse and skirt, but oh, her hair! She unwove her ratty braid, snatched up the brush lying on a ceramic tray on the vanity marble top, and brushed her tresses until they crackled. Then she gathered the wavy strands into a tail and secured it with a piece of ribbon from a small drawer in the vanity. Satisfied her appearance wouldn't shame Mama, she selected a dime, two nickels, and five pennies—the standard twenty-five-cents spending money Mama allowed on weekend visits—from a dish on the tray. She dropped the coins and the list Mama had given her into a velvet drawstring pouch and hooked it on her wrist.

One more glance in the mirror confirmed she was presentable for a visit to town. She descended the stairs, this time with her hand on the polished railing and at a sedate pace. She exited the house via the back door, locked it behind her, and followed the sidewalk around to the front. Now that she was dressed appropriately, she didn't need to sneak through alleys. The sun—so welcome after the valley's shade—beamed down bright and cheerful, and a soft breeze carried the scent of Aunt Delia's abundance of sweet william blossoming in the beds at the base of the porch. A sudden shaft of delight filled Jennie. She'd walked the pipeline by herself countless times, but not once had she ventured into Cañon City's downtown all alone. A sense of freedom and adventure accompanied the *click-click* of her heels on the concrete sidewalk.

Although she still wondered why Mama had chosen to stay home today, she decided to enjoy herself. In fact, before she filled the shopping list, why not treat herself to a soda at the drugstore? Mama wouldn't mind. The two of them usually ended their shopping excursion by sharing a tall glass of fizzy, sweet soda pop. She could drink the whole thing today. Anticipating the treat, she was tempted to hurry. But the pinching shoes dictated a more relaxed pace. Why hurry, anyway? She didn't have to answer to anyone but herself.

Smiling, she swung the little pouch and clicked steadily toward town.

Etta

Etta had fully intended to go into town with Jennie that morning, as they'd done the first Saturday of every month since moving out to this cabin above the center point of the pipeline. But the young college student's visit yesterday evening squashed her intentions. Watching Jennie's delight in hosting a visitor close to her age awakened Etta to all her daughter was missing. After lying awake and praying well past her bedtime, she decided that she and Claude needed to have a serious talk. About the pipeline and Claude's continued reluctance to use his leg, but mostly about Jennie. About the future Jennie was being denied.

Could she have talked with him during a time when Jennie was walking the pipeline? Of course. She and Claude were alone at the cabin for hours each day. But she sensed the conversation would anger and frustrate him. This new Claude, the one who sat in a chair all day instead of going off to work, sometimes harbored resentment. Multiple times since his accident, he'd broken their wedding-day promise to never go to bed angry. At least if he broke the promise again tonight, Jennie wouldn't be there in the morning to witness its lingering effects.

She glanced at the clock. Nearly ten-thirty. He'd limped to the outhouse two hours ago, then returned to their bedroom. But instead of getting himself dressed, he'd gone back to bed. Another habit the old Claude would never have formed. How she longed for the Claude she'd once known—the proud, hardworking family man who showered affection on his daughter and treated his wife with respect and concern.

She clasped her hands beneath her chin and bowed her head. *Please, Lord, let him listen with understanding ears. Let him see how his behavior hurts and hinders his precious child. Restore him to the man he used to be. Oh, please, dear Lord, restore him to us.*

Bolstered by the brief prayer, she squared her shoulders and entered the bedroom. He lay propped up on the pillows, eyes open, his gaze angled toward the window. Etta approached the bed, and he rolled his head and aimed a scowl at her.

She teasingly shook her finger. "Do you know what time it is? You should have had your breakfast hours ago. Why are you still lying there?" She sat on the edge of the squeaky mattress and linked her hands in her lap. "I hope you aren't feeling sickly."

He stared at her, unblinking, for several seconds. Then he huffed. "Why are you here?"

She drew back, uncertain. "In the bedroom?"

"At all." He growled the simple statement. He jammed the heels of his hands against the mattress and pushed himself higher on the pillows. "You should've gone to town today. You should've stayed there. You should've given up on me months ago." He slapped at the leg he'd broken in a fall on that August day almost two years ago. "I'm worthless to you. Why are you here?"

He couldn't have hurt her more if he'd slapped her. Did he think so little of her and the vows she'd made? She promised before God and man to be faithful whether in sickness or health. How could she abandon him in his darkest hours of need? "I'm here, Claude, because you're my husband and I love you. Jennie's here because you're her daddy and she loves you." An uncomfortable thought tiptoed through her brain. "Are you trying to drive us away?"

He looked aside. "It'd be better for you if I did."

She gripped his whisker-dotted chin between her thumb and fingers and turned his face to her again. "Don't ever say that again. You and I—we're one, Claude. What God put together should not be torn asunder. If I lose you, I lose myself. Why don't you understand that?"

He caught her wrist and pulled her hand down. "Why don't *you* understand you can't be whole when you're bound to me?" He pressed his fist to his forehead, his eyes closing so tight his face crumpled. "I can't work anymore. I'm nothing but a burden. Catch that train and go to Cañon City. Live with your sister. Forget about me."

He could work again. The doctor in Cañon City who'd set his leg said so. The break was bad—it had shortened his left leg and he'd always have a limp. But most of his weakness was from all the sitting. The doctor insisted that if he got up, if he exercised his leg, he'd one day walk the pipeline again. Maybe not as fast, but he could do it. If only he would. And if he returned to his job, they could let Jennie move to town with Delia and Prime, finish school, and enjoy a year of being unfettered before taking a full-time job or starting a family. But as long as Claude stayed abed, Jennie'd never be free. The girl's love and loyalty to her mama and daddy would trap her here forever.

As much as Etta wanted to talk and make Claude understand, she held all those words inside her. He was too distraught to listen to reason. She shifted around and tucked herself under his arm. With her head nestled on his chest, she wrapped her arm across his torso and held tight. Talking would wait. For now, she would pray.

Restore him, Lord. Do whatever's needed for Your will to be achieved for Jennie, Claude, and me.

Chapter Five

Jennie

Jennie slurped up the last few drops of cherry soda from the bottom of the glass. She'd lingered so long over the drink that the striped paper straw was soggy, but she didn't care. She enjoyed every sip of the sweet soda. She also enjoyed the store's bustling activity. Chatter and laughter, plinks and dings of a cash register, the rustle of brown paper being wrapped around a purchase—noises so different from the sounds of nature to which she'd become accustomed since moving to the cabin.

When she arrived almost an hour ago, several tables and half the barstools were already taken. She'd settled on a stool at the far end of the long bar. Her back was to the little tables and well-stocked shelves filling the drugstore floor, but the large plate-glass mirror in the ornate shelving behind the bar reflected the entire room. So she sipped and observed people coming and going or sitting and chatting, all the while listening to the voices and whir of the various appliances used by the soda jerk, her chest fluttering at being even a small part of the social liveliness.

Her attention returned frequently to two young men at a table in the middle of the area set apart for diners. They'd arrived just a few minutes after her, sauntering in like a pair of rich businessmen even though they were pimply faced adolescents. And were they ever noisy. They talked loud and laughed loud, their voices carrying above everyone else's. She suspected they were purposefully loud to draw her attention, because every time she sought out their reflections, their grinning gazes were on her. Her own reflection sported pink cheeks, partly embarrassment and partly from the enjoyment of being noticed.

How would it feel to walk over and sit with them? Wouldn't it be grand to talk for a while the way she used to with friends when she was younger? Mama's warnings about proper behavior for a young lady kept her on the stool, but temptation still niggled. Would it hurt to engage, just once, in idle flirtation?

"Have fun, but behave yourself even though I'm not with you."

Mama's voice whispered in Jennie's memory, and she sighed. She'd spent enough time dallying over her soda. She should go to the general store and do what she'd been sent to do—fill the supplies list.

She put two pennies beside the glass for a tip and turned on the stool. A startled gasp escaped her throat. The pair of young men stood so close she nearly bumped the taller one with her knees.

"Hi." The tall boy ran his hand through his unruly red hair, sweeping the thick strands away from his forehead the way a swashbuckling storybook hero might. "I'm Bart. This is Donny." He grabbed his buddy's elbow and pulled him a few inches forward. The two of them formed a human barricade, leaving Jennie no room to slide down from the stool onto the floor.

The boy named Donny blushed crimson and bobbed his head in a greeting. "What's your name?"

She'd contemplated going over and talking to them, but being hemmed in dissolved the desire. Unease now prickled her skin. She looked from one smirking face to the other. Most of the customers had departed, leaving only two older ladies quietly visiting and sharing a sandwich at a round table. The soda jerk busily arranged little jars on the shelf behind the counter, whistling. No one seemed aware of her discomfort. If she answered the boys, would they go on and leave her alone? She could try. "I'm Jennie."

Bart jammed his hands into his pockets and rocked on his heels.

"We've seen you in here before now and then, but we ain't really met."

Of course they never approached her when she was with Mama. They wouldn't have had the nerve. Maybe being alone in town wasn't so wonderful after all.

Jennie cleared her throat and eased off the seat. She stood in the little space between two stools, her spine pressed against the edge of the counter. She offered a weak smile and gestured to the screen door perhaps a half dozen yards from her spot. "Well, now we've met. If you'll excuse me, I—"

Bart yanked his hands from his pockets. "Where are you goin'? We wanna talk to you."

But she no longer wanted to talk to them. They were pushy and obnoxious. Their attention felt less innocent than it had from a distance. She peeked over her shoulder at the soda jerk, hoping he might intervene, but he went on clanking the little jars of colored liquid onto the shelf. She faced the boys again. "I'm sorry, but—"

"Oh, come on." Donny's tone turned pleading. "We saw you lookin' at us. We know you wanted us to come over here."

Is that what her casual glances communicated? How had she gotten herself into this fix? Mama and Daddy expected her to follow the biblical instruction to treat others the way she wanted to be treated. She didn't like being brushed off as unimportant, so she shouldn't be rude to these two, who probably thought they were flattering her with their attention. At the same time, she only wanted to escape them. During her years living beside the waterway, had she lost all ability to interact with others?

She swung her little velvet pouch. "I'm sorry, but I've finished my soda and I have shopping to do. So if you two will—"

"Come watch us play tennis." Bart spoke forcefully—a demand, not an invitation.

Jennie drew back, connecting painfully with the counter's sharp edge. She grimaced. "I already told you, I have shopping to do."

Donny snorted. "Stores're open until six. You got plenty of time." He braced his hand on the counter, blocking her in place. "A whole bunch of fellows meet Saturday afternoons at the tennis court behind the high school. They'll all want to meet you, you bein' such a pretty girl."

So that's what this was about—they wanted to show off for their friends by bringing someone new. Although it had been several years since she'd attended school, she recalled some of the petty games young people played. These boys weren't interested in her as a person as much as a tool to impress others. The thought irritated her and made her all the more anxious to leave. But neither boy seemed willing to budge. Could she push past them? It wasn't a ladylike thing to do, but she wouldn't call them gentlemen, so maybe it didn't matter. What would Mama advise?

Mama, help . . .

"Well, hello there, Miss Ward."

The friendly voice directly following her inward plea nearly buckled Jennie's knees. She looked toward the sound and spotted Leo Day crossing the floor. His gaze and easy smile latched on to her face. Relief flooded her, and her lips automatically lifted in response. The pair of young boys inched backward at Leo's approach, sending narrow-eyed frowns at each other.

Jennie stepped off the little rise at the base of the counter and met Leo on the floor. "Hello again, Mr. Day. How nice to see you." Her words wheezed out on a note of gratitude. *Nice* was an understatement. She'd never been happier to see another human being.

He shifted his attention to the boys, skimming each with an unsmiling examination. "Are you going to introduce me to your friends?" Next to the teenage boys, Leo appeared mature and masculine—even more so than yesterday. And he seemed to bristle with protectiveness. No wonder the boys acted cowed by his presence.

"We ain't exactly her friends." Donny took another step in reverse, bopping Bart on the arm with the back of his hand. "We just saw her sitting there all by herself and asked if she wanted to watch us play tennis."

"That's right." Bart side-stepped around Leo and joined his pal. "But she said she had shopping to do, so I guess we'll go on without her."

"Very well." Leo tipped his hat at the pair. "Have fun at the courts, boys." The two departed in a hurry, letting the screen door slap into its frame. Leo watched after them until they disappeared beyond the drugstore window. Then he put his hands on his hips and settled a concerned look on Jennie. "Are you all right? I happened to glance in as I was passing by, and something told me you weren't comfortable in their presence. Did they harm you in any way?"

They'd intimidated her with their brashness, but she couldn't honestly say she'd been harmed. "No, they were just persistent."

He chuckled softly. "Mm-hmm. Sometimes boys their age can be a nuisance, especially when they want to impress a pretty girl."

He thought she was pretty? The younger boys had said so, but she appreciated the compliment more from Leo. He stood as close as the boys had, but she didn't view him as a nuisance. Or intimidating or obnoxious. No, she welcomed his presence. The realization made her pulse hiccup. She wrung the little pouch between her hands, seeking something to say that would keep him there. "I didn't want to hurt their feelings, but I didn't want to leave with them either. Thank you for getting rid of them for me."

A warm smile lit his eyes. "No need to thank me. I would've done the same thing had some young hooligans been badgering one of my little sisters."

Her fluttering heartbeat fizzled into a normal rhythm. He viewed her as a younger sister? The admission was kind. Even gentlemanly. So why did disappointment sting? "Th-that's very kind."

He glanced around. "Aren't your parents with you?"

She shook her head, trying to discern if he disapproved of her being in town alone or was merely curious.

He sighed. "Oh. When I saw you, I hoped they might be." He rested his elbow on the counter and beamed at her. "I talked on the telephone with Mr. J. D. Figgins this morning. He's the director of the Denver Museum of Nature and Science. I told him about the bone your daddy's dog brought home, and he was very interested in it. I have some more questions for your daddy. Are you meeting up with your parents soon? If so, may I tag along with you?"

She didn't like comparing him to those boys who'd only wanted to use her to show off for their friends, but it seemed she was an end to a means for Leo, too. She forced a light laugh to chase away the uncomfortable thought. "Mama and Daddy didn't come into town with me." Actually, Daddy hadn't been to town since his appointment to have his cast removed, but nobody was supposed to know that. "I'll meet up with them tomorrow afternoon, after I attend church with Aunt Delia and Uncle Prime. If you want to talk to Daddy, you'll have to go to our cabin."

Leo tapped his chin with his finger, his brow puckering. "Mr. Figgins was so eager, I hate to leave him waiting too long for answers to his questions. Do you have a telephone at your place? Might I be able to call your daddy?"

A telephone? The idea was so ludicrous that this time her laugh trickled out involuntarily. "I'm afraid not. We didn't even have running water until a year ago, and we live right next to the river. Can you imagine trying to string telephone wire all the way out to our place?"

A sheepish grin climbed Leo's clean-shaven cheeks. "I didn't think about that. You're right. But you folks are so isolated out there. How do you summon help if there's an emergency?"

"We send a message with the train engineer, or one of us rides into town to fetch help." They'd discovered the challenge of being completely on their own when Daddy took his fall and she and Mama had to find a way to carry him home. Had they caused more harm by dragging him on a blanket up the craggy hill? If they'd been able to get him doctoring sooner, would Daddy's leg have healed better? She shrugged, trying to dislodge the guilt that still weighed on her. "It's not an ideal method, and it takes a while for help to come, but Mama says it's better than nothing." Mama also said God was always only a prayer away. All their prayers hadn't fixed Daddy's leg, though.

Admiration glowed in Leo's eyes. "I'm beginning to feel rather spoiled by my city life. My family isn't wealthy—few ministers' families are—but our parsonage in Denver has running water, electricity, and even a telephone in Father's study. Sometimes I forget not everyone is so blessed." A shadow seemed to fall across his expression. He gave his head a little shake, and the odd sadness departed. "Since it seems I'm only able to speak with your daddy face-to-face, would you be opposed to me taking the train with you tomorrow?"

An impish thought entered her head. "Not at all. You can help me tote the month's worth of supplies I'm in town to purchase. I wasn't looking forward to doing that all by myself."

To her surprise, he burst out laughing. "I'm quite accustomed to carrying young ladies' packages, and it would delight me to provide assistance. In fact . . ." He tipped his head, his dark-blue eyes narrowing slightly. "I promised my parents I would find a church to call my own while I'm in Cañon City. Would you consider me forward if I asked to attend with you and your aunt and uncle?"

Jennie didn't even think about her answer. "Of course not. And afterward you can join us for lunch." Guilt nibbled at her. Leo hadn't been forward in asking to come to church with her family, but Mama would say asking a young man to dine with her aunt and uncle without first securing their permission was forward.

Even brazen. She assured herself that Aunt Delia, who was as hospitable as Mama, wouldn't mind. "Then we'll be ready to board the train at the same time."

Delight burst across his square, honest face. "Perfect!" He stuck out his elbow. "And now let me accompany you on your shopping expedition. We can't have those youngsters accosting you again."

Oh, how Jennie wanted to slip her hand into the bend of his arm and experience being escorted through town by a handsome college boy. But he'd said he was acting as a big brother. He was only interested in gaining information from her daddy. Once he'd found what he was seeking, he would board the train and go home and she'd never see him again. She would accept his help loading and unloading the crates of goods tomorrow, but she should guard herself against anything more personal.

"The general store is just next door. I shouldn't run into trouble between here and there. I'll see you at the First Presbyterian Church tomorrow morning. Enjoy your day." She scurried out alone. The same way she'd gone in.

Chapter Six

Leo

D espite his best efforts to simply listen, Leo privately critiqued the minister's delivery during the church service held at the red-brick Presbyterian church. The minister was good. His message, taken from the first chapter of James, was biblically sound and he spoke with conviction, even giving Leo a thought or two to ponder later in the day. But the bane of having sat under Father's skilled and emotionally charged preaching was that other ministers never seemed to measure up. The way he'd never measured up in Father's eyes.

He pushed the thought aside as the congregation rose for a hymn. The organist played a series of reverberating opening notes, and across the sanctuary, voices joined in Charles Wesley's "Love Divine, All Loves Excelling." Leo shared a hymnal with Jennie and enjoyed hearing her sweet yet unassuming soprano. He wished he could make sense of her change in demeanor. The Jennie who'd held up the old dinosaur bone like a club, teasingly called him "college boy," and strode across the top of that warped wooden pipeline with the agility of a—his lips twitched with his effort to hold back a grin—young mountain goat had dissolved into a completely different person.

Upon meeting on the sidewalk before service began, she'd politely introduced him to her aunt and uncle. Here in the church building, she politely invited him to sit with her family, politely shared her hymnal, and politely passed him the velvet offering pouch. He couldn't fault her behavior, but her reservedness put him on edge. He'd seen her transform before his eyes yesterday when he offered to accompany her to the mercantile. He'd witnessed his sister Myrtle's rapid changes from cheerful to churlish and back again as she moved out of childhood. Maybe Jennie was merely exhibiting a girlish mood swing. Even so, he felt as if he'd done something wrong, but he didn't know what. The way he'd so often felt when he was a boy living under Father's watchful eye.

" 'Finish then, Thy new creation; pure and spotless let us be . . . ' "

The entreaty found in the hymn's lyrics brought his thoughts back to his father, and he winced. Would he ever be pure and spotless as far as Father was concerned? From his earliest memories, he'd done his best to please his father. He followed every rule whether dictated by God or man, behaved respectfully, put forth his best efforts in every pursuit whether academic or athletic. Other parents held him as the shining example for their children to emulate. But unless he changed his course of study, donned a cleric's garb, and stepped behind a pulpit, Father would forever find fault with him.

The hymn ended. Jennie closed the book and returned it to the hymnal rack without glancing up at him. The song leader moved aside, and the minister stepped to the edge of the dais. He sent a warm smile across the congregation. "Let us carry with us, no matter what conflicts we might be facing, the wise words shared in James one, verse three." He closed his eyes. " 'Knowing this, that the trying of your faith worketh patience.' " He opened his eyes again and offered a solemn nod. "Our God is not wasteful. Even our trials can be used for good when we continually trust in Him. Now the grace of the Lord Jesus Christ, the love of God, and the communion of the Holy Spirit be with you all. Amen."

Many people, including Jennie and her aunt and uncle, echoed, "Amen." Then folks gathered their Bibles, handbags, and restless children and began milling toward the front door. Jennie's aunt and uncle, the wife's hand tucked in the bend of her husband's arm, fell in with the others leaving. Leo considered offering his arm to Jennie, but after yesterday's strange reaction to his gentlemanly gesture, he feared a refusal. So he grabbed his hat from the pew and trailed behind her up the aisle and out the door into the midday sunshine.

Jennie's aunt, Mrs. Flankston, sent a smile over her shoulder past Jennie to Leo. "Did you enjoy the service, Mr. Day?"

"Yes, ma'am." He settled his hat into place. "I found the message encouraging and thought-provoking. The singing was quite nice, and I appreciate how the song leader chose hymns that supported the Scripture passages cited in the sermon." As people passed him, several offered nods or paused to shake his hand. He added, "The people are friendly, too. So, yes, it's been an enjoyable experience."

A light, trickling laugh spilled from the woman's smiling lips. "I don't think I've ever heard such a well-thought-out answer to a simple question." Her eyes shone with warmth, reminding him of Jennie's mother. "That is wonderful to hear. I was a little nervous after Jennie told us how your daddy and granddaddy are preachers."

Leo glanced at Jennie and caught her staring at the ground and shifting blades of grass with the pointy toe of her shoe. She'd shared information about him with her aunt and uncle, hmm? Maybe she wasn't as indifferent to him as her current behavior intimated.

Mr. Flankston exhaled a huff, making Leo think he'd been holding his breath. "We weren't sure how you'd take to our reverend. He's fairly young and inexperienced, but his heart is in the right place. We believe he'll grow into an excellent speaker as time goes by."

Although the preacher's delivery wasn't as skilled as Father's or

Grandfather's, Leo had seen fervor in his expression and heard passion in his voice. Clearly, the man had heeded God's calling and would, as Jennie's uncle stated, grow in his ability to share biblical messages in a meaningful manner. Father would likely approve of this young preacher. If only Father could find it in his heart to approve the calling Leo had received. Could only ministers influence lives with truths from God's Word?

"He's already an excellent speaker." Leo heard a hint of defensiveness in his tone, and he almost laughed at himself. Was he defending the new preacher to Jennie's uncle or himself to Father? "As I said, I enjoyed the service." He glanced across the street at the Baptist church. "I might visit each of the churches in town, though, before I decide which to attend regularly over the summer weeks. I've not experienced other denominations' services. It could be interesting and enlightening."

Mr. Flankston turned toward the sidewalk, guiding his wife forward. "I agree with you. New experiences can inspire and grow us. I'm sure you'll enjoy the opportunity to explore. But for now, I'd like to explore the restaurant menu at the hotel. Let's go eat."

Leo enjoyed the hearty meal of stewed beef with potatoes, carrots, and onions in a thick gravy. The dessert, a towering slice of chocolate cake, also pleased his taste buds. More than the food, though, he enjoyed the conversation. Mrs. Flankston was as friendly and personable as her sister. Mr. Flankston matched her in congeniality. Although the man did more listening than talking, he maintained an interested countenance, much the way Jennie had when Leo joined her family at the cabin for supper on Friday evening.

If Mr. Flankston took Jennie's role, she assumed her father's. She barely looked up during the meal and contributed to the conversation only when someone directly addressed her. Even then, her responses were mostly monosyllabic, nothing like the answers she'd given to his questions when they walked the pipeline to-

gether. Although his acquaintanceship with her could be measured in hours rather than days or weeks, he found himself pining
for the Jennie he'd first met and pondering how to bring her back
again.

"I'm curious . . ." Mr. Flankston's pensive tone pulled Leo from
his reflections. "Why did you choose Colorado for seeking dinosaur bones? Do you really think there's anything left to discover
after Marsh and Cope finished their intensive competition?"

Leo blinked in surprise. He knew all about the fierce rivalry
between fossil hunters Othniel Marsh and Edward Cope that
lasted for years and ended in financial and personal ruin for both
men. His college professor had lectured at length about their finds
as well as their change from friends to rivals. But the war between
the two paleontologists had ended in 1892, more than two decades
ago. Leo'd presumed it was forgotten by most people.

He swiped his mouth with his napkin. "Marsh and Cope, and a
handful of others, certainly made diligent searches in Colorado,
but they mostly scoured the western regions. I came armed with
hope that if those beds were rich with fossils, other areas of Colorado will also hold evidence of life from long ago." He couldn't
help tossing a quick grin at Jennie. "And my hope proved true
when I spotted Jennie atop the pipeline, carrying a bone. I've
prayed for an opportunity to make a significant contribution to the
field of paleontology, and it seems as if God honored that prayer
by crossing my path with hers the same day she chose to tote the
bone on her route."

Jennie put down her fork and turned to Leo, fully facing him
for the first time since they met up that morning. "Do you really
think you looking out the train window and seeing me holding
that old bone is an answer to prayer?"

God hadn't answered his prayers concerning Father's attitude
toward his son's scientific pursuits, but Leo clung to a shred of
hope that God wasn't completely ignoring his heartfelt appeals.

He wanted to believe that seeing the bone in Jennie's hand was due to God's timing and intervention. He nodded. "I do." Then he sighed. "Of course, much work lies ahead. A single bone is the start, but unless I locate the skeleton from which it came, it's likely I'll lose Mr. Figgins's interest."

"Mr. Figgins?" Jennie's aunt arched a brow. "Who is he? One of your professors?"

"No, ma'am, he's the director of the Denver Museum of Nature and Science." The flicker of hope that resided deep within Leo flared. "Interestingly enough, he and my father were classmates in their younger years." If anyone could convince Father of the importance of these archaeological finds, J. D. Figgins could. And if Father became convinced that Leo wasn't wasting his life by digging around in the past, maybe, just maybe, he'd finally offer his blessing on Leo's plans for the future.

Without conscious thought, he closed his fist, an attempt to hold to his hope. "The museum doesn't yet have any complete Jurassic dinosaurs on display, and Mr. Figgins is quite interested in expanding their paleontology exhibit. I would love to contribute a substantial find."

Jennie's uncle pushed his plate aside and propped his arms on the edge of the table. "That's a mighty big aspiration for someone who's not too far along in years and experience."

Although the statement could be perceived as condescending, Leo read only interest in the man's somber gaze. "I suppose so, but if one has no goals to which to aspire, he has no true purpose in living. My father proclaims from the pulpit that a man's life is futile if he is not about God the Father's business. I've known since I was twelve years old that I wanted to find evidence of the biblical creation story. Many might scoff that the discovery of dinosaur bones plays a role in proving the Bible is an accurate historical document." In fact, one of his college professors had ridiculed him in front of his classmates. "But I view the findings differently.

Consider the literal field of skeletal remains discovered near Morrison in the late 1870s. Even scientists with leanings toward evolution agree some sort of catastrophic event wiped the dinosaurs out. Who's to say it wasn't the flood sent in Noah's time?"

He suddenly realized Jennie was staring at him, eyes wide and mouth slightly open. In awe? Or maybe disbelief. His uncertainty in determining the reason for her focus brought him up short. He sat back and folded his hands in his lap. "Of course, as you tactfully pointed out, Mr. Flankston, it will take more than a college student's suppositions to convince seasoned paleontology experts to change their stance. But who knows? Maybe God will lead me to a key piece of evidence that points directly to His hand in not only the creation of but also the extermination of the great beasts that once roamed the earth."

Chapter Seven

Etta

With the dishes washed, dried, and back on the shelf, Etta's lunch chores were done. She glanced at the mantel clock. Still a half hour until the train would round the bend. She had fifteen minutes before she needed to start her trek to the bridge with their hand wagon. Fifteen minutes to convince Claude to get up out of his chair and walk with her.

She crossed to him, fixing a smile on her face as she went. "It's a pretty day. Hardly any wind at all." He often complained the wind made him unsteady. "And the pathway is dry since we've not had rain in two weeks." He also fussed about wet and slippery ground. He couldn't use that excuse today. "So why not put on your shoes and hat and accompany me to the bridge? What a fun surprise it would be for Jennie to find both of us waiting for her when she arrives with our goods."

Claude slowly turned from the window and gaped at her. "It's a good quarter mile down to that bridge, Etta. I can barely make it to the outhouse and back, and you want me to walk all the way to the bridge? You'd end up toting me in the wagon instead of the goods."

"Now, Claude . . ." Etta placed her hand on his shoulder and gentled her voice. "Remember what the doctor told you when he came out? Your leg's all healed up. Yes, it's shorter than it was before, but it still works. The fact that you can get yourself up and around and to the outhouse proves it. But you have to exercise it to regain full strength. A walk to the bridge and back would be good exercise." She rubbed a circle on his shoulder, trying to relax the tense muscles. "A few walks like that and pretty soon you'll be ready to walk the—"

He shrugged her hand away and aimed his gaze out the window again. "Don't say *pipeline*. I won't ever be able to climb up on that pipe and walk its length. There's no sense thinking about it."

Oh, he was stubborn. But it was despondence talking. The Claude she'd known before his fall was buried somewhere inside this surly, defeated shell. If only she knew how to draw him out again. She sent up a silent prayer for guidance and opened her mouth. She surprised herself by saying, "All right, then. I'll go by myself."

She fetched the wagon from the shed attached to the small chicken coop and set off slowly down the hill, silently berating herself with every step. Why had she given in so easily? She'd planned to use this weekend alone with Claude to stir him to action for Jennie's sake. Here she was, down to the final minutes, and she'd walked away from one last opportunity. Why hadn't she said what she wanted to?

"You need to think about it and then do it so your daughter has a chance to live her own life instead of taking care of you. Until you regain your strength, you'll never regain your self-respect. So get up, Claude, and walk to the bridge with me." She spouted the statement to the rolling expanse of towering, boulder-strewn mountains on the opposite side of the river. Their stony silence reminded her too much of Claude's often brooding muteness.

She shook her head, aggravated with herself. Doc Whiteside had advised her not to mollycoddle Claude, as she was enabling him to give up. Yet time and again, she hid her true feelings. Out of kindness or simply an unwillingness to stir contention? She couldn't be sure.

Etta paused and lifted her face to the clear blue sky overhead.

"God, did You stifle my words, or did I let cowardice take over? I try so hard to honor You in what I say and do. Your Word instructs us to turn the other cheek, to treat others the way we want to be treated, to love even our enemies. Claude isn't my enemy—he's my beloved husband. But at times, his actions and the things he says makes him seem like an enemy." Tears blurred her vision, and she blinked them away. "Tell me what to do to bring my husband back to me, please."

The breeze tousled her hair and whispered through the grasses, and she listened hard, but no voice spoke from the canopy of sky. She sighed, took a firmer grip on the wagon handle, and continued her trek down the sloping ground to the footbridge. She parked the wagon, then sat on the flatbed and waited for her daughter.

Within minutes of her arrival, the train's whistle signaled its approach. She stood, pasting on a smile for Jennie's sake, as the train screeched to a stop. The conductor hopped down from the caboose's back landing, his round, ruddy, friendly face angling in Etta's direction. The hissing steam and *chug-chug* of the pulsing engine created too much noise to allow conversation, so she waved a hello and he responded in kind.

She watched as he lifted crates one by one from the caboose and stacked them next to the train. Midway through the transfers, she realized someone other than Jennie was handing the crates to Mr. Jenkins. Recognition dawned. Apparently, Leo Day had decided to return for the dinosaur bone. Thank goodness. It unnerved her to have the old thing in her otherwise clean house.

Mr. Jenkins tipped his hat to Etta and hopped back up on the landing. Jennie climbed down and Leo closely followed her. They both waved, presumably to Mr. Jenkins, and the train squealed into motion. Jennie reached for a crate, but Leo touched her arm and shook his head. He said something, Jennie frowned, and he said something else. She shrugged and headed for the footbridge. She made her way across the bridge slowly, watching her feet, then clambered the short distance to her mother.

Etta pulled her daughter into an embrace, savoring the tight squeeze Jennie delivered. "Did you have an enjoyable weekend? How are your aunt and uncle?"

Jennie pulled loose. "They're fine. They send their love and said you and Daddy should come next time. The hotel owner hired a new baker for the restaurant." Hopefulness glistened in her rich-brown eyes. "Uncle Prime said that when Daddy comes, they'll have the baker make pound cake with strawberries. The bed behind the hotel is producing well this year."

Etta forced a soft laugh. "The promise of his favorite cake just might lure your daddy to town."

Jennie sighed, and Etta interpreted the meaning behind it. Jennie had heard the lack of confidence in her mother's tone. Eager to set aside the cloak of sadness that had fallen over the two of them, Etta turned to Leo, who'd crossed the bridge and now stood beside the wagon with a crate balanced against his front. "I wish I'd known you were coming. I could have brought that old bone down for you. Then you wouldn't have to stay and wait for the return train."

He set the crate on the wagon and whipped off his hat, giving a nod to Etta. "It's all right. Jennie told me there's no real way to send messages out here. Besides, I'd like to visit with your husband." He sent a glance toward the cabin. "Is he available for company today?"

Etta couldn't guarantee how Claude would respond to an unexpected visitor, but he was awake, dressed, and sitting in his chair. "He is."

"Good." He settled his hat into place again. "I'll get the rest of your crates and pull the wagon around for you."

Etta held up her hand. "If you need to speak with Mr. Ward, why don't you go on to the cabin? Jennie and I are accustomed to taking care of the goods."

Determination squared his shoulders even while his friendly smile remained intact. "Ma'am, my mother would have my hide if she knew I could have helped and didn't. I'll see to the crates today for you ladies." He strode back to the bridge.

Etta slid her hand through the bend of Jennie's arm and pulled her close. "He's a polite young man."

Jennie nodded, her pensive gaze seeming to follow him. "He is. I think he could be a good friend if . . ."

Etta waited, but Jennie didn't finish her sentence. She gave her daughter's arm a gentle squeeze. "If you weren't stuck out here away from town?"

A flush filled Jennie's cheeks. "Even if I was in town, he's only here for the summer. Then he'll go back to college. So it doesn't really matter."

The regret in Jennie's voice pierced Etta. Whether Claude ever walked the pipeline again or not, they could no longer hold Jennie captive out here. Etta drew Jennie a short distance away from the wagon, then spoke in a low tone. "Honey, it does matter. Having friends matters. I'll sit down this afternoon and write a letter to Delia informing her you'll be moving to town at the end of the summer."

Jennie's eyes flew wide. "Mama, I can't move to town. Who would inspect the pipeline?"

Etta lifted her chin, feigning confidence. "Your father, of course. We'll use these summer months to build his strength. By fall, when school starts again, he should be able to resume the route. It might take him longer to walk the full distance than it did before he broke his leg, but he can do it. He *needs* to do it." She believed that from the depth of her being. Claude *needed* to walk that pipeline again. "As long as you're available, he'll sit in his chair and brood."

Tears swam in her daughter's eyes. "Mama, I can't be selfish and run off to town. If it wasn't for me, Daddy wouldn't have been hurt in the first place."

Etta drew a sharp breath. "What do you mean?"

"I . . . I . . ."

The creak of their wagon's wheels interrupted. Leo pulled the wagon alongside them, aiming a curious look from daughter to mother to daughter again. "Is everything all right?"

Jennie turned her back and rubbed her fist under her nose. Etta nodded, waving her hand in a dismissive gesture. "Yes, we were just catching up after our time apart." Such a bald lie. She hoped God would forgive her, but she didn't know what else to say. Why would Jennie blame herself for Claude's fall? She hadn't even been with him at the time. "Thank you for loading those crates for us. You're a very kind young man." She gave her daughter a gentle nudge. "Jennie, you run ahead and let your daddy know Mr. Day wants to talk to him. Mr. Day and I will be along shortly."

"Yes, Mama." Jennie darted off.

Leo watched after her. "Jennie seemed upset. I hope my presence isn't making her uncomfortable."

Etta's heart rolled over. He was a nice young man, exactly the kind of friend she wanted Jennie to find. "It isn't you at all." She started up the path, and he accompanied her, pulling the wagon. She held to a slow pace partly to prevent spilling the crates and partly to prolong their time together. "Jennie always experiences a touch of the doldrums when she returns from town. It's very quiet out here, don't you agree?"

He switched hands on the handle. "Yes, I do." His gaze swept the area, a smile twitching at the corners of his lips. "I find it a nice distraction from the busyness of the college grounds, but I suppose it would be different if I lived here. The quiet and seclusion might lead to being lonely."

His astuteness surprised her. It also lent further evidence to his kind nature. "You're right. And it has. One weekend in town every month doesn't allow time for Jennie to develop friendships."

To her further surprise, he laughed. "Well, if she stayed longer than a day or two, I think friends might pop up from behind every bush. I actually witnessed a pair of boys doing their best to win her favor."

Etta raised her eyebrows. "Oh?"

His grin turned mischievous. He shared about her trying to escape some boys' overly friendly advances at the drugstore counter. "I'm sure they were harmless, but I think they intimidated her with their enthusiasm."

She imagined the scene, then sighed. "Likely so. Jennie hasn't had any real interaction with people her age since she was a child. She's probably forgotten how to relate to others." The longer her daughter stayed out here, the harder it would be for her to form friendships. Should she arrange to send Jennie to town right away instead of waiting until school started again?

"Well . . ." Leo swiped perspiration from his brow. "Depending on what your husband tells me about this area, it's possible I will spend quite a bit of my summer break near your home. With your permission, I could stop by occasionally and visit with you folks."

Etta appreciated him including her and Claude. He seemed to be an honorable young man. How many visits would he make before he grew weary of Claude's morose countenance? Then he would stop coming around, and Jennie could be hurt. He was waiting for an answer, but she didn't have one. She gestured to the open doorway of the cabin. "Thank you for your help, Leo. Please leave the wagon next to the stoop. Jennie and I will bring the items inside while you visit with Mr. Ward."

Chapter Eight

Leo

When Leo was seven, he got a splinter in his foot. It went deep into his heel and then, because he walked on it the rest of the day, broke into three pieces and eventually caused an infection. It took Father holding him down and Mother digging with a needle for three quarters of an hour to remove every bit of wood from the bottom of his sore foot. In retrospect, the lengthy, painful procedure was easier than drawing information from Jennie's disagreeable father.

After his third question was met with a grunt and shrug, Mrs. Ward stopped stacking cans on shelves and crossed to Mr. Ward's chair. "Claude, you know the answers to what Mr. Day is asking." She spoke as kindly as Leo's younger sister did to butterflies that visited their mother's flower garden. "He came all the way out here from town to gather information for the director of the big museum in Denver. Why won't you tell him what he needs to know?"

Mr. Ward's brown eyes narrowed. "Why does that fellow in Denver need to know bones are layin' half-buried on the ridges? What business is it of his?"

Leo stifled a sigh. If a person opened the dictionary to the word *curmudgeon,* they'd probably find an image of Claude Ward. "If I locate something of note, such as more of the bones that go with the one Jennie gave me, Mr. Figgins wants to be sure it isn't from privately owned land. If it is, he needs to seek permission to access the area. He wants to avoid charges of trespassing."

The man's expression remained sour. "And likely doesn't want a battle over ownership."

Ah, he was more knowledgeable than he wanted to let on. Leo nodded. "Absolutely. The museum's reputation could be tarnished if it was forced to engage in litigation." The world of paleontology didn't need another war over dinosaur bones.

"Far as I know"—Claude drawled the words, as if too weary to participate in conversation—"the acreage on the waterway side of the river is claimed by the Cañon City Water Works Department. They let hunters and trappers roam out here without having to ask first. I've warned a few of 'em away from the pipeline and our cabin. Don't want a stray bullet poking a hole in the staves or, worse, hitting my wife or daughter."

Now that he'd gotten his vocal cords working, he seemed to have a lot to say. Leo listened for information that Mr. Figgins would find of use.

"I don't reckon they'd mind you *hunting* for bones. But if you want to do any kind of digging, you'll need their permission. Depending on how deep you go, it could affect the stability of the mountainside. They won't want an avalanche coming down and damaging the pipeline."

Leo nodded, amazed by the man's lengthy speech. His sullen, uncooperative attitude had led Leo to wonder if he wasn't quite bright. Clearly, he was intelligent. For whatever reason, he simply chose to keep his knowledge to himself.

The man aimed an impatient look at him. "That all you want to know?"

Leo believed he'd garnered what was necessary to proceed. He nodded and started to rise.

"Then lemme ask you a question."

Something in Mr. Ward's tone made the hair on the back of Leo's neck stand up. He settled in his chair again. "All right."

"Who all is gonna be doing this snooping for bones? You, or a whole passel of people?"

Mrs. Ward and Jennie both paused and looked at him. They seemed to hold their breath.

Leo shifted in his seat. "Just me, sir, for now."

"For now?" The man almost growled the query.

Leo gave a hesitant shrug. "Well, yes. But if I find something of value, and if the water-works owners approve a dig, a team of paleontologists secured by Mr. Figgins will likely come out to excavate the site. That could involve"—he borrowed Mr. Ward's term—"a passel of people."

Mr. and Mrs. Ward exchanged a glance. Mr. Ward rubbed his stubbly chin. "Then I don't know if I want—"

Jennie scurried to her father. "We're getting ahead of ourselves, Daddy. There's no guarantee Leo will find the remainder of the skeleton."

"That's true." Leo grimaced. "You folks can't know for sure where your dog found it. It might be a futile hunt."

Sadness shadowed the man's eyes. "Too bad Rex ain't around to lead the way. He was a good dog. Never had a better dog."

Jennie bit down on her lower lip and stared at Mr. Ward with such sympathy Leo wished he hadn't mentioned the dog. But it was too late now. He had to ask one more question, but not for Mr. Figgins's sake. He crossed to the doorway and picked up the bone Mrs. Ward had leaned against the corner. Then he returned to her husband.

"When I was here last, you named a possible location where the bone was found." His pulse thrummed in hopeful double beats as he locked eyes with Jennie's unsmiling daddy. "I'm not familiar with this area, but you are. If I paid you for your time, would you take me to the place you mentioned?"

The man bristled, and his hands balled into fists on his knees. Jennie stood quiet and wide-eyed behind her father, staring at the back of his head. On the other side of the room, Mrs. Ward seemed to turn into a statue, her eyes fixed on her husband's face. Leo waited uncertainly. Apparently, he'd broken some kind of unwritten rule, but what?

Jennie suddenly took a step forward and placed her hands on Mr. Ward's shoulders. "Leo, Daddy can't take you up on the mountain."

Leo recalled him saying as much last Friday when Jennie asked him to show Leo the spot. He should have remembered. He cringed. "I'm sorry. If he doesn't have time, it's all right. I understand."

"It's not about the time it would take." Jennie's expression seemed to plead with him, further confusing him. "You see . . ." She gulped. Mr. Ward stared out the window, and dejection seemed to wilt him. "Daddy can't do all that walking. His leg . . . he hurt it, and . . ."

Leo slowly put pieces together in his mind. Jennie had said she was examining the pipeline for her father because he'd been sick. She'd told a half-truth. He wasn't sick after all. But why lie about something like that? There was no shame in having an injury.

"If you bring a lot of people up here, the waterway men will know."

Leo tilted his head, confused. "Know what?"

Jennie gritted her teeth. "That Daddy is hurt."

Based on Jennie's tone, the situation was dire, but Leo still didn't understand. "They don't already know?"

Mr. Ward sat straight-up and pinned Leo in place with a fierce glare. "No. And you ain't gonna tell them. You ain't gonna do any bone hunting around here either. We can't risk—"

Jennie wrapped her arms around her father from behind. "It's all right, Daddy. You can let Leo look for more bones. We can trust him not to say anything to anyone. I know we can."

Mr. Ward wriggled, his expression fierce. "How do you know?"

"Because—" She swallowed. "I know." She released her father and slowly stood upright. Her gaze drifted to Leo's and remained steady. "I just . . . know."

Jennie

Please, Daddy, believe me. Jennie couldn't say the words out loud, but her thoughts begged. Daddy had to let Leo look for dinosaur bones. Because if Leo found more bones, then maybe she could start to believe again that God answered prayers.

Her reasoning was so jumbled even in her own mind she wouldn't be able to explain it. Was confusion part of being at a tumultuous age? When Leo had said he believed that God orchestrated her path crossing with his while she was carrying that awful old bone, something deep inside her had come alive again. She knew what the something was. Hope. Hope that God did hear prayers. Hope that God did answer prayers. Hope that God was watching and caring, the way she'd believed when she was a little girl. She missed believing. She wanted to believe again. But she had to see in order to believe. If she saw Leo's prayers fully answered, then maybe she could trust God with her own.

Mama came close to Daddy. "Claude, Jennie's right. Until we know for sure if there's more dinosaur bones up on the hill, there's no sense in stewing about people coming around and finding out she's really the one walking the pipeline."

Daddy struggled to his feet and turned a sour look on Mama. "I guess there's no reason to tell him not to look for bones since you spilled the secret we've been holding. Tell him whatever you want to. I'm gonna take a nap." He limped to his bedroom door and closed himself inside.

Leo sat back in the chair next to Daddy's and placed the bone across his knees. He looked from Mama to Jennie to Mama again. "I'd never divulge something that could bring harm to all of you, but I don't understand why it's such a secret that Jennie's walking the pipeline."

Mama sat sideways in Daddy's chair. She reached out and caught hold of Jennie's hand and cradled it between hers. "The waterway men hired Claude. They didn't hire Claude's little girl. All this time, they've kept paying a salary meant for a grown man. It won't matter to them that Jennie's done the same job her daddy did before he got hurt." She chuckled, peeking up at Jennie. "She's maybe done even a little more, because she makes drawings of what she finds so they have a better idea of the problem." Then Mama sighed. "They might think we've been pulling the wool over their eyes. They could ask for some of that money back or even kick us off this place. And if they do . . ."

Mama didn't need to say more for Jennie to understand, but would Leo? Jennie added, "We won't have a place to live or money to support us. Daddy"—she sucked in a breath—"can't work anymore." Her air whooshed out with the admission. She didn't want to shame her father, but Leo had to know the truth of everything. Then for sure he wouldn't tell anyone. "And he depends on Mama to take care of him during the day."

Should she say the rest of what she was thinking? Leo was, after all, still pretty much a stranger. But she wanted to trust him. Wanted to think that maybe he could be a friend if only for a little while. "Mama thinks Daddy can get his strength back and start walking the line again by the end of summer, but I don't think it'll happen. It's not just Daddy's leg that's broken. There's something inside him that broke when he fell off the pipe. Probably because he lay there, hurting and helpless for so long. All his pride drained out of him."

She'd never forgive herself for not going with him on that drizzly summer morning. August 8, 1913—the day everything changed. She had followed Daddy on his route Monday through Thursday of the week, like always, but that Friday she begged off so she could wash her hair in readiness for the next day's train ride into Cañon City. When Daddy was late coming home, she and Mama first thought the wetness delayed him. The pipe would be slippery—he had to go slower. But when full dark came and he still wasn't home, Mama lit a lantern and she and Jennie went looking.

An image of her beloved daddy lying on the rocks near the river, his face contorted into a mask of agony, was forever seared in Jennie's memory. She knew now that not all the agony was from physical pain. Her strong, capable daddy didn't feel strong and capable anymore. He never would. And it all could have been avoided if she'd gone with him. If she'd been there, she would have witnessed his fall. She could have fetched help right away. He wouldn't have had to lie there for hours, brooding over his powerlessness.

Mama patted Jennie's hand and released it, stubbornness jutting her jaw. "If your daddy gets his strength back, his pride will return, too."

To Jennie's way of thinking, Daddy needed his pride in order to work at getting his strength back, but she wouldn't argue with Mama. Especially not in front of a guest.

Mama went on in her certain voice. "He'll keep sitting around moping unless we *make* him get up. He needs motivation. And you"—she shook her finger at Jennie—"doing his job for him will not motivate him to get out of his chair."

Jennie huffed. "Mama, I can't just stop inspecting the line!"

Mama pursed her lips. "Of course not. But we need to tell him you're going to school this fall. Then he has no choice except to get strong enough to be the linewalker again."

Leo had sat quietly while Mama and Jennie talked, but now he leaned forward. His fingers curled over the bone in his lap as if fearful they would yank it away from him. "Ladies, would it be better if I chose another location—one far away from the pipeline—to search for bones?"

"No," Mama and Jennie said at the same time.

Leo blinked in surprise, his gaze flitting between the two of them. He gently cleared his throat. "Are you sure? It seems my presence here has created angst. I don't want my personal aspirations to cause problems between you and Mr. Ward."

Jennie swallowed a knot of longing. Oh, to have a friendship with this kind young man. Why did he have to be a college boy who was only passing through? He couldn't be the friend she'd prayed for. Maybe only selfishness made her want to be more than part of the answer to his prayers. If he could be unselfish, she could be, too.

Mama started to say something, but Jennie jumped in. "We know for sure there are dinosaur bones somewhere in these hills or Rex wouldn't have found that one." Leo glanced at the bone, then settled his attention on her. "The quicker you find the rest of the skeleton, the sooner you'll know if it's something the museum wants. It isn't your fault Daddy got hurt and I had to take over his job, so you shouldn't have to give up your search because of us. I think you should look where—"

She sucked in a startled gasp. The realization of what she planned to say surprised her so much she lost her ability to speak for a moment. Both Leo and Mama sat looking at her as if she'd suddenly sprouted mule ears like the characters in her childhood picture book *Pinocchio*. She almost giggled. She whispered, "Where God led you."

Mama's eyes swam with tears. She nodded. "Yes. Yes." She grabbed Jennie's hand again and squeezed it while beaming at Leo. "Young man, I believe God sent you here to aid us in Mr. Ward's recovery. So you will hunt these hills for dinosaur bones. And Jennie will be your guide."

Chapter Nine

Etta

Monday morning, Etta sent Jennie out the door with a hug and whispered promise—"Only three months, honey, and you can go back to being our daughter instead of our breadwinner."

She watched Jennie trot down the rise, her braid bouncing on her spine. So carefree she appeared. For a moment, Etta worried she'd made a promise she couldn't keep. But the girl deserved to be set free. God had great plans for her. How would she find her God-given pathway if she didn't have the opportunity to explore?

Stepping out onto the stoop, she looked up at the sky. "I will keep the promise to Jennie. With Your help, God, I will keep it."

Saying the prayer aloud bolstered her, and she headed to her bedroom, where Claude still lay flat on his back snoring, one foot out from under the light covers and an arm flung above his head. She paused and smiled at his relaxed position. A part of her hesitated to disturb him, but he needed to break his habit of sleeping late. With determination, she marched to the bed and put her hand on his chest.

"Claude?"

He gave a little jerk. His eyes popped open, then quickly narrowed to slits. "What?"

"It's breakfast time. Come and eat."

He brought his arm down and rubbed his nose. "Not hungry."

Etta hid a smile at his grumbly tone. "Not even for pancakes and maple syrup?" She always purchased a quart tin of maple syrup with their monthly groceries, but it never lasted to the end of the month. Claude liked to drown his pancakes, as he put it.

He licked his lips. "That does sound good."

"All right, then. Visit the outhouse, get dressed, and come to the table. I'll have a short stack ready for you."

Etta had already sprinkled a pancake with sugar and rolled it into a tube, which she'd eaten with Jennie. But she enjoyed a second one flat on the plate with syrup while Claude ate his drowned stack. She waited until he was using his finger to scoop the last smears of syrup, then delivered the speech she'd practiced in her head after bedtime last night.

"Now that you've got your belly filled, you can help me stack the mercantile's empty crates on the wagon and tote them down the hill for Mr. Jenkins to collect when the train comes by."

Claude paused with his sticky finger halfway to his mouth. "What'd you say?"

She repeated it all word for word, in exactly the same nonchalant tone, like it was something she asked of him every day of the week.

He wiped his syrup-smeared hand with his napkin. "They're still here?"

She forced a soft laugh. "Of course they are."

He grunted. "Figured you'd ask that young fellow to take 'em back since he helped cart 'em in. He had to meet the train last evening anyway."

Etta shrugged and rose. "I suppose I could have." She'd actually thought about it, but then she'd decided taking those crates down the hill would be good exercise for Claude. She gathered their plates and carried them to the sink. "But he'd already helped enough by pulling the full wagon up the rise. I didn't want to take advantage of his kindness."

Claude pushed up from his chair and limped to the stove. He

refilled his coffee cup, then leaned against the counter, slurping the brew and watching her pump water into the basin. As she lowered the dishes into the water, he plunked the empty cup onto the counter. "I already told you it's a hard walk to the footbridge. Don't see myself being able to get that far and back again."

She kept her eyes on her hands running a sopping cloth over her plate. "You won't know unless you try. And we don't have to be in a hurry. The train won't come by until midmorning." She glanced out the window. "The sun hasn't even cleared the mountain peaks yet. We can go slow, let you rest as often as you want to." She sneaked a peek at his frowning countenance. "It'd be a real treat to go out walking with you this morning, Claude." Etta set the clean plate in the dish drainer and looked him full in the face. "Please?"

He stared at her unblinking for several seconds, his lips puckered into a half scowl. She held her breath, waiting, hoping, praying he'd agree. Finally, he lurched away from the counter, a huge sigh heaving from his chest. "I'm just not up to that walk, Etta."

Her spirits sank.

"But I reckon I can stack the crates on the wagon for you if it'd help."

A smile formed without effort. "That would be a real help. Thank you, Claude." *And thank You, God, for this little step forward.*

Jennie

Jennie reminded herself to slow down as she inspected the pipeline's staves and steel bands. She was still the linewalker. She needed to do a good job. But her mind refused to focus. Too many exciting, scary, unsettled thoughts cluttered her head.

Would Mama really convince Daddy he was able to do this work again? Would she really get to move to town and stay with

Aunt Delia and Uncle Prime at the end of the summer and finish her education in a classroom? She wanted to believe it, but she was afraid to. There was a verse somewhere in Proverbs that said hope deferred made the heart sick. If she believed—really believed—and then Daddy didn't get better and take over and she didn't get to move to town, her heart might never recover. She'd end up the way Daddy was now. Morose. Uncommunicative. Trapped in a constant state of despair.

And what if she did get to go to town but she was too far behind to keep up with her classmates? When she was younger, she was a good student. She got high marks and praise from her teachers. She'd wither up from mortification if she failed tests or had to attend classes meant for students younger than her age. What if she ended up in the same class as those obnoxious boys who'd pestered her at the drugstore? Maybe it was best if she finished her schooling with Mama instead. She wouldn't go to college anyway. She had no important aspirations. Not like Leo, who needed training to become a paleontologist.

But if she went to school in Cañon City, she could take an art class. Aunt Delia said she had a real knack for drawing—that it was a God-given gift and she should make the most of it. How could she do that if she didn't go to school?

And now she couldn't remember if she'd even looked at the pipeline. She released a huff of aggravation and carefully turned around. She swept her gaze across the pipe, taking slow, cautious forward steps. No cracks or breaks in the staves. No signs of weakness in the reinforcing bars. No leaks or rot or other signs of damage.

The river's song roared in her ears. The wind tossed her hair. Her heels squeaked on the dew-damp redwood staves. She held her balance and advanced, step-by-step, just the way Daddy had done.

There was no need to hurry, anyway. Yesterday, after she got

Mama's permission to be Leo's guide, they'd planned it all out. He would hop off the afternoon train and meet her near the spot they'd encountered each other last week. She stifled a snicker. This time, though, she wouldn't pretend she might clop him with a bone and he wouldn't sit and wait for her to finish her route. He said he wanted to walk the pipeline with her, build up his muscles for trekking over the hillsides.

Maybe he'd end up setting an example for Daddy.

She stopped for a moment, contemplating the thought. She'd prayed for Daddy to get better and for a friend. Leo had prayed for dinosaur bones. He believed God aligned his pathway to meet hers. Was Leo's answer to prayer also *her* answer to prayer . . . for Daddy?

The question was still rolling in the back of her mind when the train rumbled by. She waved as always, then remained in her place, watching the pile of boulders for Leo. When he popped into view, a laugh burbled up. Where was his fancy suit and bowler hat? The college boy had been transformed into a . . . she didn't know what to call him. He wore a light-brown button-up shirt with buttoned patch pockets on the chest, trousers the same color as his shirt, and a darker-brown belt with flat leather pouches hanging from it. Wide canvas straps over his shoulders held a good-sized well-worn knapsack on his back. He'd tucked his pant legs into nearly knee-high brown lace-up boots, and on his head was a wide-brimmed hat of some sort of heavy tan-colored material secured by a string under his chin. She'd never seen the like.

He splashed across the river, then clambered on top of a large partially submerged boulder along the bank and grinned up at her. "Were you laughing at me, Miss Mountain Goat?"

His teasing query only made her laugh again. "I guess I was. I'm sorry if I hurt your feelings, but . . ." She swallowed her amusement and gave him a slow toes-to-hat perusal. "You look so different in those clothes."

He held his arms outward and glanced down at himself. "When I was in high school, I was a junior leader for a boys' scouting group. This is my uniform, which is perfect for camping or hiking. See?" He patted one of the leather pouches. "This holds my folding knife. This one"—he pointed to another pouch—"has flint and steel in case I want to build a campfire." He shared the contents of each pouch and shirt pocket, then chuckled. "I'm much better prepared for mountain climbing in this gear than I was the last time we met out here."

She had to admit, his current clothes were more appropriate, but she'd become accustomed to his formal bearing. The uniform, as he'd called it, gave him a youthful, relaxed countenance that she found both appealing and a little frightening. This Leo seemed even more approachable than the dignified version. She would have a harder time guarding herself from growing too attached to him.

"You're probably right about that." She gestured to the upward slope behind the pipe. "Better come on over and pull yourself up on the pipe. I've got a route to finish." She gave herself a stern warning to pay attention, too.

Leo remained a few feet behind her the remainder of her daily examination. To his credit, he didn't speak to her, which should have helped her stay focused on the task at hand. But just knowing he was there proved distracting. And comforting. An odd combination Mama would probably blame on Jennie's tumultuous age. Had her traipsing after Daddy been both distracting and comforting to him? She wished she could ask him, but she never knew how he would respond to questions anymore. And what did it matter, anyway? Her days of following Daddy were done. If he did take over the route again, she'd be in Cañon City with her aunt and uncle. Those days of following his footsteps and peppering him with questions were long gone.

She reached the end of the pipe and released a big sigh of satisfaction. She pulled out the little pad of paper and wrote "7 June 1915—no issues." Proud of herself for remembering the correct way to write the date, she slid the notepad back in her shirt pocket and turned to face Leo.

"That's it for the day. Let's walk the pipe back to my cabin. Mama said she'd pack us a few sandwiches to take along when we go up on the hillside."

He grinned and waggled his eyebrows. "Ah, there's no need to backtrack to the cabin." He shrugged one arm free of the knapsack strap and brought the bulky pouch to his front. "I asked the hotel cook to pack a picnic supper for us. We can go straight to exploring."

Jennie cringed. "Isn't that kind of expensive?" He'd told her his family wasn't wealthy. Paying to stay at the hotel all summer long was costly enough. She shouldn't expect him to feed her, even if she was acting as his guide.

He slid his arm back through the strap and bounced a couple of times, settling the sack on his back. "I suppose it would be if I paid for it outright. But I hired on at the hotel."

"You did? Are you a clerk or a porter?" Many young men served in those capacities at the St. Cloud.

"Neither." He struck a regal pose, made all the more ludicrous by the floppy hat and its dangling strings. "I scrub pots and pans and see to the trash bins. For my labor, I receive a room, three meals a day, and fifty-cents spending money each week." He chuckled and slid his hands into his trouser pockets. "Granted, the job isn't as glamorous as discovering prehistoric species embedded in rocks and dirt, but it will allow me to stay in the area and do what I set out to do."

Leo was raised by a preacher, lived in a house with many amenities, and attended college. He could consider himself above such menial tasks, but he didn't. Her admiration for him increased again. She wanted to tell him so, but bashfulness held the words inside. So she drew on impishness.

She sat and slid off the pipe, then looked up at him with one fist propped on her hip. "Well, what are you waiting for? Let's go hunting."

He released a hearty laugh, then saluted. "Yes, ma'am." He slid to the ground, and they took off up the hill.

Chapter Ten

Jennie

For the remainder of the week, Jennie and Leo followed the same routine established on Monday. When the afternoon train made its slow curve, Jennie paused and waited for Leo to join her on the route. When she was done with the daily inspection, they searched for signs of prehistoric life until the shadows grew heavy and Leo needed to meet the evening train at the footbridge.

How she savored those late-afternoon hours spent with Leo, roaming the hills and talking. At first she thought he would want quiet and focus in case he'd miss something, the way she did when walking the pipeline. But he claimed he could search *and* talk. So they talked. Endlessly. About their families, their closeness to their mothers and the emotional distance they felt from their fathers. School, his chosen classes at college and the classes she hoped to take in Cañon City. Everyday things, their likes and dislikes, living in the city versus living far outside of town, childhood memories, and much more. She hadn't realized she had so many words in her, and Leo seemed interested in everything she said.

She reminded herself often and firmly not to grow accustomed to his company. Once he found the bones he was seeking, their time together would end. But it didn't matter how often she inwardly cautioned herself—she continued to open up to him. To not only converse but also laugh with him. And just once, late in the week when talking about Daddy, got teary-eyed with him. She'd never forget the tender look in his dark-blue eyes or the gentle squeeze he gave her shoulder. Hardly a touch at all it happened so quickly, but the deep feeling behind it left her almost giddy with gratitude. He cared. He really cared.

His kindness on that breezy Thursday afternoon made her all the more determined to find bones for him. To gift him the way he had gifted her. At the same time, she understood that finding bones could potentially expose the secret her family kept. Knowing what a discovery would cost her created a tumult of emotional angst, but she held to her determination to repay him the only way she could—by locating the remainder of the skeleton from which Daddy's old shepherd dog had taken a bone.

Early in their hunting, Leo had indicated they'd be more likely to find bones in rocky outcroppings, so Jennie gravitated toward the places where layers of sediment were exposed. Friday afternoon, about an hour into their explorations, they encountered an area perhaps twelve feet wide. It was four feet high at its center but tapered down to mere inches at both ends. She nearly dismissed it, reasoning that such a small expanse of rock wouldn't be able to hold the remains of a dinosaur. But Leo approached it with eagerness, so she trailed after him, enjoying watching him go into what she had secretly dubbed his detective mode.

He bent forward until his face was only inches from the exposed rock, then worked his way across, his finger tracing a line from left to right as if he were reading text from a giant book. Then he reversed the search, tracing right to left with his finger a bit lower than the first sweep. He moved slowly, meticulously, sometimes pausing and squinting one eye shut and staring hard at a spot. She stood to the side, biting down lightly on the end of her tongue to prevent herself from talking and interrupting his concentration.

He was making his fourth slow sweep when he jolted and sucked in a breath. With his gaze locked on the rock, he pawed one of the belt pouches open and withdrew his knife.

Jennie darted forward, her hands clasped beneath her chin. "Did you find it?"

He laughed, unlocking the blade. "That depends on what you mean by 'it.'"

"The skeleton!" The statement squeaked out. Her heart pounded as exuberantly as if a drummer had taken up residence in her chest. Both hope and a sense of doom warred within her. He was poking at the rock with the knife blade, seemingly unaware that she awaited a reply. She rocked in place, eagerness to know what he'd found making her want to climb out of her skin. She couldn't stay quiet. "Leo, did you find the skeleton?"

"Ta-da!" He pinched out a chunk of rock and held it aloft, beaming. "Look!"

She looked, but she couldn't see anything of worth. "What is it?"

He laughed again, a joyful laugh that chased the element of doom from Jennie's chest. He cradled the bit of sediment in his palm. "Look there in the middle. Do you see something smooth and almost glassy half-buried in the rough stone?"

His description helped her locate a small triangle a bit darker and much smoother than the surrounding rock. She nodded.

He curled his fingers around the chunk of rock, his smile bright. "It's a tooth, Jennie."

Her jaw dropped. "A dinosaur tooth?"

"A shark tooth."

She drew back, suspicious. Was he making a joke? "How do you know?" She scanned the rock wall, seeking further evidence. "Where's the rest of it?"

He chuckled. "Sharks don't have bones. They're all cartilage, and cartilage breaks down. You'll never find a shark skeleton." He pulled a handkerchief from his trouser pocket and folded it around the broken piece of stone that contained—supposedly—a shark tooth. "But they have lots of teeth. Literally rows of them, and they lose teeth quite frequently."

She'd read in a science book about sharks' teeth regenerating, so she didn't doubt the truth of what he'd just said. Even so . . . "How'd a tooth get way up here? That doesn't make any sense."

"Sure it does." He shrugged out of his knapsack and tucked the bundle into a little buttoned pouch on the outside of the pack. "Shark teeth and fish skeletons have been found far inland from oceans—in the middle of prairies and high up on mountain peaks." He settled the knapsack in place and gazed at her with his brow furrowed. "Jennie, think about it. When God sent the great flood, the creatures of the seas didn't stay where they'd been before. They were able to swim all around the world. Of course, when the waters receded, not all those fish made it back to the ocean. Their fossilized remains show where they died. Or where they lost a tooth." He grinned. "I know it sounds a little fishy, if you'll pardon the pun, to imagine a shark swimming along these hillsides, but the tooth proves it. This was once all underwater."

She tried to think of something intelligent to say in response, but all that came out when she opened her mouth was, "Wow . . ."

He nodded. "Exactly." Then he frowned. "I wish there was a way to take a photograph of where we found the tooth. I'd like to commemorate our first discovery."

He'd said *we* and *our,* including her in the finding. A happy shiver wiggled down her spine. She snatched out her little notepad and pencil. "I don't have a camera, but I can make a drawing." She plopped down on the ground, balanced the pad on her knee, and made a sketch. The paper wasn't large enough to include the whole mountain—or Leo standing there smiling with the sediment-crusted tooth in his hand—but on the back of the page, she recorded their approximate location based on distance from her family's cabin and the river. She hoped it would do. When she finished, she gave it to him.

He stood looking at her sketch for a long time with as much concentration as he'd given the bank of exposed rock. Then his gaze lifted from the paper and settled on her. "This is really good, Jennie."

His praise made her feel light as air. She rose, slipping the paper and pencil back into her shirt pocket, then rocked gently on her heels. "It's not much. It would be better if I had my big sketch pad and the fancy drawing pencils Aunt Delia gave me."

He shook his head. "Don't belittle yourself." His serious expression held her captive. "That you made such a detailed drawing on a small piece of paper with only the nub of a pencil proves you are very talented."

His words delighted her but also embarrassed her. Uncertain how to respond, she dipped her head.

He lifted her face with his finger under her chin. An easy smile formed on his face, framed by the hat's silly brim and the strings beneath his chin. "Don't hide from a compliment. Just say 'thank you' and move on."

She swallowed the bashful chortle threatening to erupt and said, "Thank you."

"You're welcome." He lowered his hand, then winked. "You need to start thinking of yourself as an artist, Jennie Ward."

Maybe. Later. For now, she was just the linewalker's daughter. But Leo's statement gave her hope that she might be something more someday. She took a step in the direction of the cabin. "I think we better move on."

His laughter rolled as he followed her. They wove their way down the rocky, sloping expanse of ground. When they encountered an exposed wall of stone, they paused and Leo gave each inch a thorough perusal, but he didn't find anything else of note. If he was disappointed, he gave no indication. They continued their winding trek, and when they neared the cabin, he pointed ahead.

"I think I see your daddy sitting at the window."

Jennie slowed her pace, a hint of sadness intruding on the pleasure of finding a fossilized tooth. "Yes, probably." An ache settled in the center of her chest. Mama kept telling her not to give up hope, but when would they see a change in Daddy? Five whole days had slipped by since Mama promised she would get Daddy strong again, and the only thing he had done besides sit was stack empty crates on the wagon. He'd never get stronger if he didn't do something more. "Sometimes I think that chair has a magnetic pull on him."

"I don't think it's the chair that has the pull," Leo said in a musing tone. "I think it's the view beyond the window."

Jennie stopped and turned a puzzled frown on him. "What do you mean?"

Leo folded his arms over his chest. "Look at the view, Jennie. What do you see?"

She sent her gaze from the patch of grassy ground where the cabin and the outhouse stood, down the rock-strewn rise to the pipeline, across the wide ribbon of rippling water to the sharp climb leading to the man-carved flat path for the railway lines, and finally up the sheer rock wall behind the steel lines. She'd seen it all so many times it held no real significance anymore. She shrugged. "I see where we live."

He nodded as if she'd said something wise and important. "You see where you live. All the places you've been on a daily basis. Where you've walked, climbed, and explored. Yes?"

She nodded.

"Well, so does he."

Jennie scanned the view again, wondering if she'd missed something. It looked the same. "I don't know what you mean."

The kindness she'd seen before warmed his eyes. "When he looks out the window, he sees where he used to be. Remembers what he used to do. I think a longing to return to those days draws him to the window, where he can pretend he's out walking, climbing, working, being."

Unexpectedly, anger flared in her middle. "Then why doesn't he get up and *do*? If he really wanted to, he could. The doctor said he could. He just won't." She turned sharply away from Leo's probing gaze and stared across the river at the rock wall. If she hollered at Daddy to get up, her voice would hit that wall, bounce back, and reach his ears. Maybe if she yelled it again and again, it would penetrate deep enough to bring him out of his chair.

She pulled in a full breath, ready to try.

"He won't," Leo said so quietly that Jennie barely heard him over the rushing river and whistling wind, "because he hasn't found a strong enough reason yet." He put his hand on her shoulder. "But he will, Jennie. Keep praying. Keep prodding. Hold on to hope."

Her eyes stung. She sniffled hard and stepped free of his light hold. "I think hope is Mama's domain. I'm pretty well empty."

Leo nodded, that same gentleness glimmering in his eyes. "Then stand in her echo until you catch some of it." He rolled his eyes upward, as if seeking something in the sky. When he met her gaze again, the corners of his lips turned up in a sweet, encouraging smile. "Remember what it says in Isaiah 40:31—those who wait on the Lord will renew their strength. Patiently waiting on the Lord is the essence of hope, Jennie. So wait. But don't give up, okay?"

Her cheeks twitched with an effort not to smirk. "You sounded like a preacher just then."

Pain creased his brow, but only for a moment. He released a soft chuckle. "Don't say that around my father. It'll give him ideas."

Guilt struck hard. Leo had shared on one of their excursions that he felt like a failure because he had no desire to follow in his father's and grandfathers' footsteps. Her comment must have stung. She inwardly kicked herself for being so thoughtless, especially in light of his kindness. He'd told her she should express gratitude when paid a compliment. Well, she should express remorse after delivering a blow.

She grazed his arm with her fingertips. "I'm sorry, Leo."

He shrugged. "It's all right. You meant no harm. And, Jennie?" He leaned forward slightly, intensity lighting his eyes. "Your father doesn't mean you harm by staying in that chair. I don't believe he's deliberately seeking to hurt your mother and you. He's fighting a battle inside himself. Fighting is exhausting. Remind yourself of that when you're tempted to lose patience with him."

Leo's statement pushed aside a bit of her resentment and brought sympathy forward. She glanced toward the cabin, biting on her lip. "Should Mama and I stop pushing him to get up? Should we let him sit until he's ready?" They'd waited so long already. Would another year pass before Daddy finally got out of his chair? How long did the Lord expect her to wait?

He grimaced. "I wish I knew how to answer. My semester of psychology gave me just enough knowledge to be dangerous. In fact . . ." He sighed. "You know your daddy better than I do. Maybe you should ignore what I said."

But much of what he'd said made sense. She'd thought herself that Daddy was fighting an inner battle. Her mind skipped backward in time to when she was little and followed him everywhere he went, asking questions and sticking her nose in the way of whatever he was doing. He'd always responded patiently. The fall had changed him in many ways. Maybe it had even knocked all the patience out of him. But maybe his impatience wasn't so much with her as it was with himself.

"No, I won't ignore what you said." She shook her head, making her braid bounce. "You've given me a lot to think about."

He raised one eyebrow. "And pray about?"

She couldn't resist teasing, "You're preaching again."

This time a hearty laugh rolled. "I suppose I am. You can't grow up in a preacher's house and not pick up a few preacher habits."

They set off for the cabin, Leo's comment echoing in her mind. All her childhood, Mama and Daddy had modeled faith, hard work, and respectfulness. Would she let Daddy's current behavior strip those lessons from her? Leo had said to hold on to hope, but it seemed she had some other things she should strive to keep hold of as well.

Chapter Eleven

Etta

On her knees in the lumpy dirt, Etta yanked out another weed from the base of a green pea bush and tossed it aside. Their trio of chickens, which she'd released from their pen a half hour ago to peck in the grass, waddled over, wings flapping, and battled over the wilted plant. She parted straggly leaves from the scrawny bushes and searched for more scraps of green that didn't belong in her vegetable plot. Sometimes she wondered why she bothered trying to nurture a garden. Given the limited sunlight that reached her valley home, the plants' production was paltry at best. But she loved gardening, loved seeing a seed blossom into a plant that budded then bore fruit. Even if the bounty was small, she pushed seeds into the soil each summer and thanked God for every bit of sustenance she could coax from her garden.

If only she could coax Claude into bearing fruit. She closed that thought down quickly lest it lead to bitterness. She didn't want a negative seed to take root in her soul, but this past week, she'd needed much prayer to hold it at bay.

A movement caught her attention, and she turned. Jennie was trudging up the slight rise toward the line strung from the back of the outhouse to a post Claude had pounded into the ground the year they moved out here. The girl balanced an overflowing basket of wet laundry against her front. The way she staggered as she walked proved the burden taxed her. In years past, Claude carried the full basket to the line and then Etta or Jennie hung the clothes.

Did Claude not see his daughter struggling? Or had he ceased to care?

And now her thoughts were leaning toward bitterness again. She stood and caught up to Jennie, wiping her hands clean on her apron as she went. "Wait, honey, let me help."

Jennie shot a weary grin over her shoulder. "Thanks, Mama." She plopped the basket down and they each grabbed a handle.

Even sharing the load, the weight tugged at Etta's arm, but together they reached the sagging line and set the basket on a flat, smooth rock.

Jennie swiped the back of her hand across her forehead. "Phew. I won't fill the basket all the way before bringing it out next time."

Etta gave her daughter's braid a light tug. "Or you could ask your daddy to carry it for you." Even if he liked to act as if he were in a little world all alone, they shouldn't play along. They needed to include him, the way they used to.

The girl's face clouded. "I did. I asked if he'd take one side and help me. He didn't even answer."

Frustration billowed in Etta's middle, but she forced a smile. "He's probably lost in thought and didn't even hear you."

Jennie pulled one of Claude's shirts from the basket. She gave it several brisk snaps, raising the scent of lye soap, then secured it to the line with wooden pins. "Leo told me Daddy doesn't like who he is right now any more than we like it and I should be patient with him, but"—she blew out a mighty huff of breath— "sometimes it's hard."

Etta raised one brow. "You and Leo talk about your daddy?"

A soft smile fluttered on Jennie's face. "Leo and I talk about . . . well, everything. He's the nicest boy I've ever known."

Etta added a shirt to the line, observing her daughter from the corners of her eyes. When they moved to the cabin, Jennie hadn't yet reached the age of noticing boys. Since then, with the exception of their monthly visits to town, her only companions were her parents. According to what Leo told Etta, Jennie had spurned the attentions of some other young boys. But apparently she wasn't completely indifferent. If Etta's instincts were correct, her daughter was smitten with Leo Day.

She passed behind Jennie and removed another damp clothing article from the basket. "He's a very polite, personable young man." She applied the pins and peeked at Jennie between the gently waving shirts. "And handsome, too."

Jennie shrugged and looked aside. "I suppose."

Etta laughed softly. She stepped close and briefly cupped Jennie's flushed cheek. "There's nothing wrong with acknowledging a fellow's pleasant features. Truthfully, your daddy's broad shoulders and velvety brown eyes were what caught my attention first."

Jennie giggled.

"It's true." Etta winked and picked up another of Claude's shirts. "But it was his honest character, kind spirit, and dedication to the Lord that won my heart."

A pensive frown creased Jennie's forehead. "You just described Leo, Mama. And those are all things I like about him." She hung a pair of trousers. "Even though he isn't a preacher, he sometimes talks like one. He tells me things he thinks I should know—like what he said about Daddy—even if it might be hard to hear. But even when he says hard things, he says them in a way that lets me know he really cares." She yanked another pair of trousers from the pile and crushed them against her front, staring across the landscape. "I like everything about him. And I think he might have come to Cañon City because I—" She clacked her jaw shut and flopped the trousers over the line.

Etta's curiosity drew her to Jennie's side. "He came because . . . why?"

Jennie pursed her lips for a moment, then said in a rush, "I prayed for a friend."

Etta's heart swelled. She squeezed Jennie's upper arm. "I know you're lonely out here. But it won't be much longer."

Jennie untangled one of Etta's aprons from the pile of wet laundry, blowing out a noisy breath. "Please don't get my hopes up, Mama. It's been a whole week already and Daddy's still stuck to his chair." The bitterness Etta wanted to evade came through in her daughter's tone. "You can't know for sure I'll get to finish school in town." She clipped the apron to the line with jabs of the pins.

Maybe Jennie was right. Maybe Etta shouldn't make promises. But she knew deep in her heart that this smart, talented, friendly girl should have the opportunity to attend school and be with others her age. Leo was meeting her need for friendship now, but he would leave at summer's end. Maybe even before. Jennie's loneliness would intensify after having enjoyed his companionship.

Etta sent up a silent prayer for guidance, then said, " 'The effectual fervent prayer of a righteous man availeth much.' "

Jennie paused in hooking a dress into place on the line and turned in her mother's direction. Her brow was pinched, but she didn't seem angry. More contemplative.

Etta smoothed a few wind-tossed wisps of hair from Jennie's cheek. "You prayed for a friend. Leo came. Does this not prove God answers prayer?"

Jennie's eyes flooded. "Sometimes He does."

"Always He does," Etta gently corrected.

Jennie hung her head. "Mama, you say God always answers, but . . ." She swallowed. "Sometimes He says no. Like He has about Daddy all these months. He might say no about me going to school."

Etta couldn't bear her daughter's sadness. She pulled her into an embrace and held her tight. "There's one more answer God sometimes gives. What is that one?"

"*Not now.*" The words were muffled against Etta's shoulder.

"That's right. *Not now.*" Etta kissed Jennie's temple and released her hold. "Consider my garden over there. Do the plants spring forth and become heavy with beans and peas and tomatoes overnight?"

A slight grin quavered on Jennie's lips. "No. Of course not."

Etta chuckled. "That's right. Because seeds need time and rain and sunshine to grow and produce their bounty. Sometimes we need time and maybe a little rain or sunshine, too, while we wait. But when the time is ripe, we receive His answer. Don't give up."

Jennie rubbed her nose. "Yes, Mama." She slid the laundry basket closer and resumed hanging clothes.

Etta scuffed across the grass to the garden plot, her gaze fixed on the cabin. From this angle, she couldn't see the window where Claude spent most of his day. But he was no doubt in his chair, staring. At what? Something outside, or something within? She didn't know, and it stung that she didn't know. Shouldn't she know everything about this man who was the other half to her whole?

She knelt and reached for a weed, but her hand stilled before grasping the pesky intruder. She'd told Jennie that prayers availed much. She was already on her knees. She bowed her head and folded her hands.

Leo

Leo hung the last freshly scrubbed pan on its hook above the massive iron stove, then wiped his chapped hands down the front of his bibbed apron. If any of his college pals saw him now, they'd do plenty of teasing. He wouldn't blame them either. He'd always considered dish washing a duty for girls. After all, his mother and sisters saw to the cooking and cleaning up at home. But the job offered shelter in a small but cozy room, kept his belly filled, and allowed him several hours each day to search for dinosaur bones. He couldn't ask for a better setup.

He pulled the apron over his head and dropped it into the laundry bin by the back door, then stepped into the alley behind the hotel. He stretched his taut muscles, his face aimed at the slice of cloud-dotted sky exposed between buildings. The sun didn't penetrate the alley, but he felt its warmth anyway. It was always warmer in the city than on the hillside near the river where Jennie's family lived.

Thoughts of Jennie's family raised a prickle of concern. When he'd told Jennie he believed Claude Ward was fighting an inward battle, he hadn't stated the term his psychology professor used. *Melancholia.* The definition from his textbook appeared in his mind's eye—*a quiet form of insanity displayed by unending despondency.*

He shuddered. How awful. And equally awful were some of the ways it was treated. He wouldn't share the term that seemed to fit Claude's current state of mind, because he didn't want Jennie to ask how to fix it. He wouldn't be able to lie to her, but thinking of her beloved daddy being shocked with electricity or having a portion of his brain removed would destroy her tender heart. No, he'd keep his knowledge to himself and encourage her to be patient, to gently prod him to get up and move. Exercise, his professor had indicated, was showing promise in decreasing the symptoms of melancholia. If Claude would get out of his chair and *do,* as Jennie had so despairingly said, change could come. But Leo would never utter the term *melancholia* and plant ugly pictures in her mind.

A discarded upturned crate lay against the foundation of the hotel's red-brick wall. Leo sat on it, crossed his ankles, and leaned against the warm bricks. He linked his hands on his stomach and sighed. On the other side of the wall, the kitchen workers were already scurrying around in preparation for the evening diners.

The city sidewalks and streets bustled with Saturday shoppers. But the alley, although smelly from the spoiling food in the waste bins, was quiet. A good spot for introspection.

With his head resting against the warm bricks, he closed his eyes and considered how he might be able to help the Wards. He already prayed for them each day, but was there something more—something tangible—he could do to encourage them? Mrs. Ward had kindly shared meals with him. Maybe he could ask the cook for some day-old sweet rolls to bring as a gift. Would Mr. Ward read a magazine? There were several interesting periodicals for sale in the drugstore. Father enjoyed *The Saturday Evening Post,* with its variety of articles. Leo didn't have a large sum of pocket money available, but he could afford to spend five cents on a magazine.

He liked the ideas for Mr. and Mrs. Ward, but what about for Jennie? His sisters enjoyed receiving new hair ribbons and lace handkerchiefs, but he wasn't sure if Jennie would have much use for them. At least not living where she did now. A smile tugged at his cheeks. How sweetly feminine she'd looked in her church dress last Sunday. But she moved much more freely and gracefully in her boots and britches than she had in the full skirt and dainty shoes. He'd never met a girl as unpretentious as Jennie, and he liked the ease with which she carried herself. If he gave her ribbons or lace, she might surmise he thought she needed to gussy herself up. She might start feeling conspicuous in her everyday clothes. He shook his head—frippery wasn't an option. What could he give her that would be practical yet personal so she'd know he put some thought behind it?

Just like that, he knew. He bolted to his feet, reaching into his pocket for the change he carried. He counted out the coins, eagerness building in his chest to make the purchase, already envisioning her delight. Surely, thirty-five cents would be enough. He turned toward the opening to the street, but a noise—a whimper?—

drew him up short. Something was in distress. He cocked his head, an ear tipped in the direction of the sound.

Scuffling noises came from behind the rubbish bins, and another distinct whimper followed. Rats, feral cats, and an occasional raccoon sometimes rustled through the bins, but none of those animals made the kind of sound he'd heard. So what was back there? Leo slowly advanced toward the bins, moving as quietly as possible to avoid startling the creature, whatever it was.

He stopped next to the bins and leaned sideways, peering behind, and his heart lurched. He slowly lowered himself to a crouch and extended his hand. "Hey there. Are you lost?"

The pup, filthy and so thin its ribs showed, flattened itself to the ground and stared at Leo with wide brown eyes. It quivered from speckled head to scrawny tail. Its obvious terror made Leo want to cry.

He wiggled his fingers. "C'mere. I won't hurt you." But the puppy inched backward until it was out of sight. Leo pinched his chin, considering his options. If he chased it, it might bolt into the street. He couldn't bear the possible consequence of such an action. Somehow he had to coax it to come to him. Food could convince it. He'd noticed quite a bit of leftover ham on the lunch plates he'd emptied into the scrap bucket. Would he be able to retrieve some of it from the barrel?

He straightened and looked into the barrel. Yes, a few pink pieces of meat were half-hidden in the disgusting mix of garbage. Grimacing, he rolled his sleeve back and reached in. He pinched out two good-sized slices, then returned to his crouched position. He tore a sliver from one of the slices and tossed it in the direction the pup had disappeared. At once, its little nose poked out and its sharp teeth snatched up the bit.

Leo continued plying the pup with pieces of meat, luring it closer with each toss. When the puppy was within arm's reach, Leo dumped the remaining greasy chunks on the ground. The moment after the pup gobbled the last bite, he scooped it into his arms. It flailed its legs, yelping as if he'd struck it, but Leo tucked it close under his chin and murmured, "Sh, sh, you're all right. I won't hurt you."

Apparently, the pitiful animal had little fight left in it, because it slumped in his arms and hid its face in the bend of his elbow. Although it smelled awful and its dirt-caked paws left smears on Leo's clothes, he stroked its trembling neck and continued to soothe it, his chest aching with compassion. The poor little thing wouldn't survive on its own. But what could he do with it? If he got caught with a smelly dog in the hotel, he'd be fired. Even if he managed to keep it hidden until he left town, the college wouldn't welcome a canine attendee. And never mind taking it home to his family. Mother had never allowed them to have a pet—they were messy, she said.

But what about the Flankstons? They had their own house, and by the end of the summer, Jennie would be with them. She'd love having a puppy, wouldn't she? If he did a good enough sales job, he could probably convince Jennie's aunt and uncle to take in this poor little dog.

He lifted the pup's head with his hand and smiled into its sad brown eyes. "You come with me. You're getting a bath. And then I'll make you look spiffy by tying a ribbon around your neck." Pink or blue? He sneaked a glance at the pup's other end and grinned. Blue. Perfect. The pup would look a county fair prize with a big blue ribbon under his chin.

Chapter Twelve

Jennie

Mama shut the worn leather cover on her Bible, bowed her head, and closed her eyes. Jennie mimicked her pose. While Mama talked out loud to God, Jennie battled temptation to peek and see if Daddy had bowed his head or if he was still sideways in his chair, staring out the window, the way he'd sat through their version of Sunday service.

Sunday had been Jennie's favorite day of the week from the time she was little. Even when they lived in town and attended services at church, her family slept a little later and got themselves ready for the day a little slower. Since moving to the cabin and only going to church services in town once a month, Sunday mornings were even lazier and more relaxed. Sometimes they didn't have breakfast until almost nine o'clock, which meant a late lunch, too. But nobody minded, because it was Sunday. A relaxed day.

But it was also the Lord's day, as Mama said, so they worshipped. Their home service was nothing elaborate. They didn't have an organ to play or a preacher to listen to. But they spent time with God, and Mama claimed that was what mattered. Until he got hurt, Daddy led their home services. Jennie had loved listening to him read words from God's Holy Book in his deep, rumbling voice. In her girlish mind, it was like hearing God Himself speak. But she wasn't sure if Daddy still read his Bible on his own. And he never led them in worship anymore. Most Sundays he stayed in the bedroom while Mama read Scripture to Jennie and shared her thoughts about it.

But today he'd limped from the bedroom as Mama was opening her Bible to read. Jennie's heart had given a leap of joy when he pulled out a chair and joined them. Having him at the table today was a treat, even though he didn't sing along when she and Mama sang the hymns Jennie picked out. She'd chosen "Onward, Christian Soldiers" because Daddy used to sing it when the two of them went traipsing, and "Redeemed, How I Love to Proclaim It!" because it was a happy, bouncy song. How could anyone sing the words to Fanny Crosby's hymn about being redeemed by the blood of the Lamb with a sad voice? She'd thought for sure those hymns would put some joy in Daddy again. He had them memorized, the same as she and Mama. He could've sung them if he wanted to.

She reminded herself again that he was at the table with them. Him being at the table for their simple worship was something to celebrate. Even so, she wished he'd sung. She missed hearing joy in her daddy's voice.

"Amen," Mama said, and Jennie realized she hadn't paid a bit of attention to her mother's prayer. A bit ashamed, she echoed, "Amen," and hoped God would forgive her for drifting away in her thoughts.

While Daddy shaved his stubble and combed his hair, Mama and Jennie prepared a simple lunch of fried ham, stewed tomatoes, baking-soda biscuits, and some wild mustard greens Mama wilted in the meat drippings. While they were eating, the midday train rumbled by as usual at half past one. The cabin vibrated, and Mama's porcelain teacups in the cupboard softly *tink-tink*ed against one another. Jennie was so used to the train's coming and going she hardly noticed it anymore. But Daddy paused and looked out the window while it passed. Was he thinking, as Leo had said, about the times he'd ridden the train to town and taken his family to the Presbyterian church on Sunday mornings?

When they finished, Jennie helped Mama with kitchen cleanup. Now that Daddy had his belly filled, Jennie expected him to close himself in the bedroom. Both Mama and Daddy rested on Sunday afternoons. Jennie preferred to take out her sketch pad and pencils. As long as she was quiet, her parents didn't mind how she entertained herself. On this Sunday, though, Daddy limped to his chair by the window, sat, and stacked his forearms on the sill.

After a few minutes of sitting and staring, he leaned forward and propped his chin on his arms. Something in Jennie's middle stirred with a desire to draw him the way he was just then. The pose seemed to carve years away, making him look like a little boy yearning for Santa Claus's sleigh to appear in the sky. Eager to get out her drawing materials, she sped up drying and stacking dishes. Just as she put the last plate on the shelf, Daddy sat straight-up.

Jennie stifled a huff. It was always easier to draw something when she was looking at the subject. Would she be able to do the drawing from memory? She waited, hoping he would resume the position, but he pointed out the window and glanced over his shoulder to Mama and Jennie.

"Did you know Prime and Delia were comin' out today?"

Mama's eyebrows pinched. "I sure didn't."

"Well, here they come up the rise. Looks like Prime's totin' a picnic basket."

Mama hurried to the window and looked out. She sighed. "Oh, my. I'm happy for the company, but I wish I'd known they planned to come by. They could've eaten with us instead of bringing their own food." She went outside.

Jennie stood in the open doorway and watched Mama half skip the distance to meet their unexpected visitors. The sisters embraced, and Aunt Delia turned Mama toward Uncle Prime. He lifted a flap on the picnic basket. Mama peered inside and immediately drew back, her hands flying up in surprise or delight. Jennie's mouth automatically watered. They must have brought something good from the hotel kitchen to share. Dessert, in all likelihood. Maybe pound cake and strawberries. Daddy would love that.

Mama and Aunt Delia linked arms and headed for the cabin. Uncle Prime followed, holding the basket with his arms wrapped around it the way Jennie carried a full laundry tub. When they got close, Mama called, "Jennie, you and your daddy come outside. Prime has something to show you."

Jennie looked at Daddy. He looked at her. Their matching brown eyes stared unblinking at each other for a few seconds. Then they shrugged in unison, which tickled Jennie more than she understood. He pushed up from the chair, and the two of them ambled out.

A sliver of sunlight fell across the basket Uncle Prime set on the sloped ground. He grinned at Jennie and Daddy, his hand braced on one of the slatted flaps. "You ready?"

"For what?" Daddy said.

Uncle Prime winked. "You'll see."

Excitement—an excitement she couldn't explain—filled Jennie's middle. She linked her hands and pressed them to her chest. "I'm ready."

Uncle Prime folded back the flap. A puppy dog with a tan-speckled white face and floppy ears—one snow-white, one tawny brown—poked its head from the basket. The bow from a wide blue ribbon hung cockeyed around its skinny neck. It wriggled for a bit, then plunked one thick white paw on the edge of the basket and released a sharp yip.

Jennie gasped, all thoughts of dessert abandoned. She scooped the pup from the basket. She expected it to be heavier based on the size of its head and paws, but the animal seemed to be mostly skin stretched over bone. "Oh, you poor little thing." She tried to cradle it, but it squirmed so much she was forced to put it down. It scrambled on gangly legs to the basket and hunkered next to it, looking around the circle of humans with round, uncertain eyes.

Jennie turned to Uncle Prime. "Where did you get him?"

He rolled his eyes. "We didn't *get* him. One of our employees found him behind the hotel near the waste cans. He brought the dog to us and asked us to take him in."

Aunt Delia held out her hands in a gesture of futility. "Oh, the temptation . . . but after talking it over, common sense prevailed. We can't keep the dog at the hotel, and we aren't home enough to take proper care of a pet."

"So we decided to bring him out here and see if you folks were interested in raising a pup." Uncle Prime leaned over and ruffled the dog's ears. "I think he's got some hound dog in him, which is a real smart breed. And if he grows into those feet, he'll be big enough to be good protection for Jennie and Etta." He grimaced. "But he sure needs some fattening up. And a big dose of patience. He's pretty skittish."

Jennie sat on her bottom and crisscrossed her legs. She laid her hand palm up on the ground a few inches from the pup's moist black nose. "Hey, little fellow. Nobody here will hurt you. Won't you let me pet you?"

The pup's wary brown eyes shifted from Jennie's fingers to her face—up and down, up and down. Its apprehension nearly broke her heart. She sensed he wanted to come close, to be loved, but fear held him captive. Uncle Prime was right—he needed a lot of patience. For some reason, the verse from James that the reverend in town shared at the close of last week's service whispered through Jennie's memory.

Knowing this, that the trying of your faith worketh patience.

Were the trials with Daddy over the past two years, trials that tested her patience, meant to increase her faith? Might the effort needed to win the confidence of this scared little dog help her grow even more in faith? Awareness brought a rush of warmth through her frame. She whirled on her seat and turned a pleading look on her father.

"Daddy, may we please keep this puppy? He'll grow up into a good watchdog, don't you think?"

Daddy scratched his ruddy, freshly shaved cheek. "I don't know, Jennie. He might chase the chickens."

"I can teach him not to."

Daddy's lips twisted into a doubtful scowl. "He's a scrawny thing. It's gonna take a lot of food to put meat on his bones. And you're gone most of the day. Who'll look after him? Your mama sure doesn't need more to do around here."

Although his words carried resistance, she witnessed a glimmer of desire in his eyes. She stood—slowly so she wouldn't frighten the pup into bolting—and took Daddy's hand. She hadn't held his hand in a long time. So much softer than she remembered, its calluses smoothed out from lack of activity. It didn't feel right. She swallowed a lump of longing for what used to be and squeezed his fingers. "If you'd keep an eye on him until he's a little bigger, he could walk the line with me the way Rex used to do with you. Remember?"

He shifted his head aside, his gaze turning inward. "Yeah, I remember."

She gave his hand a little tug, and he looked full in her face. She gave him a hopeful smile. "Please, Daddy? I know you miss old Rex. We all do. I think we need this sad little pup as much as he needs us."

Daddy stared hard at her for several seconds, chewing the inside of his cheek. Jennie held her breath, preparing herself for his refusal. Then he sighed. "I reckon if you want to give him a try, it's fine with me. As long as your mama doesn't mind."

Jennie aimed her smile at Mama. "Mama?"

Mama crouched down and ran her fingertips over the puppy's wrinkly forehead. "I don't mind."

Jennie released a little squeal of happiness and grabbed Daddy in a hug. "Thank you!"

After a moment's pause, his arms closed around her and his hand patted her back a couple of times. Then he pulled loose and shook his head. "I don't hold out much hope for him to be half the dog Rex was."

Jennie blinked back happy tears. "That's okay, Daddy. I've got enough hope for both of us."

Mama waved her hands the way a hen guided its chicks. "Everyone, let's go in and introduce the puppy to its new home."

Uncle Prime returned the puppy to the basket, and they all trooped into the cabin. Mama and Delia settled on their lone settee. Jennie perched on its arm next to Mama, and Daddy went to his usual spot by the window. Uncle Prime sat at the kitchen table. He set the basket on the floor and opened the flap. Leaning sideways, he toyed with the dog's ears. "Have you got a name in mind for the pup, Jennie?"

Jennie nodded. It had come to her when she locked eyes with the cowering creature. "Oliver, after the little orphaned boy in the story by Charles Dickens. I'll call him Ollie for short."

Daddy released a little *humph*. "Oliver . . ."

Jennie peered past Mama and Aunt Delia to her father. "You don't like the name?"

"There was a boy named Oliver in my neighborhood when I was growin' up. He was a sneaky little tattletale who made up affronts if no real ones happened just so he could get other kids in trouble."

Mama and Jennie exchanged a look. Daddy hadn't talked so much at one time in weeks. Months. Jennie's heart fluttered. Could she keep him talking? "I can see why you wouldn't want a reminder of that boy. It was just a suggestion, anyway. Do you want to call him Rex, instead?"

Daddy shook his head. "Already had a Rex. This one . . ." The pup's shining eyes peered over the rim of the basket, his white ear hitched slightly higher than the brown one. "He's no Rex."

Uncle Prime leaned back in the chair and crossed his legs. "How'd you come to choose the name Rex for your shepherd dog, Claude?"

Daddy sat quiet for a bit, long enough that Jennie wondered if he'd drifted away somewhere again. Then he sucked in a breath, as if gathering fortitude. "I'd read somewhere—don't rightly recall where—that the name *Rex* means 'king.' Even when Rex was a puppy, he had a regal bearing. Remember, Etta?"

Mama chuckled softly, her eyes holding a sheen of moisture. "Oh, yes, I do. He pranced around as if he owned the world."

Daddy pointed at the puppy. "Nothing like that little scaredy-cat."

Uncle Prime peered into the basket, his lips quirking into a wry grin. "I agree this dog is more like the storybook character Oliver Twist than any king. What do you expect? He got plucked up out of a lonely, stinky alley. But now he's in a place where he'll be treated well." He snickered. "Since Oliver Twist and the puppy are both rags-to-riches situations, maybe you should stick with the name Ollie."

Daddy shook his head. "Not Ollie. We'll call him"—he turned a side-eyed peek at Jennie—"Rags."

Chapter Thirteen

Leo

When Leo reached the familiar meeting spot along the pipeline, he noticed something different about Jennie. She always smiled and waved when he arrived, but today her eyes shone a little brighter. She stood a little straighter. Waved a little more enthusiastically. It seemed a burden she'd been carrying had fallen away, and he sent up a silent prayer of thanks to the One he'd been asking to lighten her heart.

He pulled himself up on the pipe behind her, then placed his hands on his hips and arched one eyebrow. "Good afternoon. You seem in fine spirits today."

She beamed at him. "I suppose I am."

He wanted to ask the reason for her cheerful mood, but she was still on duty. His question should wait. He adjusted the straps on his knapsack, then gestured up the line. "Lead on, Miss Sunshine . . . er, Mountain Goat . . . er, Linewalker."

She set off, her laughter ringing. Leo grinned and followed. Her joyful spirits lifted his, and he found himself whistling as he trailed behind her for the remainder of her inspection.

At the end of the line where the pipe seemed swallowed by the hillside, she whirled around and exclaimed, "Guess what?"

Leo held his hands out in defeat. "Can't guess. What?"

"Aunt Delia and Uncle Prime came out to visit yesterday afternoon, and they brought us a puppy."

He gave a jolt, surprise nearly toppling him from the pipe. He caught his balance and gaped at her. "They did?" Why hadn't they told him they weren't going to keep the dog? He slapped his forehead. And why hadn't he thought of giving the puppy to the Wards? She'd talked about her daddy's dog, Rex, dragging home the dinosaur bone, so he knew they'd once owned a dog. He could have been the one to make her light up with joy. Unexpectedly, jealousy struck.

She nodded and flicked her braid over her shoulder. She sat, then slid down from the pipe. "Daddy named him Rags because one of the hotel workers found him near the rubbish bins behind the hotel."

"Rags, huh?" He envisioned the skinny pup with floppy mismatched ears. The name fit. He slid down to the ground. Why hadn't the Flankstons told Jennie's family he'd found the pup? It would sound like he was trying to steal the credit for Jennie's happiness if he claimed responsibility now. "And your daddy was open to having a new dog?"

Jennie started up the rise, angling slightly southeast. He'd begun to think of their excursions as systematically following the ribs on a giant opened Chinese fan. On their first Monday, she'd led him as due west as possible. Each day, she ended a few yards east of the preceding day's exploration. Her leading gave true meaning to the phrase *fanning out.* He admired her ingenuity. She applied her penchant for intense examination of the pipeline to seeking out fossils. God couldn't have provided him a better guide.

"At first he wasn't sure." Jennie swung her arms as she went, a bounce in her step. "After all, the puppy is nothing like his old dog, and he loved Rex so much. He was brokenhearted when he died."

Leo searched his memory but didn't think Jennie had ever mentioned what happened to the dog. "When was that?"

"About a month before Daddy fell." Jennie's pace slowed as she talked. "We'd noticed Rex sleeping a lot more that last winter, but we just thought he was getting older. That the cold affected his joints. Mama even let him stay in the house instead of putting him in the shed. But spring came, and he didn't perk up the way he had in years past. He stopped following Daddy and me on the route and stayed at the cabin with Mama instead." Her feet slowed to a stop, and her tone turned pensive. "Then one day he wandered off and didn't come back. Daddy and I went looking for him and found him curled up underneath some bushes, like he was taking a nap. But he was gone." Her shoulders heaved in a mighty sigh. "I'd never seen Daddy cry before. It was a hard day."

Leo closed the distance between them and put his hand on her shoulder. "I'm sorry I made you think about it. We don't have to talk about Rex anymore."

She gave him a sad smile. "It's all right. Like Mama told both of us when we buried him, Rex lived a good life. He'd loved and been loved, which was more than some people can say at the end of their lives." She tipped her head, her forehead puckering. "I think remembering the hurt of losing Rex made Daddy hesitant to take in another dog, but in the end, he said yes. And then"— unshed tears brightened her eyes—"we hugged. I can't remember the last time Daddy and I hugged." She laughed. "It felt like Christmas and my birthday and having a three-layer chocolate cake to myself, all at once."

He couldn't resist giving her shoulder a quick squeeze. "Good, huh?"

"The best." She set off again, her gaze sweeping the landscape as she went, and he followed, his gaze fixed on her happy face. "I've been praying and praying for Daddy to be Daddy again, if you know what I mean. I was ready to give up. But yesterday I got a peek at who he was. And not just because we hugged."

She shared all of Sunday's events with him—about her father sitting with them for a worship time, visiting with the family when her aunt and uncle came, and choosing a name for the dog. Gratefulness for those happy moments swelled in him, and he sniffed to hold emotion at bay. But worry also teased. According to his studies of mental diseases, melancholia was an unpredictable illness. Sufferers could experience temporary lifts followed by deep plummets into despair. Jennie's heart might break if Mr. Ward fell into a sudden dark decline after she enjoyed such a hope-filled day.

Maybe Leo should tell her about the possibility of his mood swinging in the opposite direction. Surely, it would be better if she was prepared for it, just in case. But how could he mention an abrupt disposition change without telling her why it might happen? Besides, he couldn't be certain Mr. Ward suffered from melancholia. The symptoms seemed to fit, but only a trained psychiatrist could make such a diagnosis.

Jennie breathed out another sigh, this one carried on a note of joy. "I felt like God lifted the curtain of sorrow that's hidden Daddy from us all these months and let us see his real soul again. He wasn't out of bed yet when I left the cabin this morning, so I don't know how today is going for him. But I pray the curtain will stay open. Maybe Rags will be the one to hold it that way."

Leo shrugged, pondering her final statement. "We never know what God will use to work His will. But we can say for sure that living behind a curtain of sorrow isn't what He wants for any of us. He sent His Son so we can have abundant life. My father calls it the fullness of joy." Leo would have his fullness of joy when the man he admired most in the world finally offered his blessing on Leo's calling. "Your daddy's misplaced his joy, but it's still there, waiting for him to discover it again."

Jennie nodded, her mouth slightly open. "Yes. Yes, that's how it felt yesterday. That he'd forgotten how to be joyful but suddenly stumbled over it."

He liked the word picture she'd painted in his head. Maybe God would let him stumble over a dinosaur bone. That would bring a joyful explosion in his soul. He smiled. "I'll pray that yesterday's reach for joy will become your daddy's new habit and he will be fully restored to joy."

"Thank you, Leo." She crinkled her nose. "Someday I'd like to hear your father preach. He's obviously very good at what he does, considering how many of his teachings you find important enough to share with me."

Leo scratched behind his ear, pushing his hat askew. "To be honest, it sometimes surprises me when I hear Father's words come out of my mouth." But why should it surprise him? He'd spent his entire life listening to his father expound upon truths found in God's Word. Had Father not said again and again that God's Word does not return void? Of course the Scriptures would take root in Leo's soul. "I suppose whatever we take in will also come out."

Her eyes widened. "Yes." A smile split her face. "Yes!"

Leo stared at her, confused and curious. What discovery had she just made?

She aimed her face skyward for a few seconds, her brown eyes glowing, then met his gaze. "I've been taking in too much of Daddy's hopelessness and not enough of Mama's hope. But no more. I'm going to stand firmly on hope. And if I join Mama in a firm stance of hope, it'll be two hopeful souls against one whose hope is lost. Won't Daddy then be swayed to our side?"

What Leo knew of melancholia didn't necessarily support what Jennie said. The illness went deeper than mere mindset to an imbalance somewhere in the brain. But even if Mr. Ward did suffer from melancholia, positive attitudes exhibited by others wouldn't do the man any harm. He nodded and offered a smile of encouragement. "Remember also to pray. Pray for your daddy to be fully restored to joy and for yourself to avoid the temptation of letting hopelessness take hold again if he slides into sadness. As Jesus told His disciples, the spirit is often willing but our flesh can be weak. So bolster yourself with prayer."

Her wide, attentive eyes never wavered from his face. "I will. I promise, I will." She drew in a breath. "And, Leo, I'm going to pray for your father, too."

Leo raised his brows. "Mine? Why?"

"So he'll be happy to have a son who is a paleontologist."

A knot of intense longing filled Leo's throat. Oh, for Father to be happy with him. He swallowed hard, then again, before he could speak. "Thank you, Jennie. Nothing would please me more than to have my father's support and approval."

"Not even finding the dinosaur skeleton of that . . . that . . ." She scrunched her lips into a scowl of frustration and rolled her eyes upward. "What did you call it?"

He hid a grin. "Allosaurus."

"That's right. Allosaurus. Finding it would make you happy, too, wouldn't it?" For a moment, a hint of uncertainty shadowed her expression, but she gave her head a tiny shake and her joy returned.

Happy, yes, and validated. He'd talked over the telephone with Mr. Figgins on Saturday afternoon and assured him he hadn't yet given up locating the remainder of the skeleton and correctly identifying it. Fortunately, the museum director hadn't given up on him. Mr. Figgins shared the name of a local businessman who might be interested in joining Leo on his explorations. Leo had written down the man's name, but he wasn't ready to involve someone else. He preferred to stick with his current guide, who was standing in silence before him, waiting for him to say something.

He chuckled, embarrassed at having drifted off into thought for so long. "Indeed it would. And I appreciate your assistance in making it happen. But even more, I appreciate your prayers for my father to accept this vocation I've chosen. As you know, it isn't pleasant to be at odds with someone you love."

She released a little half laugh, half huff. "No, it isn't. But remember what you keep telling me." Her fine eyebrows rose, and a teasing grin appeared. "What do you keep telling me?"

He pinched his chin, pretending deep thought.

Jennie laughed. "You aren't fooling me. I know you know."

He laughed, too. "Hold on to hope. I promise . . . I'll practice what I preach."

"Good." She set off, tossing a smirk over her shoulder. "Let's go, college boy. We've got a skeleton to find."

Chapter Fourteen

Jennie

Despite their intense searching, they didn't find skeletal re-mains of an allosaurus or any other large prehistoric crea-tures. But Leo discovered the shell of a beetle-type bug imprinted on a flat stone. The rock was too big to carry and too hard for him to chop out the section, even with the chisel he carried in one of his pockets. Jennie took out her little notepad to draw the beetle for him, but he told her to wait. Then he removed a large sketch pad from his knapsack and gave it to her.

"Thank you, Leo!" She hugged the pad, giving him her bright-est smile.

A sheepish grin climbed his cheek. "You're welcome. I wanted to thank you somehow for your help. I hoped this would please you."

"Oh, it does." How well he already knew her. Her heart gave a funny little flutter. To hide the unfamiliar reaction, she plopped onto the grass next to the stone. She balanced the pad on her knee and opened the cover. While she painstakingly created a pencil replica of the insect fossil, curiosity prompted her to ask, "Is this beetle as old as the dinosaurs?"

"Well, I'll answer the way one of my professors would." He sat on the edge of the stone and pushed his hat back, letting it droop by its strings against the knapsack. "According to evolutionists, in-sects evolved during the Paleozoic Era. The Paleozoic Era began more than five hundred million years ago and ended with the dawn of the Mesozoic Era, somewhere around two hundred fifty million years ago. The dinosaurs lived during the Mesozoic Era, so insect fossils are potentially older than dinosaur fossils."

Jennie gaped at him. "You mean I could be drawing what's left of a bug that lived five hundred million years ago?"

He wagged his finger. "*Could* be." He braced himself up on the rock with one arm, stretched out his legs on the grass, and crossed his ankles. "The years attached to various prehistoric eras are speculations. Although the concept of the earth's age dating back as far as five billion years to the Azoic Era is commonly taught, I can't accept it as fact. After all, there are no records to validate it. Not even primitive ones, such as drawings found in caves."

Jennie added a few strokes to the beetle shell while Leo went on in his serious yet fervent tone.

"I believe in biblical creationism. If you add up all the years recorded in the Bible—even taking into account that a year in God's measurement of time could be very different from the way we measure a year today—the earth's existence doesn't seem to stretch back that far."

Jennie paused and squinted up at him. "But dinosaurs really lived on our earth, didn't they?"

"Of course they did." A hint of teasing glinted in his eyes. "There wouldn't be skeletal remains if there hadn't been actual creatures with skin, muscles, blood veins, and internal organs to go with those bones."

Heat filled her cheeks. "I guess I meant to ask, *when* did they live?"

Leo shrugged. "Based on my study of Scripture, I believe they existed up to and even after the great flood of Noah's time."

"Study of Scripture . . ." Jennie put the pencil down and gawked at him. "The Bible talks about dinosaurs?" She'd never encountered them in her reading. Maybe she needed to dig deeper.

His expression turned introspective. "Scripture doesn't use the term we attach to the fossilized remains of extinct animals, but there are mentions of particular beasts many Bible scholars believe refer to the giant creatures that roamed the earth. For instance, Leviathan."

"Leviathan . . ." Jennie savored the name, trying to envision a creature to match it.

"It's described in Isaiah as a gliding or coiling serpent. The writer of Psalm 104 included a reference to the same beast frolicking in the sea. The Leviathan is mentioned in the book of Job, as well as in the Lord's instructions to look at Behemoth, a beast that fed on grass like an ox. Scholars suggest the Behemoth was a woolly mammoth."

She released an awe-filled huff of breath. "I never realized."

A knowing smile curved his lips. "Few people think about it. Why should they? Those creatures are long extinct. Although the opinions of the professors at college would differ, my personal belief is that God created the dinosaurs at the same time He created the other animals of the earth—on the fifth day of the Creation. And as He said when He finished, He deemed His creation good."

Jennie leaned forward and examined the two-inch-long series of half circles resembling scales imprinted in the stone. "I've probably seen little things like this dozens of times since we moved from town, but I didn't know what I was looking at. Now that I know, it . . ." She pressed her hand to her chest. "It makes me feel smaller, yet somehow bigger inside." She turned to Leo. "Does that make sense?"

He nodded. "I think so. I remember visiting my grandparents in Massachusetts when I was a boy. They took me to see the Atlantic Ocean. When I looked across the water stretching so far it seemed to touch the sky and listened to the pounding surf, I was filled with a sense of how small I was in comparison to the earth. At the same time, the sight and sound and smell so engulfed me I sensed God's presence in a way I never had before. The wonder of His creation swelled inside me the way the ocean waves swelled and surged. I've never forgotten it."

The awe and wisdom in Leo's tone and expression as he shared his remembrance touched her. When she'd prayed for a friend, she longed for someone to laugh and talk with. A companion. She hadn't expected a friend who would prompt her to look at herself and her relationship with God differently. The verse about Him giving exceedingly and abundantly above what one asked seemed truer than ever.

The emotions swirling inside her couldn't be stifled. She blurted, "Leo, I really like you."

His eyebrows shot up, and then a pleased smile spread across his face. "Well, thank you, Jennie. I like you, too."

For several seconds, they sat smiling at each other, him on the rock and her on the grass. The breeze tossed the strings under his chin and sent little strands of hair across her face. If they were in a storybook, he might lean forward, smooth her hair with his fingers, and place a kiss on her cheek. Slowly, so slowly she thought she might be imagining it, he bent his legs to the side and leaned toward her. Had he read her secret thoughts? Her pulse skittered. His face came nearer, nearer, and then his gaze dropped to her sketch pad.

"How's the drawing coming along? Nearly done?"

Her fanciful thoughts dissolved, and embarrassment swept in. She flipped the page around and held it up. "Good enough, I think."

He nodded, his grin wide. "More than good enough. Thank you, Jennie."

Slipping her pencil into her pocket, she pretended to search the sky. "The day's getting away from us. We better head for the cabin."

He stood and shrugged out of his knapsack. "I'll tuck your drawing pad into my bag for safekeeping."

"That's fine." She turned her back and headed down the rise, trusting him to follow.

Neither of them spoke during the long walk to Jennie's home. Leo whistled, proof that his cheerful mood was intact. But the shine had been rubbed off her happy day, and she was aggravated with herself for allowing it. Hadn't she just inwardly praised God for sending her such a good friend? She hadn't asked for a beau, so why expect Leo to act like one? And she'd made a pledge to take on hope-*full*-ness instead of hopelessness. By being glum, she was acting like Daddy. She huffed. Mama was absolutely right—seventeen was a tumultuous age.

How did Mama consistently hold so tight to her hope? The answer swooped in with such force that she stumbled, as if she'd actually tripped over the thought. "I've got to tell Daddy."

Leo's puzzled "What?" came from behind her shoulder.

She didn't realize she'd spoken aloud. She grimaced. "Sorry. I was talking to myself."

His soft chuckle rumbled. "Now that you've pulled me into your private conversation, I'm curious. What do you intend to tell him?"

She came to a stop. She kept her gaze forward as she answered. "He needs to pray more." And so did she. "He used to pray at meals and when we had our private worship services on Sundays. But I haven't heard him pray in over a year." She'd stopped talking to God as often as she should, too. It needed to be fixed.

Leo drew up alongside her. She sensed his worried gaze pinned on her profile.

Jennie went on, not looking at him. "Now Mama does all the praying. But even before she took over meal praying and such for our family, she prayed a lot. When she was a girl, she read a poem about taking one's burdens to Jesus in prayer, and it became her lifetime habit. I can't ever remember a day that Mama didn't pray. So that's her hope, right?" She sent a side-eyed glance at him.

"The One to whom she offers the prayers is her source of hope, but, yes, the prayers are her connection to Him and the hope He gives."

Funny how he always knew the right way to put things. He would make a good preacher. She turned and fully faced him. "Daddy got hurt, then he stopped praying, and now he's sad all the time. If he prays again, it should boost his spirits because he'll be connecting himself to the source of hope."

He winced as if she'd pinched him. "Well . . ."

His uncertainty was squashing her hope. She considered pinching him for real. "Well, what? Does prayer help or not?"

"Of course it helps. We rob ourselves of peace and contentment when we wallow in troubling thoughts." He answered quickly and with such confidence Jennie sighed in relief. He put his hand on her shoulder. "We're emotional beings. We all have times when we feel sad or discouraged. Emotional feelings are fickle. They can change on a whim."

She nodded, too aware of how her feelings had gotten the best of her when her wishful thinking painted an unrealistic picture in her head.

"Talking to Jesus, especially letting Him carry whatever is burdening us, can draw us out of sadness or discouragement. But, Jennie, there are some feelings that take hold deep inside and consume a person until he can't seem to shake them loose." His grip tightened on her shoulder. "Continual despair can move beyond an emotional feeling and become a sickness, no different than a lingering physical ailment. And sometimes illnesses don't go away."

Jennie frowned, fear creating a bitter taste in her mouth. "Are you telling me prayer won't help Daddy?"

He released her shoulder and jammed his hand through his hair. For several seconds, he stood with his fingers clenched around thick, wavy strands of his hair, his brows pulled low. Then he abruptly straightened and dropped his hand. "The apostle Paul was an example of a man who prayed often. Bible scholars say his knees resembled camel knees because he knelt for so many hours a day."

Remembering a picture she'd seen of a camel's bulbous knees, she cringed. "Ouch."

Leo nodded. "Indeed. Would you say he was a man who knew how to leave burdens with Jesus?"

The minister in Cañon City often talked about Paul's amazing conversion and his strong faith. He held Paul up as an example for others to follow. "Of course."

"Yet in spite of how much time he spent praying, he was also a man who battled, as he put it, a thorn in his flesh—a problem that constantly tormented him. He prayed repeatedly for the thorn to be removed, but God didn't take it away. Instead, He told Paul that His grace was enough for him." He blinked several times as if battling tears. "Having the affliction would let him lean on God instead of depending on himself."

Jennie was beginning to understand, but she didn't like what he was saying. Only a couple of days ago, she'd told Mama she preferred yes answers. But if Leo said yes to the question she wanted to ask, she might never ask another question again. She gathered her courage. "Do you think God will decide it's better to let Daddy stay sad for the rest of his life?"

She held her breath while Leo stared across the landscape beyond her shoulder. He was quiet for so long she wondered if he'd decided to ignore her. Finally, his head wagged back and forth, and her breath whooshed from her lungs in a rush of relief.

He met her gaze. "I can't say for sure what God will choose. Who am I to know the mind of the almighty God? But I know what He tells us in His Word. He loves us. He never forsakes us. He gives us His strength when ours is gone." He brushed her arm with his hand. "I know it's hard for you to see the sadness your daddy wears, but I'm proud of you for making the choice not to let *his* sadness become *your* sadness. Continue to pray for him. And, yes, encourage him to pray."

"And hope?" Jennie's query emerged in a husky whisper.

He smiled. "Always hope." He sobered, then looked past her again. "Sometimes the battle a person is fighting isn't so much for the warrior's benefit as for someone watching from the wings. God won't waste your daddy's struggle, Jennie. Wait and see. Good will come from it."

A wry laugh left her throat. "That's hard to imagine right now."

He turned a soft look on her. "But isn't that faith in action? Believing even before you see?"

She shook her head in part wonder and part amusement. "Are you sure you aren't a preacher in a paleontologist's suit? I feel like I just came from church."

He laughed so heartily she couldn't help grinning at him. He reined in his humor and winked at her. "I'm starting to think my father orchestrated our original encounter so he'd have someone on his side coaxing me into the ministry."

He had a preacher's knowledge, but she'd seen him light up over an old bone, a shark's tooth, and the remains of a centuries-old beetle. He was, at heart, a fossil hunter. Maybe God sent this preacher's son down the path of paleontology to help other scientists see God's hand of creation wherever they looked. He'd already taught her a great deal. She made a silent vow to enjoy her time with him and not let silly emotions interfere in their budding friendship.

A series of shrill yips seemed to echo from miles away. They both looked in the direction of the sound, then at each other.

"I wonder if that's Rags," Jennie said.

"Is that your dog barking?" Leo asked at the same time.

They chuckled in unison.

Another quick succession of yips followed by a throaty bark

met her ears, and Jennie clasped her hands in a prayerful position. "Oh, I hope it's Rags. The only sounds he made yesterday or last night were whimpers. But those are happy noises!"

Leo waggled his eyebrows. "It sounds to me like someone is playing with him and getting him riled up."

A rush of anticipation set Jennie's feet in motion. "Let's go see who it is."

Chapter Fifteen

Etta

E tta tossed the misshapen ball she'd made by tying a sleeve from one of Claude's old shirts into a series of tight knots. The puppy's bright eyes followed its path, and then he lunged as it neared the grass. He missed catching it, but he pounced on it. He yipped his joy between alternately trampling the wad of chambray cloth with his oversized feet and clamping it in his jaw and shaking it.

She couldn't hold back a grin. She hadn't wanted to play with the dog. She should be preparing supper for her family and Leo. But when she caught Rags chewing a rung on Claude's window-watching chair, she exclaimed the pup needed to be diverted from destructive behavior. She'd meant she wanted Claude to take him outside and play with him. Claude ignored her hint and told her to give *that dog,* as he'd referred to him all day, a stick or something else to chew on.

So now, instead of cooking, she entertained Rags. And Claude observed them from his place behind the window. He might act disinterested, but twice during the day, she'd seen him give the pup a scratch behind his ears. He'd also dropped a few bits of his lunch sandwich into his lap and then brushed them to the floor, pretending it was an accident. He wasn't a good faker—she knew he meant to share with the dog. But she didn't say anything.

Those interactions, small though they were, had given her heart a lift. Eventually, Rags would win him over. Only a heartless person would be able to refuse the pup's winsome face and adorably clumsy prancing. Despite his current state, Claude was not a heartless person.

Suddenly Rags dropped the cloth ball and went tense. His brown ear spiked straight-up, and a little whimper rolled in his throat before he gave a hearty yap. Etta looked where the pup was focused and spotted Jennie and Leo cresting the hill behind the cabin.

She crouched beside the dog and placed her hand on his quivering back. "Good boy for alerting me that someone's coming. But there's no need to be frightened of our girl. You know Jennie. And Leo is a friend. So—"

Rags bolted from her and took off in a stumbling run, his ears flapping as if he meant to take flight. Etta pushed to her feet and started after him, but then she stopped and watched the puppy take a weaving path toward the approaching young people. She expected Rags to go straight to Jennie. After all, Jennie had fed him and tucked him into a folded blanket on the floor at the end of her bed last night. But the dog ducked past Jennie's reaching hands and jumped against Leo's legs.

Leo picked up the squirming bundle of yipping fur, swiveling his head away from Rags's swiping tongue. But Leo was laughing, as was Jennie. Etta waited for them to join her in the yard, and then she took the puppy from Leo and put him on the grass.

"My goodness!" Etta shook her head, smiling at Leo. "That was quite the greeting you received. He treated you like a long-lost friend."

Leo rubbed his finger under his nose, his grin sheepish. "Yes, well . . ." He flicked an almost embarrassed glance at Jennie. "I hadn't planned to admit this, but *I* found the puppy and brought him to the Flankstons."

Jennie's mouth dropped open. "You did? I wonder why they didn't say so?"

Etta bent over and ruffled Rags's velvety ears. "Maybe they didn't want us to feel obligated to take him since you and Leo have become such good friends."

The pair exchanged grins.

"I guess so," Jennie said before giving Leo a light bop on his arm. "But why didn't you tell me you'd found him? I feel kind of foolish now, the way I went on about the dog when you already knew about him."

He put both hands in the air as if in surrender. "But I didn't know they'd given him to you. So we both got a surprise."

Jennie laughed again, shaking her head. "Well, he sure remembers you."

"Or maybe he just smelled these." Leo shrugged out of his knapsack and unbuckled the flap. He lifted out a wax-paper-wrapped package and gave it to Etta.

Rags bounced at Etta's feet, half lunging at the bundle. She *tsk-tsk*ed at the dog, then turned to Leo. "What is it?"

"Cherry-filled rolls from the hotel." Remorse twisted his lips. "I'm afraid they got a little squashed in my pack. I hope they'll still taste all right."

His thoughtfulness warmed her. "Squashing won't remove the flavor. Thank you, Leo. This is very kind of you."

A blush stained the young man's chiseled cheeks. "It isn't much, but I wanted to thank you for sharing meals with me and letting Jennie guide me around the hills. I appreciate all you've done for me."

"You're quite welcome. We don't get many visitors out here, and we've enjoyed becoming acquainted." Etta headed to the house. The dog and both young people trailed her inside. She held the package of rolls out toward Claude as she passed him. "Leo brought us a treat from the hotel." Claude stared out the window as if he hadn't heard her. She placed the package on the table, then crossed to the sink and pumped water to wash her hands. "Leo, did you have any luck today at finding more of the dinosaur skeleton?"

"No, ma'am, but we're not giving up."

Etta turned a startled glance on him. His use of *we* seemed to carry significance.

Jennie was beaming up at Leo. "But we did find something important, didn't we? A fossilized beetle from the"—she crinkled her nose, her eyes rolling upward—"Paleozoic Era." She fixed a hopeful look on Leo. "Did I say it right?"

"You did." Leo removed his hat and tucked it under his arm.

"According to evolutionists," Jennie went on brightly, "it could possibly date back as far as five hundred million years ago."

Leo's smile turned warm and encouraging. "It's amazing you remembered all that. It took me more than a week to memorize the names and estimated time periods of the eras. You're a good student."

Suddenly Claude snorted and pushed himself to his feet. "I don't hold with evolution. Adaptation? Sure. Over time, as the environment changes, critters have to change for survival. But one type of critter turning into another one? That's pure nonsense. Goes completely against what the Bible says about how things came to be. I won't allow that kind of talk in my house, and I won't have you teachin' it to my daughter."

Jennie gasped. "Daddy! Leo isn't—"

Claude pointed at her. "He just now called you a good student. You spouted some big word you've never said before. So don't tell me he isn't filling your head with whatever he's learning at that fancy college."

Etta grabbed a hand towel and hurried to her husband's side. "Claude, there's no need to get yourself worked up. I don't think Leo's teaching Jennie things that will harm her."

"No, he isn't." Jennie's voice turned shrill, even panicky. Rags went flat on the floor and peered up at her, his round eyes filled with worry. "Leo *is* studying the theory of evolution at college. It's part of his training in paleontology. But he believes—"

Claude made a vicious swipe with his arm. "I don't want to hear anything more about it." He aimed a fierce glare at Jennie, who trembled as badly as the frightened pup on the floor. "We were foolish to let you go traipsing with him. Two young folks wandering around out there without supervision . . . Heaven only knows what all you could be up to."

Leo drew back as sharply as if he'd been struck. "Sir, I assure you, I—"

Claude jammed his palm in the air. "Nope. I said I'm done listening. I'm telling. You're no longer welcome here, young man. You wanna keep hunting for bones, hire somebody from town to take you. But Jennie ain't gonna be picking up on any more lies."

Jennie wrung her hands, tears swimming. "But, Daddy, Leo and I—"

"I said *no more!*" Claude roared the command.

Rags scuttled under the table, and Jennie burst into tears. She ran to her bedroom and slammed the door behind her, but the heartbreaking sounds of her weeping filtered past the planked wood.

Etta touched Claude's arm. "Claude, please, let's talk about this."

Claude jerked free of her light hold and plunked onto the chair. "Got nothin' more to say." He peered out the window, his jaw jutting in an obstinate angle.

Etta sighed and gestured for Leo to follow her outdoors. She moved well away from the cabin, then offered the stricken college student a sorrowful look. "Leo, I know you haven't done or said anything to deserve Claude's railing. I'm sorry about the accusations he threw at you."

Leo swallowed, his Adam's apple bobbing. "It's not your fault, ma'am. Jennie told me about Mr. Ward's troubles. His sickness was talking just then, not him."

What a kind, understanding way of responding to such unwarranted treatment. Etta's respect and admiration for Leo increased. "Even so, he owes you an apology. Since he won't give it, I will. I'll also talk to him when he's calmed down. It—" Suddenly the full meaning behind his words settled in her mind. "Did Jennie tell you her daddy is sick? Because he isn't ill. According to the doctor, his leg is fully healed. It just didn't heal straight, so he can't walk as well as he used to."

Leo looked aside for a moment, and when he turned back, his eyes seemed to hold a steely resolve. "Ma'am, I'm not a doctor. I won't even pretend to be. But Mr. Ward's behavior matches the symptoms I learned about in one of my college classes." Red streaks flooded his cheeks. "If I tell you about it, can we keep it between the two of us? I don't want Jennie to know. She's hoping so much for Mr. Ward to be himself again, and I don't want to knock the hope out of her."

Clearly, Leo cared about Jennie. Etta heard it in his voice now. She'd witnessed it in the way he acted around her. She understood his desire not to discourage Jennie, but she feared whatever he said might discourage her own heart. Some days her hold on hope was more tenuous than she wanted anyone to know.

The young man waited for her to grant or deny permission to speak. *Lord, what do I tell him?* An explicable peace whispered through the center of her soul—the Holy Spirit giving an answer. She placed her fingertips on his arm. "Please tell me. I'll keep whatever you say in confidence."

She listened while Leo shared the details of a mental disease called melancholia. So many of the symptoms—overwhelming sadness, unwarranted irritability, sleeping too much, lack of energy or desire to participate in previously enjoyed activities—described Claude so well that gooseflesh broke out on her arms in spite of the mild summer temperature.

"Sometimes there's no explanation for its occurrence," Leo

said, "but other times it seems to follow a significant emotional trauma. Jennie told me earlier today that Mr. Ward lost his beloved dog shortly before he injured his leg. Rex's death may play as much a role in his feelings of despondence as his inability to walk as well as he once did."

Etta glanced over her shoulder. Claude's unsmiling face was framed in the window, and his low-lidded eyes stared at . . . what? Another chill attacked. She needed to end this conversation and return to the cabin as quickly as possible lest another emotional storm was brewing under his surface. Jennie had been through enough for one day.

"I appreciate you telling me about this illness." She nibbled her lower lip for a moment, her need to return to the cabin warring with her desire for more information. "Is there . . . a cure?"

Leo ducked his head and scuffed grass-blades with the toe of his boot. "There are treatments, but no known cure." He lifted his face. Did she glimpse a small element of hope in his expression? "However, there are recorded cases when the melancholia lifted as mysteriously as it arrived." He grimaced. "Of course, there aren't guarantees it won't come back at a later time. But at least there is a possibility of a reprieve in the depressive symptoms."

Suddenly he gripped Etta's hand. "I pray that I'm wrong. That Mr. Ward doesn't have melancholia. But if he does, you—all of you—need support from a good doctor."

A sad chuckle found its way from Etta's chest. "Claude has re-fused to go to town since Doc Whiteside told him his leg had healed incorrectly."

"Then *you* go." The corners of Leo's lips lifted into a sheepish grin. "Please pardon me for being so bold, but I . . . I've come to care about your family. And if I'm not allowed to see any of you anymore, I'd like to leave with the assurance that things will be better for you by and by."

She blinked hard against the threat of tears. What an amazing young man. The type of young man Etta would choose for her daughter . . . for more than a mere friend. But what was she thinking? She'd always known Leo would be in Cañon City for only a short time, and now Claude had banished him. She shouldn't allow such thoughts for even a moment. "Thank you, Leo. When I'm in town next, I'll stop by the doctor's office and visit with him."

He breathed out a huge sigh laden with relief. He put on his hat and tightened the strings, then removed his knapsack and pulled out a wire-bound drawing pad. "This is Jennie's. Would you return it to her, please?"

Etta took it. "Of course."

"And this is for Mr. Ward." He slowly removed a periodical, as if now fearful of giving it. "You'll notice there's a painting of children on the cover. The magazine features works by various artists on its covers, but don't let the subject matter mislead you. The articles aren't written for children. My father takes the *Post* and always enjoys its contents. I hope it will provide a pleasant diversion for Mr. Ward."

Etta stacked the magazine on top of the sketch pad. "Thank you, Leo. It was kind and generous for you to think of him." Especially considering how inhospitable Claude had been on previous visits. After tonight's eruption, Leo could have decided not to leave the gift. That he chose to give it anyway said much about his character.

Leo swung the knapsack onto his back. "I'll go watch for the train now. Thank you, Mrs. Ward, and . . ." His gaze drifted to the cabin. He swallowed. "Please tell Jennie I'm grateful to have met her. She's a very special girl." He turned and scuffed down the hill, his shoulders as bowed as if the pack on his back was filled with boulders.

Etta pressed the items he'd given her to her pounding heart. She returned to the cabin, her steps slow and labored. Could Leo be right about Claude? As he'd made clear, he wasn't a doctor, but he was an intelligent young man who, she truly believed, wouldn't bear falsehoods. Could it be that Claude wasn't merely being stubborn about his perceived inability to work again but had a true illness that kept him captive in the cabin every day?

Lord, I've asked You to restore Claude. But what restoration does he truly need—physical or mental?

Chapter Sixteen

Leo

Leo spent a restless night, tormented by guilt and worry. What if Mr. Ward had another outburst after he'd left the cabin? What if it went beyond verbal to physical? According to his studies, people with melancholia could engage in violent eruptions. He would never forgive himself if Jennie or Mrs. Ward suffered harm because of him. Deep down, he knew he wasn't responsible for the man's erratic behavior. But he'd inadvertently caused it by talking to Jennie about evolution. If only Mr. Ward would have let him explain his personal beliefs concerning the earth's beginning and growth. But the man's ability to reason was buried somewhere inside him. Leo had made the right choice to leave without a fuss, but how his heart hurt.

Was it true he'd known Jennie for only ten days? It seemed their friendship was decades old—older, even, than their chronological years. He'd told her he believed God intended for their paths to cross, and he still believed it. But was the intersecting of their lives meant for only a few days? He struggled with accepting the possibility.

He eventually drifted off to sleep and awakened to the sounds of clanking pans and muffled voices. He bounded out of bed and scrambled into his clothes, prepared for a verbal dressing-down for going into work late. But the chef must have recognized the lingering anguish weighing Leo's soul and took pity on him, because he just told him to jump in and get busy. Leo did so.

The morning flew by in a flurry of activity, and by the end of his shift, he was drained. He ate his late lunch, then returned to his room. His bed beckoned him to nap instead of catch the train. Why not? After all, he didn't have a guide anymore. The prospect of searching on his own held little appeal after his delightful afternoons with Jennie's company. Then he remembered the conversation with Mr. Figgins from the Denver museum. Leo had written down the name and telephone number of a Cañon City businessman interested in fossil hunting but laid it aside because he was content to search with Jennie. With that option ripped away, he needed a guide. Where had he put the paper holding the information?

A brief search through the desk tucked at the foot of his bed uncovered the paper. He flicked it with his finger, contemplating whether or not to give Mr. DeWeece a call. This uncertainty wasn't like him. He came here so driven. Why was he now waffling on continuing his hunt? Would he let Mr. Ward's behavior steal his determination to find the remainder of the skeleton?

He pushed the paper holding Mr. DeWeece's telephone number into his pocket and went to the hotel's lobby. The concierge granted permission for Leo to use the telephone. A female voice answered almost immediately, and Leo asked to speak to Mr. De-Weece. A few moments later, he heard, "This is DeWeece. To whom am I speaking?"

Leo cleared his throat. "My name is Leo Day, sir. I'm a student from the University of Denver, studying the field of paleontology."

"Very well, Mr. Day. What can I do for you?" His tone wasn't overtly friendly—he sounded as if Leo had pulled him away from something important—but he'd opened the door to conversation. Leo would walk through.

"The director of the Denver Museum of Nature and Science, Mr. Figgins, gave me your name. He said you have an interest in locating the remains of prehistoric animals. I'm in possession of a single bone found a few miles west of Cañon City." The concierge lingered near, aiming his ear in Leo's direction. Leo turned his back on the man to keep himself focused on Mr. DeWeece. "It's my goal to discover the entire skeleton, but I'm not familiar with the area surrounding the city. Are you interested in helping me search for the fossils?"

"I am quite interested in seeking out new discoveries."

The immediate agreement lifted Leo's spirits.

"But I run a business, son. I limit my fossil-hunting excursions to weekends."

Only the weekends? What would Leo do with himself the remainder of the week?

"If this suits your schedule, we can arrange to meet this coming Saturday and Sunday—that would be June 19 and 20." The sound of pages ruffling carried through the line. "Should I add you to my calendar?"

Leo chewed the inside of his cheek. He needed help. He wanted to find the skeleton. But searching on Sunday, when he should attend worship services, went against his conscience. "I, um . . ."

A slight huff of air spoke of impatience. "Son, we can further discuss this when you know your weekend plans. In the meantime, give me your telephone number and address so I'll have it for my records."

Leo shared the telephone number and address for the hotel, then said, "I'll contact you as soon as I know whether this weekend will work for me."

"Fine. Good day, now." A click severed the connection.

Leo settled the telephone handpiece in its cradle but didn't release it. There was another call he felt compelled to make. To his father.

The realization so startled him his knees wobbled. He leaned against the sturdy counter and checked the grandfather clock tick-ing from the corner of the lobby. Given the day and hour, Father was likely in his office. If he was deep in study, he would ignore the telephone's ring, but he might pick up. And if he did, what would Leo say? Would Father listen or launch into another lecture about Leo's choice of study? In his current state, both weary and heartsore, he wouldn't respond well to criticism. Yet the desire to tell his father about Jennie's family, to ask him and Mother to pray for the Wards, was too strong to ignore.

He glanced at the concierge, ready to ask if he could make another call, but the man's not-so-subtle eavesdropping on his conversation with Mr. DeWeece stifled the request. The Wards' situation was too personal to share on a public telephone. He thanked the concierge and returned to his room. He sat on the edge of the bed and contemplated his options. His gaze drifted to the desk, and he rolled his eyes at his own inability to see the obvious. Why not write a letter?

The day he'd arrived in Cañon City, he sent a picture postcard of the hotel to his parents so they'd know where to reach him if need be. A couple of days later, he mailed a postcard with a watercolor image of columbine to his sisters so they wouldn't feel left out. This past Saturday, a fat envelope with notes from every family member arrived.

He crossed to the desk and sat in the creaky chair, then took out the short missives. Each person had included at least one question. Daisy wanted to know if he'd found a candy shop, no doubt hoping he'd send her a treat for her July birthday. Myrtle begged him to send more pretty postcards to paste on her wall. Mother expressed concern about whether he was eating right, and Father inquired if he'd located a church where he felt at home. He'd planned to write a lengthy letter on Saturday since his weekdays were taken with work in the morning and searching for fossils in the afternoon. But he wouldn't go out today.

He took his journal and pen from the desk drawer and turned

to a clean page. He started to write, "Dear Father, Mother, and Sisters," but decided against it. His sisters needn't be privy to Jennie's situation. Instead, he wrote, "Dear Little Pests." His sisters would find it amusing. He kept the note short, letting Daisy know there was no designated candy shop but that a good variety of sweets could be had at the drugstore. He asked what she liked better, gumdrops or licorice whips, knowing full well she preferred fruit-flavored hard candies because they lasted longer.

What was Jennie's favorite candy?

With a grunt of irritation, he pushed the thought aside and focused on writing a little something for Myrtle. He promised to collect a variety of penny postcards and send one each week as long as Myrtle agreed to ask permission before applying paste to a wall in the parsonage. He ended their missive with, "Enjoy your summer break, but be good helpers for Mother. I love and miss you." Amazingly, he did miss them. More than he'd thought possible before moving away from home. He'd actually been lonesome for them. How lonely it must be for Jennie to be the only child and so far from town.

And now he was thinking of Jennie again. Gritting his teeth, he signed the girls' letter and started on a fresh page.

Dear Mother and Father,

I pray you are both well. I am doing fine. Since I work in the hotel kitchen, I am provided with meals by the hotel. The chef's cooking is very good. Not as good as Mother's, of course. How could it be? But I am well-fed, and you can tell the girls I have dessert every day. Won't they be envious?

I attended the Presbyterian church on my first Sunday in town. Yesterday, I visited the Baptist church. There are three other churches in Cañon City, and I plan to visit each before choosing one for the rest of my weeks here.

If he began hunting dinosaur fossils with Mr. DeWeece, though, he wouldn't be in church at all. Guilt nibbled at him. Should he tell his parents about his dilemma? Then he decided against it. He already knew what they would say to him—honor the Lord. If he confessed he was even considering something else, he would hurt and disappoint them.

He went to a new paragraph—the paragraph he needed to write to unburden himself.

> *My very first Friday here, I planned to take the train to Pueblo, but I didn't get all the way there. I was watching out the window, and I saw a girl carrying what I could tell was a fossilized bone. So I disembarked early and asked the girl if I could examine it. As it turned out, I became friends with the girl—her name is Jennie—and her parents, who live along the pipeline that delivers water to Cañon City. Jennie's parents, Claude and Etta Ward, gave Jennie permission to show me some places on the mountain where more bones could be found.*
>
> *You're likely wondering why her father didn't offer to show me. He was injured in an accident some time ago and suffered permanent damage to his leg. He no longer does a lot of walking. Jennie has assumed his duties as inspector of the waterline, which means she isn't able to attend school. Additionally, the loss of mobility has affected Mr. Ward's mental well-being. He's become emotionally unstable.*

He stared at what he'd just written. Should he have put that down? The statement could be perceived as harsh and critical. Yet he wanted his parents to understand the problem so they would be able to pray specifically for the family. After a moment of internal debate, he chose not to scratch it out and continued the letter.

During our excursions on the mountainside, I had the opportunity to encourage Jennie and share verses I hoped would comfort her. But yesterday her father became angry about

His fingers froze. If he truthfully recorded what precipitated Mr. Ward's outburst, it would give Father fuel to dissuade him from continuing his course of study. He didn't want to lie, though. Maybe saying Jennie's father became angry was enough of an explanation. A man who was emotionally unstable likely wouldn't need much of a reason. It would suffice.

He marked through the word *about* and continued, sharing how he'd been forbidden from seeing Jennie again. A lump filled his throat, and he blinked to clear his vision before he could add another paragraph.

I'm concerned about Jennie's and her mother's well-being. I encouraged Mrs. Ward to visit a doctor for suggestions on how to help Mr. Ward overcome his state of despondence, but I wish I could do more. Would you please pray for the Ward family? I'm sure the Lord will direct you in how to pray, but I ask that you plead healing for Mr. Ward, safety for Mrs. Ward and Jennie, and freedom for Jennie to go to school this fall. She's very bright and a gifted artist. She drew the location where we found a fossilized shark tooth and also a beetle embedded in rock. Both sketches were very well done.

He jolted. When he gave Mrs. Ward the sketchbook for Jennie, he didn't remove the drawing of the beetle. A sense of loss fell over him. He pinched the bridge of his nose, his eyes closing. After a few minutes of silent self-recrimination, he lifted the pen and went on.

Jennie wants to study art, but unless she is released from what should be her father's duties, she won't have the opportunity. Please pray she will be able to use the gifts God gave her and won't lose heart. She has faith, but it's being tested. Please pray hope will reign victorious in her soul.

He finished by telling them a bit about his job and co-workers and ended with a promise to write again soon. He signed the letter, then set it aside so the ink could fully dry before folding it and sealing it in an envelope.

The afternoon loomed in front of him—long, lonely hours. He missed Jennie. And Mrs. Ward, who had made him feel welcome from the very first time he crossed the threshold of that little cabin. If only he could check on them and make sure they were all right. The anguished sound of Jennie's weeping echoed in his mind. Her look of betrayal when her daddy claimed he couldn't be sure what the two of them had been doing those hours alone was embedded in his memory as permanently as that beetle's scales were in rock.

Had the man calmed down and asked forgiveness for the hurtful things he'd said? Leo doubted it. But he hoped that at the very least Mr. Ward had held his tongue and resisted inflicting any more verbal wounds on his daughter. Leo stood and paced the length of the room, running his hand through his hair. There had to be a way to check on Jennie without violating Mr. Ward's order to stay away.

Just like that, an idea came to him. He trotted to the desk, yanked up his pen, and began to write.

Dear Jennie . . .

Chapter Seventeen

Jennie

At the end of the pipeline, Jennie stopped and arched backward, grinding her fists at the base of her spine. A groan eased from her lips. What a day. What a long, miserable, lonely day after a long, miserable, lonely night because she'd stayed in her bedroom through supper and until daybreak.

She plopped down, dangled her legs, and stared at the rushing river a couple of yards beyond the toes of her boots. When she was younger, she liked to toss a flower or twig into the river and watch it sail away. If only she could send the uncomfortable feelings coursing through her middle away so easily. Tumultuous? Oh, yes.

Strange how quickly she'd become accustomed to having company on the final miles of her route. For close to two years, she'd inspected the pipeline by herself. She'd been lonely sometimes, but she hadn't dwelled on it. Walking the route alone was her responsibility, so she did it and sought out moments of joy along the way—like waving at the passing train, watching a hawk soaring overhead, and laughing at a bunny she'd startled into a zig-zagging escape. But without Leo's company, the pipeline seemed twice as long, the responsibility complete drudgery. She hadn't seen one thing all day that gave her spirit a lift. Because she hadn't looked.

Hadn't looked . . .

Guilt pressed down on her, and she sucked in a hissing breath. She pressed her hand to the little notepad where she'd recorded a leaking split between two staves only a quarter mile from the place where the pipeline entered the hillside. She knew from experience that breaks could happen quickly. It was the nature of the pipe's wood construction. But breaks were more common when the weather turned cold. She wasn't expecting one during the warmest months of the year. Had she been distracted by Leo's presence and therefore missed something? Would catching the spot earlier have prevented an actual leak from forming? There was no way to know now, but she hoped the waterway men wouldn't blame her—or, rather, Daddy—for the leak.

But maybe she really did want them to blame Daddy. Maybe she wanted them to accuse him of wrongdoing the way he'd accused her and Leo. Maybe she wanted his feelings to be stomped the way he'd stomped hers. Maybe she even wanted the waterway men to—

Another wave of guilt, this one stronger than the first, washed the ugly thoughts away. She peeked skyward and grimaced. "I'm sorry, God. I know I'm supposed to be kind to others, tenderhearted, and willing to forgive. But when Daddy sent away the friend You gave me, he kind of broke my heart." Her chin quivered, and tears distorted her vision, making the clouds waver. "That's pretty hard to forgive."

She sighed and stared at the water again. It would be easier to forgive Daddy if he apologized. But she couldn't count on that. Once upon a time, Daddy would've admitted he was wrong and made amends. But she didn't have that daddy anymore, and she feared she never would.

Her chest went tight, so tight it hurt to breathe. She looked across the river to the sheer rock wall behind the train tracks. Without thinking about what she was doing, she pulled in a full breath, cupped her hands beside her mouth, and yelled, "I need hope!"

The mountain bounced back "hope, hope, hope," each repetition softer until the wind whisked it away completely.

Her dry, aching throat advised against more yelling, but she couldn't seem to stop herself. "God, give me hope!"

The echoing "hope, hope, hope," although it was only her own voice coming back to her, somehow brought a flutter of assurance to her soul. She turned around on the pipe and clambered onto the patch of ground above the pipe's end. She paused, then looked back to the spot in the bend where Leo used to join her. A silly thing to do. He wouldn't show up again after what Daddy had said. But he wouldn't stay away out of resentment. He was honorable. He wouldn't go against Daddy's wishes.

Funny how well she knew him after such a short time. An odd thought sneaked into a far corner of her mind. Had she attached herself to him so thoroughly because he was the only person close to her age she'd been able to spend significant time with since moving to the cabin? Was it not Leo himself but only the opportunity to engage with another young person that inspired their friendship?

As quickly as the idea came, she discounted it. She'd encountered those two boys in the drugstore and hadn't longed for more time with them. Yet from the time she closed herself in her bedroom yesterday evening, she'd pined for Leo. For her friend.

A plan took shape on the heels of her dismal thought. She rolled her eyes upward, envisioning the calendar that hung in their kitchen. The first weekend in July was two weeks and four days away. She would ride the train into Cañon City for shopping and church. Would Mama stay with Daddy again, like she had last time? If so, Jennie would be able to do whatever she pleased, as long as she got the shopping done. When she visited the hotel, which she and Mama always did, she would most likely encounter Leo.

Her heart thrummed in anticipation. Then her conscience pricked. But stubborn rationalizing rose above the tickle of guilt. Daddy had banished Leo from coming to their cabin, but had he forbidden her from seeking him out? She chewed her chapped lip, reasoning she wouldn't be disobeying Daddy if her path crossed with Leo's in town. Deep down, she knew what Daddy meant when he sent Leo away. But it was such an unfair declaration. Jennie knew—as did Mama, Aunt Delia, and Uncle Prime—that Leo was not a bad influence. Leo was her God-sent friend. Daddy should not have sent him away.

After this dismal day, she needed to anticipate something good. Seeing Leo again would be something good. Something even better than good. It would give her a splash of that hope she was hollering about. What would it hurt to seek out Leo in town? Daddy would stay behind at the cabin, so he wouldn't even know.

But God would know.

Jennie gritted her teeth. She squinted at the sky. "But, God, he was wrong."

Honor your father and mother.

Oh, why couldn't she ignore what she'd been taught? Because she loved her parents and they'd taught her to obey God, that's why. She kicked at a clump of grass. It would be so much easier if she didn't love Daddy. Then his morose attitude and untrue suppositions about Leo wouldn't matter. But she loved Daddy and missed him so much. The loving and missing him was a constant ache in the center of her chest. She wanted the daddy from her growing-up years to return to her.

She jerked in the direction of the wall and screeched, "Ho-o-ope!"

"Ho-o-ope! Ho-o-ope! Ho-o-ope!"

With the mountain's echo rolling in her heart, she set off on the lonely walk home.

On Tuesday morning, Jennie sent a note with the train engineer about the leak she'd discovered. Wednesday, a different kind of engineer, dispatched by the waterway men, met up with Jennie mid-route, and she showed him the split. The man asked for Mr. Ward, which made Jennie's stomach churn in nervousness. But when Jennie said Mr. Ward was under the weather and couldn't come out, the man didn't seem bothered. He measured the area, made several notes in an official-looking notebook, and then thanked Jennie for her assistance and left, none the wiser that he'd spoken with the actual linewalker.

Mama expressed relief at suppertime that their secret hadn't been uncovered, but Daddy kept eating as if nothing of concern had taken place. Mama told Jennie she didn't need to help with kitchen cleanup and sent her outside with Rags. "Someone needs to run the energy out of him," Mama said, but Jennie suspected Mama was really giving Jennie a chance to escape Daddy's presence.

So Jennie romped on the lawn with the puppy, aware of Daddy watching from the other side of the window. Back when she played with Rex, if the dog did something funny, she looked to see if Mama or Daddy saw it so they could laugh with her. But no matter how cute Rags was while wrestling with his tied-in-knots shirtsleeve or barking at grasshoppers that had the audacity to invade his domain, she never once glanced Daddy's way. She didn't want to witness his disinterest.

Thursday morning, Mama walked out with Jennie into the long morning shadows and pressed a sealed envelope into her hand. "Will you please flag down the train, give this note to Mr. Rawling, and ask him to deliver it for me? I know this will waylay you setting off on the route, but it's important."

Jennie glanced at the envelope. Mama had addressed it to the doctor who'd tended Daddy's broken leg. A chill exploded across her frame. "Why are you writing to Dr. Whiteside? Are you sick?"

Mama chuckled softly, giving Jennie's cheek a sweet pat. "I'm right as rain, sweetheart. Don't worry. I want him to know I intend to stop by his office for a little visit on July 3 when we're in Cañon City."

Jennie released a little huff. "I'd forgotten our next time in town will be Independence Day weekend. Do you think Daddy will come with us since it's a holiday?" She knew she shouldn't even consider disobeying Daddy. She'd prayed repeatedly for God to take away the desire to see Leo. But temptation to meet with him at the hotel still pulled hard. If Daddy went to town, too, there'd be no chance of sneaking a few minutes with Leo. Maybe it would be best. Her guilty conscience would haunt her forever if she carried through with her plan. But never seeing Leo again might also haunt her forever.

Mama's expression turned pensive. "Your daddy used to love going to the parade, the community picnic at the park, and fireworks when we lived in town. Remember?"

Jennie remembered. The memories of those happy days were fuzzy, though, as if they weren't really hers at all but only something someone else had told her about.

Mama sighed. "Even if I did convince him to go, it's hard to know if he'd enjoy it now."

Jennie hung her head. "He doesn't enjoy anything now. Not even Rags. I thought for sure after he picked out the pup's name he'd show some interest in him."

A sly yet still-sad smile curved Mama's lips. "He does—just not when he thinks anyone is looking. Give it time. Rags will win him over. I believe your daddy will one day walk the hills with Rags the way he used to with Rex."

Jennie didn't say anything because she didn't want to disappoint her mother. But Mama would have to believe by herself. Until Jennie saw it with her own eyes, she wouldn't believe it.

"Hurry to the bridge, now, so you'll be there when the train comes around the bend." Mama pressed a kiss on Jennie's cheek.

"I'll see you at noontime. Well, probably closer to an hour past noontime since you'll get a late start."

Daddy would probably be napping by one o'clock. That suited Jennie fine. She waved goodbye to Mama and ambled down the rise to the footbridge. As she approached it, something caught her eye. A brown piece of paper was rolled and stuck between two boards on the far side of the bridge. Could it have blown out a train window and gotten jammed there? It didn't seem likely. Someone must have put it there.

Curiosity propelled her across the footbridge as quickly as possible. She pulled the paper loose and unrolled a large waxed envelope. A startled gasp escaped. Someone had written her name in a bold masculine script right across the center. Even before she opened the flap, she knew who'd left it. She looked over her shoulder toward the cabin, then up and down the line. Certain she wasn't being observed, she scurried over the lines of track and leaned against the rock wall. Only then, tucked fully into shadow, did she peel back the flap and peek inside.

A single sheet of paper—a letter, she realized—waited for her. Her heart thumping like the bass drum in a parade band, she pressed the page flat and read.

Dear Jennie,

I trust this missive finds you. I apologize for resorting to such unusual means of communication, but I didn't know how else to reach you.

First, a sad confession: I miss our daily talks. But though I do not see you daily, I think of you and pray for you. I pray especially that your daddy will find complete healing and that you will cling to hope and not harbor bitterness.

Jennie gulped as she read "not harbor bitterness." Sometimes she thought Leo knew her better than she knew herself. Mama had taught her from the time she was small that God the Father gave His children good gifts. He'd given one of the best when He brought Leo into her life. Mama also said she could trust her heavenly Father to bestow what she needed. She needed hope—there was no question about it, and she was doing her best to not let it go. But did she *need* Leo's friendship, or did she merely *want* it?

The bitterness Leo was praying against tried once more to sneak in. Jennie tamped it down and returned her attention to the letter.

Next, I doubt any guide will make hunting as fun as my mountain goat friend did, but I have contacted a local businessman who is as interested as I in locating the remaining bones. I thought you might be glad that I don't have to give up seeking. He and I will be in your area on Saturday. And this leads me to a request.

When we parted on Monday, I neglected to remove the drawing of the beetle from your sketchbook. I would very much like to have it—a memento of our time together. Would you be kind enough to place it in this envelope and return it to its spot at the footbridge? I will retrieve it on Saturday.

Jennie sucked in a breath and stared at the gap between boards where she'd found the rolled envelope. Would Leo spend every Saturday with this businessman now that Jennie wasn't guiding him? If so, she could set aside anticipation of seeing him in town on Independence Day weekend. The thought stung her heart, but at the same time, she was a little glad. Knowing he wouldn't be available removed any chance of her disobeying Daddy. Maybe God was sparing her conscience.

There was one more paragraph written on the page.

Lastly, when I came to Cañon City for the summer, I asked God to lead me to a historical find but also to like-minded friends. He blessed me with you, your mother, and your aunt and uncle. Although my time with you has proved short in duration, our hours of togetherness will linger always in my dearest memories.

Give Rags an ear scratch for me. I hope to find a reply from you at the footbridge.

Fondly,

Leo Day

Jennie crushed the letter to her chest. Of course she would leave a reply. She'd made the drawing for him—he should have it. And she would write a long letter telling him all he meant to her. Words began tripping through her mind, and her fingers itched to record them on paper. But first she must give Mama's note to the train engineer. Then she had to inspect the line. The letter would have to wait.

Chapter Eighteen

Etta

C laude limped from the bedroom, yawning. He crossed to the table and scowled at the skirt and needle in Etta's hands. "Why're you working on mending now? Shouldn't you be getting supper started?"

Etta had decided to fix a late supper, knowing Jennie's return would be delayed given her morning errand. She pushed the needle through the soft cotton, closing the L-shaped tear one of Rags's claws caused when he jumped on her legs earlier that day. "I'm going to wait until Jennie's home so it'll be hot and fresh for her."

He yanked out the chair next to Etta's and plopped onto its seat. "If I eat much past six, I get indigestion. She'd best not be too late."

Etta started to tell him that if *he'd* walked the line that day, she would have made sure *his* supper was hot and fresh, but she held the comment inside. If Leo was right about Claude suffering from an illness over which he had no control, she shouldn't deliberately aggravate him.

"Well," she said as she knotted the thread, "it will be worth waiting for, because I baked applesauce cake." Jennie was particularly fond of applesauce cake laden with raisins and chunks of walnuts, especially when served with sweet white sauce. The cake was already in the oven. She would make the sauce later.

Claude yawned again, rubbing his belly. "Wish you'd make pound cake."

Etta glanced up. "Well, I suppose I could, but it'll mean no eggs for breakfast for a couple days. Pound cake takes a lot of eggs, and we only have three chick—"

"And put some sliced strawberries on top." Was he even listening to Etta? He went on as if she hadn't spoken. "Haven't had that in so long I've about forgot what it tastes like." A frown of disgruntlement marred his face. "It's summertime. Summertime means strawberries. It always has."

Was he getting himself worked up? Etta's anxiety rose a notch. She patted his hand, then rose and draped the mended apron over the back of her chair. "Now, Claude, you know how hard I tried to grow strawberries out here. The first three years, I brought out starts from Delia's garden and planted them, remember? But we don't get enough sun on our garden for them to take."

Claude sent a brooding look toward the window.

"If you're really hankering for a slice of pound cake with strawberries, we could take the train to town and visit the hotel dining room." She watched his profile for signs of an impending outburst. "We could even go tomorrow if you wanted to."

He worked his jaw back and forth as if working loose a seed from his tooth. "Can't leave that dog unattended."

Etta glanced at Rags sleeping soundly on a folded blanket next to the stove. With his paws folded under his chin and the white ear flopping over his eye toward his nose, he looked so sweet and innocent. If only she could shake the notion that he was storing up energy for further mischief. "Well, then, Saturday. Jennie would be here Saturday to keep an eye on him, if you're worried about him."

Claude snorted. "Not worried. Just saying he shouldn't be left on his own. Not while he's still a pup."

She hid a smile. He was worried or he wouldn't have said anything. The peek at her husband's heart bolstered her spirits. "Then do you want to take a trip to Cañon City on Saturday and have some strawberries and pound cake at the hotel?" She held her breath, warning herself not to get her hopes up. But he needed interaction with people. He needed to see something besides the view from the front window. He needed to—

"Reckon so."

Her breath rushed out with such force spots danced behind her eyes. She blinked twice. Should she pinch herself? Maybe she was dreaming and wasn't awake at all. "You . . . you want to go?"

He nodded—one unsteady bob of his head. "Probably need to pick up a few extra stores since you fed supper to four people instead of three all last week." A sullen edge entered his tone.

Etta made her own voice happy and light to counterbalance it. "Oh, maybe some coffee, flour, and sugar, but that won't cost much." She eased close and smoothed the tufts of hair sticking out above his right ear. "It'll be nice to ride the train with you and spend a little time in Cañon City. Just the two of us, the way we did back when we first wed. Remember?"

He turned his face up to her. Something unreadable glimmered in his brown eyes. Did she see a spark of longing to live those days again? To be the man he was back then? He pushed up from the table and shuffled to the chair in front of the window. He settled in his usual spot and released a slow sigh. "Yeah," he said.

His back was to her, but he'd answered. And he remembered. It was enough for now.

The scent of applesauce cake drew her to the stove, and she peeked inside. The domed top looked brown and ready. She protected her hands with a dish towel and removed the steaming cake from the oven, then set it on the windowsill to cool. As she inhaled the spicy aroma, she couldn't keep a smile from forming. Jennie had been so sad all week. A big piece of her favorite cake should give her a lift.

"Keep an eye out for Jennie, Claude." She chose a can of peas from the shelf, then rooted in the potato basket for several small potatoes. She tumbled a handful of them into a basin and reached for the pump. Then her hand stilled on the handle. How would Jennie react to her parents' plan to visit Cañon City by themselves? Would she be happy her daddy wanted to go to town, or would it sadden her to stay behind?

While Etta prepared the potatoes for boiling, she sent up a quick heartfelt prayer that her daughter would choose joy over disappointment.

Jennie

Jennie closed herself in her bedroom after supper. She'd not eaten much the past few days, too upset over Leo's banishment to be hungry. But Mama's applesauce cake with white sauce brought her appetite racing back. She'd eaten two pieces after a full plate of peas, potatoes, and ham chunks swimming in gravy. Her stomach ached from too much eating, but it was worth it. Her taste buds were still tingling with the flavors of cinnamon and nutmeg.

She retrieved a writing pad and pencil from a basket on the top of her dresser, then sat on the edge of the bed and balanced the pad on her lap. Leo's letter, crumpled from being rolled and then shoved into her waistband beneath her shirt, lay next to her. Her gaze settled on the line "I hope to find a reply from you at the footbridge."

Rolling the pencil between her fingers, she pondered how to reply. She'd never written a letter to a boy before. There was so much she wanted to say that it probably wouldn't all fit on one page. But should she write it all down? What if someone else—his parents or one of his sisters—came upon it someday and read it? She would die of mortification to have her personal feelings for Leo exposed. And how would she leave a note for him now?

Her pulse tripped as she recalled Mama's astounding announce-

ment at suppertime that she *and Daddy* were going to Cañon City
on Saturday. Equally shocking, they wanted her to stay behind—to
tend to chores and keep an eye on Rags. They'd not only let her go
to town and do the shopping on her own at the beginning of the
month, but now they trusted her to stay at the cabin alone. They
must see her as close to grown. She couldn't deny puffing up a bit
at the news. And their leaving her alone cracked open a door of
opportunity.

Since Mama and Daddy would meet the train at the footbridge,
she couldn't leave a letter there as Leo had requested. They'd see
it, too, and it might send Daddy into another rage. But according
to Leo's letter, he would be out here on Saturday searching for
dinosaur bones. With chores to do, she couldn't run off and join
him and the businessman he'd mentioned. But she could wave
him down and give him the beetle-shell drawing. Steal a moment
or two of his time. Long enough to once again bask in his warm
smile, peer into his dark-blue eyes beneath the wide brim of his
funny hat, and grasp one more memory to cherish.

Of course, she might look like a real ninny to the other man if
she let herself get caught up in staring into Leo's face. She'd better
hand off the envelope and depart. But she would put a note in the
envelope.

With worry about someone else possibly reading the missive
rolling in the back of her mind, she chose her words carefully.

Dear Leo,
   Here is the drawing of the beetle you found embedded in
volcanic rock on the rise west of my cabin. Thank you for
the gift of the sketch pad so I could record it for you.
   Good luck finding other fossils in the mountains near
the pipeline.
   Your friend,
   Jennie

She read what she'd written, satisfied with her penmanship but disappointed in how impersonal it sounded. Particularly when compared to what he'd written her. She slid the note and drawing into the envelope and put it on her dresser underneath her writing pad. Then she settled against her pillows and read Leo's letter again. And again. And again. Until she'd memorized one small section.

She closed her eyes and whispered, " 'I miss our daily talks. But though I do not see you daily, I think of you and pray for you.' " His words on paper were the words in her heart.

Then the next line from the letter played in her mind's eye. *I pray especially that your daddy will find complete healing and that you will cling to hope and not harbor bitterness.*

She opened her eyes, and unexpectedly a warm tear rolled down her cheek. She whisked it away with the back of her hand, then pulled herself out of bed. She knelt and folded her hands, the way her parents had taught her to humble herself before God. Did Daddy ever kneel and pray? She didn't know if his leg would allow it even if his soul desired to do so. But whether he did or not, *she* needed to.

On her knees, head bowed, fingers clasped so tightly they ached, she begged God to honor Leo's and Mama's and her prayers for Daddy to find complete healing. She begged for the ability to keep hoping for change even when it seemed impossible that he'd change. And as tears sneaked from beneath her closed eyelids, she pleaded for God to root all hints of bitterness from her soul. Then, nearly spent, she made one more plea.

"Please change Daddy's mind about my spending time with Leo again so I can tell him how much his friendship meant to me. Thank You, God. Amen."

She folded the letter from Leo, tucked it in the back of her Bible, then slid between the sheets of her bed. She'd spent several restless nights in a row, but that night, Jennie slept like a log and awakened refreshed. She ate applesauce cake for breakfast on Friday morning and then set off for her route with a bounce in her step.

It must have sprinkled during the night, because the grass was more than dew wet. She reminded herself to be cautious on the pipe, as the wood would be slick until the moisture dried. It would have to happen by evaporation because the sun wouldn't touch the pipe until nearly noon. By midmorning, she'd ceased worrying about sliding on the pipeline's surface. She'd also paused and admired a particularly fluffy bank of clouds way in the east, watched a mud turtle's laborious journey along the rocky edge of the river, and blinked into the full sunlight cresting Pikes Peak. Each short acknowledgment of her surroundings made her heart feel lighter, more joyful.

She marveled at the shift in her spirit, so unlike the middle of the week when bitter sorrow weighted every step. What brought the change? She would still finish the complete route alone. She wouldn't wander the hills with Leo when her duties were done. Today was no different than Tuesday, Wednesday, or Thursday in those regards, yet she was enjoying herself again. Why?

A vibration traveled from the pipeline through the soles of her boots and up her frame. She angled herself on the pipe and faced the passing cars. She waved both hands over her head and smiled at the engineer, the passengers peering out the windows, and finally Mr. Jenkins, who held a blue handkerchief out the caboose window like a flag and winked at her. As the locomotive rolled out of sight, she resumed her inspection and her introspection.

Were her spirits better today because she'd gotten a solid night of sleep? Mama always said sleep was good for what ailed a person. Or did her joy stem from Daddy choosing to go to town for the first time in over a year? His decision wasn't comparable to miracles in the Bible, but it felt somewhat miraculous to Jennie. Or was it because she would likely see Leo, if only from a distance, tomorrow? Probably a combination of all three.

Whatever the reasons, she gloried that her tumultuous emotions had swung in a more cheerful direction. She tossed a smile and a whispered "Thank You" heavenward, then continued her route with a happy heart.

Chapter Nineteen

Leo

Leo glanced across the aisle to Mr. DeWeece. The businessman was examining a map he'd brought with him. A bulging pack with a looped rope tied to its outside filled the other half of De-Weece's seat. He looked so official. So knowledgeable. So in charge.

Leo braced a hand on his roiling stomach. Was the uncomfortable churning in his middle caused by the train's rocking motion or by worry? Had he made a mistake by asking Mr. DeWeece to join him on his search? Leo was only a college student, and De-Weece was a seasoned businessman involved in several philanthropic endeavors in the community. Given their ages and levels of experience, it made sense that DeWeece would take the lead. But where did that leave Leo?

Whether he liked it or not, he couldn't reverse time. He'd opened the door to the man by agreeing to search with him on Saturday. But not on Sunday. DeWeece had snorted under his breath when Leo told him he couldn't go out on Sundays because he attended church, but then the man had shrugged and said, "Fine, I can always go out on my own." Another reason for Leo's angst. What if DeWeece came upon the skeleton when Leo wasn't there? This was supposed to be Leo's find. Leo's moment of glory. Leo's means of gaining favor with Mr. Figgins and, in so doing, impressing his father. Would DeWeece take all that away from him?

The wheels screeched and the locomotive slowed. They were coming up on the footbridge, and he and Mr. DeWeece would get off the train. Leo slung his knapsack on his back and sat sideways, readying himself to disembark. The moment the train shuddered to a stop, he stepped through the doorway onto the little landing. He nearly plowed into Mrs. Ward, who was already there.

A smile automatically tugged at his lips. "Good morning, ma'am." Then he spotted Mr. Ward waiting on the ground next to the steps. Leo looked past the man, expecting to spot Jennie, but she was missing.

"Good morning, Leo." Mrs. Ward's warm greeting yanked Leo's attention to her. "It's very nice to see you."

"You, too. Are . . . are you going to town?" He could hardly believe it.

She beamed at him. "Indeed we are. Mr. Ward has a hankering for pound cake and strawberries from the hotel restaurant, so we're going to get some."

Delight exploded in his chest. "Well, then, let me get out of the way so you and Mr. Ward can come in." The knapsack hooked on the doorframe as he edged backward, nearly sending him sideways, but he caught his balance and moved around the corner.

Mrs. Ward came on in, but Mr. Ward didn't budge. The man's fingers gripped the iron handrails and he glared up at Leo. "What're you doing out here?"

Leo's happiness dissolved. His mouth went dry. "I'm going to search for the remainder of the dinosaur skeleton." He gestured Mr. DeWeece forward. "Mr. Ward, do you know Mr. DeWeece?"

A brusque shake of his head gave a reply.

Leo went on in a conversational tone although his insides churned with unease. "He is also interested in finding the remains, so he's guiding me today. Mr. DeWeece, this is Mr. Claude Ward. His family lives in the cabin on the rise and keeps watch over the pipeline."

DeWeece leaned past Leo and stuck out his hand to Mr. Ward. "It's nice to meet you, sir. Thank you for serving the community in such a worthwhile way."

After a moment's hesitation, Jennie's daddy gave the man a brief handshake. "Nice to meet you." He settled his frown on Leo again. "You ain't going out to my cabin."

It was more a command than a query, but Leo shook his head. Emphatically. "I am not, sir."

The train's conductor poked his head from the caboose's doorway. "Folks, we need to be moving on. Get off, come aboard, whatever needs doing . . . do it quickly, please. We have a schedule to keep."

But Mr. Ward didn't move, preventing Leo and Mr. DeWeece from disembarking.

Mrs. Ward rose from her seat and peered around the corner. "Claude, do you need a hand coming aboard?"

Jennie's daddy released the handrails and took two limping backward steps. "Not going."

Leo gaped at him. "But, Mr. Ward, there's no reason not to go. As I said, I won't go to your cabin. You have my word."

"Got nothin' to do with you." Jennie's daddy spoke with force, but perspiration was dotting his face. His frame trembled. "Changed my mind is all. It's too far to go. Too much walkin'. Should've known it'd be—" He clamped his mouth closed and shifted his gaze to his wife. "Etta, come on out o' there. I wanna go home."

Leo caught a glimpse of Mrs. Ward's distraught face before she skirted past him and Mr. DeWeece and descended the steps. "All right, Claude." Her voice held nothing but acceptance. "Let's go, then."

Leo and Mr. DeWeece departed the car and stood against the rock wall until the train chugged back into motion. Leo stared after the Wards, who were already across the footbridge and climbing the rise, Mrs. Ward holding Mr. Ward's arm. Leo winced at the man's slow, stumbling, limping gait. Doubt that Jennie's daddy would ever take over as linewalker again struck hard and made his heart ache for her. Would she ever be released from the duty?

DeWeece was watching them, his brows tipped together in contemplation. "Did you say this is the Mr. Ward hired by the Cañon City Water Works Department to monitor the pipeline?"

Leo went cold and then hot. How could he have been so foolish? He'd only meant to make a polite introduction, but by sharing who Mr. Ward was, he might have inadvertently divulged the secret Jennie's family had been keeping. Would Mr. DeWeece tell the waterway men what he'd seen—that Mr. Ward was barely capable of walking from the train tracks to his cabin without assistance? Would he be fired? What would happen to Jennie's family then?

He licked his dry lips and gathered his jumbled thoughts. "Yes, sir. He's recovering from an illness." He chose the same half-truth Jennie had given as an excuse, praying God would understand. "But the duty hasn't been neglected. Another family member walks the line each day and reports issues."

"Interesting." Mr. DeWeece continued frowning after the pair for another few seconds, and then he withdrew the map from a patch pocket on the outside of his pack and handed it to Leo. He lifted the pack with a little grunt and hooked it over his shoulders. He held out his hand, and Leo gave him the map. "We have much ground to cover today. Let's get started." He shot off for the footbridge. Grateful for the quick change in topic, Leo followed.

Etta

Jennie was hanging clothes on the line, Rags sitting close by her. As Etta and Claude neared the cabin, Rags whirled in their direction and set up a clamor. Jennie turned quickly, and even from the distance of nearly forty-five feet, Etta saw dismay blossom on her daughter's face.

Jennie came running, and Rags galloped along beside her, his ears flapping. "What's wrong? I thought you were going to town."

"We were." Etta exercised every bit of fortitude she possessed to maintain an unconcerned tone. "But the walk to the train proved too tiresome for your daddy. He decided he wasn't up to going all the way to Cañon City."

The look Jennie turned on her father hovered between disappointment and compassion. "I . . ." She drew a breath. "I'm sorry you won't get your cake and strawberries, Daddy."

He pulled loose of Etta's grip on his arm. "I'm gonna go lay down for a while. The climb from the tracks to here wore me plumb out." He limped the remaining distance to the cabin. Rags whimpered, prancing in place, and then bounded after Claude. The two went inside.

Jennie held her hands out in a gesture of defeat. "I don't understand. He was so set on going to town."

Etta sighed. She looped arms with Jennie and they ambled toward the clothesline. "He was, but . . ." Something else, some unnamed fear, had come over him. Deep down, she knew it wasn't the worry about walking so far, and it was more than worry about Leo being in the area. She gave Jennie's arm a little squeeze. "Guess who we encountered getting off the train."

Jennie shrugged.

"Leo Day."

Jennie dipped her head. "Oh."

A guilty admission if Etta had ever heard one. She drew Jennie to a stop and peered into her face. "Did you know he'd be out here today?"

Jennie's lips formed a grimace. "Well . . . yes, ma'am."

Is that why Jennie hadn't shown an ounce of resistance about staying behind? "How? Has he been meeting you on the line after your daddy told him not to?"

"No, Mama." Her answer came quickly. "I haven't seen him since Monday evening, when Daddy sent him away."

Etta searched her daughter's brown eyes for signs of deception. Seeing none, she gave a little nod. "All right, then, but how could you know he'd be in this area today?"

Jennie confessed to finding a letter from Leo at the footbridge. She pointed to an envelope weighted down by the clothes basket under the line. "I put the drawing he asked for in the envelope. I hoped I would see him so I could give it to him, but I didn't plan to spend time with him. Honest, Mama." Her voice broke. "But it was hard to tell myself no. I . . . I miss him so much."

Etta grabbed Jennie in a tight hug. "I'm sure it was tempting. But I'm proud of you for being obedient to your daddy."

Jennie jerked loose and turned her back on Etta. "Don't be proud of me, Mama. I've had some ugly thoughts. I've wrestled with temptation. To be honest, if I had seen Leo today, I might've tossed my convictions to the wind and gone hunting with him after all." She slowly faced Etta again. The contrition in her expression spoke more loudly than words. "Are you mad at me?"

A chuckle found its way from Etta's throat. "Oh, honey . . ." She tucked a loose strand of hair behind her daughter's ear. "Do you think you're the only young person who's battled temptation? The only one who's had ugly thoughts?" Maybe she *did* think so. Who did she have to compare herself to, not having siblings or friends to call her own? "When I was your age, I inwardly railed at my parents' rules and expectations. Sometimes I did what I wanted to instead of obeying them. It's all part of growing up. Of finding your path."

Jennie's eyes widened. "You rebelled? But you're the most faithful person I know."

The praise, especially coming from her very own child, blessed

Etta's heart. But Jennie knew the broken-in version of her mother, not the tumultuous young woman she'd been. "If I'm faithful today, it's because I learned when I was young the importance of following a God-honoring path. When I obey the standards God set for His children, I live without regrets. Regret is a terrible burden to carry. I want to spare you that pain if I can."

Jennie glanced at the cabin, chewing the inside of her cheek. "I told God it's really hard to obey Daddy when I think what he's doing is wrong."

Etta took encouragement that at least Jennie was talking to God. "You can tell God anything and He'll listen and understand. But even when your daddy's being a little"—she grinned—"irascible, we still have an obligation to respect him. Yes?"

Jennie scuffed the grass with her bare toes. "Honor your father and mother. I know."

"That's right. The Bible doesn't say honor your parents if they deserve it or earn it—it simply instructs us to honor them." Etta brushed Jennie's cheek with her thumb. "And it's clear to me you'd chosen obedience over temptation even before your daddy and I left for the train."

Jennie tilted her head. "How do you know?"

She pointed at Jennie's feet. "How could you go chasing after Leo without your shoes on?"

Jennie gaped at her bare feet for a moment, then laughed. "Maybe you're right. I didn't even think about it." She sobered. "Thank you for not getting angry about me being tempted to disobey. And please don't be angry if I still think about it sometimes. It wasn't hard to obey Daddy when I was a little girl. I loved him and I trusted him to do what's best for me. But I don't feel like I even know him anymore. Even though I still love him, it's hard to honor and obey the daddy I have now."

"Then obey God the Father," Etta said firmly. She'd battled through the same feelings Jennie was expressing and emerged victorious. Her experience could help guide her daughter. "If you live in a way that honors God, you'll honor your mother and father at the same time. And you won't regret your choices. Do you understand what I'm saying?"

Jennie nodded slowly. She dropped her gaze to the envelope. "Mama, Leo and the man who's guiding him will probably get back on the train near the footbridge. May I take the envelope with the drawing I made for Leo down there and leave it for him to find? Then I won't be tempted to wave him down if he passes by."

Etta's heart rolled over. Jennie was trying so hard to do the right thing. Somehow she had to convince Claude he was being unfair to Jennie and Leo by keeping them apart. "Yes, you may. But, Jennie?"

Jennie blinked. "What?"

"Put your shoes on first. That's a rocky walk down to the footbridge."

Jennie laughed, a merry sound that heartened Etta. "Yes, ma'am." She yanked up the envelope and scampered to the house.

Etta took over the task of hanging laundry. She wasn't ready to go inside yet. She needed a little time with the Lord to release the ache in her heart over Claude's abrupt refusal to go to town. She needed to seek His discernment for the best way to approach her husband about letting Jennie guide Leo again. She needed His peace and strength because her heart was sore and weary.

By the time Jennie finished her errand and returned, Etta had emptied the basket and released her cares. Jennie grabbed up the basket and headed for the house, calling over her shoulder, "I'll get the next load washed if you want to work in the garden."

"That sounds fine, but I need to change into my chore dress first." She closed herself in the bedroom. Claude lay flat on his back, arms wide, snoring. She shook her head. How could such a short walk wear him out so? How long would it take for him to regain his strength?

She tiptoed to the wardrobe, selected a work dress, and changed. As she turned to leave, she glanced at her sleeping husband again. Then she stopped and looked long and hard. His once muscular arms seemed shriveled. His torso was no longer taut from his daily fourteen-mile walk but was softly rounded from too much idle sitting. Her eyes drifted to his legs. To his shorter, bent leg. She stared at it, remembering how he'd struggled up the hill.

And all at once, the man from town who was with Leo on the train intruded into her thoughts. Mr. DeWeece. She'd never met him, but she knew his name. She knew his reputation and his many involvements in Cañon City politics and advancements. Had he, too, witnessed Claude's clumsy progress on the hillside?

Her knees went weak. She caught hold of the rail on the iron footboard. Their secret might not be a secret anymore. It was more important than ever to get Claude strong and walking the line again.

Chapter Twenty

Leo

When Leo and Mr. DeWeece returned to the footbridge Saturday evening, Leo spotted the brown envelope held down by a football-sized rock on the train side of the river even before he crossed. Mr. DeWeece must have seen it, too. He went across the bridge first, then bent over and picked up the envelope. He pinched a corner between his pointer finger and thumb and swung it like a clock's pendulum, a half smile aimed in Leo's direction.

"Seems there's been a delivery made for you while we were on our hunt."

Over the course of the day, Leo had glimpsed a lighthearted side to the serious businessman, which had put him at ease in the man's presence. He swayed his head in beat with the envelope. "May I have it, then, before I become seasick?"

The man laughed and handed it to Leo. Leo opened it and peeked inside. The drawing he'd asked for was there along with a smaller, folded piece of paper. His heart gave a little lurch. A letter? Eagerness to read it pulled, but he would wait until he was in his room at the hotel. He took out the drawing, though.

DeWeece angled his head and peeked at the sheet of drawing paper. "What do you have there?"

Leo didn't hesitate in handing it over. "The Wards' daughter, Jennie, sketched this."

Mr. DeWeece gave the pencil image a thorough perusal. "Ah, a trilobite."

Leo blinked in confusion. "It's not a beetle?"

"I don't believe so." DeWeece pointed to the markings. "If this drawing is accurate, it's more likely a trilobite. Note the layered scales of the thorax. That's indicative of a creature that can roll itself into a ball."

"Like a pill bug," Leo said, clarifying things in his mind.

The man chuckled. "Well, a pill bug is actually a crustacean, more closely related to a crayfish than to an insect."

Leo rubbed his nose, embarrassed. He still had a lot to learn. "I see."

"What's interesting about this," DeWeece went on, "is that the skeleton appears complete. That's fairly rare. Did she embellish the rendering?"

"No, sir. She drew what we saw."

The man's face lit. "Where did you find it?"

Leo gave a brief description of where they had been when he spotted the imprint in rock.

DeWeece nodded. "I think I know the area. This is an excellent, very detailed sketch." He returned the page, and Leo put it in the envelope. "Is she an art student at college?"

Leo wasn't certain he should answer. He'd already slipped by admitting that someone else in the family currently served as the linewalker. But the man's assumption that Jennie was a trained artist brought a swell of pride. "No, sir, she's self-taught. She has a natural gift, doesn't she?"

DeWeece's eyebrows rose. "Yes, I should say so. I hope she'll have the opportunity to hone her gift. She could become an illustrator for periodicals or books."

Leo couldn't wait to tell Jennie what DeWeece had said. But then, at once, his elation plummeted. Would he have the chance to tell her? He kicked at the rock that Jennie had used to hold the envelope in place, and a plan formed in his mind. Jennie came by the footbridge every day on the pipeline route. He could treat this rock like a private post office. But he wouldn't write to Jennie. He'd taken a chance of stirring her father's wrath by requesting the drawing. Instead, he'd put Mrs. Ward's name on the missives. Jennie's mother would share the contents.

Vibrations under his feet and a distant clatter of steel on steel warned of the train's impending approach. Leo and Mr. DeWeece leaned against the rock wall and watched for the nose of the engine to peek around the bend. Mr. DeWeece waved down the engineer, and the two of them climbed aboard.

Leo flopped onto a tufted seat and sighed. They hadn't located the bones, but it had still been a good day. Despite his initial apprehension about partnering with DeWeece, he was now grateful for the man's expertise. He also appreciated the map. Mr. De-Weece marked the areas they'd searched that day, then gave it to Leo so he could use it during further exploration if he chose to hunt on his own.

As they disembarked at the train station, DeWeece said, "Let's meet here again next Saturday. If you've found the skeleton by then, you can show it to me. If not, we'll search together. Will that suit you?"

Leo drew back in surprise. "You're not going out on your own tomorrow?"

He shrugged, a slight grin lifting the corners of his mustache. "I should probably attend Sunday services. The bones aren't going anywhere." He gave Leo a hearty clap on the shoulder. "Happy hunting, Mr. Day." He hitched his pack a little higher on his back and then departed.

Leo returned to the hotel as quickly as his tired legs would carry him and closed himself in his small room. The good smells creeping under the door from the kitchen made his stomach growl. Hours had passed since he and Mr. DeWeece ate sandwiches, dried apples, and tinned gingersnap cookies for lunch. He was tempted to go to the kitchen and ask for a plate before the leftovers were tossed into the rubbish bins, but Jennie's letter beckoned.

He spilled the drawing and folded paper from the envelope onto his desk, then snatched up the note. Anticipation collapsed beneath disappointment when he saw how little she'd written. He couldn't fault the contents. Her words were kind, appreciative, and even friendly. But he'd hoped for something . . . more. And he needed to set those kinds of thoughts aside. He hadn't come to Cañon City in search of a romantic relationship. His friendship with Jennie was one he would cherish, but it was meant to be short-lived. An era, so to speak, in his life's history.

"The Jennie Era," he said to the empty room. Not as dramatic sounding as the Paleozoic or Mesozoic Eras, but definitely warmer and more personal.

Before he got sidetracked, he should write what Mr. DeWeece had said about her drawing. If Mrs. Ward knew what the businessman had said, she might be encouraged to press harder for Jennie to go to school in town. He reached to open his desk drawer and retrieve writing materials, but his stomach rumbled again. Breakfast was a long time away. He better eat now while he had the chance.

He laid out the items so they'd be ready for him when he finished eating, then headed to the kitchen.

Jennie

Clouds rolled in on Sunday evening and lingered all through Monday. Jennie hated cloudy days. Their valley received very little direct sunlight even during the summer months, so when clouds hid the sun's face and heavy shadows cloaked the entire area, she felt dreary even inside her. The lack of light also made it harder for her to see problems with the pipeline. But when she reached the spot she'd reported last week, a darker patch of wood caught her attention. She touched the wood, and her fingers came away wet. She huffed in aggravation. It was still leaking.

She lowered herself to the ground and examined the area from the underside. A slow yet steady drip fell from beneath the patch of tar the repairman had applied. She scribbled a note describing the issue, then clambered back on the pipe and finished the route.

After supper, Mama recorded Jennie's finding on a nicer piece of paper and told Jennie to watch for the train. Jennie wanted to wait until morning. With the sun now descending, it was drearier than ever outdoors. She wanted to stay inside near the glow of their lanterns. But Mama shook her head.

"The sooner they know, the sooner they can send someone to fix it correctly. It's best to hand this off to Mr. Rawling or Mr. Jenkins when the train returns to Cañon City for the night."

Jennie stifled a sigh. "Yes, Mama." Then she patted her leg. "Come on, Rags. You can go with me."

Rags's ears perked up, but he didn't budge from his spot at Daddy's feet.

Daddy looked down at him and snorted. "That dog doesn't listen very well." He gave him a light nudge on the back of his head. "Go on. Go with Jennie."

Rags whined in his throat, but he slinked across the floor to Jennie. She rewarded him with a scratch under his chin. "Don't worry. We won't be gone long."

Even though the evening shadows fell long and gray, having the pup's company made the trek more cheery than the route had been. When they reached the footbridge, Jennie sat cross-legged and pulled Rags into her lap. "Now, listen, the train will be pretty loud, but you don't need to be afraid. I won't let it hurt you." He swiped her chin with his warm, velvety tongue, and Jennie laughed. "You're welcome."

She would have enjoyed holding him longer, but he wriggled too much. She let him loose and he circled her, sniffing the grass and smacking her with his wagging tail. With each rotation, he ventured a little farther from her until he went as far as the edge of the footbridge. He stopped at the first board, seemingly mesmerized by how different it looked from the grass. Then, before Jennie realized what he was doing, he trotted across the bridge as easily as if he'd done it a dozen times already.

Jennie yelped and charged after him. "Rags!" He flattened himself to the ground, tucking his tail. She grabbed him up. "Shame on you, crossing the bridge like that. I'm not going to let you follow me if you can't stay close by." He tried to lick her face, but she arched away. You—" Her gaze landed on the rock she'd used to secure Leo's envelope to the ground. A square, lidded box twice the rock's size lurked beside it.

She set Rags on the ground and pointed at him. "Stay," she said in her firmest tone. The dog hunkered low. Keeping an eye on him, she crossed to the box and picked it up. It's heft startled her, as did the ants climbing on the outside of it. Grimacing, she flicked the bugs away.

Just then, the ground began to vibrate. Rags jumped up and barked furiously. Jennie dropped the box and grabbed the dog. She darted across the footbridge and put Rags down again. "Run home." He took off as if someone had fired him from a cannon. Jennie moved to the middle of the footbridge and held the note from Mama high as the train rounded the bend. Mr. Rawling waved an acknowledgment from the engine and applied the brakes. The screech pierced Jennie's ears, and she couldn't help wincing. The caboose was even with her when the train shuddered to a stop, so she handed the note to Mr. Jenkins and then waved farewell.

Once the train had chugged off, she retrieved the box. It had to be from Leo. Who else would have left it? Her heart pattered in anticipation of seeing what was inside. But on the top, he'd written "Mrs. Etta Ward." Jennie jolted. For Mama? Why would Leo send Mama a package?

She checked it to make sure she'd knocked all the ants off, then secured it in the bend of her arm and followed the pathway of trampled grass and patches of rocks to the cabin. Inside, she went straight to Mama and held the box out to her. "I found this by the footbridge. It's tagged for you."

Mama turned from the washbasin, her eyebrows shooting up. "For me?"

Her mother's pleased, surprised reaction erased every bit of disappointment that the box wasn't for her. Jennie nodded. "Mm-hmm. See what's inside."

Mama wiped her hands on a piece of toweling and took the box to the table. From his chair at the window, Daddy angled himself and watched as Mama removed a bit of string holding the lid in place and popped off the lid. Her face crinkling in distaste, she pinched up a single ant and tossed it out the open window. Thick layers of wax-coated paper hid the contents. Mama tore a hole in the paper, then reared back and laughed.

Jennie rested her fingertips on the tabletop and leaned close. "What is it?" With the box open and her nose over it, she already knew. Strawberries and pound cake.

Mama carried the box to Daddy and showed him. Jennie held her breath, uncertain how Daddy would respond. His eyebrows rose the way Mama's had, and he gave her a startled look. "You reckon Prime and Delia sent this out?"

Mama turned the box and peeked at every side. "It doesn't say, but that makes sense."

It made sense to Jennie, too. It probably wasn't from Leo after all. But why wouldn't Aunt Delia write Daddy's name on the box? He was the one who loved the cake and strawberries.

Daddy slowly rose, his gaze locked on the box. "Any ants get to it?"

Mama shook her head. "I don't think so. It was very well wrapped."

"Then let's have some." Daddy limped to the table and sat.

Jennie fetched the small plates they used for dessert. Mama put a chunk of crumbly cake on each plate and topped the chunks with squashed berries. She put the most on Daddy's plate. While Mama carried the plates to the table, Jennie took the box and its wad of rumpled wax paper, crumbs, and juice stains to the sink. She started to throw the whole thing away, but the box was nice enough to use for something else. *Waste not, want not,* Mama always said.

She pulled out the paper and wadded it up for the trash bucket. Only then did she notice a letter-sized envelope in the bottom of the box. It, too, had Mama's name written on it. And now she knew for sure it was from Leo. She recognized his handwriting.

She glanced over her shoulder. Daddy was enjoying his cake. If she brought up Leo's name, his mood would turn darker than the landscape outside the window. She put the lid on the box and said, "Mama, may I keep this box? It's a nice size to hold my hair ribbons and combs."

"Of course."

She hugged it to her chest, aching anew for the friend she'd lost. "Thank you."

Mama pointed to the plate in front of Jennie's usual spot. "But come eat before you take it to your room."

Jennie slid the box under her chair and sat down. When Daddy went to bed, she'd give Mama the letter. And she hoped Mama would let her read it, too.

Chapter Twenty-One

Etta

Before going to bed, Etta sat at the table and wrote a thank-you note to Leo for gifting Claude with cake and strawberries. She also thanked him for passing along Mr. DeWeece's comments about Jennie's ability as an artist. Her chest swelled with pride in her daughter. Her determination to send Jennie to school for her final year, where she would receive specific instruction to help her develop the talent God gave her, increased.

Tuesday morning, she gave Jennie the note she'd written and asked her to put it where Leo would find it when he came out to hunt for bones. Rags leaned against Etta's legs and whimpered while she stood on the stoop and watched Jennie bound down the rise. With her braid swaying against her daddy's chambray shirt, how carefree she looked. But Etta knew better. The child was burdened. Jennie would stay burdened until her beloved daddy was well again.

She ruffled Rags's white ear. "You stay quiet now. I've got some praying to do before my day gets going."

When Claude limped from the bedroom and settled at the table for his breakfast, Etta slid Leo's note in front of him. "Take a look at that while I dish up your eggs and biscuits."

"What is it?"

"Just look at it."

Claude picked it up. "Where'd this come from?"

"It was in the box with the cake."

"So that all came from Leo Day and not Prime and Delia?"

"Seems so." Etta kept her nonchalant tone. "Go ahead and read it, Claude."

He grunted but bent over the page.

She went to the stove and spooned scrambled eggs from the skillet onto a plate, peeking at Claude out of the corner of her eye. His scowl shifted to arched brows and then smoothed back to his stoic expression. He set the paper down, but his gaze remained riveted on it while she stacked two buttered biscuits on the eggs and carried the plate to the table.

She set the food and a fork in front of him, smiling. "What do you say about that? Mr. DeWeece—an important businessman—thinks our daughter is a talented artist."

Claude fiddled with his fork but didn't pick it up. "Reckon an educated fellow like him knows what he's talkin' about."

Etta sat in her chair. "I agree." She clasped her hands together in her lap, silently praying for Claude to respond favorably to the speech she'd planned out in her head. "Honey, we've got to do what we can to encourage Jennie's talent. She's got a knack, one God planted in her, but she needs training for it to grow and develop."

Claude fisted his fork. "So teach her. You been teachin' her everything else."

Etta sighed. "I would if I could. But I'm not an artist. I wouldn't have any idea how to help her. She needs to attend classes for art. Remember when Delia gave Jennie the drawing supplies? She told us the high school in Cañon City has art classes. We need to send her there." She could have added, "The way we promised two years ago," but she held the comment inside. The reminder could be seen as combative and turn the attention to him and his injury. She wanted to keep Claude focused on Jennie's needs.

"How's she gonna go to school in town an' still see to the linewalkin'?"

Etta winged another prayer heavenward. "Well, now, she can't do both. For her to be able to go to school, you'll have to take over walking the line again."

He turned his face toward the window, giving her a view of his stubborn profile.

She reached across the table and curled her hand over his wrist. "On Saturday, you walked down the rise to the train tracks and back up again. The sloping, uneven ground and all the rocks along the way make it a hard walk, but you did it. Didn't that show you that you're able to walk a piece?" She squeezed his wrist, and he gave her a side-eyed glare. She said what needed saying in spite of the warning glimmering in his brown irises. "You're stronger and more able than you think. You could walk the line like you used to. I believe it."

He jerked his arm free. "I was plumb wore out by the time I got back to the cabin. That walk to the train tracks an' back ain't even a full mile. And you think I'm gonna be able to climb up on the pipe and walk it back and forth just like that?" He snapped his fingers, fury pulsating from his tense frame. "It's fourteen miles, Etta. It's too much for my leg."

"It's too much for your leg right now because you haven't been using it." Silent prayers rolled in the back of her heart, keeping her voice gentle. "If you'd get out and walk some each day, you'd re-build your strength. Before you know it, that fourteen miles will seem like a stroll to the outhouse. You can do it, Claude. I know you can."

He pushed the plate aside, thumped his elbows onto the table, and jammed his fingers into his graying temples. "I can't."

"You can."

"I can't!"

The desperation underscoring the declaration pierced Etta

through the center of her chest. She rounded the table, sat in Jennie's chair, and put her hand on his trembling shoulder. "Why not? Tell me why not, Claude."

"I . . . I . . ." Rags propped his front feet on Claude's leg and looked at him with moist eyes. Claude sat up and gently shifted the dog to the floor, then folded his arms on the table and buried his face. "I don't know."

Tears stung Etta's eyes at his ragged admission. Claude had always been a proud man. A hardworking man. A man who found his satisfaction in providing for his wife and daughter. This shattered shell no longer housed the husband and daddy she and Jennie loved. If Leo was right and an unknown illness had stolen Claude, it would take more than walking the line again to bring him back. Maybe he would never come back.

She slammed the door on the frightening thought. She patted Claude's shoulder. "Sit up, now, and eat your breakfast before it's stone-cold. We don't have to talk anymore." *Right now.*

He slowly straightened, but he didn't reach for the fork. His hand dropped beside him and landed on Rags's head. He rubbed his fingers back and forth for a few seconds, then pushed to his feet. "Give the plate to that dog. I'm not hungry." He shuffled to his chair in front of the window, sat, and stared out.

Etta did as he asked, her heart aching. She watched Rags gobble up the eggs and biscuits. By the time the dog had finished, she'd made a decision. She intended to talk to Dr. Whiteside on July 3 if the doctor confirmed Leo's suspicion that Claude wouldn't—couldn't—ever walk the line again, then she would do it herself. With God's strength bolstering her, she would do it herself, because Jennie would go to Cañon City and finish her schooling with other young folks her age. The girl deserved a different life than this one of isolation, and she would get it.

She will, Lord. I vow, she will.

Leo

As June marched steadily on, Leo caught the afternoon train every weekday and searched the hills surrounding the Wards' cabin for the illusive skeleton that belonged to the bone on the desk in his room at the hotel. The days seemed longer and less enjoyable without someone along for company, but he went anyway. Mr. DeWeece had given him a bundle of little flags to leave if he found anything of note. He was able to place one near a rock formation embedded with the fossilized remains of some sort of fish, but his desire to circle the area containing a dinosaur skeleton remained unfulfilled.

The last Saturday in June, he and Mr. DeWeece searched together. The more Leo got to know the man, the more he appreciated him. They shared a common goal to preserve remnants of the past for future generations. From the businessman he received the encouragement to pursue his studies that he longed to have from his father. Leo listened with rapt attention to stories about previous finds, including a prehistoric bird with wings that spanned five times wider than an eagle's. He dreamed about the day he would get to see such things for himself.

DeWeece indicated he would need to bring in a team of excavation experts when they finally located the skeleton, and he promised that Leo could be part of the team if he was still in the area. Leo knew it was customary that the financial supporter would receive the recognition for its find, but DeWeece assured Leo his name would be included on official documentation.

"Even if it's found after you return to college, you recognized the significance of the bone and instigated the search, so you will be recorded as a member of the discovery team," he told Leo when they stopped for their lunch break.

Leo briefly pondered if Jennie Ward should be acknowledged. But Jennie hadn't actually found the bone—the Wards' dog Rex had. And they couldn't credit a dog, could they? He asked Mr. De-Weece, and the man laughed so heartily Leo wished he'd kept the question to himself. But he understood the man's amusement. Crediting a dog would be a strange addition to scientific documents.

He received two letters from home during the last weeks of June. The first, from his mother, included a promise to pray for the Ward family. The second, penned by Father, also stated assurance that the family was in his prayers, but it ended with his usual request to give some serious thought to making a change in his studies. "What eternal good," Father wrote, "are you accomplishing?" The query stung and begged for rebuttal, but Leo hadn't yet written a reply. He truly believed he could do eternal good by disproving scientific theories that discredited creationism. But he'd said it before and Father had discounted him. Maybe it was best to ignore the question and do as Mr. DeWeece said—continue learning about paleontology.

At the end of another fruitless Saturday search, Mr. DeWeece plopped his large pack on the seat across from Leo's, then sat sideways with his feet in the aisle and braced his hands on his knees. Despite his firm position, his body jostled with the train's motions. "I have duties at the town's Independence Day celebration next Saturday, so I won't go out on an excursion. What are your plans for the day?"

Leo preferred not to waste a day that could be spent hunting. He was on borrowed time in Cañon City. But he didn't want to miss the town picnic and fireworks. And if he stayed in town, he might run into the Ward family. He and Mrs. Ward had exchanged a couple of notes, and he appreciated receiving news about the family. But letters weren't the same as face-to-face conversation. Even if he wasn't able to talk to Jennie alone, it would do his heart good to see her, smile at her, let her know he still cared.

He gave a sheepish shrug. "I want to see the fireworks, and I doubt I'd be able to see the display from way out there."

The man laughed. "Very true. Well, then . . ." He faced forward. "I'll put July 10 on my calendar as our next search date. Unless"—he lobbed a grin at Leo—"you find the skeleton on your own and we make it an excavation date instead."

Leo's pulse skipped a beat. "Wouldn't that be something?"

DeWeece nodded, then rested his head on the tufted seatback and closed his eyes. He remained quiet for the rest of the ride to town, leaving Leo to daydream on his own.

Leo attended the United Presbyterian Church on Sunday morning. Afterward, he joined Mr. and Mrs. Flankston for dinner and conversation in the hotel dining room. He liked Jennie's aunt and uncle very much and appreciated their friendship, especially since he couldn't spend time with Jennie. That afternoon, he stayed in his room and wrote postcards to his sisters and another missive to Mrs. Ward. As he put his signature on Mrs. Ward's note, he hoped he hadn't overstepped any boundaries of protocol. But his worry about Mr. Ward's behavior continued to weigh on him, and he wanted the family to heal. He reread the paragraph troubling him.

> *I am praying Dr. Whiteside will have suggestions for helping Mr. Ward break free from his chains of despondence and be restored to his former self. If I can help in any way, perhaps with chores or delivering goods to the footbridge, please don't hesitate to ask. I won't return to Denver until late August. Until then, I am at your disposal.*

Maybe it was presumptuous to make himself available when he knew Mr. Ward didn't want him around. Should he rewrite his note and leave the section out? But the helplessness he experienced when he thought about Jennie walking the line for her father, about Mrs. Ward caring for a grown man who did nothing to contribute to the family, and even about Mr. Ward's seeming inability to help himself swept over him again. He wanted to do something to ease their burdens. So he left the note as it was and sealed it in an envelope.

On Monday, he hopped off the train near the footbridge. He placed the letter under the rock and then set off, hope propelling him forward that today might be the day he came upon the dinosaur skeleton.

Chapter Twenty-Two

Etta

Etta left Jennie at the crowded general-merchandise store to do their shopping, then headed for the doctor's office. Guilt accompanied her. Jennie already carried so much responsibility at home. Was it fair to expect her to gather their monthly stores on her own, especially since she'd seen to the task by herself last month, too? But Etta didn't want her daughter listening to the conversation with Dr. Whiteside. If the doctor told her that Claude wasn't ever going to be better, Jennie would feel obligated to stay with her folks and walk the pipeline. But Etta had made up her mind—Jennie was going to school in the fall. No matter what.

The town bustled with activity on this celebratory weekend, but the doctor's small office was quiet. The only other person in the place besides her and the doctor was his wife, who served as a receptionist and extra pair of hands in the treatment room as needed. Since Etta was only there to talk, Dr. Whiteside invited Etta into his little office behind the examination room and closed the door.

He pulled a chair from the corner and positioned it in front of his desk. "Please, Mrs. Ward, have a seat." She settled in the chair while he rounded the desk, sat down, and linked his hands on the desktop. "All right, what can I do for you?"

Suddenly the urge to cry struck hard. Etta removed a small handkerchief from her sleeve and pinched the bridge of her nose. "I'm not sure there's anything you can do."

"Well, now," he said with a light chuckle, "why don't you let me be the judge of that?"

His easygoing manner invited Etta to divulge the difficulties of the past two years. She shared about Claude's continued refusal to use his leg, his daily habit of sitting and staring out the window, his uncommunicativeness and mood swings that were becoming increasingly erratic, and the desperation she'd witnessed when he admitted he didn't know why he couldn't return to work.

"A student from the college in Denver is in Cañon City for the summer, searching for fossils in the hills along the Arkansas River. He has become acquainted with our family and was privy to one of Claude's irrational outbursts. He told me he'd studied different types of illnesses in one of his classes and suggested Claude might be suffering from a mental malady rather than a physical one. I believe he called it melancholia." She felt as breathless as if she'd just run a race, but there was more she had to say. She gathered her courage and asked the question that had plagued her since Leo's observation. "Do you think Claude might have an illness of the mind that traps him in despondence each day?"

Dr. Whiteside tapped his thumbs together a few times, his brows descending. "Mrs. Ward, I wish I could answer that for you, but to be honest, I have no training in illnesses of the mind."

Etta sagged against the chair's ladder back. "Oh."

"Your husband should be examined by a doctor of psychiatry."

She inwardly shuddered. Why did his statement seem so ominous? And how would she convince Claude to submit to such an assessment? "Is there one here in Cañon City?"

The doctor's face pursed in sympathy. "I'm afraid not. The only insane asylum in Colorado is in Pueblo."

Insane asylum? She gaped at the kindly man. "Are you saying Claude has lost his mind?"

The doctor raised one hand and shook his head. "No, Mrs. Ward. I'm saying I don't know what ails your husband. According to his last physical examination, his leg is able to support his weight, and the muscle structure is intact. Physically, he should be able to work. Yet you're saying he can't. If it isn't a physical ailment, then he could be suffering from a mental ailment. But it would take a qualified doctor to make that determination, and the doctor at the insane asylum has the training to do so."

"I . . . I see." How would she get Claude to Pueblo? How long would they have to be there? Helplessness washed over her. She had come for answers but was being filled with more questions. She pinched her nose again and cleared her throat. "Doctor, I couldn't even convince Claude to come into the city this weekend for activities he always enjoyed in the past. I know he'll refuse to board a train and go to Pueblo, and I can't force him. So what do you suggest I do?"

Compassion glowed in the doctor's hazel eyes. "I wish I could make a diagnosis for you, Mrs. Ward, and give you a pill or some other treatment that would restore Claude to the man he used to be."

She sighed out a sad laugh. "Oh, so do I."

He opened a drawer and pulled out a paper tablet and pen. "I can't diagnose Claude, but I can share information with a colleague in Pueblo. If we feed him enough information, he might be able to give you an idea of what's happening in Claude's mind. Would you like to try?"

A flicker of hope ignited in the center of Etta's chest. She crushed the hankie in her fist and sat forward. "Yes. Please."

"All right, then." He uncapped the pen and positioned it on the page. "Let's talk a bit about Claude's situation. When did you notice the onset of despondence?"

Etta searched her memory. "Well, as you know, he broke his leg in August of '13. The period of healing wasn't easy—he told me over and over again he was worthless. And he was missing his longtime companion, our shepherd dog, Rex, who died earlier in the summer. He deeply mourned the loss. But the despondence heightened in the fall and went deeper and deeper during the winter months. Emotionally, he slid further and further away from Jennie and me."

She watched the tip of Dr. Whiteside's pen record everything she said. Something occurred to her she hadn't considered before. "You know, I'd seen him distance himself emotionally even before his accident, although not to the extent we have now. It started the year we moved out to the cabin. That was in June of 1909." Her pulse sped, making her ears ring. "Yes, our first fall and all through the winter, he had what I teasingly called the winter blues. The same thing happened our second fall and winter, too. But he still went to work. He still did all his chores around the cabin. It wasn't until after his accident that he parked himself in a chair and spent entire days staring out the window. That's gone on for nearly two years now."

Dr. Whiteside paused and fixed a concerned frown on her. "These 'winter blues' . . . they came on with your move from town?"

"Yes, sir." Why hadn't she thought about it before? "He's never been fond of the shorter winter days—always claimed it was too gloomy without the sun beaming down—but he didn't suffer that way through the winter months when we lived here in Cañon City." She tilted her head, deep in thought, trying to make sense of this discovery. "Is there something out at the cabin that could be making him slip away from us?" But then why weren't she and Jennie affected? They lived out there, too.

"I don't know." The doctor wrote several lines, the pen flying. He paused and looked at her, his thick gray eyebrows forming a V. "So . . . he sits all day?"

"Looking out the window," Etta said, picturing Claude's dismal pose. "Pretty much the only time he isn't in that chair by the window is when he's eating or sleeping."

Dr. Whiteside seemed to perk up. "Have his eating or sleeping patterns changed?"

Etta couldn't hold back an amused snort. "My mother used to say we were off our feed when we were sick. But whatever ails him hasn't affected his appetite. He takes great pleasure in eating. Especially sweets. And as for sleeping, he sleeps a lot more. Goes to bed early, stays in bed late, and takes frequent naps in between. Yet he's tired all the time, which doesn't make sense since he isn't wearing himself out from work." Could continual sitting make a person tired? It seemed he should have energy to burn given all his resting.

The doctor wrote some more on the page, the *scritch-scritch* of his pen loud in the otherwise quiet office. Knowing he was recording her observations made them feel more official. Etta could only hope they would prove useful to the doctor in Pueblo.

Finally, he laid the pen aside and fixed his gaze on Etta. "Mrs. Ward, I won't make any promises about whether this is enough information for a proper diagnosis. The doctor may very well insist you take Claude to Pueblo for observation and tests. But at least we can try."

The relief that help might be forthcoming was so great that Etta blinked back tears. "Thank you for trying. Do you . . . do you have any suggestions of what to do while we wait? Do I let him sit, or should I encourage him to get up and walk?"

Dr. Whiteside sat for several minutes, his eyes seemingly locked on what he'd written. Then he clicked his tongue on his teeth and lifted his face. "Mrs. Ward, back before you folks moved to the cabin, I gave Claude the examination required by the Water Works Department owners to prove he was capable of the duties required for monitoring the pipeline. He was a strong, determined man who told me how important it was to him that you and Jennie were well cared for. I can't reconcile that man with the one you just described, and I can't help but think all the sitting has left

Claude feeling weak and, as you said a bit ago, useless. He won't feel useful until he regains his physical strength. So urge him to get out of that chair. You said he misses the sun during the shorter winter days. Well, it's summer now. Get him outside, where he can soak up as much sunshine and fresh air as possible."

Etta offered a weak shrug. "There isn't a lot of sunshine for us to soak up out there. The mountains do a good job of blocking it even in the summer. We're usually inside at the table, eating our lunch, during the brief time sunlight floods the valley."

"Then take your lunch outside. Have picnics in your yard. You said he likes to eat. He'll be catching the sun's rays while he fills his belly."

The doctor's enthusiasm stirred Etta's desire for action. "And if I spread a blanket on the ground for picnics, he'll have to get himself down and up again. That's exercise, isn't it?"

Dr. Whiteside smiled. "Indeed it is. Exercise is good for his physical well-being and won't do him harm even if he does have an illness of his mind."

Etta nodded, eager. "Anything else?"

The man tapped his chin. "Well, you said he misses his dog. Maybe get another one for him to chase."

Etta released a soft, rueful laugh. "We already have. The college student I told you about found an abandoned puppy and couldn't keep it, so now we have it. Claude hasn't bonded with it the way he did with Rex, but not because the pup isn't trying. He hardly leaves Claude's side."

Dr. Whiteside nodded. "Claude might feel he's dishonoring Rex by attaching himself to another pet. But in my experience with animals, they choose where to place their fiercest loyalties. It sounds to me that the pup has chosen Claude. Your husband is a kindhearted man—he won't be able to refuse the dog forever. And the dog could very well give Claude a reason to get up and work his muscles."

"I thought the same thing when he agreed to let us keep the puppy." Etta pulled in a big breath and let it ease out slowly. The action refreshed her and reined in her scattered thoughts. "Dr. Whiteside, thank you for listening to me and for writing to the doctor in Pueblo. I'll be back in town the first weekend in August. Do you think you'll have a reply by then?"

He gently rocked in his chair. "I don't know for sure, but we can hope so. If it comes sooner, how can I reach you?"

Etta answered without thinking. "The college student I mentioned—his name is Leo Day—works in the kitchen at the St. Cloud. As I said, he comes out every afternoon to search for fossils. He's a very responsible young man. He would deliver the reply to me." Odd how they'd already established a method for communicating. Maybe God had put the means in place for Etta to receive news that could finally point them to Claude's restoration.

The doctor wrote Leo's name on a scrap of paper and put it in a basket on his desk. Then he stood and walked Etta through the treatment room and to the front door. He paused and turned a puzzled look on her. "Mrs. Ward, if Claude is sitting in his chair all day, how does he inspect the pipeline?"

She'd held their secret close for so long. Allowing others to peek behind the curtain of protection she'd drawn sent cold chills up and down Etta's spine. She gulped and forced an honest answer. "Jennie walks the line and reports to her daddy." Then she clasped her hands under her chin. "Please don't share what I've told you with anyone. Claude might not have much left, but he still has his pride. It would shame him if the whole town knew his little girl had taken over his job." She added, more forcefully, "Besides, she won't be doing it much longer. She's moving to town for her final year of school at the end of August."

A smile softened his expression. "Then it's imperative we encourage Claude to regain his strength."

She nodded hard. "Yes."

He patted her shoulder. "I'll hold all aspects of our conversation in confidence, Mrs. Ward. Let's hope the doctor in Pueblo will answer quickly with ideas to help Claude."

Etta's only sustenance was hope. She gripped it with every ounce of her being and bid the doctor farewell.

Chapter Twenty-Three

Jennie

After Jennie finished the shopping, she and Mama attended the scheduled Independence Day festivities. They went from the parade to the picnic, then watched a baseball tournament with teams from various churches playing one another, all in good-natured fun. Then, after supper at the hotel, they returned to the park and stayed for the fireworks display.

Everywhere Jennie went, she searched the crowds for Leo, but she never saw him. Maybe he'd gone out to hunt fossils and wasn't in town at all. Or maybe the swell of people hid him from her. She saw lots of young people roving the grounds in groups from small to large. She pointed out some she thought she remembered from when she attended the grammar school. Mama encouraged her to go over and reintroduce herself, but Jennie resisted. Even though Mama had told her repeatedly she'd be living in Cañon City with Aunt Delia and Uncle Prime by the end of the summer, she wasn't ready to believe it. As it said in Proverbs, hope deferred makes the heart sick. She didn't need more reasons to feel heartsick.

After such a full, exciting day, she thought she'd fall asleep the moment she dropped into bed at her aunt and uncle's. But long after Mama's even breathing from the other side of the comfortable feather tick proved she was sleeping, Jennie lay awake. On her side with her cheek resting on her hands, she stared at the lace curtain hiding the starry sky from full view and sent her mind backward. To when she was ten years old. To the last Independence Day celebration before they moved out to the cabin.

She remembered partnering with Daddy for a three-legged race. She was so much shorter, his stride so much longer, they first went in a circle. Throughout the entire race, both of them laughed so hard they could barely stay upright. They'd come in dead last but they didn't care because they had so much fun. The memory of their joyous laughter brought a sting of tears now.

Back then, she thought the sun rose and set on her daddy. Oh, she loved Mama. She'd always loved Mama. But she and Daddy . . . they had something special. When her folks sat her down and explained that Daddy had a new job and they'd be moving from town to the cabin, she hadn't fussed a bit, because she'd still be with Daddy. Back then, he called her his little shadow, always with a twinkle in his eye that spoke of pride and affection. Now his eyes always seemed empty. Like he was dead inside. Where'd that twinkle gone?

Mama said they should hold on to hope. Leo said it, too. Jennie was trying. If she was alone on the pipeline right now, she might scream the word again to the cliff and stand in its echo. But she couldn't scream to the ceiling. She'd wake up the whole household. And if she didn't get some sleep, she'd be crankier tomorrow than Daddy on his worst day.

She closed her eyes and snuggled deeper into the soft, clean-smelling pillow. One last thought trailed through her mind before sleep claimed her.

I wonder where Leo's going to church tomorrow?

Leo

Leo strode up the sidewalk in the direction of the First Presbyterian Church. He should be attending the First Christian Church instead. It was the last one in town he hadn't yet visited. But he'd gotten a late start after staying up for the fireworks show. The Christian church was the farthest from the hotel of any church in town. He'd never make it on time. He loathed entering a service late—probably because Father said late arrival signified laziness or disrespectfulness. Neither quality was acceptable in his home. Childhood lessons, whether positive or not, always lingered. The First Presbyterian Church was a shorter walk. He could make it there on time, and he'd visit First Christian next Sunday instead.

As he turned the final corner, he spotted Jennie, her mother, and the Flankstons crossing the lawn toward the front door. Of its own volition, his pace quickened to a jog, and he drew up behind them at the base of the concrete steps leading to the sanctuary.

Mr. Flankston glanced at him, then tapped Jennie's shoulder. "Look who's here."

Jennie turned, and the delight that burst over her face sent Leo's heart flopping like a rainbow trout on a riverbank. She silently mouthed his name, as if she couldn't believe it was really him. Then her expression instantly shuttered, and her bearing became as formal as the Sunday blouse and skirt she wore. She touched her mother's arm. "Mama, would you like to say hello to Leo?"

Mrs. Ward paused on the first step, angling sideways. She held her hand out to him. "Of course I would. How good to see you, Leo."

"It's good to see you, too." He gave her hand a quick squeeze, then stepped back. He probably shouldn't have approached them. Mr. Ward wouldn't approve, and even though the man wasn't there to witness them talking, Leo should honor his preference. "I don't want to keep you from going in to worship. I'll . . ." He eased to the side of the steps.

Mrs. Ward gazed intently into his face. "Leo, would you be kind enough to meet me here when the worship service is over? I'd like a"—she sent a sideways peek at Jennie—"private word with you."

Jennie's puzzled expression matched the curiosity writhing in Leo's mind. But she didn't say anything. Leo nodded. "Of course, ma'am." They all went inside.

Jennie and her family sat in the same pew as they had during his first time here. Temptation to join them tugged hard, but he chose a seat at the back near a frazzled young couple with three squirmy children who distracted him during the entire service. Then again, maybe it wasn't the children's fault. The wavy curtain of Jennie's light-brown hair, drawn back and secured with a wide mint-green ribbon, drew his attention like a magnet. The image of her joyful face when she laid eyes on him danced in his memory. Their time apart had been hard on her, too. He couldn't decide if the realization more greatly pleased him or crushed him.

He also couldn't stop wondering what Mrs. Ward wanted to tell him. Had Jennie's father decided Leo could visit the cabin again? Would Jennie be allowed to guide him? He didn't want to presume and then be disappointed, but he couldn't help entertaining the possibilities. At the close of the service, he hoped no one asked him about the sermon, because he'd have to embarrass himself and admit he hadn't listened. But he was ready to listen to whatever Jennie's mama planned to say.

The woman guided him well away from gathered clusters of chatting folks on the lawn. Well away from Jennie and the Flankstons, too. Worry began to nibble at Leo. The message must not be a good one if she exercised such caution about it being overheard.

In the shade of a flowering shrub the size of a hippopotamus, she stopped and faced him. Her blue eyes held a sheen of moisture, increasing Leo's angst. He blurted, "Ma'am, has something happened to Jennie's daddy?" Despite their recent difficulties, Jennie adored the man. She'd be devastated if—

"No, no." Mrs. Ward patted Leo's coat sleeve with her gloved hand. "Mr. Ward was fine when Jennie and I left for town Friday evening. Well"—her lips formed a sad smile—"as fine as he ever is these days."

Leo blew out a breath of relief. But should he be happy to hear that Mr. Ward was unchanged? It removed any possibility of him allowing Leo to spend time with Jennie again.

"You said in your letter you'd be willing to help if it was needed." Suddenly Mrs. Ward seemed shy. "Did you mean that?"

"Of course I did." He pushed aside his own disappointment and focused on the woman standing timid yet hopeful before him. "What can I do for you?"

"I talked to Dr. Whiteside yesterday." Tears glistened in her eyes but didn't flow as she shared the doctor's inability to make a diagnosis. "He promised to consult a doctor from the . . . the insane asylum in Pueblo"—she whisked her fingertips across her eyelashes and erased the tears—"and garner his opinion and suggestions. We have no idea when a response will come, but obviously I'm praying it will be quickly. I beg your forgiveness for not gaining your agreement first. I suppose urgency prompted me to tell Dr. Whiteside that you would be able to deliver the information to me when it arrives. Are you . . . willing to do so?"

Leo nodded, humbled that she trusted him enough to ask. "Of course I will. I presume you told the doctor where to reach me?"

"At the hotel." A teasing glint suddenly entered her eyes. "Or wandering the hills beyond the pipeline. But I suppose you'd be a little hard to track there."

Leo laughed, more out of gratitude for her indomitable spirit than in response to her humor. "You're right about that. I will check my mail cubby every day for the information from"—he gulped back the name she'd used for the institution—"the doctor in Pueblo and will bring it out right away."

"Thank you, Leo. Now . . ." She bit the corner of her lip, glancing across the yard. "Would you care to join us for dinner at the hotel?" The query came out in a rush, as if she was afraid she'd change her mind if she didn't ask quickly. "I think that with three chaperones in attendance, Claude couldn't disapprove of you and Jennie enjoying a short chat."

Leo wanted to join them so much it made him ache. Mrs. Ward had given her permission, but worry about her husband finding out and becoming enraged held him back. "I, um . . ."

"If you have other plans, you won't hurt our feelings."

Leo arched one brow. "Not even Jennie's?"

"Since she has no idea I invited you, she won't be hurt." She tilted her head, squinting as a little ray of sunlight sneaked between branches from the shrub and landed on her face. "Do you have other plans?"

He had to be honest. "No, ma'am, I don't."

She slipped her hand through the bend of his elbow and gave a little tug. "Then come eat with us."

How could he refuse? He smiled. "All right. Thank you."

They moved away from the bush, and full sunlight splashed over them. Mrs. Ward lifted her face and sighed. "Ahh, the sun feels good. I hope it's shining through the window of our cabin right now and blessing Claude with its warmth and light."

Leo hoped so, too. He also hoped Mrs. Ward wouldn't come to regret the invitation.

Jennie

Jennie stared across the lawn, her mouth slightly open. Was Mama escorting Leo to her and her aunt and uncle? Daddy would have a fit if he knew. She held her breath, expecting the two of them to part and Leo to go another way. But they made steady progress directly to the sidewalk where Aunt Delia, Uncle Prime, and Jennie waited for Mama to finish talking to Leo.

Mama stopped and beamed at Aunt Delia and Uncle Prime. "Leo has agreed to join us for dinner." Her gaze shifted to Jennie and she winked. "Jennie, why don't you and Leo lead the way? You can chat on the walk to the hotel." Then she leaned close and whispered, "We'll have our eyes on you the whole way so Daddy won't have need to worry."

Jennie swallowed a giggle. "Yes, Mama." Bashfulness struck, an odd feeling considering how often in the past three weeks she'd yearned for the chance to talk to Leo again. "W-would you escort me, please?"

Leo took a wide step forward and offered his elbow. She took hold, and then they fell in step on the sidewalk. Her silly pinching shoes slowed her progress, but she didn't mind. It would prolong her time with Leo. For the first block, they walked in silence, Mama and Aunt Delia's soft conversation and occasional interjections from Uncle Prime providing accompaniment to the light pats of their soles against the pavement. As pleasant as it was to simply walk with Leo, she was wasting precious time. One of them needed to say something.

She sent a shy smile up at him. "Tell me, how is it going with your new guide? Do you like him as much as you like me?" Her cheeks flamed. Had she really asked such a bold question?

He threw back his head and laughed—a hearty laugh that held not even an ounce of ridicule or embarrassment. "Jennie, Mr. DeWeece is a wonderful guide. Very knowledgeable about the land and various types of fossils. I'm grateful he is willing to assist in the hunt, and I'm learning a great deal from him that will benefit me as I continue my studies. But if I might be perfectly frank, no guide, not even Georges Cuvier himself, could top Jennie Ward."

Her face was as hot as if she'd stuck her head in an oven, but she had to ask. "Why?"

"Well, for one thing, he doesn't make drawings of the discoveries and gift me with them." He bounced his elbow, pressing her fingers to his rib cage. "And for another, he doesn't have braids that catch the wind, or freckles that decorate his nose. How could he possibly compete?"

She dipped her head and swallowed a delighted chortle. Then she squinted up at him. "Who is . . ." What was the name again? "Jaw-jizz Coov-ee-ah?"

He didn't smirk even a bit. "A man many consider to be the father of paleontology. He lived in the late 1700s to the early 1800s and was inarguably one of the finest minds in history. His research established the fact of extinctive life-forms by comparing recently decomposed skeletons of animals to fossilized skeletons and citing their vast differences. Cuvier didn't believe in organic evolution. Do you know how he proved his theory?"

Jennie, enthralled, shook her head.

"By studying the mummified remains of cats from Egypt."

She gaped at him. "You're making that up."

He held up his palm. "I promise, I'm not. When Napoleon invaded Egypt, his soldiers scavenged graves and brought back, among other things, mummified cats. Their skeletons, although purported to be thousands of years old, were identical to cat skeletons found in the Jura Mountains. That the skeletons were exactly the same proved in Cuvier's mind that once a cat, always a cat."

She pondered this information for a moment. "If Cuvier is considered the father of paleontology and he didn't believe in the evolution of living beings, why do your current professors teach the theory of evolution?"

Leo sighed. "Ah, Jennie, that's a question I'm not able to answer. But I remind myself frequently that they are teaching a theory, not a fact. And I keep praying for discoveries that will prove without scientific doubt that God created living beings the way He wanted to craft them." He fell silent for a few seconds, as if he drifted away into thought, and then he gave a little jerk. "Oh, you might find this interesting, too. Do you know why cats today ignore you when you call for them?"

She searched her mind for a reason. "No, I don't. Why?"

"Because their Egyptian ancestors lived in palaces like royalty and they've never forgotten it. They are the ones who beckon. They do not heed commands."

It took a bit for her to recognize mischief sparkling in his eyes. She laughed and playfully swatted his arm. "Leo, that's not nice. I thought you were being serious."

Immediately, the humor faded to something else. He pressed her fingers to his ribs again. "I was being serious. When I said I like you as my guide better than Mr. DeWeece, I was being very serious. Remember that, will you?"

She nodded, battling a wave of emotion she couldn't define.

He gestured ahead of them. "Here we are, safe and sound at the hotel. Are you ready to eat?"

No, she wasn't, because when they finished their dinner, they would part company and she might never have another opportunity to talk with him again. But she would always remember his words—*I like you as my guide*—and the way he looked at her when he said them. She would remember and treasure the moment.

Mama, Aunt Delia, and Uncle Prime closed the distance between them. Mama eased between Leo and Jennie. "Let's get our dinner, honey. Remember, we have a train to catch."

Something else she couldn't forget. Jennie tore her gaze from Leo and sighed. "Yes, Mama."

Chapter Twenty-Four

Etta

"Thank you for your help." Etta shook Mr. Jenkins's hand. "You're always so kind to Jennie and me."

The conductor whipped off his hat and placed it over his chest. "It's a pleasure to assist you ladies." As he settled the hat back over his balding pate, his gaze bounced from the stack of full crates beside the train tracks to the opposite side of the river. "I don't see your wagon. It's not broke down, is it? How're you going to carry all these goods to your cabin?"

Etta forced a nonchalant chuckle. "I assure you, the wagon is in working condition. I imagine Claude is enjoying his quiet afternoon and didn't keep track of the time." She ushered Jennie toward the footbridge. "When he hears the train rattle by, he'll come with the wagon and help us." It stung her conscience to fib to the kindly man, but how else could they keep others from knowing the truth about Claude's condition? Folks would be understanding if the wagon was broken down, but what would they say about a broken-down man?

"Yes." Jennie raised her voice above the train's rhythmic *chug-chug* as it idled on the track. "But if you're worried, you could ask Mr. Rawling to blow the whistle." She peeked at Etta from the corner of her eye, a smirk curving her lips. "That should wake up Daddy."

The conductor released a robust laugh. "Oh, Jennie, you're an ornery one, for sure." He ambled to the rear of the caboose and pulled himself onto the landing. He leaned over the railing and waved. The engineer's arm popped out from the engine's window and wagged up and down in reply. Moments later, a cloud of smoke billowed from the engine's stack, steam hissed from behind the iron wheels, and the cars screeched forward. Mr. Jenkins tipped his hat to Jennie and Etta, then disappeared inside the caboose.

Etta waited until the train was far enough up the tracks to allow conversation, then put her hands on her hips and turned a stern look on her daughter. "Young lady, that comment about waking your daddy with the whistle was not funny. It was unkind, and I expect better of you. Regardless of provocation, we should not make sport of his current ailment."

Jennie looked aside. The stubborn angle of her jaw reminded Etta of Claude. "I'm sorry, Mama. I guess I'm a little out of sorts."

She'd been out of sorts since they left the hotel dining room. Etta didn't need a degree in psychiatry to surmise the reason why. She touched Jennie's arm, drawing her focus. "Maybe I shouldn't have invited Leo to eat with us today. I thought some time with him would make you happy."

Jennie's chin quivered. "I was happy. At the time. But as soon as he walked away, I felt the loss all over again. We'll only go to Cañon City one more time before he leaves for college. Who knows if I'll see him then?"

Etta glanced at the rock next to the footbridge. "You can write and leave messages for him."

Jennie huffed and folded her arms. "That's not the same. I prayed and prayed for a friend, and God sent me one. Then Daddy sent him away. It isn't fair."

No, it wasn't. But Jennie needed to look to the future, not the past. "Honey, it won't be long and you'll have lots of friends again. When you're in school—"

"Mama, please . . ." Jennie groaned. "You keep saying that, but how can I go? Even if Daddy jumps out of his chair today and starts using his legs, he won't be able to take over the line by the time school starts. He's sat for almost two full years. It'll take months for him to get his strength back."

Etta's heart ached at the defeat in her daughter's voice. "That may be true, but whether he can walk the line or not, you *are* going to school in the fall. Your aunt and uncle know it. Soon the school will know it, because they promised to enroll you. As I said, even if you don't see Leo again, you will have other friends. Hosts of friends, the way you did before we moved out here. You must have faith, Jennie."

The sadness didn't lift from her daughter's eyes. "I'll go get the wagon so we can tote these cartons to the house." She scuffed off, her heels dragging and her head low.

Etta sat on one of the crates and prayed while she waited for Jennie to return. She wished she'd told her to ask Claude to help her, and then she was glad she hadn't. If Claude said no, he'd only discourage Jennie more. Even though she told herself not to expect Claude, a shaft of disappointment struck when Jennie returned with the wagon alone.

Etta carried the first carton across the footbridge slowly, placing her feet carefully. Her pumps weren't as sturdy as the work boots Jennie was wearing. "Rags didn't come with you?"

"He was snoozing under Daddy's chair. He opened one eye, then went back to sleep."

Etta plopped the carton on the wagon bed. "Your daddy's in his chair?" A hint of irritation colored the query. If he'd sat there and watched his daughter leave with the wagon, knowing a load waited for them, he truly had sunk low.

Jennie lifted a carton. "No. When I looked in the house, the bedroom door was closed. He must be sleeping, too."

Etta couldn't decide if that was better or not. Claude slept far too much. She focused on transporting the crates across the bridge and then pulling the wagon home. They left the wagon next to the stoop, and Etta went inside. She called over her shoulder, "Rest a bit, get a drink of cold water, and pet Rags. Those things will keep." Then she entered the bedroom.

Claude rolled over and blinked at her. "Oh, you're back."

She sat on the edge of the bed and put her hand on his hip. "Yes, we are. The celebration was quite enjoyable. I wish you'd gone."

He snuffled. "Good thing I didn't."

"Oh? Why is that?"

"Had a visitor out here yesterday." He sat up, then leaned against the headboard, his lips forming a grim line on his whiskery face. "The feller who tried to fix the leak in the pipeline came back to do the job right. But then he came up here. Knocked on the door. I let him in."

Etta's heart pounded. "W-what did he want?"

Claude grunted. "Wanted to make sure I was alive an' kickin', I guess. He said a rumor's makin' the rounds in the Water Works Department that I ain't been seen for a while." His scowl deepened. "Who do you reckon told 'em that?"

Did anyone need to tell them? The train went by every day. People no doubt saw Jennie on the pipeline. Even if they surmised, as Leo had, that Jennie was out there entertaining herself, some might wonder why they never saw anyone else. Word would get around the way it always did in a small town. She started to say as much, but he went on.

"It was probably that college boy. Said it out of spite because I told him not to come around anymore."

Etta gasped. "Claude, I don't think—"

"Or Jennie. She was out there with that fellow who tried to fix it the first time. She must've said somethin' that—"

"Claude!" Etta had never spoken so firmly to her husband, but she wouldn't allow him to disparage Jennie. "Your daughter has

served as linewalker without an ounce of recognition or appreciation since she was fifteen years old. She assumed your responsibility and never once complained about it. She's done everything
possible to protect you since you fell off the pipe. And why does
she do it? Because she loves you. Don't you dare accuse her of
discrediting you to someone from the Water Works Department—or to anyone else, for that matter. Do you hear me?"

Claude stared at her through slitted eyelids, grinding his teeth.

She clamped her hand over the knee of his damaged leg and
wiggled it. "Do you hear me?"

"I hear you."

His tone was belligerent, but he'd answered. She took the acknowledgment as permission to say other things she'd been holding inside. "Then let me tell you something else. Leo Day is an
honorable, Christian young man who didn't deserve to be sent
away from our house in disgrace. Jennie needs friends. She *prayed*
for friends." She nodded at his raised eyebrows. "That's right—
she specifically prayed for a friend, and Leo came along. For one
week, she had a friend, and then your temper interfered. It was
wrong of you, Claude, and you need to make it right."

He shifted as if readying to slink under the covers again.

She shook his leg. "No. Listen to me. Whether you reverse
your ill-given edict about Leo Day or not, Jennie *will* have friends.
She's borne the financial burden of this family far too long. She
deserves time with people her own age. She deserves to attend
classes that will help her hone her God-given talents. I am sending
her to Cañon City at the end of the summer to finish her education in town. It's all been arranged with Prime and Delia, and the
topic is not up for discussion." She stood. "Now, I have cartons of
goods to put away. I'd appreciate your help."

For several minutes, they stared at each other—her standing
stiff and unsmiling beside the bed, him sitting slumped and sullen

on the mattress. She waited, inwardly crying out for him to get up, to help, to *try*. She held her tongue as long as she could, then asked raggedly, "Are you coming?"

He averted his gaze. His chest heaved in a sigh. Then a slow wag of his head spoke for him.

Etta marched out of the room, snapped the door closed behind her, and breezed past Jennie, who stood pale and wide-eyed in the middle of the floor. She must have heard every word. In a way, Etta was grateful. Jennie needed to know she had her mother's support. But at the same time, she regretted speaking so harshly to Claude. What a poor example of loving-kindness she'd set for her daughter.

She headed for the front door. "I need the outhouse." A bald lie. She needed privacy, and no one would bother her there. Closed inside the stuffy, smelly, shadow-cloaked ramshackle structure, she leaned into the corner and let her tears flow. She cried long and hard, unleashing her frustration and worry in a torrent the likes of which she'd never indulged before. She feared the racking sobs might collapse her chest, but they didn't. When her tears finally shuddered to a whimper, she dug under her skirt for her slip and used it to clean her face.

Closing her eyes, she rested the back of her throbbing head on the warped wall and eased out a lengthy cleansing breath. "God, forgive me for carrying on so. But I must confess, it felt good to let it out. Did You catch all those tears in a bottle?" A rueful chuckle rattled her chest. "If so, it's probably overflowing." She opened her eyes and peered at a tiny crack in the ceiling, envisioning the vast sky on the other side of the cedar shakes. "I've held to hope for Claude's restoration for so long. I know You answer in Your time, and I've always trusted You. I still do, but . . ." She swallowed a knot of agony. "I need help. Please let that doctor in Pueblo offer some hope, because I'm nearly spent, Lord."

The concession made, she smoothed her hand over her hair,

straightened her skirt, and stepped into shaded yard. She searched the sky for a moment, hoping to spot at least a ray from the sun reaching upward, but mountains shielded every bit of its glow. Disappointed, she returned to the house.

Jennie was at the table, an empty glass in front of her, and Rags sitting next to her chair. She looked over at Etta and stood. "Mama, are you all right?"

Etta could only imagine what she looked like after such a harsh crying jag. But she answered with confidence. "I'm just fine, honey."

Jennie bit the corner of her lip, glancing down at the dog before settling her uncertain gaze on Etta again. "Then may I ask you something?"

A smile tugged at Etta's lips. "You may ask me anything."

Jennie approached Etta, Rags coming along with his moist brown eyes aimed at Jennie's face. "Somebody has to walk the line. Otherwise, there's no money coming in for our family. If I don't do it anymore, and Daddy won't, who will?"

Etta shrugged, feigning a nonchalance she didn't feel. "I will."

Jennie's mouth fell open. "W-what?"

"As you pointed out, it takes some fortitude to cover that distance every day. My housework hasn't adequately prepared me for it. But we have seven weeks for me to build my stamina, and I'm sure I can do it since I haven't been sitting in a chair for two years." She squared her shoulders and lifted her chin. "Starting tomorrow, I will walk with you in the morning. We'll start with half the route. Then, as my legs grow stronger, I'll do the full distance. By the time school starts, I'll be more than able to inspect the pipeline."

Doubt glimmered in Jennie's brown eyes. "Are you sure you want to do that?"

Etta ground her teeth. Truthfully, she did not. "Someone has to or—you're right—we won't have any money to live on."

"But I can—"

Etta covered Jennie's lips with her fingers. "No. Not anymore. You've devoted two years of your youth. That's more than enough sacrifice. I will do it if your daddy isn't able." She caught Jennie's hand and swung it. "We'll have fun, won't we, walking the line together?"

The uncertainty didn't clear from Jennie's expression, but she nodded. "It'll be nice to have company."

"Indeed." She released her daughter's hand. "And in a few minutes, I'll give you some company in the front yard, where those cartons are waiting to be unloaded. But I need to apologize to your daddy first. I was truthful, but I spoke harshly to him, and it was wrong of me to use such an uncaring tone."

A hint of resentment briefly narrowed Jennie's gaze. "He talks harshly and never says he's sorry."

"That may be true," Etta said, speaking to herself as much as to her daughter, "but I'm not accountable for what he does. I am, however, accountable for my own behavior. I'll feel better after I apologize." She gave Jennie's braid a light tug. "Go on, now."

When Jennie exited, Etta went to the bedroom and tapped Claude's shoulder. He didn't move but shifted his eyes and met her gaze. Looking into the brown eyes that had captured her heart a quarter century ago, she asked his forgiveness for being curt with him. "I meant everything I said," she told him, speaking softly and kindly, "but I shouldn't have spoken the way I did. I am sorry, Claude."

For several seconds, he stared at her, unblinking. Then he nodded—one brusque bob of his head. "Don't know how you keep your patience as much as you do. If I was you, I would've given me the boot already."

There was no good response to a statement like that. She kissed his forehead and left the room. As she and Jennie transported items to the house and put everything away, Etta's mind wandered to her conversation with Dr. Whiteside. When would they hear from the doctor in Pueblo? What might he say? What if there was no cure for whatever had taken hold of Claude? Would they live the rest of their lives in this way—him sulking, sleeping, and eating, and her caring for him? She'd vowed to be faithful in sickness and in health, but she'd never imagined this kind of sickness.

The oft uttered prayer of her heart spilled again from the center of her soul. *Lord, whatever it takes, please restore my husband to me.*

Chapter Twenty-Five

Leo

Leo propped his chin in his hand and watched the landscape outside the train window. The rocking motion of the car could lull a person to sleep if not for the sounds of iron wheels grating on iron track, wooden joints popping, and the wind's discordant squeal through the open windows. Such an unpleasant chorus. But he didn't want to sleep anyway. He needed to pay attention to his surroundings.

After his many weeks of riding the train, he had become familiar with the view and used landmarks to grasp where he was. But one landmark—the spot where the dinosaur bones lay—remained unknown. Since his searching had thus far proved fruitless, his parents were encouraging him to give up and spend the remainder of his break at home with his family. But he wasn't ready to quit. Those bones were out there. God would lead him to them when He deemed best.

He spotted a rocky outcropping shaped like a pirate's ship midway up a sloping rise, which meant the curve leading to the Wards' footbridge was close. He slung the knapsack on his back and put on his hat. After tightening the strings beneath his chin so the wind wouldn't tear his hat loose, he moved out on the car's landing and prepared to jump when the train slowed for the curve.

He liked getting off at the footbridge. Even if he had to skirt around the cabin so Mr. Ward wouldn't spot him and suspect he was sneaking a visit with Jennie, it was better to go over the footbridge than slosh across a low point in the river. Sometimes if it had rained up in the mountains, the water was so deep even at the low spots that he'd get soaked as high as his waist. He didn't mind a bath, but he wasn't fond of submerging himself in cold river water that smelled like fish and minerals.

The brakes squealed and the train slowed. His leap was near. He braced himself, knees slightly bent and hand gripping the cool metal post at the landing's corner. The cars clattered and wobbled as the rails curved, but he held his footing until the landing met the center of the curve, and then he leaped onto the hard ground. The impact jarred him. He staggered forward and caught himself on the rock wall. He stayed there safely distanced from the iron wheels until the caboose passed by. Then he adjusted his hat and pack and turned toward the footbridge.

He'd taken one step onto the bridge when the sound of laughter reached his ears. Female and lighthearted. Who else was out here? He scanned the area, and he spotted two bobbing heads approaching from the west. He recognized the floppy hat Jennie sometimes wore when she walked the pipeline, but who was with her? His mouth fell open. Was that Mrs. Ward trailing Jennie?

He stood stupidly and stared while they came closer and closer. They were still perhaps ten yards away when Mrs. Ward stopped and cupped her hand above her eyes. A smile broke over her face and she waved.

"Why, hello, Leo!"

Jennie stopped and looked in his direction. She, too, lifted her hand in a greeting.

Leo moved to the center of the bridge and waved to them. He waited until they'd reached the pipeline section directly below the bridge, then bent forward with his hands on his knees and grinned down at them. "I see you've hired a helper, Jennie."

Jennie pointed to Mrs. Ward over her shoulder with her thumb. "Not a helper. An apprentice."

Leo straightened and scratched his ear. "What did you say?"

The pair exchanged grins. Mrs. Ward hollered up, "I'm taking over for Jennie at the end of the summer. She's training me in what to look for."

If Mrs. Ward was taking over the route soon, then Jennie would be free to attend school. One of his prayers was being answered in a most unusual way. A smile grew in response to the joy flooding him. "Is that so?"

Jennie nodded. "And she's doing great. On Monday, she had to turn around after only a mile in on the first half. She said her legs were tired. But each day, she's gone a little farther. Here we are on only her fifth day, and she made it all the way to the front end of the line and back to center by lunchtime."

The pride in Jennie's voice was unmistakable. Leo barely knew the woman and he was proud of her, too. He knew how much effort it took to stay balanced on top of the pipe and walk its full distance. "You walked seven miles on your fifth attempt? That's incredible. You should try out for the Olympic Games, Mrs. Ward."

"No, thank you." Mrs. Ward made a face and rubbed her lower back. "As a matter of fact, I'm going to let my youthful, nimble daughter inspect the second half on her own. I'm feeling my age." She laughed again. "We've planned a picnic lunch at the cabin, Leo. Would you like to join us?"

Leo had eaten before getting on the train, so he wasn't hungry. But it would be nice to enjoy the sunshine with Mrs. Ward and Jennie while they ate. Except . . . "I would, ma'am, but I don't want to cause problems." He didn't need to add more. They would understand.

The pair exchanged a glance, and then Jennie grinned up at him. "It's all right, Leo. Daddy isn't mad at you anymore."

Leo drew back, unsure he'd heard correctly. "He isn't?"

"No." Remorse briefly pursed her face. "He doesn't want me

traipsing all over the hills with you by ourselves, but he said if you wanted to visit the cabin, he wouldn't stand in the way."

Leo whistled through his teeth, amazed. A small miracle, for sure, considering how adamant the man had been. God was surely working things for good. "Well, then, in that case, yes, I'd love to join you. But I don't need anything to eat. I'll just chat with you all."

"That sounds fine," Mrs. Ward said.

Leo crossed the bridge and waited for the women to climb the slight rise above the pipe. Then they walked the rocky path to the cabin together. When they'd progressed far enough to see the cabin ahead, Leo noticed a kitchen chair in the middle of the yard. Mr. Ward was perched on it like a king on his throne. The sight jarred him almost as much as the leap from the train car.

Rags was lying on the grass near the man, chewing on something. As they approached, the dog looked up, yipped, and dashed toward them, his ears flapping like wings and with a doggy smile on his face. He darted to Jennie first and danced a happy circle around her legs. He then leaped at Leo, bouncing off his knees and nearly toppling him sideways on the sloped ground.

"Whoa there, Rags." Leo laughed and tried to catch the writhing ball of fur. "You're getting too big for that." He dropped to one knee, and Rags rolled on his back, offering his belly for a rub. Leo complied, still laughing. He grinned up at Jennie and Mrs. Ward. "You must be feeding him well. He's twice the size he was when I found him."

Mrs. Ward winked. "He does like to eat, as does his master. And speaking of which, I need to get the picnic items laid out. Excuse me, please." She continued to the cabin, stopping and delivering a kiss on her husband's temple on her way past him.

With Rags bounding around their feet, Leo and Jennie crossed the yard to Mr. Ward. Rags flopped down again, panting, and the man laid his hand on the dog's head while looking into Leo's face. Leo wouldn't call his expression friendly, but neither was it intimidating.

Leo stuck out his hand. "Good day, sir."

After a moment's pause, Mr. Ward gave Leo's hand a brief shake and then returned to stroking Rags's head. "Good day." He scanned Leo from head to toe. "Still huntin', huh?"

Leo removed his pack and placed it on the ground. "Yes, sir. I plan to explore the upper area of the southwest ridge. I pretty well covered the lower to mid ranges earlier this week." He'd found another shark tooth but no dinosaur bones. "If I don't have enough daylight to go all the way up today, Mr. DeWeece and I should be able to reach the peak tomorrow since we'll have the full day."

Jennie inched sideways in the direction of the cabin. "I'm going to wash up and help Mama bring out the food." Her wary brown eyes zinged between the two men as she went. "You two . . . enjoy your chat." She darted inside.

Mr. Ward stared after her, as did Leo. He didn't realize how much he depended on Jennie's presence as a buffer in case the man became unpleasant. He'd been there only a few minutes and already he was uncomfortable. He needed to increase his prayers for the family. How awful it must be for Jennie and Mrs. Ward to live under a cloud of constant tension, never knowing when Mr. Ward's mood might go dark. For the moment, though, he seemed content if not cheerful to sit in the sun and pet the dog's head. Leo sent up a quick prayer of gratitude for the peaceful moment.

Jennie and her mother returned, Jennie carrying a folded quilt and Mrs. Ward balancing a tray holding sandwiches, peaches, a pitcher, and four glasses. Jennie snapped the quilt twice and it fell in a somewhat smooth square onto the grass.

Mrs. Ward set the tray in the center, then smiled at Mr. Ward. "Are you ready for lunch? Come join us." She swung the smile in Leo's direction. "You, too, Leo. We've eaten out here under the sunshine every day this week, and it's such a pleasant change from being at the table in the stuffy cabin."

Leo waited until Mr. Ward pushed up from his chair, limped to the quilt, and plopped down somewhat clumsily next to his wife. He sat with one leg bent in front of him and the other extended off the quilt. Jennie knelt across from her father and patted the open spot across from Mrs. Ward. Leo accepted the invitation and sank down cross-legged on the faded patches.

Mrs. Ward placed her hand on Claude's knee. "Do you want to say grace?"

Mr. Ward cleared his throat. He glanced at Leo from the corner of his eye. "You go ahead, Etta."

If the woman was disappointed about his refusal, no one would know. She bowed her head and thanked God for the food, the sunshine, and the opportunity to fellowship with a friend. At her "amen," Claude grabbed a sandwich and started eating.

Mrs. Ward poured glasses of water for each of them before taking a sandwich and piece of fruit for herself. She and Jennie asked Leo about his searches, and they shared little happenings from their week—nothing of import but so very pleasant. Mr. Ward didn't say a word the entire time it took to consume the sandwiches and fruit, but he slipped bits of bread and meat to Rags, all the while pretending he wasn't doing it. Leo hid his smile so the man wouldn't know he'd seen.

When they'd finished, Mrs. Ward placed the empty glasses and peach pits on the tray with the pitcher and stood. "Well, now, that was a nice break. Jennie, don't bother with the quilt. Your daddy might enjoy stretching out on it and soaking up the remainder of the sunshine, the way he did yesterday. Am I right, Claude?"

He patted his belly and yawned. "Reckon so."

The fondness in her eyes as she smiled in her husband's direction stirred Leo's admiration. And his compassion. Despite Mr. Ward's crustiness and seemingly helpless state, she still loved him. What an arduous duty, remaining devoted to one who gave so little in response to her care.

Leo rose, and Jennie bounded up at the same time. She steepled her hands under her chin and turned a pleading look on her mother. "Mama, when Leo and Mr. DeWeece go fossil hunting tomorrow, may I join them?" She flicked a worried glance at her father. "If they find the skeleton, I'd like to be able to sketch it before it gets dug up and taken apart."

Leo's pulse skittered with eagerness. "That's a fine idea, Jennie. I believe Mr. DeWeece would appreciate it, too. The excavation team will include a photographer, but Mr. DeWeece doesn't carry a camera with him. A sketch would be the first record of the discovery." If Jennie was officially credited for the rendering, it could garner scholarship money for her to go to college.

Mrs. Ward looked at Mr. Ward, but he'd already settled on his back on the quilt and lay with an arm looped around Rags and his eyes closed. She shifted her attention to Jennie, and the regret in her expression warned Leo of a denial even before she spoke.

"Honey, we were gone last weekend. And I've been away from the house for hours each day this week. I'm woefully behind on chores. I'm sorry, but I'll need your help here tomorrow." She turned to Leo. "If you go out next Saturday with Mr. DeWeece, maybe Jennie can go then. Assuming, of course, Mr. DeWeece gives his approval."

"That will be fine. I'm sure he wouldn't object, ma'am. Especially since he's the one who suggested Jennie could make a career as an artist." Leo picked up his knapsack and shrugged the straps into place. "Thank you for letting me visit today. I enjoyed it." He shifted his gaze back and forth from mother to daughter as he spoke. "If I see you on the pipeline, I'll give a wave, but if not, I'll stop by next Saturday morning in case you're able to join the excursion." Both women nodded. "Bye, now."

He set off, and even though he didn't look back, he sensed Jennie's disappointment-filled eyes watching after him.

Chapter Twenty-Six

Jennie

If Jennie's emotions had been tumultuous before Mama's commitment to become the linewalker, they blossomed to turbulent afterward. On the positive side, she believed that Mama would send her to Cañon City for school. But on the negative side, she was certain Mama could not take care of Daddy plus Rags and the chickens, see to all the household chores on her own, and inspect the line every day. No one person could manage it all. The two opposing beliefs swung back and forth like a pendulum in her mind, nearly driving her to distraction during those days she established the routine of setting off with Mama in the morning, breaking for a picnic lunch with Daddy, then setting off again.

She faced a constant inward battle about whether or not she should go to school. Did she truly need to attend classes with others? She'd lasted this long without friends, so couldn't she continue without them? She told herself she'd be fine finishing her education with Mama here at home. But she couldn't stop thinking about the groups of young people she'd seen in town on the Fourth of July weekend. She wanted to be part of a group of friends—to giggle in the lunchroom and pass notes during class with girls her age, the way she'd done before they moved to the cabin. Taking classes beyond the rudimentary sounded so wonderful. Was it wrong to want to once again experience being something other than a loner?

Not all her thoughts were about herself and her needs. She

worried about Mama, too. Especially about her becoming despondent. Jennie relied on Mama's strength and positive attitude to keep from absorbing Daddy's morose bearing. Mama had confided on one of their treks how much it helped her when Jennie chose a cheerful countenance. If Jennie wasn't there to brighten her days, would Mama sink into sadness? Guilt plagued her that her departure could destroy Mama's hopeful demeanor.

Although the thoughts continually tormented her, she kept them to herself. She wasn't willing to burden her mother. Daddy was in no position to even listen let alone advise. She could talk to Rags. He'd keep whatever she said secret. But she'd feel like a ninny exposing her innermost thoughts to a dog. If she had time alone with Leo, she would trust him to listen, advise, and pray for her. But those days were past and she couldn't count on having private conversations with him ever again. She considered asking God the Father to calm her storm-tossed mind, but she felt selfish praying for herself. Especially when Mama's need for strength and Daddy's need for healing were so much more important than her gaining control of her silly emotional whirlwinds.

At least she had Mama's company while walking the line. At first it was awkward reversing their roles as teacher and student. She'd never been one to tell her parents what to do—she respected their authority too much. But Mama praised Jennie for her knowledge and keen eye, and soon Jennie set aside her discomfort and took pride in sharing the things she'd learned from Daddy. She complimented Mama for making it farther day by day—for noticing the places where rebar looked loose, a bolt was rusting, or an insect had chewed a worm-shaped indention in a stave. She felt grown-up saying such things to her mother, almost as if they were becoming friends. She liked the feeling.

Maybe a friend should tell Mama how funny she looked wearing Daddy's trousers, shirt, and suspenders, but she kept that to herself. Oddest looking was her ladies-style lace-up oxfords sticking out from the rolled hems of men's pant legs. Worse than the shoes' appearance, though, was their inadequacy. They weren't designed for so much walking. Jennie was convinced Mama would be more secure on the pipe and her feet wouldn't hurt as badly if she had different shoes. She needed work boots like Jennie wore.

If Jennie went to school, she wouldn't need her boots anymore. She could leave them for Mama to wear. In the meantime, her mother soaked her feet in warm water with Epsom salt at the end of each day. The sight stung Jennie's heart. Mama worked so hard, did so much. It wasn't fair that she ended her days weary and sore. Jennie wouldn't move to Cañon City for another six weeks. Mama needed better shoes now.

On Wednesday after supper, Jennie penned a note to Leo asking him to have Aunt Delia send out a pair of work boots for Mama to wear on the route. The sisters wore the same size, so Aunt Delia would be able to choose something sturdy and comfortable. She left the note under the rock on Thursday morning, and that evening she found a response written in pencil on a scrap torn from the corner of her note.

You're a thoughtful daughter. I will talk to your aunt tonight.
Keep watch for a box. —Leo

She tucked the scrap in her pocket and transferred it to her treasure box when she got home. There was no box waiting on Friday, but on Saturday morning—early, just as she and Mama were sitting down for their breakfast—someone knocked on their door.

Mama told Jennie to close Rags in her bedroom. Jennie obeyed, ignoring the pup's complaining whines, while Mama went to the door. "Good morning." Mama's tone held a cheery welcome. "You're here early."

"Yes, ma'am."

At the sound of Leo's voice, Jennie hurried over. Had he brought Mama's new shoes? She started to ask, but another man stood on the stoop with Leo. Until that moment, she'd forgotten about Leo's intentions to fossil hunt with the businessman from town. Early in the week, she and her parents discussed the possibility of her going with them, but Daddy hadn't granted permission yet. And now they'd come before Daddy was even out of bed.

Leo gestured the other fellow forward. "Mr. DeWeece, you probably remember meeting Mrs. Etta Ward a couple weeks ago. And this is the artist, her daughter, Jennie."

Jennie swelled with both pride and embarrassment at the title Leo used. She felt like she was stricken tongue-tied, so she nodded at Mr. DeWeece in a silent hello.

"Good morning, ladies." The man removed his hat, uncovering thick dark hair graying at the temples, and gave a little bow. His smile crinkled the corners of his eyes and turned up the tips of his mustache. "I trust we haven't arrived at an inconvenient time. We wanted to take advantage of as much daylight as possible, so we borrowed a handcar and brought ourselves out ahead of the train."

"It's very nice to see you again, Mr. DeWeece." Mama shook hands with him. "Your timing is fortuitous if you haven't had breakfast."

It didn't surprise Jennie a bit that Mama was willing to share. Mama was always the giver in their family. Was Leo holding something behind his back? She wished he'd bring it out so she'd know if it was a shoebox. She couldn't wait to see Mama become the receiver of a gift for a change.

"We ate at the hotel before setting out," Mr. DeWeece said, "but thank you for your offer. We stopped to see if young Miss Ward intended to accompany us today."

"And also to make a delivery," Leo added.

Jennie stifled a gasp. "What is it?"

Leo held out a rectangular box wrapped in gray-speckled white paper. On its end, a fancy border design framed the words *The Florsheim Shoe,* all stamped in crisp black ink. "Here you are, Mrs. Ward."

Mama pressed her fingertips to her bodice and drew back, her eyes wide. "F-for me?"

Jennie nearly bounced in place. "Take it, Mama."

Leo grinned, his eyes sparkling. "Yes, please, before Jennie explodes."

Heat filled her face. She was behaving like an overexcited puppy, but she didn't care.

Mama took the box, her puzzled gaze settling on Jennie. "What do you know about this?"

"I know it's something you need." Suddenly a mist of tears blurred her mother's face. Jennie wished the box contained something even better than new shoes that wouldn't hurt Mama's feet. She wished it were full of emeralds, sapphires, and rubies—jewels fit for a woman who poured herself out on others. She wished it held the answers to all their prayers. But how silly to indulge in such whimsical thoughts. Mama would say that not having aching feet at the end of the day would be an abundant blessing. "Open it, Mama."

Mama set the box on the little table near the door that held their parlor lamp and removed the lid. She folded back a layer of crinkly paper and lifted out a brown leather work boot. She turned it upside down and ran her finger along the sole from the rounded toe to the nearly flat heel. A delight-filled laugh trickled. "Oh, my, you're absolutely right, Jennie. These are exactly what I need." She aimed her smile at Leo. "How did you know?"

Leo pointed at Jennie, and Jennie hunched her shoulders and giggled. She draped her arm over Mama's shoulders. "Leo and I conspired with Aunt Delia. She did the purchasing."

Mama laid the shoe aside and hugged Jennie. "Well, I'll be certain to reimburse her when I see her next."

"No." Jennie pulled loose and shook her head. "I'll pay for them when I start working at the hotel." They'd planned, before Daddy got sick, for Jennie to work part-time at the hotel and give some of the money to her aunt and uncle for housing her. "I want to buy them, Mama. Please?" She lowered her voice to a whisper, aware of their guest close by. "If you weren't willing to walk the line, I wouldn't be able to go to school. You're giving me a big gift. Please let me gift you a little bit, too."

Tears swam in Mama's blue eyes, making the irises glisten like sapphires. She nodded and cupped Jennie's cheek with her warm hand. "All right, sweetheart. Thank you." She hugged Jennie again, then turned to the men. "Thank you so much for bringing this special delivery. Are you sure you wouldn't like some pancakes and maple syrup?"

"No, thank you. We should be going." Mr. DeWeece stepped from the stoop. "Are you coming with us today, Miss Ward?"

Jennie glanced down at her stocking-covered feet. "I don't have my shoes on." Then she looked at Mama. "And I need to make sure Mama doesn't need me here."

Mama laughed softly. "Get your feet covered, Jennie. Why you want to go traipsing on Saturday with all the walking you do Monday through Friday, I can't know, but I won't hold you back."

Jennie grabbed Mama in a hug, then snatched up her shoes from their spot by the door and sat on the edge of the sofa.

Leo cleared his throat and leaned a little closer to Mama. "Mrs. Ward, there's another special delivery in the box. Under the shoes."

Jennie's fingers stilled in pulling on one shoe, a tingle attacking her flesh.

Mama's hand flew to her throat. "Is it . . ." The unfinished query hung in the air, causing as much tension as a wasp invading the outhouse.

Leo nodded. "I pray it's good news." He straightened and looked at Jennie. "Are you ready to go?"

If he'd asked the question before giving such a secretive message to Mama, Jennie would trail the men. But Mama's strange reaction to his comment about a special delivery trampled the desire to leave. Whatever else was in the box had left Mama trembling and pale. Mama might not need help with chores, but she needed *her.*

She swung a shoe by its laces, feigning a casual air. "May I go next week? I . . . I think I should . . ."

Leo nodded, a smile of understanding softening the square contour of his jaw. "That sounds fine. Have a good day." He hopped from the stoop and followed Mr. DeWeece across the yard.

Mama carried the box to the table, her steps as slow and labored as if she'd just walked the seven miles of pipeline all the way up and back again. Jennie dropped her shoe and stayed close behind her, her pulse galloping, although she couldn't explain why. Mama lifted out the new boots and set them side by side next to the box. Then she pried out a large brown envelope, which Leo must have folded in half and pressed into the bottom of the box.

Jennie peeked at the front of the envelope. The block letters didn't resemble Leo's handwriting. And it was addressed to Dr. Whiteside in Cañon City. Why was a letter intended for Dr. Whiteside in the box with Mama's shoes?

A remembrance fell on Jennie with as much shock as if someone had dumped a tub of cold water over her head. Mama had seen the doctor their last weekend in town. She'd told Jennie she wasn't sick but wanted only to talk to the doctor. What if she hadn't told Jennie the truth? What if Mama really was sick? It would be like Mama to hide an ailment so she wouldn't worry anyone.

Jennie had wished the box might hold the answers to her prayers, but what if it held a nightmare instead?

Chapter Twenty-Seven

Etta

Etta pressed the unopened envelope to her pounding chest. "Fetch your drawing materials and then run and catch up to Leo and Mr. DeWeece."

Jennie shook her head, tipping her chin in the stubborn angle she'd learned from her father. "I don't want to. I want to know what's in the envelope."

Etta tried to deliver a carefree laugh, but it emerged more like a strangled cough. "Honey, it's just information I requested from Dr. Whiteside."

"What about?"

Heat filled Etta's frame. She waved the envelope, stirring the air. "Nothing important."

Her daughter—her helpful, obedient, rarely rebellious daughter—folded her arms. "Then let me see it."

Etta turned her back on Jennie and hugged the unopened envelope. She didn't want to divulge the contents until she knew whether the news was good or bad. If it was bad, she wanted time to pray about the best way to share it. Why hadn't she told Leo to keep the letter from the doctor a secret? But it was too late for that now.

"Mama?"

Jennie's gentle yet strained voice pierced Etta's mother-heart. She faced her daughter.

"Please tell me what's in the envelope. I . . ." Jennie gulped.

"I'm concocting things in my imagination that are probably worse than what's really there. I need to know the truth so I can set my mind at ease."

If it turned out to be bad news, neither of their minds would be at ease. Not without God's mighty peace embracing them. But she couldn't bear to torment her daughter. "All right," Etta said on a sigh. She sent up a silent prayer for God to stay close and give her strength as she crossed to the sofa and sat in the middle of it.

Jennie took the spot on Etta's right and leaned close while Etta loosened the glue holding the flap in place and removed five or six sheets of paper. The top sheet was a typewritten letter. Before reading it, she flipped through the other pages and scanned a few words—information, it seemed, about the facility in Pueblo and the various illnesses treated there. She tamped the papers back into a neat stack and laid them on her lap, the letter beginning "Dear Dr. Whiteside" on the top.

She read silently with the huffs of Jennie's rapid breathing loud in her ear. As she read, her emotions bounced between heartache and hope. According to the doctor in Pueblo, the behavior described by Dr. Whiteside—by Etta—showed a strong indication for melancholia. Seeing the diagnosis in stark black letters on a white sheet of paper made the illness seem much more dire, much more real. She wasn't sure she wanted to accept it as truth. Yet at the same time, she experienced a sense of relief that Claude wasn't choosing to hide away in a state of constant despair—rather, the disease held him captive there. If there was a diagnosis, there must be a cure.

The close of the letter almost stripped the hope from Etta's heart.

The aforementioned malady is suggested, given by my best knowledge based on secondhand informa-tion. For an accurate diagnosis, I must conduct

```
a full psychiatric evaluation at my facility.
Please advise the family to bring the patient to
Pueblo at their earliest convenience.
```

It was signed by Dr. Abraham V. Dixon, chief of psychiatry at Colorado State Insane Asylum.

Etta glanced at her daughter. Tears traced a trail from Jennie's eyes to her quivering chin. Her gaze seemed fixed on the final line. On the name of the facility. The horror reflected in her brown eyes hurt as much as anything Etta had ever seen.

She flipped the pages upside down on the sofa and grabbed Jennie in a hug. Jennie threw her arms around Etta's neck and clung, her entire frame trembling, but she didn't make a sound. Etta ached for her daughter, who loved her daddy so much. Ached for Claude, who was possibly lost in his own mind. And ached for herself, because she desperately wanted to fix it all and couldn't.

Gently rocking Jennie, she closed her eyes and reached out to her heavenly Father for guidance and strength. When she was certain she could speak evenly, she dislodged Jennie's hold on her neck and caught her daughter's hands. "I know that was hard for you to read. It was for me, too. But we should be grateful. It will be good to know what ails your daddy, am I right?" She waited for Jennie's slight nod, then continued. "And this doesn't change any of our plans for you to go to school this fall."

Jennie released a disbelieving gasp. "Mama! Of course it does. Daddy will be in the hospital for days, maybe even weeks, before he's better. You won't leave him there by himself. You and Daddy . . . you can't be apart."

Etta's throat ached from holding back a wail of despair. Jennie was right. The thought of being separated from Claude was unbearable. How would she endure its reality?

"If he stays in Pueblo, you'll stay there, too. That means there won't be anyone here walking the line." She sat straight-up, her chin lifting. "If no one's bringing in money, how will we pay for Daddy's treatment?" She shook her head hard, her brows forming a determined V. "I need to stay here until Daddy's well and home again."

Etta reached for hope. "There's no sense in changing our plan for you to go to school until—"

"You and I both know this doctor in Pueblo is going to say Daddy is sick."

Jennie's interruption was disrespectful, but she spoke with such kindness, so much grace and maturity, that Etta couldn't be offended. In that moment, Jennie seemed more a friend than her child. Etta sighed and answered the way she would a friend. "You and I also know that convincing him to be evaluated will be the hardest battle I've ever waged. He may refuse to go at all. In which case, this entire conversation is a waste of time and worry."

Jennie's eyes glistened with compassion. "For all our sakes, he has to go, Mama."

"Go where?"

Both Jennie and Etta jolted. Etta jerked her attention in the direction of Claude's growly voice. How long had he been standing in the bedroom doorway, listening to them? She rose and took a step toward him, instinctively shielding Jennie. "Why, Claude, you're awake. And dressed already." His shirt was untucked, but it was buttoned to the top, and he'd even donned socks and shoes. Such a change from his usual routine of waiting until after breakfast to change out of his sleep shirt.

He glanced at Jennie's closed door. "That dog woke me up. Heard him in there whimperin'."

Jennie scurried to her door and opened it. Rags bounced directly to Claude and rose up, resting his front feet on Claude's injured leg. Claude gave him a pat on the head, then shifted him to the floor. He aimed a suspicious scowl at Etta. "What—"

"You're probably wondering what's for breakfast. I hope you're good and hungry. I'm fixing pancakes this morning. A whole stack of them. It'll probably be the last time we have pancakes until next month, because the syrup jug is about empty." She was prattling, something she never did. But her nerves were so frayed she didn't feel like herself.

Claude shuffled closer, his frown bouncing from Etta to Jennie to Etta again. "Never mind that. Who were you talkin' about? Who's gotta go somewhere?"

Etta delivered a light squeeze to his forearm. "Now, Claude, we can discuss that later. Let's have our breakfast and then—"

Jennie darted to them. She grabbed Etta's arm and shook it. "Mama, no. Tell him. He needs to know."

What had gotten into this child, acting like she was the grown-up in the house? Etta tried to summon indignation, but it refused to rise. And she knew why. Jennie was right. Fear was holding Etta back, and fear had no place in a Christian's heart. Not when it came to doing the right thing.

She gave Jennie a slight nod and faced Claude. "Sit at the table. I'll pour you a cup of coffee. Then I'll tell you about some information I received from Dr. Whiteside."

"I'll get the coffee," Jennie said, giving her mother a look full of silent encouragement. "You go ahead and talk."

So Etta talked. Claude cupped the full mug Jennie gave him between both hands, but he didn't take a sip. His gaze never wavered from Etta's as she confessed she'd visited Dr. Whiteside and told him the details of Claude's behavior since the accident. She shared the doctor's suggestions about getting outside and moving around more and then what the doctor from Pueblo said in his letter. Claude's eyebrows lifted or descended at various points of her recital, but he didn't interrupt or show signs of fury.

Heartened by his apparent acceptance, she admitted, "There are several pages of information. I haven't had a chance to read all of them yet. Maybe we can read them together." Jennie was sitting next to her. She patted her daughter's hand. "Honey, would you fetch those papers for us?"

Jennie left the table, and Claude's hooded gaze followed her to the settee and back. As she laid the stack of papers on the table, he looked at Etta. "Is that why we've been doing picnics—because the doc said to get me out of the house?"

She nodded.

"An' is that how come Prime an' Delia brought that dog out here?"

A hint of resentment colored his tone and glinted in his eyes. A silent prayer for him to remain calm formed in the back of her mind as she answered. "No, Claude. I didn't see the doctor until after Delia and Prime brought Rags to us. They did that on their own because they thought we'd enjoy having another pet." She tipped her head, fixing him with a hopeful half smile. "You like Rags, don't you? And you've enjoyed the picnics—being out in the sunshine. Haven't you?"

He lifted the mug and took a noisy slurp. "Reckon so."

She forced her quivering lips into a full smile. "We love you, Claude. Jennie, me, Delia and Prime . . . we all want you to be better. You want to be better, too. I know you do. So . . ." She reached across the table and curled her hands around his on the mug. "Will you let me take you to Pueblo? Will you let the doctor there evaluate you?"

He stood, yanking his hands free. Coffee splashed over Etta's hands and the table. Jennie jumped up and ran to the sink. She grabbed a towel, returned to the table, and mopped up the mess. Claude watched her, his face set in something caught between an angry scowl and a pained grimace. Jennie glanced at Etta. "Did it burn you, Mama?"

The coffee sat so long it was only lukewarm. Etta wiped her hands dry on her apron. "No, honey, I'm fine. Thank you for seeing to the spill." Claude still hadn't answered her questions. The storm brewing in his eyes warned her not to ask again, but she needed to know. "Claude? Will you go?"

He jerked his gaze in her direction and stared, the muscles in his whiskered jaw twitching. Time seemed to stand still while she waited for a response. While she waited, she prayed for him to make the right decision. Finally, when she thought she might collapse from the tension, he gave an all-over jolt and opened his mouth.

"I'll let you know after I've read them papers."

Etta's heart clawed in desperation for hope's tattered hem. She forced a calm tone. "Reading the information is a good idea. Why don't you sit by the lamp and get started while I fix those pancakes I promised?"

Claude glanced at the sheets. Coffee droplets spattered the top page, but the writing wasn't smeared. He scowled at it, though, as if he couldn't make sense of it. He slowly backed away from the table. "I don't much feel like reading. Or eating." He patted his leg, and Rags scrambled to his side. Claude limped slowly toward the door with the dog staying close. "I think . . . me an' Rags'll . . ." And he went outside.

Jennie stood beside the table, twisting the stained, soggy towel in her hand and staring tight-lipped at the open doorway. Suddenly she marched to the dry sink, tossed the towel into the basin, and headed for the door.

Etta started after her. "Jennie?"

Jennie stopped.

Etta did, too. She spoke to her daughter's tense back. "Where are you going?"

"To talk to Daddy."

Etta's stomach rolled. Should she forbid her? Jennie was growing up. She'd been right about Etta needing to be honest with Claude. Maybe, given the close relationship she'd shared with her daddy, she could talk some sense into him when Etta couldn't.

Lord, will it make things better or worse? The short prayer brought to mind her wedding vows. Whatever happened with Claude, she would stay by his side. At this point, could anything Jennie said or did make things worse than they already were?

Etta pulled in a deep breath and blew it out. "All right."

Jennie walked out the door.

Chapter Twenty-Eight

Jennie

J ennie paused on the stoop and scanned the areas to the left and right of the cabin. She didn't see Daddy or Rags. Given her father's limp, he couldn't have gone too far in the short amount of time since he went outside. Maybe he was in the outhouse. She started to go look, but from the corner of her eye, she caught a movement down the rise in front of the cabin. She turned fully in that direction. Daddy was plopping down on the boulder that perched at the edge of the rocky eight-foot-high drop-off to the river.

As vividly as if it had happened only yesterday, a memory played through her mind. They'd been living at the cabin for a week or so when Daddy caught her standing on that same boulder with her back arched, arms outstretched, and chin held high, the way she'd seen an acrobat pose on the edge of a platform high above the circus floor. Daddy had jogged up and asked in the drollest tone she'd ever heard, "You ain't plannin' to jump, are you, Jennie Hennie?"

When she'd seen him coming, she thought for sure he would scold her for doing something dangerous. His question had knocked the fear right out of her. She told him that no, she wasn't. Then he asked what she thought she was doing. She answered with an eleven-year-old's logic—"I wanted to find out what it felt like to fly." He scratched his chin and said, "I've always wondered that myself." Then he'd climbed up and posed with her.

Her chest went tight, and her nose burned with the effort to hold back tears. She'd had the best daddy in the world. And now Daddy was broken. Not in bones, but in spirit. Broken bones could heal. Even if they healed crooked, they healed. Well, if broken bones could be splinted, maybe there was a way to splint a broken spirit. Maybe the doctor in Pueblo would be able to pull Daddy out from under the blanket of sadness that covered him. Daddy had to let the doctor try. They couldn't keep going the way they were.

She walked down the rise and stopped next to the boulder. Rags whined a greeting, and Daddy angled his head in her direction. She arched one eyebrow and asked, "You ain't plannin' to jump, are you?"

His lips quavered, and something—remembrance?—sparked in his eyes. Then as quickly as it lit, the spark dimmed. "Don't let your mama hear you say *ain't*."

"I won't." She climbed up and sat next to him. She hung her legs over the boulder's rounded edge the way he did and watched the water for a few minutes, absorbing the morning. The harmony of the wind's whistle, the water's burble, and birds' various chirps and cheeps came together in a tune so unique she'd never be able to replicate it in a million years. But she inwardly titled it. "Peace Song." This hillside she'd called home for six years was isolated and often lonely, but it was also peaceful.

But not inside her cabin these days. And not inside Daddy, either.

She put her hand on his knee. "Daddy, I haven't said this in a while, but I want you to know . . . I love you."

He glanced at her. "I know, Jennie."

She waited for him to say he loved her. It stung when he didn't. But maybe all the sadness had eaten up his deepest feelings, too. She tightened her grip on his knee. "And I miss you." She swallowed. "I really miss you."

He huffed a soft snort. "I'm right here."

She shook her head. "No, Daddy, you're not." She didn't mean to speak so sharply. She cleared her throat and tried again. "I miss the daddy I had before we moved to the cabin. Before you hurt your leg. You . . . you aren't the same."

He shot her a dark scowl. "Well, of course I ain't. I can never be. Not with this bum leg holdin' me down."

Her week of advising and guiding Mama had built her confidence. She looked directly into her father's eyes and said kindly yet firmly, "It's not your leg that's holding you down, Daddy. It's something else. Something inside of you. And until it gets driven out, you'll never be better. If you're never better, then neither Mama nor I can feel right either. That's how important you are. That's why it's so important for you to get better."

Daddy stared at her unblinking, his lips forming a grim line. Suddenly he raised his head and peered at her through squinted eyelids. "Do you think I'm crazy?"

Jennie didn't hesitate. "Of course I don't." She patted his knee a couple of times, then laid her hand on the dew-cool boulder. "I think you're *sad,* Daddy. Not crazy. *Sad.*"

"Then why do you and your mama wanna send me to that insane asylum?" He sounded belligerent now. But she sensed that inward pain drove his hostility. Leo had told her to be patient. She would do so.

"Because that's the place people go when they have a sickness that isn't in their body." Bits and pieces of things Leo had said found their way from her lips. "We need a doctor to make us well when our bodies are sick, don't we? Well, we need a different kind of doctor to make us well when our minds are sick. Folks who are stuck forever in sadness have a sickness in their minds. The sickness is what makes them feel sad all the time. They need a doctor to help them."

"Doctors." Daddy snarled the word. "They can't fix everything." He slapped at his damaged leg. "This here proves it. It's healed up, but it ain't the same as it was before I fell."

"But it's better than it was at first." Jennie's voice sounded shrill. She drew a breath, calming herself. "Remember how it was? You couldn't walk on it at all. Now you get yourself to the outhouse and all the way down to the footbridge. You even climbed onto this boulder so you can watch the river. It's better than it was at first, right?"

Daddy shifted his focus to the river again. On his other side, Rags nosed his hand, and he flopped his arm across the dog and pulled him half onto his lap. Rags rested his chin on Daddy's knee and watched the river with him.

For several minutes, Jennie sat and listened to the hillside's peaceful song, patiently waiting for Daddy to say something else. She waited until her supply of patience reached its end. She gave his elbow a light nudge. "Daddy, do you *like* being sad all the time?"

Very slowly, as slowly as if his neck had stiffened up, he wagged his head back and forth. He mouthed, "No."

Despite the sorrowful admission, Jennie's heart fluttered with hope. "Then do you want to get better?"

His head dropped back and stared at the sky. His Adam's apple bobbed, then bobbed again. Still looking upward, he rasped out, "Yes." He angled an anguished look at her. "But I'm scared. What if even after I see that doctor at the asylum my mind ends up bein' like my leg . . . crooked an' weak?"

"Your leg is crooked, but it still works. It's better than being broken." She put her hand on his shoulder. "Even if your mind stays a little crooked, crooked is better than broken, Daddy. And your mind might not be like your leg at all. It might get all the way fixed. But we won't know unless we try." Please, Daddy, say you'll try. The words escaped her thoughts in a ragged whisper. "Please say you'll try."

At first she feared nature's boisterous chorus had smothered her voice, because he sat still and unresponsive. But after several seconds, he gave a slight nod. "All right, Jennie. I'll try."

She forced down the elated cry straining for release. She didn't want to scare Rags into leaping off Daddy's lap into the water. She squeezed Daddy's shoulder. "Let's go tell Mama you want to see the doctor in Pueblo. It'll make her so happy." She blinked back tears. "As happy as it's made me."

She swung her legs around and stood up, holding out her hand. Daddy put Rags on the ground, then shifted to the edge of the boulder and stood, too. He looked at her hand, his chin quivering.

"No, Jennie. Ain't gonna catch hold. I need to walk the yard on my own. The way I used to walk the line. Back when I was a whole man. I can't never be a whole man again unless I can walk it . . . on my own."

Something about his statement didn't set right in the back of Jennie's mind, but she pushed the nibble of unease aside and grasped the joy of the moment. He wanted to get better! He'd said so. She clasped her hands in front of her and nodded. "That sounds good, Daddy."

They walked side by side, with her slowing her pace to stay even with his limping gait the way he used to slow down when she was a little girl so she could keep up. Her joy increased with every step across the yard. A smile pulled so hard her chapped lips felt stretched beyond their limit, but she didn't mind a bit. Leo had told her to pray, to hope, to trust, and now God was answering her prayers. Daddy would get better. He'd come back from the hospital being Daddy again. She felt like she was walking in hope's echo.

They reached the stoop, and Jennie ran inside. Mama was at the kitchen table, the papers from the envelope spread out in front of her. Jennie dashed to the table, planted her palms on its surface, and blurted breathlessly, "Mama, Daddy said he'll go. He'll see the doctor in Pueblo." She smiled over her shoulder at Daddy, who limped toward her. "Isn't that right, Daddy? You want to go and get better."

Daddy rubbed his finger under his nose. "I'm willin' to try."

Jennie whirled and faced Mama again, expecting to see happy tears flowing. But Mama's expression remained somber. Jennie's elation faltered. "What's the matter?"

"I didn't realize . . ." Mama lifted one page from the stack and held it out. "I thought seeing the doctor in Pueblo wouldn't cost any more than a visit to Dr. Whiteside. I knew we'd have to pay for a train ride and maybe even a night at a hotel, but I didn't count on . . ." She dropped the paper and hung her head.

Jennie took the page Mama had discarded and scanned it. Amounts seemed to leap out at her. The cost for the evaluation— two dollars and fifty cents. An evaluation took an average of three days, and a bed in a ward cost three dollars a day. During that time, the hospital charged extra for toilet articles, meals, and use of linens. Jennie did the math in her head, and her heart seemed to cease pumping for one painful second before stuttering into painful double beats. How would her family pay such a sum?

She held back a groan of agony. Why had God let Daddy agree to go to Pueblo when He knew how little they had in their money jar? Why had He let her hopes fly so high only to crush them again? The joyous echo in her soul faded into silence.

Leo

Leo stared at the bone Mr. DeWeece held, hope exploding through his chest. "What do you think? Is it part of the allosaurus?"

The man raised the dirt-smeared fossilized bone they'd worked free from the soil and squinted down its length. "It's possible that it is part of the same skeleton from which the bone you found originates. Given the geographic location, rain could very well carry bones from this ridge to the valley where the Wards' cabin is built. But if it is from the same skeleton, then the suspicion I've harbored may be true."

Leo frowned, confused. "What do you mean, suspicion?"

DeWeece sent an amused glance at Leo. "Now, no need to grow defensive. The bone you found bears a resemblance to the scapula of an allosaurus. At first examination, I thought the same as you. But after comparing it to other known specimens, something about the joint end of the bone didn't quite ring true for me."

He flipped the newly discovered bone and pointed to its end. "Look here. See how it's almost flattened on the top? Then look at this very slight curve from top to bottom. It reminds me a bit of our human arm bone."

Leo extended his right arm and rotated it, trying to imagine the bones under his skin. "Really?"

The man chuckled. "Have you studied human anatomy?"

"Yes, sir. Last year."

"Then you know the human arm consists of several different bones. Below our elbow, we have the ulna and the radius." As he spoke, he turned the sizable fossil this way and that, his expression thoughtful. "Now, this is mere conjecture at this point—we won't know until we find the entire skeleton—but what if this bone and the one previously found are actually the ulna and radius of a dinosaur's foreleg?"

Leo gaped at the businessman. "Wow. That would be something, wouldn't it?"

He chuckled again, nodding. "Yes, my enthusiastic young colleague, it would most certainly be something." Mr. DeWeece handed Leo the bone and then withdrew a sextant from his pack. He turned a slow circle while peering through the telescope. His fingers flipped filters and turned the dials on the navigational device with as much ease as Leo tied his shoelaces.

Their first Saturday together, DeWeece had shown Leo the complicated brass instrument and explained how it identified their location by degrees of latitude and longitude. Leo had a compass he'd used when hiking or camping in the woods, and it had proved helpful for keeping his bearings on these mountain treks. Would he one day have a sextant of his own? Recording its coordinates would be the same as placing a pin in a map.

Mr. DeWeece went down on one knee and wrote in the leather-bound journal he always carried, then returned the journal and sextant to his pack. He loosened one of the wire-stemmed flags from its bundle and pushed the wire deep into the ground. After swishing the dirt from his hands, he flicked the red fabric square flapping in the breeze, buckled the leather strap on the pack, and straightened. His gaze landed on the bone in Leo's arms, and a sly smile formed. "We're getting close, Leo. I feel it—if you'll pardon the expression—in my bones." He glanced skyward and grimaced. "I wish we could search more today, but we're an hour-and-a-half walk from the Wards' cabin. We should go."

As much as Leo wanted to press on, he wouldn't argue. They'd left the handcar near the footbridge. If they didn't have it back in Cañon City before seven, they'd risk encountering the return train on the track. "Yes, sir."

Mr. DeWeece flung his pack onto his back and started down the hillside, taking the winding path of flattened grass carved by their feet earlier in the day. Leo fell in step behind him carrying the bone. He hoped they would reach the Wards' cabin with time to spare. He wanted to show Jennie what they'd found. An idea struck.

"Mr. DeWeece, I suggest we leave this bone with Jennie at the cabin. She could do a sketch of it. If you give her the coordinates you recorded, she can add those and today's date to the drawing for later reference." The ground was becoming steeper. He shifted the bone to one arm, giving him a better view of the ground. He didn't want to trip and fall on this precious piece of history. "If she does the same with other bones we locate, the sketches with their discovery dates and locations would make a nice addition to a portfolio."

"That's a fine idea." DeWeece tossed a grin over his shoulder. "Since two bones have already been found apart from a skeleton, chances are we'll make similar discoveries of single specimens. It would be good to have a precise record of which bones were found where." They reached a slight plateau, and his pace sped, as did his words. "Perhaps after we've located sufficient bones to determine the species from which they came, I'll write an article for one of the science magazines. People might be interested in knowing how much work is involved in uncovering these evidences of life from the past."

"I like that idea." Leo smiled, thinking about Jennie's drawings printed in a national magazine. He didn't know any other seventeen-year-old girl who could claim such an honor. "It will only take a minute or two to drop off the information and the bone. Should we do that before going to the handcar?"

Mr. DeWeece gave a decisive nod. "Yes. Let's."

Leo fought the urge to break into a run, eager to show Jennie the latest find. Perhaps by the end of the week, he would discover the remainder of the skeleton. If so, she'd have a large project to draw. She'd be so excited. He could hardly wait to tell her.

Chapter Twenty-Nine

Leo

Leo's stomach was growling by the time he and Mr. DeWeece reached the shade-drenched valley floor where the Wards' cabin stood. By now, the Wards were probably around their table, enjoying their supper, and he wondered if he should interrupt them. But then he spotted Mrs. Ward on her knees beside her garden plot. Beyond the garden, Jennie was making her way down the clothesline, plucking pins and draping clothing articles over her arm.

Gripping the bone tight to his chest, he broke into a run made clumsy by the uneven ground. Mrs. Ward sat back on her heels and watched his approach. He drew to a stumbling halt next to the garden and smiled while extending the bone like a trophy. "We found another one."

The woman's eyebrows rose. She called over her shoulder, "Jennie, come look."

Jennie dropped the stack of rumpled shirts, dresses, and trousers into a basket and crossed to them, her brown eyes locked on the dirt-crusted bone in Leo's hands. When she was close enough to touch the bone, she met Leo's gaze. "Did you find the skeleton?"

He'd anticipated more enthusiasm based on previous encounters. Maybe she was tired. He hoped he wouldn't disappoint her with the answer to her question. "Not yet. But we must be getting closer."

Mr. DeWeece ambled up beside Leo. "Certainly, locating a second bone is a strong indication we're on the right path. We see the discovery of this bone as a true victory."

Mrs. Ward stood and brushed dried grass and dirt from her apron skirt. "Congratulations. We're very happy for you." Her lips curved into a smile, but her eyes remained devoid of real happiness.

Leo glanced from mother to daughter. Something was wrong, and he thought he knew what. The information he'd delivered from Dr. Whiteside must not have been helpful. Sympathy struck hard. He lowered the bone and leaned closer to Mrs. Ward. "Is there anything I can do?"

The woman gave a start. She brushed at her apron again, her gaze darting to Mr. DeWeece. "Oh, we're fine. Just weary from today's . . . labor." She slipped her arm around Jennie's waist, and another sad excuse for a smile flashed on her face. "You gentlemen didn't stay for pancakes this morning, but you must be hungry now. Would you like to join us for supper? I have a pot of stew simmering on the stove and a pan of cornbread ready to serve with it. It's nothing fancy, but there's plenty."

To Leo's chagrin, his stomach chose to rumble. He forced a laugh to cover the sound. "Thank you, but we have to get the handcar back to Cañon City."

Mr. DeWeece turned a speculative look on Leo. "The line slopes downhill toward town. I could man the handcar by myself if you'd like to stay. Then you'd have the opportunity to discuss our proposition with Miss Ward and catch the train when it comes by."

Leo glimpsed hidden meaning in the man's expression—DeWeece, too, sensed something was amiss. His obvious concern for the Wards increased Leo's respect for him. Leo gave a nod and turned to Mrs. Ward. "I would like to talk to Jennie about something important, so, ma'am, I accept your kind invitation."

Mr. DeWeece tipped his hat. "Very well, I'll leave you folks to

your evening. It was nice seeing you again, ladies. Leo, farewell."
He strode in the direction of the footbridge, the pack jouncing on
his back as he went.

Leo waited until DeWeece was too far away to hear their conversation. Then the troubling thought rolling in his mind blurted
out. "The doctor in Pueblo can't help Mr. Ward."

At his stark statement, both women winced. Jennie sucked in
her lips and looked aside. Mrs. Ward shook her head slowly, her
expression sad. "I'm afraid not."

Leo's shoulders slumped. "I'd hoped . . ." He tightened his grip
on the bone, inwardly praying for something to relieve their obvious distress. "I wish there was something I could do to make
things better for all of you."

Jennie jerked her gaze back around. "I wish there were medi-
cines for sicknesses of the mind. There are cures in the drugstore
for everything from abdominal distress to yellow fever. I read all
the labels while sitting at the counter, drinking my soda. You hand
over twenty-five cents for a bottle and your sickness is gone. Doctors are so smart. Why can't they make a twenty-five-cent medicine to cure endless sadness?"

Leo longed to hug her and take some of her pain, but all he
could do was hug the bone and offer a look of sympathy he hoped
she could read in the ever-thickening shadows. "Maybe there will
be someday." He sighed and searched their faces for a small element of hope. "There wasn't anything in the packet that gave suggestions for making Mr. Ward better?"

Mrs. Ward touched Jennie's arm. "Get the rest of the laundry,
honey, before it's too dark to see what you're doing. I'll wake your
daddy from his nap and put supper on the table." Jennie hurried
off, and Mrs. Ward turned to Leo. That sad smile formed again.
"Come inside, Leo. You can wash up and help me set the table."
Then she glanced at the bone and crinkled her nose. "But please
leave that on the stoop."

Jennie

After supper, Mama lit the lantern and gave it to Jennie. "Walk Leo down the hill, but don't dawdle, all right?" Jennie understood Mama's meaning. She wasn't to linger over conversation and accidentally share their financial dilemma. After keeping the secret for so long about being the linewalker, adding another one shouldn't be difficult. But somehow it was.

She nodded to her mother, then turned to Leo. "Are you ready?"

Leo grabbed his hat and knapsack, which he'd left beside the door. "I am." His gaze drifted to the bone he and Mr. DeWeece had located. "You'll put that in a safe place, won't you? Somewhere Rags can't reach?" His worried scowl drifted to the pup lying on his belly under Daddy's chair and gnawing a piece of rope Daddy had found in the shed.

"It'll be in my room, up high."

He raised one brow. "Could you take it there now?"

Jennie swallowed a chortle. He was as protective of that bone as a mama bear with her cubs. But she couldn't blame him. "All right." She set the lantern on the side table, picked up the bone, and placed it on her bureau. She closed her bedroom door, then rattled the knob to be sure it was latched. "Safe and sound."

He let out a little sigh. "Thank you." He crossed to Mama. She'd settled at the table with a cup of tea and her Bible—probably planning tomorrow morning's reading. "Thank you for the good supper, ma'am."

"You're very welcome, Leo. We enjoyed your company." She glanced across the room to Daddy, who sat at the window with his chin resting in his hand, staring outward. "Please feel free to stop by anytime."

Leo nodded. After a moment's pause, he crossed to the window. "Good night, Mr. Ward. Take care." Jennie held her breath, and

Leo seemed to do the same. He stayed by Daddy's chair for several seconds, but Daddy didn't even look up.

Jennie's air wheezed out, and Leo nodded, as if Daddy had thanked him for his concern. Or maybe he was agreeing with her long sigh. Jennie took hold of the lantern. "We better go so you don't miss the train." Without a word, Leo followed her out the door. As they headed down the rise, she said, "When I've finished my drawing, I'll leave a note at the rock so you know to collect it and the bone."

"Thank you, Jennie." The lantern's glow highlighted his grateful smile. "Please don't feel obligated to put off more important things to work on it. I doubt that Mr. DeWeece will start writing his planned article until we've located the skeleton or collected enough bones to make an accurate identification of the species."

A wry chuckle spilled from her throat. "I can't put it off too long. Mama will want it out of the house as quickly as possible."

He grinned, remembering Mrs. Ward's sour face as Jennie carried the bone through the cabin. "That's true enough. Maybe you'll be with us when we find the next one. Then you can sketch the location, too."

Her pulse skipped in anticipation. "That would be so much nicer than a bone all by itself on a piece of paper." The flatter ground angled to the east, and she moved in that direction. "I'll do my best to draw it accurately, though."

"I know you will." Leo's tone held confidence. "I need to bring the bone that Rex found to you so you can draw it, too. I'll drop it by Monday afternoon when I come out to explore."

She could hardly believe an important man like Mr. DeWeece had asked her to make drawings of archaeological finds. When Leo shared with her and her folks the possibility of having her sketches being printed in a magazine, she'd nearly swooned. The news wasn't as good as being able to send Daddy to Pueblo, but the request had flattered her and given her heart a much-needed lift.

"Bring the"—she'd forgotten the word he used to describe precisely where the bone had been unearthed—"numbers you want written on the page for the new bone. I'm sorry we don't know exactly where Rex found the first bone."

Leo shrugged. "It would be nice to know, but"—a grin split his face—"it'll make a good story, won't it? How a dog dragging home a bone set off a hunt for an entire skeleton."

Jennie couldn't stifle a snicker. "I can imagine the title, 'Dog Digs Up Bone, Discovers Paleozoic Creature.'"

Leo threw back his head and laughed. "Write that down and I'll show it to Mr. DeWeece. He might like it enough to keep it."

A smile tugged at the corners of her lips. Absolutely nothing had changed for Daddy, but even so, she was smiling. All because of Leo. He was medicine for her soul. She stopped and faced him. Yellow light from the lantern encircled them as if they were caught in a beam of moonlight. She gazed up at him and cracked the door to her heart. "I'm going to miss you when you leave Cañon City."

Tenderness softened his expression. "I'll miss you, too. You're very dear to me, Jennie. I'm grateful to have met you." He gave her shoulder a light squeeze. "I realize you and your mama were disappointed by the news you received today from Dr. Whiteside, but please don't sink into despair. No doctor can give the final word. Only God can."

Jennie ground her teeth, resentment boiling. She'd longed for an opportunity to share with her friend the many emotions churning within. Now he stood before her, compassion glimmering in his dark-blue eyes. She could ask him why Jesus had made the blind see, the lame walk, and the dead resurrect but didn't fix Daddy's mind. In fact, it seemed He was trying to *not* fix Daddy. Why else would He make them aware of the Pueblo hospital, inspire Daddy to agree to go, then yank the chance away from them? While she tried to form her thoughts into words, a tremble tickled the soles of her feet. The train was coming.

Leo must have felt it, too, because he took a step away from her and sent his gaze up the rails. Regret pursed his face. "I'd better get across the footbridge or I'll miss my ride."

Miserably, she nodded. "Yes, you need to go."

She followed him to the bridge. It was dark enough that the engineer might not see him if she didn't signal with the lantern. Leo went all the way to the other side of the tracks and leaned against the rock wall, but Jennie stayed in the middle of the bridge, holding the lantern out. The rumble and clatter of the cars grew louder.

Suddenly Leo cupped his hands beside his mouth. "Jennie!"

She hollered back, "What?"

"Remember . . . hold on to hope!"

Tears stung. She'd promised him weeks ago she would do so. He'd been a good friend to her—she wouldn't break her vow. On the tail of her inward commitment, she remembered the preacher's admonition from the pulpit the Sunday in June when she and Leo attended church together. His words tiptoed through her memory.

Knowing this, that the trying of your faith worketh patience.

Patience—another virtue Leo had encouraged her to practice.

Scripture snippets from other times, other sermons, whispered to her. Challenged her.

Rejoicing in hope, patient in tribulation, continuing in prayer . . .

The train bore down, shaking the bridge. The noise and movement made her pulse pound in her temples and brought an attack of dizziness. She set her feet wide for stability and swung the lantern back and forth. Mr. Rawling must have noticed, because brakes squealed, the ear-piercing sound reverberating against the rock wall.

As the locomotive shuddered rhythmically on the track, it seemed to chant, "Patience-hope-prayer-patience-hope-prayer . . ."

She stayed in place while the train heaved into motion again, then watched it disappear around the bend. Finally, she turned toward home. The train's clamor faded, but the reminders of being patient, harboring hope, and continuing in prayer stayed with her every step of the way. Until she reached her stoop.

She stood outside the door, her fingers on the doorknob, worry sealing her in place. Out there with the river singing and the breeze whispering, it was peaceful. Even under her skin at that moment, thanks to Leo's encouragement and reminders from God's Word, she'd found an element of peace. But when she went in—when she saw Daddy's morose bearing and Mama's weariness—would her peace once again shatter?

Chapter Thirty

Etta

If Etta lived to be a hundred, she would likely still remember that third week of July 1915. She discovered the Lord's presence in a deeper sense than ever before by tapping into His strength to endure Claude's downward spiral after realizing they couldn't afford to go to Pueblo. She walked the entire seven-mile-long pipeline from one end to the other all five days and got home in time to put a decent supper on the table, proving a physical strength she hadn't known she possessed. And, of much lesser importance, she discovered the difference shoes made. The final two days of the week, even after all that walking, her feet didn't hurt badly enough to need a soak in hot water.

Her greatest joy all week long was sending Jennie off each afternoon with Leo. Claude hadn't wanted the two young people roaming the hills alone, but Etta trusted her daughter and she trusted Leo. She no longer trusted Claude's ability to make rational decisions. Even though Etta returned from the route by herself each day and Jennie and Leo arrived together hours later, he never questioned it. Either he didn't reason that the two were traipsing or he'd ceased to care. Either way, she was grateful the young people could continue their friendship. Time with Leo did Jennie good, and Etta enjoyed chatting with him over supper.

Three different days, the pair returned giddy about new findings. Leo decided not to collect them, though, which suited Etta. She didn't care to play hostess to old bones. Instead, he marked their locations with flags Mr. DeWeece had given him. "He'll be so surprised when he comes out tomorrow and sees the small army of flags dotting the rise," Leo told the family on Friday evening while they ate creamed peas and chopped ham over potatoes. "They all seem to be parts of a leg, but I agree with him now that they're most likely not from an allosaurus. The allosaurus walked on two legs. The parts we've found this week seem to be the smaller bones from feet and toes, which means this creature likely walked on all fours."

Jennie listened, wide-eyed and attentive. She seemed to soak in all Leo said, and Etta smiled to herself, envisioning her daughter applying the same focus in a classroom in the fall. Maybe after she finished high school, she'd even go to college. She should be given the opportunity to grow and develop her talents. Considering their financial status and Claude's situation, maybe Etta shouldn't allow herself to contemplate something so lofty, but she couldn't help it. A girl with Jennie's intelligence and passion for learning could accomplish just about anything.

Etta lifted the water pitcher from the middle of the table and refilled Claude's glass, then her own. "Have you done drawings of those bones for Mr. DeWeece, too, sweetheart?"

Jennie shook her head. "I wanted to, but it takes time to do a decent sketch. The locations are far enough from the cabin that I wouldn't make it home before dark if I took the time to draw them. It'll have to wait until I can spend a full day. Or"—she hunched her shoulders and grimaced—"several days. There are quite a few little pieces. Like Leo said, we've got about a dozen flags waving up there."

Leo wiped his mouth with his napkin and draped it over his empty plate. "I spoke with Mr. DeWeece on the telephone this morning. He and I plan to make use of the handcar again tomorrow and come out ahead of the train. We can get a lot of ground covered in those extra three hours. May Jennie go with us? If we do come upon the bulk of the skeleton, Mr. DeWeece will want a rendering of its location to add to the portfolio."

Etta pushed a pea back and forth on her plate, observing Claude from the corners of her eyes. Was he listening to their conversation? "I have no objection to her going. How many drawings does he want?"

He shrugged. "He hasn't given a specific number, but he said the more illustrations the better. He'll use all of them for his personal records, but he also wants lots of options to send with the article he intends to write. Initially, he planned to query *Scientific American,* but there's a new periodical soon to release called *The Scientific Monthly.* Since they're gathering articles for its upcoming editions, he might submit to it first."

Etta experienced a delight-filled shiver despite the warmth of the stove-heated room. "Jennie's drawings will really appear in a published magazine?" Was Leo right that such an honor could earn college scholarship money? Maybe the dream of college for her daughter wasn't so far-fetched after all.

"Yes, ma'am, if there's space and the editors like the drawings enough."

Those were very big ifs, but Etta's heart continued to flutter in hopefulness. She put her hand over Claude's wrist. "Honey, did you hear what Leo said? Mr. DeWeece wants to send Jennie's drawings to a magazine. She could get published. Isn't that exciting?"

Claude looked up from his plate and sent his gaze around the table as if he only just realized he wasn't eating by himself. "Drawings of what?"

"The dinosaur bones, Daddy." Jennie's lips quivered in a hesitant smile. "The one Rex found and all the others Leo found."

"Oh." His brows pinched together. "Didja find more bones, Leo?"

"Yes, he did, Daddy." Jennie's voice was kind yet subdued, the tone she'd used with Claude all week. "Quite a few of them on the ridge south and west of the cabin, just like you predicted he might."

It pained Etta to see Claude slip so far away from them after his desire to go to Pueblo was squashed, and it must hurt Jennie, too. But the girl seemed to have gained control of her wavering emotions and maintained an even, positive front for her father. She was growing in maturity.

Etta's pride swelled anew. She patted Claude's wrist, hoping to keep him engaged in their conversation. "They just might find the whole skeleton of a dinosaur up there, Claude. Wouldn't that be something?"

Claude stared at her for a moment, his face expressionless but his eyes seeming to search for something. "Find the whole skeleton?" He slurred the question, extending each word as if uncertain he was pronouncing it correctly.

"That's right." Etta chose a perky tone to offset his dismal one.

He shook his head, his eyebrows forming a deep crevice. "More folks'll be comin', then. To dig it up an' carry it off. Don't need more folks out here, Etta. Don't want 'em."

Weeks had passed since his last outburst. Was one building now? Both Leo and Jennie were also watching him, apprehension evident in their stiff bearings.

Etta rubbed his arm. "It'll be folks we already know. Just Leo and Mr. DeWeece. There's no need to worry."

Claude stared at her for another few seconds, then stood. "Where's that dog?"

The sudden change threw Etta. It took a moment for her to process the question. The answer might very well inspire aggravation, but she said, "I put him out in the shed so we could eat in peace." Rags had developed a bad habit of sitting beside Claude's chair and begging, something they'd never tolerated from Rex. The pup needed to learn better manners, and Claude needed to break his habit of spoiling him.

Without a word, Claude limped across the room and out the door.

Leo watched him go, then turned to Etta. "Mr. DeWeece will bring a team of excavators out if we find a fairly intact skeleton. It could take as long as two or three weeks for them to remove and catalog each bone for transport to the warehouse Mr. DeWeece uses to store the specimens he finds. Will their coming across this area be too much for Mr. Ward? I don't want to cause further harm."

Etta sat back in her chair and looked past Leo to the grounds beyond the open cabin door. "Leo, if I thought telling you to give up the search would make Claude better, I'd do it. It would be selfish of me, knowing how much the discovery means to you, but I'd do it." She met Leo's sympathetic gaze. "But whether Mr. DeWeece brings a team out here or not, unless God works a miracle, Claude isn't going to change. So do what you need to do to find the skeleton."

The young man's eyes glinted. "Just don't stack the bones in your house, right?"

She appreciated his attempt at humor—clearly, he wanted to reduce the tension still hovering after Claude's odd behavior—but she couldn't respond in kind. Not with Claude wandering out there in an almost trancelike state. She gave him a quick nod and stood. "Excuse me. I'm . . ." She hurried out the door in search of her husband.

Jennie

After five afternoons of enjoying Leo's undivided company for several hours, Jennie had a hard time sharing him with Mr. DeWeece on Saturday. The men's acquaintanceship was short, but the two were completely at ease with each other. She supposed it shouldn't surprise her. Leo was a very personable young man. He'd won her family's favor—well, hers and Mama's—in a single visit. Part of her had hoped his ease with her was unique to her, making her someone special. But after observing him with Mr. DeWeece, she realized he was comfortable with everyone he encountered. Maybe because he was comfortable with himself.

She followed the men, listening to their conversation but staying quiet, letting her thoughts roam. Before Daddy banished Leo from coming around, she'd promised to pray for Leo's father to accept his son's choice of career. Since then, she'd continued to pray for Reverend Day to change his stance. Leo's lighthearted attitude on this summer Saturday indicated he didn't have a care in the world. She truly hoped the father and son had mended their fences. She also truly hoped she and Daddy would one day completely mend theirs.

If only they could take Daddy to the doctor in Pueblo. He fell deeper in despondence each day since he expressed desire to go and then had the opportunity snatched away. Mama and Jennie were still holding on to hope, but Daddy had none. No wonder he was so sad all the time. Without hope, there was no real reason to live. Somehow they had to help Daddy grab hope. Even if it was only the echo of their hope, it would be enough. After all, she'd stood in Mama's hope-echo and eventually it penetrated. How to get him to reach for it—that was the greatest challenge.

"Oh, my . . ."

Mr. DeWeece's awed murmur pulled Jennie from her thoughts. The two men had stopped, and she moved up beside Leo. Then she understood Mr. DeWeece's astonishment. From this angle, the dots of red looked like bright poppies blooming in a mountain meadow. They stood out even against the profusion of wildflowers peppering the ridge.

Leo chuckled. "I told you we found a bunch of bones."

"You did, but I hadn't imagined . . ."

Jennie peeked past Leo to the businessman. "We put numbers on the flags so you'll know the order we found them. I wrote down the numbers with the date for your records, too." Her record taking for the waterway men had prompted the idea. "When I draw the bones, I'll have the right date to put with each picture."

Mr. DeWeece gave her a bright smile. "Excellent thinking." He clapped Leo on the shoulder. "All right, future paleontologist, you decide. Should we spend today recording the coordinates for each of these finds, or search for more bones?"

Jennie chorused with Leo, "Search for more." They looked at each other and grinned.

Mr. DeWeece rocked with laughter. "Very well. It's unanimous. Let's continue on."

At the businessman's suggestion, they fanned out across the landscape, staying close enough to talk while they searched but far enough apart to cover three times as much territory. The climb got steeper the farther they went, yet Jennie was able to continue without a great deal of difficulty. Walking the line must have strengthened her muscles more than she'd realized. Taking over the linewalker's responsibility hadn't been easy, but she appreciated the benefit today. Would she look back someday at the difficult journey she and Mama were walking with Daddy and find reasons to appreciate it?

"Mr. DeWeece! Jennie! Come and see!"

Jennie whirled toward Leo's voice. The curve of the hillside hid most of him from view, but she saw his waving hands. She ran as fast as the landscape allowed in his direction, her heart pounding in eagerness. He'd exhibited excitement over the single bones they'd discovered, but his shout held an element of delight far beyond what she'd heard before.

Even before she saw it, she already believed it. He'd found the skeleton.

Chapter Thirty-One

Leo

Leo's pulse pounded hard and fast. His legs trembled. He slowly lowered himself to a crouch, then dropped to his knees, his gaze never drifting from the row of pale-gray rocks that weren't rocks at all forming an arched row maybe twenty feet long. He'd seen photographs and hand-drawn images of prehistoric remains in his textbook at school, but they couldn't compare to seeing it in person. He was certain he was looking at bones from a large Jurassic creature.

Jennie and Mr. DeWeece panted up next to him from opposite directions. Jennie stood and stared, open-mouthed, but Mr. DeWeece caught hold of Leo's shoulders and half lifted, half pulled him away from the exposed lumpy protrusions.

"You could be on top of its rib cage. Back up. Back up."

Jennie scrambled backward while Leo regained his footing. They moved several feet away from the find, then stood elbow to elbow. In silence. Almost in reverence, the way he felt in church during times of silent prayer. Except up here, wind slapped the strings from his hat against his chest and tossed Jennie's braid. Birds scolded from nearby brush. His and his companions' chests heaved as if they'd all finished a footrace, something he'd never experienced during prayer. But inside him, a hush had fallen, a reaction far beyond anything he'd expected.

Thank You, Lord, for leading me to this place. To this find. To this gift.

"All right, Leo, now the work begins." Mr. DeWeece's determined statement trampled the hush, but Leo didn't mind. He was ready to work. "Unless I miss my guess, these bones are vertebrae. I hope they're still lined up the way they would have been when the creature fell or lay down here. Not only will it make our task easier, it will paint a more accurate picture of its size." The man pulled his journal, pencil, and sextant from his knapsack and gave them to Jennie, talking all the while. "Miss Ward and I will visit each of the flags and make note of their coordinates before collecting and wrapping the bones you two found earlier in the week. While we're doing that, I want you to go to the other side of the creature's spine. The removal of earth, grass, and roots will start there. After unearthing the length of the spine, we'll work our way toward what would have been its belly."

He pulled a leather pouch from his knapsack and plopped it into Leo's hands. "This contains tools for extraction. Use the coarsest brush and scrape away as much earth as possible from the knobby side of each bone. Keep in mind, as you remove dirt, you'll likely uncover more bones. Keep going until you run out of them. If it's intact from head to tail, it could extend for sixty to eighty feet."

Leo tried to imagine such a thing, but he couldn't conjure it. He gripped the pouch and nodded. "Yes, sir."

"Now, remember, give a wide berth as you go. Move slowly and look before you step. You don't want to inadvertently trample a part of the skeleton."

Leo thought his heart had pounded when he encountered single bones. That pound was a mere flutter compared to what was happening in his chest now. He had trouble drawing a full breath. He'd thanked God for the find—now he thanked Him for Mr. DeWeece. He needed the man's knowledge and experience. He gasped out, "Yes, sir. I'll be careful."

Mr. DeWeece gave him a clap on the shoulder and grinned. "Well done, Leo. Well done. You found it. I'm proud of you."

Basking in the man's affirmation, Leo set to work. And *work* it was. Hard work, but satisfying work. Sweat dribbled into his eyes, but he wiped it away with the sleeve of his shirt and continued brushing, scraping, plucking grass. Mr. DeWeece and Jennie finished their recording and packaging and joined him. They stopped long enough to eat the sandwiches Mrs. Ward had sent with them, and then they returned to work. By late afternoon, they'd exposed what Mr. DeWeece deemed the sacrum, two cervical vertebrae, ten dorsal vertebrae, and a dozen caudal vertebrae, as well as several inches of three dorsal ribs of a Jurassic herbivore.

"What's an herbivore?" Jennie asked as the three of them gathered up their supplies and organized them for the walk back to the cabin.

Mr. DeWeece lobbed a smile in her direction. "Dinosaurs are classified as either herbivores or carnivores—plant eaters or meat eaters, respectively. Predominantly, herbivores walked on four legs rather than two. The spine on this one reminds me of a skeleton found in the 1870s. It proved to be a plant-eating dinosaur. Fossil-hunter Othniel Marsh named it Brontosaurus excelsus, which means 'noble thunder lizard.'"

Jennie grinned. "Noble thunder lizard . . . I like that."

The man chuckled. "Yes, well, as large as it was, when it walked by, it probably sounded and felt like thunder was rumbling somewhere."

Leo shrugged into his knapsack, looking at the bones they had unearthed. "Do you think this is a brontosaurus?"

Mr. DeWeece glanced at the exposed bones as he tugged the strap on his pack and gave it a pat. "I don't honestly know yet, Leo. We'll know more when we're able to uncover more of the skeleton." He started down the rise, and Leo and Jennie fell into step behind him.

"Mr. DeWeece," Jennie said, "how long will it take to dig it all up?"

Leo grinned at Jennie. She'd been quiet earlier in the day, seem-ingly cowed by Mr. DeWeece's presence. But she had shed her shyness. He was glad she asked questions, because he was inter-ested in the answers, too.

The businessman sent a sheepish grin over his shoulder. "It could be weeks or it could be months, depending on how deeply the skeleton is buried and how many hours I can carve away from work each day. To protect the site, I'll come out tomorrow with a few men who've helped me on previous explorations and cover the area with a tent."

Leo wanted to participate in every bit of the process of uncover-ing the skeleton, which included erecting the tent, but his con-science wouldn't allow it.

"Leo, we'll take the midday train if you'd like to join us."

Startled, Leo stumbled, then caught himself. "Did you say the midday train?"

DeWeece's head bobbed in a nod. "That's right."

The midday train left at one. He'd still be able to go to church in the morning. "Yes, sir! Shall I meet you at the train station?"

"That will be perfect."

Leo gave a satisfied nod. Yes, it would be. He smiled all the way down the hill.

At the cabin, Mr. DeWeece and Leo thanked Mrs. Ward for pro-viding their lunch. Mr. DeWeece passed the cloth-wrapped single bones Leo and Jennie had discovered to Jennie for sketching. He teasingly assured her he didn't expect to retrieve the renderings tomorrow, and Jennie teased back that the sooner she got it done, the happier her mother would be. "And they'll be safer from Rags if they're with you," she added, gesturing to the exuberant puppy tossing a knotted-up clothing article around in the yard. The man feigned worry and they all laughed.

Mr. DeWeece tipped his hat. "Take all the time you need, Miss Ward. I trust you'll take good care of these priceless specimens."

He turned toward the footbridge. "Enjoy the rest of your evening, ladies."

Mrs. Ward and Jennie said goodbye, and Leo and Mr. DeWeece headed to the footbridge to wait for the train. They stepped over the track, removed their packs, and leaned against the rock wall. Leo sighed, physically spent but still wound up from the wonderful day. When he got back to the hotel, he intended to call his parents and tell them he'd done what he'd set out to do—he had discovered a dinosaur skeleton. How he hoped they'd be happy for him.

"I'm curious about something..." DeWeece's musing tone captured Leo's attention. "When we stopped by the Wards' cabin last week to inquire about Miss Ward joining us, her mother commented that the girl does enough walking Monday through Friday. What exactly does she do that requires so much walking?"

Leo scrambled to find a plausible reason without giving away her family's secret, but he didn't want to tell a falsehood. "Well, she . . . uh . . ." Nothing came to mind.

Mr. DeWeece shifted, propping himself against the wall with his shoulder, and faced Leo. "Is Jennie Ward performing the inspection duty for the pipeline on a daily basis?"

Leo couldn't respond with anything but the truth to such a direct question. But his throat had closed up. He pursed his lips and nodded.

"I see." The man turned forward again. He fell silent, chewing the edge of his mustache.

Leo waited, tense, but when several minutes passed without further queries, he released a relieved breath, grateful to let the subject lie.

"I presume," Mr. DeWeece suddenly said, "from the women's excitement over the pair of men's boots you delivered that day, Mrs. Ward also inspects the line."

Leo wished they would talk about dinosaur bones instead of

discussing the Ward family's activities. He'd be a traitor if he told what he knew and a liar if he refused to answer. But hadn't he learned over the past few weeks that Mr. DeWeece was a reasonable man? Surely, he would understand why the women in the family had assumed responsibility for the line's inspection.

He stepped away from the wall and stared across the river toward the Wards' cabin. "Sir, Mr. Ward took a terrible fall and broke his leg. Unfortunately, it didn't heal correctly, which affected his ability to walk long distances."

"Yes, I heard something about an accident at one of the city administration meetings. I believe they sent out a substitute inspector for a few weeks while Mr. Ward recovered. It was quite a while ago, though." DeWeece moved next to Leo and fixed him with a concerned look. "I didn't realize he was still struggling."

Leo gritted his teeth for a moment. "Well, he is. Before his accident, Jennie often accompanied her father on the route. She learned what to watch for and how to report it so the repairmen could be prepared when they came out to address damages. I can assure you, the pipeline receives diligent attention."

The man looked across the river, too. "I don't doubt their diligence. Granted, the water supply to Cañon City has suffered a few delays over the years, especially during the winter months when pipelines are prone to freeze. But considering its construction, occasional issues are to be expected. There hasn't been an adverse increase in delays over the past months, which would be a sign of neglect." He went on as if speaking to himself. "The family is handling the responsibility. But to have a pair of women performing such a strenuous duty, particularly when the weather turns frigid . . ."

Leo touched the man's elbow. "Sir?" Mr. DeWeece shifted his gaze to Leo. "The Ward family depends on the income from the Water Works Department. Given Mr. Ward's . . ." What should he call it? He would not divulge the deeper reason Mr. Ward didn't walk the line. "Well, his infirmities, he might not be able to find another job. If he's released from being the linewalker, the family loses not only their source of income but also their place to live. You . . . you won't say anything, will you?"

Mr. DeWeece's brows tipped inward. He didn't look angry—just seemed merely puzzled. "To be honest, Leo, I'm a little surprised that you support their duplicity. They are, in essence, misleading the Water Works Department."

Leo hung his head. He'd grappled with his conscience about keeping their secret. Maybe it was wrong, but they trusted him. He couldn't betray their trust. "The women are only doing it until Mr. Ward is able again."

"I see."

The familiar vibrations and rumbles alerted them to the approaching train. Mr. DeWeece flagged it down, and the two of them boarded. They sat across the aisle from each other, leaned against opposite windows, and remained quiet for the ride. At the station, Mr. DeWeece reminded Leo to meet him tomorrow at one, then headed off. Leo hoped they'd put to rest the subject of the linewalker for good.

At the hotel, he put his knapsack away and changed out of his hiking clothes. Then he went to the lobby and asked permission to use the telephone. The concierge slid the telephone his way, then said, "Since you're here, I'm going to go out front and have a cigarette. I'll watch for new guests and come in with them as needed." He sauntered off.

Leo took advantage of the privacy and requested connection to his family's home from the switchboard operator. After a single ring, he heard his father's rich baritone voice say, "Hello. Reverend Day speaking."

A knot filled Leo's throat, a mix of loneliness and apprehension. "Hello, Father. It's Leo."

"Good evening, Leo." Warmth underscored his tone, decreasing Leo's apprehension. "Mother, girls? It's Leo on the phone."

Leo heard a squeal, the patter of feet, then a rustle.

"Leo? It's Daisy." She sounded breathless, and a smile tugged at Leo's cheek. He envisioned her as he recalled her on Saturday nights—clad in a cotton nightgown, her blond hair in pin curls, her beloved rag doll tucked in the bend of her arm. "Are you calling to tell me happy birthday? It's not until next week, but you can tell me early. I don't mind."

A muffled argument ensued, then—"Leo, hello!" Apparently, Myrtle had wrestled the earpiece from her sister. "I sent a letter yesterday. You didn't get it already, did you?"

"No, I didn't, but I'm sure I will soon. Have you received my postcards?"

"Yes, three of them, but I'll gladly take more. I want to make a whole display on my new *bulletin board*." The emphasis came through loud and clear. If she'd been given a bulletin board for the purpose of pinning up postcards, he'd better send more.

"I'll see what I can do. Please tell Daisy I'll call on her birthday. May I talk to Father now?"

"Mother is here now."

He listened to more rustling and whispers while hoping he'd have a chance to tell his parents about the dinosaur find before the concierge returned and he had to clear the line.

"Leo?" Mother's sweet voice brought a rush of longing for home. "How are you doing? We pray you're well."

"I'm fine, Mother." A couple entered the lobby from the dining room and passed the desk to the stairs. He watched them go up the spindled stairway as he spoke. "In fact, I'm better than fine. Can Father hear me, too?"

"I can. I'm right here."

Leo leaned closer to the telephone's mouthpiece. "Today when

I explored with Mr. DeWeece—he's the businessman I wrote to you about, remember?—we made an incredible discovery. Mr. DeWeece said it's the spine of a large plant-eating dinosaur. We only uncovered a portion of the spine and a few ribs so far, but he is confident we'll find much of the creature's skeleton intact as the excavation continues. He's going to write an article about the find for a science magazine, and if it's published, I will be credited as one of the discoverers." His mouth felt dry. He licked his lips, swallowed, and went on. "He said I can participate in the excavation, too. I'm learning so much from him. I really believe God orchestrated our meeting, just as He orchestrated my meeting with the Ward family. It's been an amazing summer so far. As much as I miss all of you, I'm grateful I came. Thank you for allowing it."

For a few seconds, he heard only breathing from the other end of the line. Then, "You're welcome, Leo." Father's voice, husky and kind. "We're grateful it's been a good experience. We had planned to call the hotel tomorrow afternoon and ask if you'd come home next week to celebrate Daisy's tenth birthday. It's the only thing she asked for."

Guilt stabbed.

"But it sounds as if you'll be quite busy with an excavation," Father went on. "So would you object if we change our plans?"

Leo's pulse skipped a beat. "What do you mean?"

"What if"—Mother was speaking now—"we treat Daisy to a train ride for her birthday and come see you? We could stay at the hotel, meet Mr. DeWeece and the Ward family."

"Maybe even visit the excavation site."

Leo pulled the earpiece from his ear and stared at it. Had Father truly mentioned visiting the site? He smashed it against his head again and spluttered, "Th-that would be wonderful."

Laughter trickled through the line—Mother had taken over again. "Good! Daisy's birthday is the twenty-eighth. We'll plan to arrive on the twenty-seventh. One of us will call on Monday and confirm the plans."

Leo laughed, stunned by this sudden turn. "I can't wait to see all of you." The concierge came in with a gentleman. Leo needed to get off the telephone. "I'll talk to you on Monday. I love you. Goodbye." He placed the earpiece in its cradle and strode out of the lobby, his heart so light he might as well have been floating.

Chapter Thirty-Two

Jennie

M onday morning, Daddy scuffed into the kitchen earlier than usual and plopped into a chair. "Coffee," he said on a sigh as wearily as if he'd trekked across a mountain to reach the chair.

Jennie exchanged a worried look with Mama, then poured a cup. She set it in front of him and gave his bony shoulder a rub. "Here you go, Daddy. Strong and hot, just the way you like it."

He gripped the mug between his palms and lifted it to his lips. He blew on the surface of the brew, then noisily sucked in a sip. He braced his elbows on the table and sat with the cup under his chin, staring ahead without drinking or talking.

Jennie returned to the stove where Mama stirred the bubbling pot of Quaker Oats. "Mama?" She held her voice to a mere whisper even though it seemed Daddy was far inside himself, unaware. "Remember what Leo told us yesterday when he came by after the men put up the tent on the mountain?"

Mama shifted the pot to the edge of the stove's surface, away from the hottest area. "He told us several things."

Indeed he had, and Jennie had been happiest about his family coming to visit. He'd seemed so surprised and excited. Might this reunion be the answer to her prayer for Leo's father to be at peace with Leo's choice of profession? She hoped so. But one other thing he'd said had played through her mind during the night. Seeing Daddy's condition this morning made her certain the decision she'd reached was the right one. Now to get Mama to agree.

"What he said about the magazine article and my drawings maybe being published." She hugged herself, reining in a delighted shiver. "Remember? He said I could be paid for the sketches."

Mama spooned gloppy oatmeal dotted with raisins into bowls. "I remember."

"Well, I want to—"

Mama whirled on Jennie, her expression fierce. "No."

Jennie drew back. "But I haven't said what I—"

"No!" Although whispered, the denial was sharp and cutting. "If any money comes from the magazine, it will be yours, Jennie Henrietta Ward. You will deposit it in the bank for college or whatever else you decide to do with it when you're finished with school in Cañon City."

Mama had guessed. Which meant she had also thought about using the money to send Daddy to Pueblo. Jennie curled her hand around Mama's arm and leaned closer. "More than anything else, I want Daddy to get better. I know you do, too. It's like God is making the way for us to get him the help he needs. Will you tell God no?"

Mama blinked several times, her lips pursed so tightly they nearly disappeared. She shook her head. "Of course I won't tell God no. But I'm telling you no. You've already given enough of yourself to help your daddy. God knows it as well as I do, and He wouldn't expect you to pay for his treatment."

"But—"

"No! I won't hear one more word of it." Mama plunked a bowl of hot cereal into Jennie's hands. "Grab a spoon and eat before this gets as cold, hard, and dry as those bones on the ridge."

Jennie did as she was told, but she couldn't stop thinking about what she might be paid for her sketches. Would it be enough to buy train tickets and pay the bill for an evaluation and treatment?

When they finished eating, Mama took Jennie aside. "Your daddy's really low. I don't feel good about leaving him by himself today. Would you stay here while I inspect the front half of the pipe?"

Midway through breakfast, he'd gotten up and wandered to his usual window-watching chair, leaving his cereal untouched. The sadness emanating from him stabbed Jennie's soul. "Sure, Mama. Or if you want to stay, I'll walk the route today."

Mama shook her head. "I need to go out so I don't lose my momentum. If you don't mind, though, I'll let you inspect the back half and I'll stay with him with this afternoon. You can still meet Leo and go up to the excavation site if you want to."

Jennie wanted to go with Leo. The summer was more than half gone. He'd leave in a few weeks, and she didn't want to waste an opportunity to spend time with him. She looked over at Daddy's still figure on his chair. At the tufts of gray hair sticking up on the back of his head, his wrinkled nightshirt and bare feet. Such a sorry sight. A fear swooped in that she might not have much more time with Daddy, either, if he didn't get better. He seemed to be withering away.

She turned to Mama. "I'll inspect the back half for you, but then I'll come home."

Mama gave Jennie a hug. "All right. I'll see you at noon. Have a good morning."

Jennie fetched Rags from the shed. His enthusiastic greeting made her laugh. She hoped he'd have the same effect on Daddy. She brought him inside, then tidied the breakfast mess and mixed a batch of dough for their week's bread. While the dough rose, she sat at the table with her drawing materials and sketched a couple of the small bones she and Leo had found. Daddy got up twice—to visit the outhouse and to go to his bedroom. When he emerged from his room fully dressed from shirt to shoes, Jennie asked if he'd like her to comb his hair. She didn't say so, but it needed it. He went to his chair without a word and stared outward.

Rags lay on the floor beside his feet, and Jennie hoped Daddy might lower his hand from the windowsill and give the dog a few scratches, but he didn't. When the clock's hands pointed to eleven, she crossed to his chair and stepped into his line of vision.

"Daddy, would you like to take your chair out on the lawn?" She glanced out the window. The cloud cover was thick, but a few sunbeams might sneak through. "You can throw the rope for Rags and give him some exercise while I fix our lunch." She waited, but he didn't look up. She laid her hand on his shoulder. "Mama'll be back soon. She'll be ready for our picnic when she gets here."

Daddy let out a tiny sigh. "I'm fine right here."

Although it heartened her that he responded, she wished he'd go outdoors. He might not have the chance tomorrow. Dark clouds were building over the mountains, and they could bring a full day of rain. "Are you sure? Mama will worry if she doesn't see you when she comes home."

Daddy shrugged her hand loose. "Leave me be, Jennie."

Jennie went back to the table.

At noon, when Mama came trudging up the rise, Jennie had the quilt spread out in the yard and a pitcher of water, sandwiches, and cookies ready. Mama sank down and drank a full glass of water. She sent a peek in the direction of the house. "How was your daddy?"

Jennie wished she could say he was cheerful and active, but she answered truthfully. "Quiet. He got himself dressed, but he's sat in his chair all morning. He wouldn't even come out with Rags."

Mama patted Jennie's knee. "Well, maybe the afternoon will be better."

Jennie held her bitter opinion on the likelihood of Mama's *maybe* and ate lunch. This picnic wasn't nearly as pleasant as last week's, and not only because Daddy didn't join them. Gusting wind tore at the quilt and toppled Jennie's water glass. Two cookies went rolling, which Rags gobbled before Jennie could rescue them.

Mama sent a worried look skyward. "Looks like we're going to get some rain. Be sure to wear your daddy's hat to keep your head dry."

Jennie laughed. "Mama, one of those gusts would send Daddy's hat across the river. I'll be all right." Mama pinched her lips in an uncertain scowl, but she didn't argue.

When they were finished eating, Jennie gave Mama a hug and set off for the afternoon inspection. She tried to stay focused on the pipeline, but her thoughts kept drifting back home to Mama and Daddy. Had Mama been able to coax Daddy to comb his hair? To eat? To talk? By the time Leo joined her at their usual spot by the pipe, her worries had grown into a tangled, aching mass in her midsection.

Leo took one look at her and asked, "What's the matter?"

Jennie threw her arms wide. "Everything."

He climbed up on the pipe and sat, then patted the spot beside him. "Tell me."

She straddled the pipe, facing him, and shared it all—Daddy's continuing plummet into a sadness that seemed to have no end, Mama's refusal to let Jennie use any money she might receive to help pay for treatment, even her worries about moving to Cañon City for school and leaving Mama and Daddy alone. "Mama had me stay with him this morning instead of walking the route with her. She didn't go out on her own to prove to herself she could— she was scared to leave Daddy alone. But she'll have to leave him by himself when I'm not here to help anymore."

She blew out a breath of frustration. "I keep praying and praying. I know Mama does, too. But Daddy . . ." She looked into Leo's compassionate eyes and swallowed the desire to dissolve into weeping. "Nothing gets better. Are you sure God is listening?"

Leo reached out and placed his hand over her clenched fists. "He is. Even when it doesn't feel like He is, He is."

The warmth of his palm was a soothing balm, especially when compared to the cooling wind whooshing across the river and peppering her with little water droplets. They should get up and moving before the weather got worse. But questions still writhed within her. "How do you know?"

"Because the Bible says so." The confidence in his tone made Jennie's heart flutter with hope. "Yesterday in church, the minister shared from Psalm 34. When you get home, look it up and read it for yourself. The psalmist cried out the same way you are right now. God encouraged him to 'hearken' unto Him—to listen and learn from Him. And God rescued Him from his troubles. God is rescuing you, too, Jennie."

She gaped at him. "No He isn't." The wind blew her braid over her shoulder. It slapped against her cheek and she winced. She caught the tip and held tight. "I already told you. Nothing's getting better."

A soft smile lit his face. "But it is."

She drew back. "How?"

The tenderness in his expression stole her ability to breathe for a moment. "In you, Jennie. He's changing you. I've seen you exercise patience and kindness during trying times with your daddy. I've watched hope unfold in you. It's been a beautiful thing to watch."

The tears she'd been holding back flooded her eyes and spilled. She couldn't stop them. His sweet affirmation touched her deeply and washed over her a wave of gratitude. But at the same time . . . She sniffled and admitted in a croaky voice, "But I want *Daddy* to change."

Leo offered a sympathetic smile. "I know. I do, too. But God isn't finished with him yet. As long as he has breath, there's hope. Rest assured, God hears your cries, Jennie. He will answer in His perfect time in the way that's best for all of you."

Jennie wiped her eyes with her sleeve and stood. Hands on her hips, wisps of hair tickling her cheeks, she forced a grin. "Well, thank you for the sermon. I needed it." Then she stared past Leo, envisioning Daddy behind the cabin window. "When I'm done with the route, maybe you can deliver it to Daddy. See if it does him any good."

Leo stood and lightly grazed her upper arm with his fingers. "There's a powerful hold on your daddy right now, but there's no power stronger than God the Father's. Before we start off again, how about we pray together for him? Will that help you feel better?"

She grabbed his hand and clung as tightly as she would to a rescue line if she were drowning. "Yes. Please."

Leo thanked God for always being with them. He asked God to heal Daddy's mind and strengthen his body. He thanked Him again for working all things for good in their lives and expressed confidence that He was in control. When he thanked God for holding Jennie close and growing her faith through trials, she squeezed his hand in a silent thank-you.

"And now, dear Lord," he said as the wind howled and Jennie braced herself against its force, "lead us safely onward. Amen."

They opened their eyes and their gazes collided. Leo gave her a smile, one eyebrow high. "Do you feel better now?"

"Yes." She scanned the gray clouds cloaking the landscape. "But the wind's really picking up, and those clouds are getting uglier by the minute."

He tightened the strings on his hat. "You're right. Let's finish the route as quickly as possible and get you home."

Chapter Thirty-Three

Etta

E tta went to the open doorway and looked out again. The clock had chimed the sixth hour a few minutes ago. Suppertime. But the darkened landscape made it seem close to bedtime. She wrung her hands, worry plaguing her. Why hadn't she thought to give Jennie a lantern and matches before the girl left to finish today's inspection? By noon, the clouds were already thick overhead and appeared gray and ominous over the northernmost peaks. The way the wind had started gusting while she and Jennie ate their picnic lunch, Etta should have surmised the weather would take a turn. Her concern for Claude was consuming her too much. But other concerns rolled through her now.

Had Leo joined up with Jennie, as he'd done all last week? If so, at least Jennie wasn't out there alone. Yesterday, Leo told them he planned to go up to the dig site and work. Surely, the unpleasant weather changed his mind. But what if it hadn't? What if he'd gone after all, and what if Jennie went with him? As dark as it was, they might not be able to safely find their way back again.

The scent of scorched broth sent her scurrying to the stove. She moved the pot to the tile in the middle of the table and gave the beans and ham a stir. After placing the lid over the steaming beans, she rounded up every lamp and lantern in the house, lit them all, and put one on each windowsill. Except Claude's. He wouldn't want the bright light in his eyes. But the glow could guide Jennie and Leo in. Then she returned to the doorway. She squinted across the grounds, seeking any sign of her daughter.

Suddenly Claude was beside her at the doorway. She hugged his arm to her side. "It's getting stormy." A ridiculous thing to say, especially since he'd spent every hour since waking sitting at the window, watching the storm roll in.

"I need the outhouse."

She released him and reached for the closest lantern. "Better take this with you. Otherwise, you might trip on something."

He shook his head. "I'm fine." He moved out the door and off the stoop.

Rags trotted over, his toenails clicking on the floor, and rubbed against her leg. He whined, what she interpreted as permission to be excused, too. Etta shook her head at the pup, a smile of affection pulling at her lips. "You can't let him out of your sight, can you? Well, all right. Go with him. He won't mind."

Rags darted out, and Etta observed the two of them cross in front of the cabin and then disappear around the corner. She turned her attention to the northwest, where Jennie should appear. The wind roared down the ravine and flapped Etta's apron skirt. It chilled her, an odd sensation for late July, usually their warmest month. Maybe she should go inside and close the door against the wind. But her feet didn't move. She stayed in place, eyes aimed at the slope. After what seemed an eternity, she saw what looked like a hat bobbing. Then two young people, one a head taller than the other, topped the slope and came steadily toward the cabin.

Etta released a little sob and ran out to greet them. She embraced Jennie, laughing to keep herself from crying. Holding her daughter brought a rush of relief so great, her knees felt wobbly. She curled her arm around Jennie's waist and caught hold of Leo's arm. "Come on, you two. Supper's waiting. Let's go warm up. I don't think it's ever been this cold out here in the middle of summer."

"Or as dark this early in the day." Jennie shivered. "It'll feel good to get inside. That sky looks like it could let loose any minute." When they stepped over the threshold, Jennie looked toward Claude's chair. "Is Daddy asleep already?"

"No." Etta took bowls down from the shelf and carried them to the table. "He went to the outhouse." She laughed lightly. "And Rags followed." She added napkins and spoons to each place. "That dog'll probably follow your daddy right inside the cabin and sit here and beg during supper. It'll be hard to break him of his begging if we aren't consistent in leaving him in the shed when we eat." She turned a hesitant look on Leo. "I know it's frightful out there, but would you mind going and asking Mr. Ward to put Rags in the shed before he comes back in? You can tell him I'll fetch the dog to the house myself after we've finished eating."

Leo grinned. "I'll be glad to." He'd removed his hat already, but he settled it back in place and tightened the chin strap as he left.

Jennie washed her hands and sliced a loaf of bread. She stacked the slices on a plate, which she placed next to the pot of beans. "Should I pour water, or do you want me to make coffee?"

"Coffee," Etta said with an emphatic nod. "It'll take the chill off."

Jennie set to work grinding beans and filling the percolator. She put the coffeepot on the stove to heat, then crossed to the table and sat. She sent a glance in the direction of the door. "Mama, shouldn't Leo and Daddy be back already? It isn't that far to the outhouse."

Etta looked at the clock and gave a start. More time had passed than she'd realized since Claude left to visit the outhouse. She hurried to the door and swung it wide. A gust of wind, damp and cold, nearly drove her backward. But she stepped onto the stoop, cupped her hands, and yelled, "Claude? Leo?"

Pounding feet carried over the wind's roar, and Leo rounded the corner. He panted up to her and flung his arms outward. "Mrs.

Ward, I've looked everywhere. Mr. Ward and Rags . . . they're gone!"

Jennie

Jennie stood so quickly she tipped the chair over. On trembling legs, she scrambled to Mama and grabbed hold of her arm. "Mama?" The single-word query quavered out, carried on a note of terror.

Mama shook Jennie's hands loose and grabbed her coat and scarf from the peg on the wall. "You two stay here. I'm going to—"

Leo stepped forward and took her coat from her. "No, ma'am. You stay in case he comes back. I'll look for him."

"But you said you already looked everywhere around the cabin." Mama's tone rose, her eyes wide and fear filled. "That means he's wandered farther off. You aren't familiar with the ground around here. I am."

Jennie had stood against the wall, hugging herself and listening, but suddenly she gasped. "Mama! I think I know where he went." She scuttled to the row of pegs, grabbed Daddy's rain poncho, and flung it over her head. "Stay here while I check. If I'm wrong, I'll hurry back and . . ." She darted out the door without finishing her sentence. Mama called after her, but Jennie raced down the rise at a dangerous pace considering the large stinging raindrops now pelting her face and making the ground slippery. But she had to reach him. He was there. She knew he was there.

His sad voice echoed in her mind as she ran. *"I need to walk the yard on my own. The way I used to walk the line. Back when I was a whole man. I can't never be a whole man again unless I can walk it . . . on my own."*

As she neared the footbridge, she wished she'd taken time to grab a lantern. It was nearly as black as pitch, and she might miss the bridge completely and tumble into the river. At least the river couldn't make her any wetter than she already was, she reasoned with a hint of humor. In all their years at the cabin, they'd never experienced a rain like this one.

The wind roared and turned the rain into a sideways curtain, slashing her with its furious power. But God's power was stronger than anything, and she inwardly pleaded with Him for His strength to endure as she reached the footbridge and braced herself to clamber down the nature-carved ravine to the man-made pipeline, where she was sure she would find Daddy. The minute she found him, she would tell him he was wrong to want to walk the line on his own.

She slid down the bank, bumping her tailbone on rocks as she went. Then the soles of her boots met the bottom, nearly pitching her forward. She caught her balance and paused, gaining her bearings in the dark and noisy night. Fat raindrops sounded like drumbeats on the wooden surface of the pipe, adding percussion to the wind's whistle. Pressed against the cold, wet bank, the river's flow roaring in her ears, she screeched over the storm's noise, "Daddy! Rags!"

Raucous barking exploded from somewhere on her left. She jerked in that direction and screamed their names again. If Daddy answered, she didn't hear him, but Rags continued to bark and yip without pause. She inched toward the sound, blinking against the darkness and rainwater flowing down her face. She'd gone perhaps a dozen feet, bouncing her shoulder along the bank, when a bundle of white fur darted from the deep shadows and plowed against her knees.

With a cry of delight, Jennie scooped up the sodden pup. He licked her face, wriggled, and yipped in her ear with such exuberance he tugged her off-balance. She put him down so he wouldn't knock her into the river. "Take me to Daddy, Rags," she bellowed over the storm's raging song.

The little dog bounded off in the direction he'd come, and Jennie followed, one hand scraping the ravine's wall to keep herself on course. And she stumbled onto Daddy, huddled under the pipeline with Rags curled on his lap. Joy, relief, and gratitude exploded through her with such tumultuous force she couldn't stay upright. She sank to her knees beside them. "Daddy . . . Daddy . . ." No other words would form.

She whipped off the poncho, snuggled in as close to Daddy as she could, and draped the poncho over him and Rags. Under the cover of thick rubber-coated cloth, she rested her head on Daddy's shoulder and took several deep, calming breaths. When she could speak without gasping, she asked a simple question. "Why, Daddy?"

He tipped his head sideways and pressed his whisker-roughened chin to her temple. "I had to try. I had to know. It was raining the day I fell off the pipe, remember?"

Jennie nodded, her chest aching with the same intensity it had the day she and Mama found Daddy's crumpled form beneath the pipe.

"I figured . . . if I could come out here now . . . maybe I could prove to myself . . ." A huge sigh heaved his chest. "I'm a fool, Jennie Hennie."

He hadn't called her Jennie Hennie, his childhood nickname for her, since he'd taken the fall. His using it now was a gift—a reminder that the daddy she'd loved as a little girl was still inside him, struggling to find his way out. She threw her arm across his chest and burrowed into the curve of his neck. She choked out, "You're not a fool, Daddy. Not a fool at all. But you don't have to walk the line or anywhere else all on your own. None of us can do what needs doing on our own. We all need God. He helps us. He'll help you, Daddy, if you let Him."

A shuddering breath vibrated Daddy's chest. "You think He ain't forgot about me?"

Jennie shook her head, swallowing tears. "I know He hasn't. He loves you too much to forget you." Something else occurred to her, and she said it before the thought escaped. "And Mama and I love you, too. We loved you before you got hurt, we love you now, and we'll always love you, no matter what."

Suddenly a thunderous roar exploded from the heavens, and something—a rock?—landed on Jennie's shoulder. She yelped in surprise. Daddy slung his arm around her and pushed her face-down on the rocky bank. Somehow Rags got caught under her arm, and the pup squirmed, but she instinctively held tight. Then Daddy stretched out on top of her. He released little grunts of pain while the earsplitting onslaught seemed to go on and on forever. Jennie cried against the wet, cold pillow of rocks under her cheek and prayed for God to calm the storm and bestow His peace.

Then, when she'd feared it might never end, the steady beat of thuds slowed to sporadic single clunks. The fierce gusts of wind calmed. The steady, heavy patter of rain became a gentle drip-drip. And only then did Daddy roll off Jennie's frame. She shifted to her knees, and her hands encountered ice-cold chunks. Although a drizzle still fell, the heaviest clouds had blown away. In the murky shadows, she saw a sea of chunks, some as large and round as the grapefruit that came by train at Christmastime, covering the bank. With her ears still ringing from the storm's fury and her pulse racing, she couldn't make sense of what the pieces were. She picked one up, and understanding dawned—they'd been through a hailstorm. And Daddy had shielded her from its assault.

Her shoulder ached from being struck by a single hailstone. What must Daddy have endured? She crawled to him and touched his face. "Daddy, are you hurt? Can you move?"

He groaned and struggled to sit up. "I . . . I don't know."

She caught hold of his shoulders and gently pressed him back down. "Stay here. I'll get Leo and Mama. We'll get you home."

She spread the rumpled poncho over him, then leaned down and touched her cheek to his in an awkward hug. She whispered through tears, "I love you, Daddy. I love you."

His eyes slid closed. "I love you, too, Jennie Hennie."

He didn't need to say it. She already knew. He'd proved it.

Chapter Thirty-Four

Leo

Leo awakened Tuesday morning to the sound of rain. But then a distinctive aroma met his nostrils, and he realized he was hearing the sizzle of bacon in a pan. Mrs. Ward must be fixing breakfast.

He sat up on the settee, stifling a groan. He propped his elbows on his knees and buried his face in his hands. When he'd collapsed on this settee a little before midnight, he'd held a foggy hope that the evening's activities were only a bad dream. But if he was still at the Wards' cabin, then Mr. Ward's disappearance, the fierce storm, the frantic race to close all the shutters just before the hail began, and Mr. Ward's rescue after the storm passed had all happened.

Worry gnawed the corners of his mind. What would the kitchen manager think when Leo didn't show up for work this morning? Would he be fired from his job? At least he'd be in town when his folks arrived at the hotel for Daisy's promised birthday trip. But if the storm covered most of the state, would they still be able to come?

"I wonder if the trains'll run today."

"What did you say?"

Leo looked up and found Mrs. Ward peering across the room at him. He must have spoken his thought. He cleared his throat and stood. "I wonder if the trains will run today. Do you think the hailstones were large enough to damage tracks?" He'd never seen such hail before—something reminiscent of a biblical plague.

"I don't know, but I hope not." Concern crinkled her brow. "Claude is bruised all up and down his back and legs. He has a couple of nasty knots on his head, too. I want Dr. Whiteside to come out and see him."

Leo chastised himself. How could he think about his own troubles after what Mr. Ward had suffered last night? He crossed to her and put his hand on her shoulder. "I'll meet the morning train and ride into Cañon City. Before I go to the hotel, I'll visit the doctor's office and tell Dr. Whiteside what happened. Hopefully his schedule will be clear and he can come out this afternoon."

The woman sighed, her relief evident. "Thank you, Leo. And thank you for helping last night. Jennie and I were in such an emotional state that we wouldn't have been able to get Claude home on our own."

Leo disagreed. They could've done it. Mrs. Ward and Jennie were two of the strongest people he'd ever met. But it was nice to be appreciated. "You're welcome, ma'am. I'll pray that Mr. Ward isn't badly injured." The man didn't need yet another setback. "I'll gather up my things and go down to the tracks now."

"No, no, sit and have some breakfast first. The train won't pass by until a little past nine. You have time to eat."

The food smelled so good he couldn't refuse. While Mr. Ward and Jennie slept, he and Mrs. Ward ate bacon-and-biscuit sandwiches and visited. He hoped his family would make it to Cañon City, the way they'd intended. He wanted his family to meet the Wards. Mother and Mrs. Ward would get along well. Father, with his endless well of wisdom, could be a real encouragement to Mr. Ward. Leo's sisters would love Jennie, and she, them. Maybe it was silly to contemplate the two families forming a friendship given the distance between Cañon City and Denver, but he enjoyed considering the possibility.

When he'd finished eating, he thanked Mrs. Ward and then headed down the rise. The air held a nip, but the sky was clear.

Birds sang, adding harmony to the river's melody. If not for the flattened wet grass and sloppy patches of mud he was forced to skirt, he might not have believed a storm roared through yesterday evening. Would the river be high above its banks after the rain and hail that fell? If so, he hoped the footbridge was still intact.

He approached the footbridge, the river's roar growing louder with every step. He gave the simple bridge a thorough examination. He noted a few chips on some edges but no outright breaks. He stepped gingerly onto the footbridge, the river's wild churning loud in his ears, and sent his gaze up and down the rushing water. And something else caught his eye—as far as he could see, water flowed from jagged holes in the pipeline.

He stared in mute horror, his mouth hanging open. Hailstones had broken through the staves. He looked left, then right, back and forth. So much damage. How would Jennie or Mrs. Ward be able to record it all? And how would they be able to inspect it now? The river climbed the banks, leaving no place to walk underneath, and they wouldn't dare walk on top of the damaged staves. With Mr. Ward lying in bed, maybe badly injured, they didn't need this additional concern.

He crossed the footbridge, then went down on one knee. He opened his knapsack, dug out a pad of paper and pencil, and scribbled a note.

Mrs. Ward or Jennie, when I get to Cañon City, I will call the Water Works Department and tell them the pipeline was damaged by hail. There's no sense in inspecting today. Stay with Mr. Ward. I pray the doctor will come soon. —Leo

He secured the note under the message rock, as he'd come to think of the large gray stone, then stood and sent a mournful look up the pipeline. He would never have imagined hail causing such destruction. Then he gave a jolt, and his gaze jerked in the direction of the dinosaur remains. He couldn't see the site from this distance and angle, but an ugly picture filled his mind. Had the tent and bones been battered, too?

Etta

Early in the afternoon, as Etta returned the freshly washed dishes to their places on the shelves, the mutter of men's voices drifted through the open front door. She removed her apron and hurried to the doorway, hoping to see Dr. Whiteside coming. Claude needed the doctor's attention. She wanted Jennie's shoulder checked, too. The girl hadn't said a thing about being hurt. If Etta hadn't seen her wince while putting on her jacket, she wouldn't have known a hailstone had struck her.

She spotted the doctor walking up the rise with three other men, and she breathed a prayer of thankfulness. But her hand flew to her throat when she recognized the man striding purposefully in the lead—the Water Works Department president, Mr. Wilmer Cambrie. The day her family settled in at the cabin, he'd come out to thank them for seeing to the important duty. She hadn't seen him since, although he'd sent a note of condolence after Claude broke his leg. Leo's call must have greatly concerned Mr. Cambrie for him to personally visit.

She gave the cabin a quick perusal and found everything tidy, but she should brew a fresh pot of coffee. Such an important man would expect refreshments. She hurried to the counter and removed the bag of beans from a drawer. Even before she managed to grind them, there was a knock on the doorjamb.

Smoothing her hair as she went, she returned to the doorway. "Good afternoon, gentlemen. Please come in."

Mr. Cambrie entered first, removing his brown bowler as he

crossed the threshold, and Dr. Whiteside came behind him. The other two men, who wore work clothes rather than suits, remained on the stoop. The doctor crossed to Etta, his brow etched with concern. "Leo said Claude took quite a beating last night."

"He did." Etta pushed aside the distressing images plaguing her mind and pointed to their closed bedroom door. "He's in bed. Jennie is keeping watch. She suffered a blow on her right shoulder. I'd appreciate you looking at it."

The doctor nodded and went straight to the bedroom. Etta watched him go in and close the door, then turned and found Mr. Cambrie frowning after him. A chill attacked her scalp and tiptoed down her spine. She cleared her throat and offered a weak smile. "Mr. Cambrie, I wish I had a cup of coffee or a sweet to offer you. I . . . I didn't realize I'd have visitors today."

The man remained standing near the door, his hands behind his back. "There's no need to make a fuss, Mrs. Ward. Thank you for sending word about last night's destruction. I came out with the engineers to assess the damage for myself. They'll also examine the cabin while we're here and will arrange for any necessary repairs." He angled a look at the men and gave a nod. The two of them headed toward the river. Mr. Cambrie faced her again. "I would like to speak with you about a concern."

Etta's knees began to tremble. "Of course." She moved to her rocking chair and sank into its smooth seat. "Would you please sit and make yourself comfortable?"

Mr. Cambrie reached the settee in one wide stride and sat on the front edge of the cushion. He laid his hat aside and clamped his hands over his knees. "My concern involves your husband, Mrs. Ward."

Etta's pulse thrummed as forcefully as last night's raindrops had pelted the cabin roof. Her mouth went dry, and it felt as if her tongue was swollen. She couldn't speak. She gave a slight nod of acknowledgment.

"Although we've not yet made an official study of the entire line, the brief view we received upon arrival indicates last night's storm did significant damage covering at least a mile of the pipeline. It will likely be several weeks before the entire line is repaired and fully operational again."

Etta envisioned repairmen coming out each day for several weeks and working on the pipeline. Their family's long-held secret would come to light very quickly. She should confess who had been inspecting the line since Claude's accident and face the consequences. She swallowed and drew a deep breath. "Mr. Cambrie, I—"

He held up one hand, silencing her. "Let me finish, please." His gray eyes beneath thick steel-gray eyebrows gave him a fierce appearance, but no anger tinged his voice. He seemed more sad than upset. "During the time it takes to repair the pipeline, there won't be any need for a linewalker."

She'd expected him to fire Claude on the spot. She tipped her head, uncertain she'd heard correctly. "Only . . . while the pipe's being repaired?"

"Yes, ma'am." He shifted slightly, placing his elbows on his knees and linking his fingers. The position brought him closer to her, allowing her to glimpse the genuine concern in his gray irises. "To be perfectly honest, after taking the train ride to reach the cabin this afternoon, I'm pondering the sensibility of housing the workers in this cabin until the repairs are done. With the hours saved by the workers not traveling each day, the pipeline repairs will be completed more expediently and the town will have its water source restored within a more reasonable amount of time. But I realize such a decision temporarily displaces your family."

She'd often pondered what they would do, where they would go, if the waterway men fired Claude. In the past, the contemplation raised fear and worry. Strange how the thought of leaving this cabin didn't strike fear into her now. She felt more relieved than anything. "Sir, please don't worry about us. We're only one family. All of Cañon City's residents and businesses rely on the pipeline to meet their needs for water. The sooner the pipeline is repaired, the better it will be for everyone."

The man sat up, and the first hint of a smile softened his stern expression. "You're very understanding, Mrs. Ward. Thank you."

The bedroom door opened, and the doctor came out. Mr. Cambrie stood, and Etta hurried to the doctor. "How are they?"

Dr. Whiteside gave her arm a light pat. "Very badly bruised. Not surprising, considering the size of the hailstones. Praise God, neither Claude nor Jennie seem to have suffered any broken bones. However, it will take a while for their deep bruising to heal. In the meantime, please watch for excessive swelling or specific areas where the pain seems to be growing worse. Blood clots sometimes form in deep bruises, and they can be serious."

While the doctor spoke, Mr. Cambrie slowly moved closer, his lips set in a grim line.

"I'm also concerned that Claude may have suffered a concussion. I gave Jennie instructions on his care for now, but I'd feel better if he stayed with my wife and me for a few days, where I can monitor his recovery." A grin climbed the doctor's cheeks. "I know how stubborn he is. He might not agree. And it might be hard to separate him from the scruffy little dog standing guard on his bed. I'm fortunate the protective mutt allowed me to conduct an examination at all."

Mr. Cambrie pushed his hands into his trouser pockets and lifted his chin. "If Mr. Ward requires around-the-clock care, I will personally arrange for his transport into Cañon City as soon as I return to my office."

Dr. Whiteside chuckled. "You might be the only one who can convince him to go. Thank you. You've eased my mind considerably."

"And mine," Etta said. "Thank you very much."

Mr. Cambrie waved one hand as if dismissing their appreciation as unnecessary. "Doctor, please send all bills for his care to me. The Water Works Department will cover his medical expenses and"—he turned to Etta—"a hotel room for you and your daughter until better accommodations are made available to you."

His unexpected kindnesses overwhelmed Etta. She extended her hand to the Water Works president, and he took hold. "That's very generous of you, sir. I don't know how to thank you."

"Your family has done a commendable job in the past for us, Mrs. Ward." Had he emphasized the words *your family,* or did she merely imagine it? "The least we can do is make these next weeks as free of stress as possible." He gave her hand a light squeeze and released it, glancing around the room. "Most of these furnishings are your personal belongings. You won't want them used by the men on the repair crew. I'd be happy to make storage arrangements for them in a warehouse owned by Mr. Dall DeWeece. Are you familiar with the town businessman and philanthropist?"

"Yes, we've met."

Mr. Cambrie's smile broadened. "He happens to be a good friend of mine."

And, Etta suspected, had talked to Mr. Cambrie about more than housing their furniture. The family's secret was no longer a secret.

"I assure you, he will keep your belongings safe. Well . . ." He took a backward step. "I'm sure you want to check on your husband and daughter. Please give them my regards and well wishes for a speedy recovery. I will be in touch with you soon concerning your move. Have a good day, now, Mrs. Ward." He picked up his hat and waved farewell with it as he left the cabin.

Dr. Whiteside looked at Etta, sympathy glistening in his eyes. "It sounds as though things are rapidly changing. Are you reeling?"

Etta examined her thoughts. She should be reeling. Any normal person would reel after receiving such unexpected news. But she wasn't. She shook her head slowly, pondering her strange state of . . . what? Numbness? No. More calm acceptance. "I'm not. I suppose it appears that my life is falling apart, but I feel it's more like God is working His will."

The doctor's warm smile showed his admiration. "You've got some work to do to prepare for a move to town. I'll get out of your way. I left some analgesic powders on the bedside table for Claude and Jennie. Mix a teaspoon with water when they need pain relief." He glanced toward the closed bedroom door, and a wry grin lifted the corners of his lips. "I'll have my wife ready a bed for Claude. I'm sure Mr. Cambrie will let me know when to expect him."

Chapter Thirty-Five

Leo

Leo finished the lunch cleanup and headed to his room, grateful to still have a job. The kitchen manager had stood with his arms crossed and a scowl marring his face while he listened to Leo's explanation about being trapped on the mountain. But by the time Leo finished, his supervisor's stance had softened. He'd clapped Leo on the shoulder and said, "Son, you've always been reliable and worked hard for me. I can't see any reason to let you go over one situation that was out of your control. Just plan on some extra duties at lunchtime to make up for the lost time." Leo had gotten right to work and didn't even break to eat lunch.

Now, with the supper staff arriving, he changed out of his work uniform and donned his best suit, fresh from the cleaners, to greet his family at the train station. He'd already put the gifts he'd collected—new handkerchiefs for Father, a tiny bottle of rose-scented perfume for Mother, several postcards for Myrtle, and the biggest tin of Washburn's hard candies available at the drugstore for Daisy—on the bureau in the room he'd reserved for them on the second floor. He hoped they'd be happy with his choices. He hoped they'd be happy to see him. He was surprisingly eager to see all of them.

He gave his reflection a quick perusal in the little mirror above his washstand, then dashed out of the hotel and set off on the walk to the train station. On the way, he heard a train's whistle. Was it the Denver and Rio Grande engine pulling the car with his family in it? He had to be on the boardwalk when it arrived. He broke into a run and skidded to a halt in front of the station just as the locomotive wheezed to a shuddering stop. He scanned the windows, seeking the faces of the people he loved, but they must have already left their seats.

He shifted his attention to the passenger cars' landings, bouncing his gaze up and down the line of cars in the hopes of spotting his family. His heart thudded with such force he feared it might leave his chest. Why was he so nervous? He couldn't settle on a reason. He only knew he was bound up in both excitement and anxiety. When he saw Father's face, he'd know which feeling to latch on to.

He leaned one way and then the other, peering around disembarking passengers and those waiting for arrivals, and finally, when he was sure he couldn't last another second, he saw Mother's travel hat—green felt with a pheasant wing sewn on the side. He leaped in the air, waving his arms over his head the way Jennie waved at the train passing by the pipeline. Mother looked in his direction, and a smile burst over her face. She reached back for someone, and Myrtle and Daisy popped into view. Right behind them came Father—Father, in his best Sunday suit, black ribbon tie, and black derby. Mother pointed Leo's way, and Father's dark-blue gaze connected with Leo's. Father tipped his hat. While not an exuberant greeting, it was a friendly acknowledgment. The outer layer of Leo's apprehension melted away.

Leo wove between people, muttering, "Excuse me," as he went. Daisy came running and met him midway. She jumped into his arms, forcing the breath from his lungs, but he didn't mind. He swung her in a circle, laughing. He gave Myrtle the same treatment, earning a wild squeal. Then he reached for Mother.

She playfully slapped at his hands. "Don't you spin me, young man. A hug will suffice."

He grabbed her close, breathing in the scent of lilac toilet water and old feathers—a combination that would never sell if bottled but was one of his favorite fragrances in the world. "I've missed you, Mother," he said with his cheek pressed against the pheasant wing.

She sighed in his arms. "And I, you, my boy."

Father stepped forward and extended his hand. Leo gave it a firm shake, his smile intact but quavering. "Father . . . it's so good to see you."

Before Father answered, someone grabbed Leo's coattail and gave a mighty tug. Leo wriggled loose and looked down.

Daisy placed her fists on her hips and tipped her head at a saucy angle. "Excuse me, but I have a question."

Leo imitated her stance. "You do? Well, what is it?"

"Did you get me a birthday present?"

Leo tweaked her nose. "Maybe I did, and maybe I didn't, but you won't know until tomorrow, because tomorrow is your birthday."

She smirked at him. "You did. I can tell." She grabbed his hand and swung it. "Can we go now? Father said I could have ice cream at the drugstore, and I want strawberry."

Leo preferred to take them to the hotel. There were many things he wanted to discuss with Mother and Father. But this was Daisy's birthday trip. They should do what she wanted. Besides, he'd skipped lunch, and ice cream sounded good. "Yes, as soon as we collect your luggage, we'll go."

They moved in tandem toward the loading dock, where workers had stacked the passengers' various travel cases and trunks. Father located their large veneer-covered case and pulled it from the stack. Leo took it from him, then turned toward town. "This way for ice cream."

Daisy squealed, "Yippee!"

As Leo led his family to the drugstore, he tried not to read too much into Father's silence. But he couldn't help worrying there was a secondary reason they came to Cañon City—to convince him to come back to Denver.

Jennie

Jennie sat beside the bed and watched Daddy sleep. Dr. Whiteside said if he had a concussion, he should be awakened every two hours and asked questions to validate his lucidity. He'd fallen asleep a little before three. She would let him sleep another fifteen minutes, then wake him, just in time to get ready for supper. While she waited for the clock's hands to tick away the minutes, she petted Rags, listened to Daddy's even breathing, and thought about what Mama had told her about them leaving the cabin.

"Temporarily," she'd said, but the way she said it made Jennie think they wouldn't ever come back. For months, she'd wanted to leave. To leave the cabin's isolation, its endless chores, its secrets. But now that Mama was packing for them to leave, a little part of Jennie was sad. She'd miss listening to nature's "Peace Song," waving at the train engineer and conductor, and traipsing over the hills. She'd first hiked the mountains with Daddy, then with Leo. But those days were ending now, never to be relived. Regret pricked her heart.

If they weren't out here much longer, would she get to participate in excavating the dinosaur skeleton Leo found? She was supposed to draw it for Mr. DeWeece. Her hand stilled in Rags's fur and she rasped, "The dinosaur . . ."

Tiptoeing as quickly as she could, she left the bedroom and went to the sitting room. Mama was wrapping her pieces of china in towels and stacking them neatly in an old orange crate she must have dragged in from the shed. Jennie grabbed the top rung on the closest ladder-back chair and gripped hard. "Mama, the storm last night . . . If the hailstones were hard enough to break staves on the pipeline, do you think they could have broken bones on the dino-saur skeleton?"

Mama's brow crinkled. "Granted, Jennie, they were big hail-stones. I'd never seen the likes of them before. But aren't fossil-ized bones much harder than wood?"

Jennie searched her memory for anything Leo might have said about the hardness of fossils, but nothing came to mind. "I don't know." She glanced at the clock and figured in her head the num-ber of hours before the evening shadows grew thick. She sighed. There wasn't enough time to get all the way to the excavation site and home again, especially if the ground was muddy and slick. She should have set out after lunch instead of near suppertime. Maybe she'd go tomorrow, since her family had been relieved of linewalk-ing duties.

She started to ask permission, but Mama said, "Thank you for helping with your daddy today. I know he finds your presence a comfort."

Jennie cringed. What was she thinking? She couldn't go check-ing on old bones when she was needed here—not only to check in on Daddy and give him the powders if he needed them, but also to help Mama pack up their belongings. They didn't know when Mr. Cambrie would send men to cart their things down the hill to the tracks. They had to be ready. Mama hadn't let her help with packing today. She said to give her bruised shoulder a rest. But tomorrow would be different.

She glanced at the clock. Almost time to wake Daddy. Almost time to sit and eat their supper. A pot simmered on the stove. Veg-etable stew, from the smell of it. "I'll set the table, Mama, then get Daddy up. After, I'll see to the dishes. You can sit with Daddy this evening. You deserve a rest, too."

Mama sent Jennie a grateful smile. "Thank you, honey. It has been a long day after a very long season of uncertainty. But . . ."

She turned her gaze to Daddy's window, to the familiar view of a little patch of grassy yard leading to the river's ravine, train tracks, and tall rock wall. "Things will look brighter soon."

Jennie went to Daddy and Mama's room without answering. Mama's last comment rolled in her mind. Daddy was still sick. They wouldn't have a home much longer or any source of income. Maybe even something sad waiting would seem brighter when compared to what they had right now.

Leo

"I work until noon tomorrow, but I'll have the whole afternoon and evening free to spend with you." Leo perched on the edge of the desk in his family's hotel room. Myrtle and Daisy slept in the bed farthest from the door, worn out from the excitement of their first train ride. He kept his voice low. "When you said you'd be coming, I'd planned to take you to the ridge where I found the dinosaur skeleton. But I'm not sure if I should now."

Mother and Father sat side by side on the end of their bed, their attention pinned on Leo. Mother lifted her hands in a gesture of query. "Why would you not take us now?"

Leo felt the reasons were obvious, but maybe Mother was too tired to surmise. "The storm left the hillsides quite mucky, Mother. You and the girls won't want to trek over that kind of messy landscape. And after seeing what the hailstones did to the wooden pipeline, I'm not sure there will be anything of worth left at the site."

Father leaned forward slightly. "Have you spoken with Mr. De-Weece about it?"

"No, sir." There hadn't been time for a phone call. If he was honest with himself, he was afraid to talk to the man he'd come to think of as his mentor. If Mr. DeWeece said the bones were most likely lost, his hope would be crushed.

"Before you decide to give up on it, you should confer with him. He seems to be the local expert on the subject."

Leo blinked in surprise at his father. Since when did Father encourage him to pursue paleontology? Shouldn't this setback give him an excuse to sway Leo toward a different vocation?

"It's too late to call him now," Father went on, "but do you have a scheduled break time in the morning?"

Leo nodded. "Every worker is allowed a fifteen-minute break between the breakfast cleanup and lunch preparation."

"Call him on your break tomorrow." Father spoke with his usual authority. "After you've spoken with him, we can decide whether to go to the site or not." He placed his hand over Mother's and gave her a concerned look. "But if the landscape is as unpleasant as Leo indicated, perhaps you and the girls should stay at the Ward cabin while he and I go to the site."

Mother laughed softly. "I don't mind forgoing the climb, and neither will Myrtle. But do you think you'll be able to leave Daisy behind? She's still at that fearless age. She would think climbing a mountain to look at dinosaur bones a fine way to spend part of her tenth birthday."

Leo looked at his sleeping little sisters. Myrtle had already lost her childish chubby cheeks and was fast becoming a lovely young woman. But Daisy, although not ill-mannered or obnoxious, retained the impetuosity and giddiness of a little girl. Mother was right—Daisy would delight in trekking up the mountain. Leo hoped he'd be able to give her the opportunity to see bones from a creature that lived thousands of years ago half-buried in the side of a Colorado mountain. What other little girl could make such a claim?

He turned to his parents. "Did you bring clothes appropriate for the excursion? I'd hate to see her spoil a good dress or ruin her shoes." His family didn't have money to squander. This trip to Cañon City must have stretched their budget to the extreme.

A soft smile curved Mother's lips. "I packed a nearly outgrown dress leftover from Myrtle, who received it as a hand-me-down from one of our parishioners three years ago. It's seen plenty of use, so I won't fuss if she spoils it. And patent leather is easily cleaned, so no worries there, either." Mother cast a fond look toward the sleeping girls. "It won't be long before they'll be all grown-up and assuming grown-up duties. I'd like her to have a fine adventure to remember from her childhood." She covered a yawn with her hand. "Oh! Please excuse me. I believe the day's busyness is catching up with me."

Leo wished they could talk more. He hadn't yet expressed his concerns about the Ward family's situation. But they could talk tomorrow on the train. He stood. "I'll let you get your rest, then. Breakfast is available in the dining room between seven and nine-thirty, so feel free to laze about in the morning. I won't be able to join you since I'll be working in the kitchen, but I'll meet you in the lobby at one, after you've had your lunch and I'm released from duty. We can catch the train and ride to the Wards' cabin then."

Mother rose and gave Leo a hug. "That sounds fine. Sleep well."

Leo released Mother, shook Father's hand, and wished them good night. Then he headed to his little room at the back of the kitchen. When he moved to his bureau for a nightshirt, his gaze encountered the bone he'd seen Jennie carrying. He picked it up, smiling at the memories it evoked. This bone had started his search, budded a dear friendship, and introduced him to a man who'd encouraged and inspired him.

Even if tomorrow's trek to the excavation site resulted in disappointment, he still had much to treasure. He thanked God for the reminder of his blessings, placed the bone on his desk, and readied himself for bed, his burden lifted.

As he slipped between the scratchy sheets of his cot, his mind drifted to the Wards' cabin—to Jennie, Mrs. Ward, and Mr. Ward. He prayed their burdens were lifting, too.

Chapter Thirty-Six

Jennie

Jennie picked at her sandwich, dropping little bits over the edge of the table for Rags. Mama watched her do it but didn't say anything, a sure sign that Mama's thoughts were far away.

One thing Jennie'd say about Mr. Cambrie was he knew how to get things done. Men showed up at their door early yesterday evening with a stretcher. Daddy was so shocked, he didn't even make a fuss, and the men carried him down the rise to the train. She and Mama had never spent a night in the cabin alone before. Odd how unsettled it had left her. She'd slept very little, aware of every creak and moan. She wondered if Mama had slept, but she didn't ask.

Usually, Mama kept their front door open to allow in the breeze, but today it was closed. All morning long, men had walked up the rise from the pipeline and utilized the family's outhouse—another unsettling situation. Mama assured her Mr. Cambrie wouldn't hire dangerous people to work on the pipeline, but she still closed their door. Which meant Mama found their sporadic coming and going unnerving, too. Jennie wished they'd all been taken to town when Daddy went.

But she and Mama had work to do. The men who came for Daddy also brought a cartful of empty crates and a bundle of rags for packing their belongings. During the morning, Mama had packed most of their small items from the sitting room and kitchen, except necessary items for meal preparation. Jennie sorted and boxed everything from her bedroom. She'd made certain the bones Mr. DeWeece had left for her to sketch were separate from everything else.

She put the bones and the finished sketches in the box Leo had used to send the cake and strawberries for Daddy way back in June. More than a month ago. Hardly any time at all in the grand scheme of life, but so much had happened in those five short weeks, it seemed she'd lived half a lifetime.

"Jennie, if you're not going to eat, you might as well toss the sandwich out the front door and let Rags have it."

Mama's weary voice pulled Jennie from her ruminations. She looked at Mama in surprise. "You told me to keep Rags inside so he wouldn't bark at the workers."

"Well, I don't want him eating in here and making a mess."

Now Mama's tone turned sharp. She rarely lost her temper. Jennie reached across the table and put her hand over Mama's. "You didn't sleep well last night, did you?"

Mama slid her hand free, picked up her napkin, and wiped her eyes. "No, I didn't, but that's no excuse for snapping at you. Forgive me, Jennie."

"It's all right. I miss Daddy, too." Maybe it was best they couldn't send Daddy to the hospital in Pueblo. If the doctor said he had to stay, Mama might drift into melancholia, pining for him. Daddy and Mama . . . they were meant to be together. She sent up a silent prayer for them to be reunited soon.

She stood and patted her leg. "Come on, Rags." The puppy pranced alongside her to the door. She opened it and gave the sandwich a toss. Rags dove on it as if he'd never seen food before. She chuckled at his ill manners, left the door open, and returned to the table. "Mama, why don't you go in and take a little nap? I'll clear the table and wash these things. I'd like to wash our laundry and get it hung so it'll be dry enough to pack. No sense in packing dirty clothes."

Mama rose, her movements slow and weary. "I should say no,

but I believe a nap is exactly what I need. Thank you, sweetheart." She gave Jennie a hug on her way to the bedroom. "Wake me in half an hour, will you?"

Jennie nodded, but she intended to wait an hour. Mama deserved a good rest.

Rags wandered in, crumbs caught in the fur on his chin, and flopped onto the braided rug under the table. Jennie considered closing the door, but the breeze felt good. She'd leave it for a little while and let the cabin air out.

She sang to herself—her favorite hymn, "Redeemed, How I Love to Proclaim It"—while she worked. The perky tune and encouraging words bolstered her spirits, and some of the morning's dreariness melted away. As she placed the last cup on the shelf, Rags suddenly bolted to his feet and began furiously barking.

She spun toward the door, expecting to find someone on the stoop, but there wasn't anyone there. Even so, Rags continued his racket. She reached for him. "Rags, hush," she hissed. "You're going to wake Mama."

The dog skittered away from her hands and darted out the door. Jennie dashed after him on bare feet, calling, "Rags, come back here!" He took off in the direction of the footbridge. Jennie ran partway after him, then slid to a stop. No wonder he was barking. But not angry barks. These were excited barks. He ran straight to Leo, who was leading a small group of people up the rise. Mr. DeWeece was with them, and the others were probably Leo's parents and sisters. Leo glanced in her direction and waved, his smile bright.

Jennie offered a little wave and curled her bare toes into the grass. She rocked in place, comparing her baggy trousers and worn chambray shirt, dusty from the morning's work, to his family's fine clothing. She'd never been so embarrassed, but there was nothing she could do about it now. She waited while each member of the party gave Rags a pat or scratch. When they began ambling in her direction, she forced her feet to scuff forward and meet them.

Leo swung his arm toward her, smiling at the group. "Father, Mother, Myrtle, Daisy . . . this is Jennie Ward. Jennie, this is my family. You already know Mr. DeWeece."

Jennie bounced a quavering smile across each of them. "It's very nice to meet all of you. And to see you again, Mr. DeWeece." She scooped up Rags and held him against her hip. "I hope he didn't jump on you and snag your clothes. He hasn't learned his manners yet."

The smaller of the sisters stepped forward and cupped Rags's face in her hands. She delivered a kiss on his nose, then beamed at Jennie. "He's so cute. He can jump on me all he wants to, because Mother says this dress is nearly in tatters already. That's why she brought it along. So I can climb the mountain with Leo and Father and Mr. DeWeece. We're going to look at the dinosaur bones Leo found. Myrtle and Mother aren't going. They don't want to"—she rolled her eyes upward for a moment—"overexert themselves. But I don't mind getting overexerted. Are you coming, too?"

Leo chortled and put his hand on Daisy's shoulder. "You might say Daisy hasn't learned her manners yet either."

Daisy crinkled her nose at him, then shrugged. "It's my birthday. I can do whatever I want today."

Reverend Day leaned down and spoke into Daisy's ear. "Within reason, young lady. Birthday or not, manners are not optional."

Myrtle snickered and Daisy's grin turned sheepish. "Yes, Father."

Jennie put Rags down and took a step toward the cabin. "Would you like to come in? My daddy isn't here, but Mama will want to meet all of you."

Mr. DeWeece adjusted the large backpack hanging from shoulder straps. "I believe I'm going to head up to the site. Leo, I'll see you a bit later, yes?"

"Yes, sir." Leo watched after Mr. DeWeece for a moment, his

brows tipped together, then turned a worried look on Jennie. "What happened? Where's your daddy?"

As they walked up to the cabin, Jennie explained about the Water Works Department president arranging for Daddy to receive care at Dr. Whiteside's place. "He's where he needs to be, especially if he has a concussion, but Mama and I sure miss him. It doesn't feel right out here without him. And . . . I'm a little embarrassed by the state of the cabin. Mr. Cambrie is moving us into town while the pipeline is repaired. He wants the workmen to stay out here. We've been packing, and . . ." She paused at the stoop and gave them what she hoped was an apologetic smile. "Well, it's something of a mess."

Leo's mother stepped forward and curled her gloved hand around Jennie's arm. "My dear, we didn't come to see the cabin. We came to see you."

Jennie didn't know if that was better considering how she was dressed. She twisted her raggedy braid. "Thank you, ma'am. Please come in."

As they entered the cabin, Mama emerged from her bedroom. For a moment, surprise registered on her face, but then a smile replaced the startled expression. She walked forward, her work-roughened hands held out in welcome. "Leo, how nice to see you again. May I assume this is your family?" She reached Leo's mother first. "I'm Etta Ward, Jennie's mama."

Leo's mother clasped Mama's hands. "I'm Martha Day. It is wonderful to meet you. Leo has told Paul and me so much about you and your family that I feel as if we're already friends."

Jennie now knew why Leo was so personable. He'd inherited the trait from his mother, who exuded warmth and friendliness.

Mama's eyes glistened. "Thank you." She gestured to the settee. "Please, won't you all sit down? I'll make a pot of coffee, and—Jennie? Aren't there some cookies left in the jar? I imagine these pretty young ladies would enjoy an oatmeal-raisin cookie."

Daisy licked her lips, and Myrtle turned a hopeful look on her father. "May we?"

Reverend Day held up one finger.

Mama laughed. "One each. Jennie, fetch the cookies. We have canned milk, or we can offer a cup of cold water."

Jennie brought down the cookie crock from the shelf and set it on the table, then laid out a stack of napkins in case the others wanted a cookie, too.

Daisy danced in place. "Ma'am, may I eat my cookie on my way up the mountain? Mr. DeWeece has already gone. Leo is going, and so is Father, and so am I. I want to see the dinosaur bones in the dirt."

Jennie cringed. In what shape would the bones be? She hoped Daisy—as well as Mr. DeWeece and Leo—wouldn't be disappointed by what they found.

Daisy swung her eager gaze on Jennie. "Are you coming, Miss Jennie? Leo said you found the first bone and gave it to him and that's why he knew this was a good place to hunt for more bones. So you should come, too." She grabbed Leo's hand. "Right, Leo?"

Something in Leo's dark-blue eyes as he met Jennie's gaze captured her fully. He didn't say a word, but she knew he wanted her to go with them. He wanted her at his side when he reached the site. And she wanted to be there, to offer sympathy if needed or celebrate if the bones were still intact.

He still hadn't said anything, but Jennie turned to Mama. "May I go with them? I'd . . . I'd like to . . ." She hoped Mama read the meaning behind her senseless babble.

Mama nodded. "Go ahead, and take some cookies to eat on the way." She glanced at Jennie's feet. "But first put on your shoes."

Chapter Thirty-Seven

Etta

Etta made a pot of coffee, and then she and Martha, as Leo's mother insisted she be called, spent a pleasant hour becoming acquainted. It had been so long since Etta chatted over coffee and cookies with a woman her age she'd nearly forgotten how easy it was to get lost in conversation. She and Martha discussed little things, like their favorite recipes, and serious things, such as their dismay over the war raging in Europe. Martha was more familiar with current events than she was. Etta's infrequent forays into town shielded her from much of what was happening in the world outside her little valley home. She soaked up the information, storing away snippets to share with Jennie or Claude later.

While the women talked, Myrtle, after asking what she could do to help, swept the floor and swished a feather duster over every piece of furniture in the house. Rags followed her and tried to ambush the broom bristles and the turkey feathers, but Myrtle didn't seem to mind. Even so, Etta said, "I can put Rags in the shed if he's being a pest. He usually spends his day with Mr. Ward. I'm sure he's wondering where his favorite person has gone."

Martha clicked her tongue on her teeth. "Poor little scamp. Yes, I'm sure he's confused by all the changes happening. I doubt he's bothering Myrtle, though. All my children love animals, and I've always regretted that they couldn't have a pet of their own. But we've never owned our own home. We've lived in houses provided by the churches Paul has pastored. I didn't feel comfortable bringing pets into what was, in essence, someone else's home."

Myrtle hung the duster on its hook, then crossed to the table and folded her hands in a prayerful position. "Mother, may I take Rags outside and play with him? I found a piece of chewed rope under the settee. I bet he'd fetch it if I threw it."

Martha laughed. "Go ahead, but stay close by." She watched Myrtle pick up the rope from the floor and head outside with Rags leaping at her hand, then turned to Etta. "Do you already have a house picked out in Cañon City?"

Etta shook her head, worry sneaking in. "No. Mr. Cambrie, the president of the Water Works Department, said he would store our furniture and pay for hotel rooms until we can find a place. But, to be honest, I don't know how we'll be able to rent a house. I haven't held a paying job since Claude and I got married, and now Claude's income will cease since we won't be paid for linewalking." Should she be so open with someone she'd only just met? Although their acquaintanceship was new, Martha had a way of putting one completely at ease. She went on, her gaze on the mug of coffee in front of her. "My sister and her husband offered us a room in their house, which would be fine if it were only Claude and me or Jennie and me, but all three of us?" She shook her head. "That's much less than ideal."

Martha delicately cleared her throat, and Etta looked up. The woman reached across the table and cupped her hand over Etta's. "I hope you won't think me forward, but Leo shared some of the troubles your husband has experienced. He asked Paul and me to pray for you. There's something about praying for people that opens our hearts to them, and I'd like to speak frankly with you. From a place of concern." She angled her head slightly, her fine eyebrows lifting. "May I?"

Etta wanted to hear what Mrs. Day would say. Without a moment's hesitation, Etta said, "Please."

"Leo expressed grave concerns about your husband's future ability to provide for your family unless he's delivered from the illness that has befallen him."

Such a kind way of phrasing the situation. Etta had wondered how people would react if they knew about Claude's mental state. At least the Day family didn't hold contempt. The realization gave her hope that others might be compassionate, as well.

"It's my understanding that this type of illness requires a doctor who specializes in psychiatry. Leo mentioned there is a psychiatric hospital in Pueblo. I presume you've looked into it?" Etta nodded. Martha patted Etta's hand. "And may I also presume you found the costs beyond your means?"

Martha's straightforward yet kind approach garnered Etta's complete trust. She sighed and admitted, "The evaluation alone is more than we could afford. A lengthy stay, which would most likely be recommended, is completely out of reach. We had to lay the idea to rest, although it was devastating to do so. Claude wants to get better, but he needs help. I keep praying for God to make the way for us, like He did for the children of Israel by dividing the Red Sea." When would He finally answer? Tears threatened, but she blinked them away. "I won't stop praying until Claude is my Claude again and Jennie has her daddy back."

For several seconds, Martha sat staring at Etta, her face pinched into a thoughtful frown. Then she sat up and huffed out a soft breath. "Etta, is it imperative that your family remains in Cañon City?"

Etta drew back. "Why do you ask?"

"A few months ago, a representative from the University of Denver spoke at our church about a new program being offered to train doctors in the field of psychotherapy. Are you familiar with the term?" She spoke in a rush, as though the words had lain dormant, waiting for an opportunity to be spilled. "The recognition that mental illness is actually a medical condition isn't new. The ancient Greeks acknowledged the connection. But it's taken time for the idea to gain popularity among doctors who treat patients with mental issues."

She leaned forward slightly, her eyes lively. "Two doctors named Sigmund Freud and Josef Breuer combined forces, so to speak, and are credited with formulating effective methods of psychotherapy."

Etta found the information interesting, but she was puzzled. "What does all this have to do with your question about us remaining in Cañon City?"

Martha laughed, covering her mouth with her hand. "Forgive me, Etta. Paul often teases me about getting overly excited about new ideas. You see, the program organizers are seeking patients to help their trainees hone their skills in psychotherapy. Treatment will be given under the instruction and supervision of a licensed psychotherapist, but there will be no charge to the patient."

Etta's mouth fell open. "Free? They would treat Claude for free?"

"If he qualifies for the program." Martha's eyes glowed with excitement. "Based on what Leo has shared with us, I believe he'd be accepted. Of course, it would mean relocating your family to Denver, but it might be worth it if Claude received the help he needs to, as you put it, be *your* Claude again."

Etta considered what Martha had told her. She'd lived most of her life in Cañon City. Her only remaining relatives beside Claude and Jennie worked and lived there. She'd never considered living anywhere else. Yet her scalp was tingling as if lightning had struck. Was God dividing her Red Sea?

Leo

Leo pointed ahead. "There it is." The words scraped past his dry throat. They'd done little talking on the trek up the ridge. He wanted to engage Jennie in conversation. How many more op-portunities would they have, especially if she moved into town? She wouldn't be at the cabin to join the excursions. If the site had been destroyed, Father would most likely want Leo to go back to Denver with him and Mother. But Daisy talked nonstop the first half mile, all of it to Jennie. Leo didn't have the heart to tell her to give someone else a chance to talk. Not on her birthday. By the time she'd run out of things to say, they'd been walking long enough they focused their energy on clambering up the steepest part of the ridge. Now here they were, within a stone's throw of the site. If there was still a site.

Daisy left Jennie's side and grabbed Leo's wrist with both hands. "What is it? Is it the bones?"

He offered a wobbly smile, hoping she wouldn't be disappointed. "It's the tent we used to protect the bones, Daisy. Do you see it?"

She squinted ahead. "You mean that wadded-up green thing?"

Leo laughed. He couldn't help it—she looked so disgusted. "That's exactly what I mean." He rose up on tiptoe and spotted someone moving around on the far side of the pile of crumpled canvas. Mr. DeWeece, already at work. Leo's pulse pattered. There must be something left to work on. "Come on. Let's go see what Mr. DeWeece is doing."

The four of them trudged forward, Leo torn between running and delaying. To his surprise, Jennie passed him and half trotted to the far side of the tent. He watched her face for a hint. She was always expressive. By her reaction, he'd know whether there was something worth salvaging.

She looked down, her eyes widened, and she clapped both hands over her mouth.

Leo stifled a groan. Elation or dismay? Which did the action mean?

Then she flung her arms outward and yelled to the sky, "Thank You!"

Somehow he knew to whom she spoke. He clasped Daisy's hand and took off at a clumsy run, pulling her along with him. They rounded the downed tent, and Leo laid eyes on the row of vertebrae. The rain had forced dirt down the hill and covered parts of what he'd exposed, but points signifying cervical or dorsal vertebrae remained visible.

Mr. DeWeece was on his knees, a brush in hand. He waved at Leo, then stood, laughing. "I'm so glad the tent was up before the storm blew in. When I got here, the cover was lying over the site like a mother robin spreading her wings across a nest. It doesn't look as if the hail battered it. Or, if it did, the canvas offered enough protection." He shook his head, his gaze drifting to the line of vertebrae. "To be honest, Leo, I feel we were granted a small miracle. As hard as the rain came down, the whole spine could have been buried by sludge. The bones we exposed could have been broken to bits by the hail. But here it is, seemingly intact, under a protective barrier of mud and canvas."

Leo couldn't stop smiling. He nodded. "It's . . . wonderful."

DeWeece laughed again and threw his arm around Leo's shoulders. "And now that you're here, we've got work to do. Unless"—he shot a glance at Father and Daisy—"you just wanted to show your father and sister the site." He gave Leo's shoulder a pat and dropped his arm. "It was a long walk for the little one. She's probably ready to go back."

Daisy bounced in place. "No! I want to find more bones. Bigger bones. Bones as big as an elephant!"

DeWeece chuckled. "Believe it or not, you'd have to line up six elephants end to end to be as long as one brontosaurus."

Daisy's eyes grew round, and her mouth fell open. "I would?"

The man nodded. "People wonder why we don't see living creatures anymore like the ones buried here on this ridge. Can you imagine how much food an animal so big would eat every day?"

"More than Leo, that's for sure," Daisy said with confidence, and everyone laughed.

"Definitely more than Leo." He crouched down to Daisy's level, his expression serious. "There probably wasn't enough food for these large creatures to eat, and they eventually died out. It's sad to think about an animal God created no longer living. And it isn't just the dinosaurs that aren't still here. There are other animals, such as the Dodo bird and a sea creature called Stellar's sea cow, that are also extinct."

Daisy's lips formed a sad pout. "What happened to them?"

DeWeece rubbed his finger under his nose, then glanced at Leo. "Well, people didn't do what they were supposed to. You see, when God gave man dominion over the animals He created, He meant for us to protect the animals—to take care of them. When we don't do what God expects of us, there are consequences. Sometimes the consequences mean an animal can't survive anymore. That's bad for the animal, but you know what? It's also bad for us."

Daisy tilted her head. "How?"

Father moved up closer to Leo as the businessman went on.

"We'll never be startled by a Dodo bird waddling out from the bushes or watch a Stellar's sea cow float in the ocean. The only way we even know they once existed is there are written reports about them and we have their skeletons to prove they were real." He put his arm around Daisy and drew her a little closer to the vertebrae forming a chunky picket fence in the dirt. "Your big brother is helping others know that dinosaurs were real. Maybe it will encourage people to take good care of the animals on the earth so we'll never have only bones to look at. We'll be able to enjoy seeing the living animal, flying or swimming or leaping from rock to rock on the mountainside, the way God designed them to live."

Daisy nodded, her pixie face pursed into a determined scowl. "I'll always take good care of animals. I promise."

DeWeece smiled. "I know you will." He straightened and held

out the wire brush. "Leo, do you want to help your sister uncover a bone?"

Jennie hurried close. "I'd like to uncover one, too. My family and I are moving from the cabin, so this is probably the last time I'll get to be up here. I'd like to have a hand in exposing the skeleton, even if it's just a tiny bit."

"Of course." DeWeece removed another brush from his pack and gave it to Jennie. He stepped aside as Jennie and Leo knelt on either side of Daisy. "So, you're moving to Cañon City, hmm?"

"Yes, sir."

"When?"

A sigh left Jennie's throat, one that held both longing and acceptance. "As soon as we get everything packed."

"I see."

Leo's senses went on alert. The man sounded a bit too nonchalant. He guided Daisy's hand in scraping away dirt, his ears tuned to DeWeece's voice.

"My friend Wilmer Cambrie asked if I'd have space in my warehouse for your family's belongings, but he didn't mention when the items would arrive."

Jennie shrugged. "In the next day or so, I reckon." She sat up, flipping dirt onto Daisy's hand. Daisy shook it loose and kept scraping. "I almost forgot . . . I'm working on the drawings of the individual bones Leo and I found. I still have three more to draw. Mama and I started packing, but I kept the bones away from our boxes. If you'd like to take the finished sketches and their matching bones home with you today, please come by our cabin. I'll have them ready for you."

Mr. DeWeece nodded. "Thank you, Jennie. I'll do that."

Jennie returned to brushing, and Father and Mr. DeWeece stood to the side and chatted softly. Leo soaked up every detail of the moment—the feel of his sister's small hand in his, the scent of moist earth stirred by the brushes, the sounds of wind and rasping tools and murmured voices. Occasionally, he glanced Jennie's way, and nearly every time, she peeked in his direction and caught him looking. With each exchange of glances, they smiled, she blushed, and his heart caught. He was going to miss her.

After a half hour or so of digging, Daisy sat back on her heels and swiped her hand over her forehead. "Father? I'm tired and thirsty and starting to feel cranky."

Leo stifled a snort of amusement. She might be only just-turned-ten years old, but she knew her own mind.

Father strode over and helped her up. "You're ready to leave?"

"Yes, sir." She yawned, then shook her head hard, making her wind-tossed blond curls flop. "When we get back to the hotel, I would like some cake."

Father's chortle rumbled. "I believe that can be arranged." He looked at Leo. "Are you staying?"

Leo had no idea he'd be given a choice. He was tempted to stay, but this was Daisy's birthday. She wanted to spend it with him. He should go. He suspected that he and Father would take turns carrying Daisy down to the Wards' cabin. He stood and brushed off his knees. "No, I'll go with you." Jennie stood, too, and Leo asked, "Are you coming?"

"Yes. Mama needs my help. I should go back." She sent a lingering look at the exposed bones. "Mr. DeWeece, I hope I'll have the chance to draw it all when you've uncovered the whole thing."

The man took the brush from her hand, then squeezed her shoulder. "You will. I'll see to it." He smiled. "I can't finish the article without my illustrator's help." He bid them farewell, knelt next to the bones, and returned to work.

Daisy yawned again. "Let's go, Leo." He took her hand. Father took the other, and then Jennie fell in step next to Leo. Together, they headed down the ridge.

Chapter Thirty-Eight

Jennie

Jennie was amazed at how much of the distance Daisy walked. She possessed determination. She allowed her father or Leo to piggyback her for short stretches, but then she wanted down to go on her own. Jennie decided she was small but mighty, and she hoped the little girl would always remember her tenth birthday. Not only the miles she traversed, but the things Mr. DeWeece told her, the experience of exposing millennia-old bones, and sharing the experience with her big brother.

As their little band neared the cabin, the sound of laughter carried on the breeze. At first she thought she was hearing the workers, but the tone was too light and airy for men's hearty guffaws. Then she recognized Mama's sweet laugh. A smile tugged at her lips. Mama and Mrs. Day must be having a good time together. She was happy. Mama needed friends as badly as Jennie did.

She jogged the final yards and found the cabin door propped open. The women were sitting at the table, napkins dotted with cookie crumbs and empty coffee mugs between them. Mama looked over as Jennie came in, and she held out one arm. Jennie pattered across the floor and hugged Mama's neck. Mama stood, keeping her arm looped around Jennie's waist.

"Sweetheart, I'm glad you're back. Take the washbasin to my room and change into one of my dresses. We're going into town this evening."

Jennie reared back. "We are? But . . . but what about the packing? What about Rags? What . . ." She ran out of what-abouts.

Mama laughed again, the sound music to Jennie's ears. "Rags will be fine in the shed. We're going to—"

Leo, his father, and Daisy came in, and Daisy scampered to her mother. The little girl started to say something, but Mrs. Day put her finger over the child's mouth, and Daisy pursed her lips. She might have even held her breath.

"—have a late dinner at the hotel with the Day family," Mama went on as if no interruption had occurred. "If Prime and Delia are available, I'll ask them to join us. There's much we need to discuss."

Jennie blinked at her. "There is?"

"Yes, there is." She sighed, a happy, relief-laden sigh. Then she released Jennie and flicked her fingers at her. "Hurry, now. The other mountain climbers need to freshen up, too, and there's not much time."

Jennie hurried through a wash, her thoughts tumbling. What was Mama up to? Why did they need to include Uncle Prime and Aunt Delia? And what about Daddy? It didn't feel fair to leave him out of the evening's activities.

Mrs. Day sat with Mama for the train ride to town. The girls crowded onto a bench with Mr. Day, which left Jennie with Leo. With each rocking motion, their shoulders bumped. Even though the connection aggravated her bruise, she didn't try to move away. If they would soon part, she wanted to make as many memories with him as possible. Even ones as silly as bumping shoulders on a rocking, noisy train car.

Uncle Prime was at the hotel, overseeing the filling of water barrels for the guests' bathing needs. With the water pipeline closed, none of the spigots in the hotel produced water. He was too busy to join them for dinner, but he telephoned Aunt Delia, and she came.

Reverend Day ordered the special—roast duck, mashed yams, buttered green peas, and rolls with an assortment of jams—for everyone, but he let Daisy choose the dessert. She wanted chocolate cake, and the server promised to reserve the biggest piece in the cooler for her. They chatted as they ate the delicious dinner but said nothing of great importance. Jennie found herself getting impatient. Why had Mama made such a big to-do about including Aunt Delia if they were going to talk only about the latest fashions and the many ways the pipeline's break affected the hotel's efficiency?

By the time the server delivered Daisy's cake to the table, Jennie was a bundle of nerves. They sang to the little girl, who beamed in delight, and then Reverend Day laid his arm across the back of Daisy's chair and turned a serious look on her.

"Daisy, we've had a very nice day and a very nice dinner. You received many nice gifts, and you are about to eat the most beautiful slice of cake I've ever seen. You've had a good birthday celebration, yes?"

The child sat with her fork gripped in her fist, her eyes glued on her father's face. "Yes, sir."

"Good. Now I need you to be very quiet and allow the grown-ups to talk. You are not to interrupt or ask questions. And later, you are not to repeat anything you hear us say." He glanced at Myrtle. "That goes for you, too, young lady." Myrtle gave a somber nod. He kissed Daisy's forehead. "Eat your cake."

Daisy dove in.

Reverend Day held his hand to his wife. "Martha, you are the planner of this entire chain of events, so please . . ."

"Thank you, dear." Mrs. Day sent a smile around the table and began to talk. She spoke about a program at the university offering psychoanalysis sessions for no cost to the patient. She talked about the variety of job opportunities for women in the city—everything from store clerk to seamstress to bakery worker. She talked about the good schools, including their art, music, and athletic programs. She talked about a parishioner of their church, a kindly gentleman who owned three apartment buildings. "He often bemoans the difficulty of finding suitable tenants," she said with a little shake of her head, "and I know he'd welcome a respectable, responsible family like the Wards."

Jennie listened, trying to understand the purpose of this information windfall, and suddenly it all clicked in her mind. She gasped. "Mama, are we—"

"Etta, are you moving to Denver?" Aunt Delia spoke over Jennie, her voice shrill.

Mama immediately patted her sister's hand. "Delia, are you listening? Have you heard all the reasons why Denver would be a good choice for our family?"

Jennie, on Aunt Delia's other side, leaned forward and caught Mama's eye.

"I don't understand. You've never talked about moving to Denver. Why now?"

Mrs. Day *tsk-tsk*ed, her face wreathed with regret. "Oh, dear, I'm afraid I've upset everyone. That wasn't my intention. But after praying for Claude, Etta, and Jennie for so many weeks and asking God to direct their paths, it seemed as if He was carving a pathway for them to follow and it led to Denver. If I've offended you with my zealous appeal, please forgive me."

Jennie couldn't find it in her heart to be angry with Leo's mother. She hadn't acted in malice—she'd only taken Jennie by surprise. And Aunt Delia, too. Jennie leaned sideways and brushed shoulders with her aunt. "There's nothing to forgive, Mrs. Day. Right, Aunt Delia?"

Aunt Delia nodded stiffly, but her expression remained flustered.

Mama cleared her throat. "Delia, no decisions have been made. I wouldn't make such life-impacting changes without talking to

Claude. But after praying with Martha this afternoon, I do think this is a good option for us. The Days even offered to let Claude and me stay in Leo's room until I locate a job and an apartment opens up. Don't you see?"

Aunt Delia hung her head. "I'm sorry for being such a baby, Etta. But you . . . you're all I have left of family. You've always been close by. It's hard to imagine you so many miles from Prime and me."

Suddenly Leo sat up. "Wait a minute. If you've offered the Wards the use of my room, does this mean you aren't going to insist I go home for the rest of the summer?"

Jennie hadn't even considered how the invitation displaced Leo from his house. But thinking about it now sent a shaft of joy through the center of her heart. She looked at Reverend Day, her pulse skittering, and waited for him to confirm what she was hoping.

"Son . . ." The reverend lowered his head for a moment, then peered past Daisy, who was making a terrible mess of her cake. A slow smile lifted the corners of his lips. "Your friend Mr. DeWeece made a valid point this afternoon. When we don't do as God directs, we suffer consequences, and often those consequences affect more than the one who strays. God has clearly directed you to the study of paleontology. I was wrong to push you down a route of my choosing. Stubborn pride inspired my determination. But watching you today and hearing how Mr. DeWeece has been impacted by your determination to align your findings with biblical truths humbled me. I won't stand in your way anymore. I will cheer you on."

Leo pushed his chair back and rounded the table. He stopped next to his father's chair and stuck out his hand. "Thank you, sir."

Reverend Day stood and took Leo's hand. Then he pulled Leo into a bear hug of an embrace. For a moment, Leo stood with his arms limp, as if too shocked to react. He had once told Jennie that his father wasn't a demonstrative man. But Leo was now on the receiving end of the biggest, tightest, most public hug she had ever seen, and it came from his father. After a few seconds' pause, Leo threw his arms around his father's neck, and the two men rocked back and forth, patting each other on the back.

The view went blurry—Jennie was looking through a sheen of tears. She'd prayed for Leo's father to be happy with his son's career choice. God had answered. Were the suggestions Mrs. Day made also God's answers to their prayers? The thought of being in a big city full of strangers unnerved her, but at least they'd have the friends around this table. Maybe moving to Denver wouldn't be so bad.

The men separated and settled into their chairs again. Jennie wiped her eyes and turned to Mama. "If you believe God is directing us to Denver, I'll go without a fuss. He knows best. Yes?"

Mama released a happy sigh. "Yes, He does." Then she sobered. "But before we make travel plans, we must get your daddy's agreement."

Reverend Day cleared his throat. "Please allow me to talk to Mr. Ward. I have some experience in counseling parishioners. He might be more willing to listen to a stranger."

Jennie remembered how unresistingly Daddy had gone to Dr. Whiteside's office with the men Mr. Cambrie sent out. Reverend Day might get through to Daddy better than she or Mama could. Except . . .

She leaned past Leo toward the preacher. "Sir? If you want to get Daddy's attention, ask the server to wrap a piece of pound cake with strawberries and take it along. Daddy can't resist it."

Mrs. Day clapped her hands together and laughed. "What a coincidence! We have a strawberry patch in our backyard, and I bake pound cake every Saturday for our fellowship meals after Sunday service at church."

Leo winked at her, and Jennie sat back, shaking her head in

amazement. She almost thought she heard a wry chuckle drift from the heavens. She'd called out to the Lord, waited patiently . . . mostly, and He had answered her cries in the most unexpected ways. Daddy would agree to go to Denver—she knew he would. But there was still one more problem yet to be solved. How would she be able to draw the dinosaur skeleton for Mr. DeWeece if she was in Denver?

Daisy tugged her father's sleeve, and he looked at her. She rasped in a whisper that carried across the table to Jennie's ears. "Father, if Mr. and Mrs. Ward are going to sleep in Leo's room, does that mean Jennie will sleep in me and Myrtle's room?"

"That should be 'Myrtle's and my room,'" the reverend said.

"Myrtle's and my room?" Daisy sent a shy smile at Jennie. "Because I want her to share my bed."

Myrtle released a little huff. "My bed is bigger. She can share with me."

Jennie's heart warmed at their unselfishness. Fondness swelled for every member of Leo's family. When she'd prayed for friends, she hadn't expected a whole group.

Reverend Day cleared his throat. "That's kind of you girls, but I believe Jennie's mother has something else in mind for Jennie."

Jennie whipped her attention to Mama. She did? What other change was coming?

Chapter Thirty-Nine

Jennie

Reverend Day didn't divulge what he said to Daddy when he visited him at Dr. Whiteside's office after dinner on Daisy's birthday, but it was effective. On the last Saturday of July—only two days after the Reverend and Mrs. Day, Myrtle, and Daisy boarded the train for their return trip to Denver—Jennie told Mama and Daddy goodbye at the station.

Jennie hugged Daddy, and then the conductor helped him board while Jennie and Mama shared a longer goodbye on the boardwalk. Mama's hug was especially tight, proving how hard it was for her to leave Jennie behind. A piece of Jennie's heart was breaking, but she knew they'd made the right decision. Someone needed to stay behind and arrange shipment of their belongings when they'd found an apartment. Mama offered to stay, but Jennie insisted that Mama and Daddy should be together. The few days of separation while Daddy stayed with Dr. Whiteside was awful for both of them. How would they survive potentially weeks apart? Besides, her staying in Cañon City would allow her to keep the promise she'd made to Mr. DeWeece.

"Be a good girl for Aunt Delia and Uncle Prime," Mama said while rocking Jennie, her voice tearful.

"I will, Mama."

"And check on the chickens when you're out near the cabin. See that the workmen give them fresh water every day."

"I will."

"And make sure Rags behaves himself at your aunt and uncle's place. Don't let him get into mischief."

Jennie swallowed a knot of half sorrow, half amusement. "Don't worry, Mama."

Mama released a heavy sigh, her warm breath brushing Jennie's ear. "The Days have a telephone, and Delia said you can call as often as you want to."

Jennie kissed her mother's soft cheek. "And you can call me. Leo says talking on the phone is like sitting across the table from each other. Before we know it, I'll be in Denver, too."

Aunt Delia touched Mama's back. "Etta, the conductor's checking his watch, and he looks grumpy. You'd better go."

Mama delivered three noisy smacks in a row on Jennie's face and stepped back, sniffling. "All right, I'm going." Then she pointed at Aunt Delia. "Take good care of my little girl."

Aunt Delia captured Mama in a quick hug. "You know we will. Now, go, before I dissolve into a puddle of tears."

Mama boarded the train, paused on the landing for one more tear-wet smile and blown kiss, then disappeared into the car. Aunt Delia slid her arm around Jennie's waist and they stayed on the boardwalk, waving, until the train rolled past and the tail end of the caboose rolled out of sight. Then, arm in arm, they headed for the hotel, moving slowly, the heels of their pointy-toed shoes clicking a funereal beat in unison on the sidewalk.

Neither of them spoke for the first block, and then Aunt Delia sighed. "Be honest, Jennie. Any regrets about staying here for the rest of the summer?"

"Only one." Jennie peeked at the toes of her shoes. "Mama said I can't wear my work boots in town. Do you have Epsom salts? I'm probably going to need them."

Their joined laughter chased away the remaining vestige of tears.

Although the changes came quickly, they fell into place so neatly

Jennie couldn't help but believe they'd all been orchestrated by Someone who knew what He was doing. She settled in well with her aunt and uncle, and even Rags seemed content in their fenced backyard during the day and sleeping at the foot of Jennie's bed each night. She worked at the hotel in the mornings, readying rooms for guests, and spent her afternoons at the dig site with Leo and a team of experienced excavators hired by Mr. Figgins from the museum in Denver.

Mr. DeWeece agreed that this discovery shouldn't be stored in his warehouse. When all the bones were recovered, they would be shipped to Denver and reassembled there for visitors to enjoy. Mr. Figgins was already planning a big celebration for when the skeleton was ready for exhibit and had told Mr. DeWeece, Leo, and Jennie they would be his special guests. Jennie was a little nervous about being included, but she was so happy for Leo. She'd gladly go and support his first significant paleontological discovery.

The days slipped by one by one, filled with work, uncovering bones, sketching, chats with her aunt and uncle, playtime with Rags, and long talks with Leo. Full days. Happy days, even though she missed her parents. The telephone calls helped, especially when such cheeriness carried through the line. According to Mama, Daddy was doing better in Denver.

"I don't know if it's because we're on a plain and there are hours of sunshine each day, or because we're surrounded by people, or because he no longer feels guilty about you walking the line in his place," Mama said when she and Jennie spoke in mid-August, "but he seems to be sneaking out of his doldrums. The psychotherapy program coordinators approved his participation, and he'll start therapy the seventh of September. I believe it will bring even bigger changes." Mama's voice broke on a happy sob. "Keep praying, Jennie. Rejoice in hope."

"I will, Mama. I promise."

Then Mama told her she'd found a job—working in the college

cafeteria. Mama laughingly said, "Warn Leo that I'll be able to keep an eye on him, so he needs to behave himself."

When Jennie passed the message to Leo, he feigned concern, then laughed. "The campus will be a lot friendlier with Etta Ward there every day. I'll enjoy seeing her. I really like your mother."

And Jennie liked Leo more every day. Sometimes she worried she was growing too accustomed to his company. When they went to Denver, he would be at college and she in high school. They wouldn't have these hours together each day. His sudden absence might send her into melancholy. At night, in the privacy of her room at Aunt Delia's house, she pondered a serious question. Did she love him? Mama's comment about Jennie being at a tumultuous age and Leo's solemn words about emotional feelings sometimes being fickle rolled in her mind and fed uncertainty. But one thing she knew without a doubt—her favorite hours of the day were those spent in his company.

They met after each workday in the hotel lobby, rode the train to the footbridge, hiked up to the site, and helped the excavators, who had set up camp at the dig site. She savored working side by side with Leo, appreciated his patient way of answering her questions, and basked in his sincere praise of her many renderings. Every evening, they had supper together at the hotel. They always found something to talk about and never grew weary of each other's company. She once asked if he was jealous of how much progress took place on the ridge while he was working in the kitchen. He'd looked at her in surprise, then shook his head.

"History is being uncovered, Jennie. It's a delight to go out each day and see how much more of the animal's skeleton is revealed." His eyes turned dreamy. "One of these days, we'll top that ridge and view its entire length, from its nose to the tip of its tail. What an amazing day that will be!" He grinned and waggled his eyebrows. "I just might turn a cartwheel."

She couldn't resist teasing, "And tumble all the way to the bottom of the mountain?"

He winked. "It'd be worth every bruise."

Mr. DeWeece accompanied them on Saturdays. Jennie's fondness for the businessman increased over those summer weeks. He always asked about her parents and seemed genuinely glad when she gave positive reports. Clearly, he cared about preserving the past. Why else would he spend so much time and energy on digging up old bones? But he also cared about the present and the years to come. She lost count of how many times he encouraged her to continue using her artistic skills.

"I see a bright future for you as an illustrator, Jennie," he told her the last Saturday of August on their hike up the mountain. "Even if the magazine doesn't purchase the article and sketches of this discovery, don't let it discourage you. Keep honing your skill. A gift like yours shouldn't be shoved in a drawer and forgotten."

She hid his words away in the corner of her heart and treasured them, just as she treasured the waning summer days with Leo.

On that Saturday, when they reached the ridge, they found the excavation team sitting around the camp. Mr. DeWeece checked his timepiece, then sent a frown across the group. "Why aren't you working yet? You're wasting precious daylight hours."

Hank, the man who served as organizer of the dig, pushed his hat to the back of his head and flashed a huge grin. "It's done. Take a look."

Jennie and Leo exchanged a startled glance, then trailed Mr. DeWeece along the entire length of the exposed spine. Hank followed, pointing to various parts of the skeleton as they went.

"The lower jaw is missing, and all that's left of his legs is one femur."

DeWeece shook his head. "We have an ulna, a radius, and one complete foot. We found those pieces scattered over the ridge."

Hank arched a brow. "That so? Well, good. Scavengers must've gotten to some of the bones over the years. Or people carted off pieces. We can't really know." He pointed. "As you can see, the two middle ribs are snapped in half, but Mr. Figgins will have someone fuse them together again." He put his hands on his hips and looked up and down the length. "Even missing its legs, it's quite a find. The entire spine is all lined up nice and neat, from the head to—"

Leo and Jennie chorused, "The tip of the tail," with him, drowning out his voice.

Hank laughed. "You got it."

Jennie teasingly poked Leo with her elbow. "Well?"

His gaze tracing to the line of vertebrae, Leo said, "Well what?"

"Where's that cartwheel you promised?"

He burst out laughing and grabbed her in a hug. It lasted only the length of three heartbeats, but oh, how glorious to be held in his arms!

Hank winked at Jennie. "All right, Miss Illustrator. Get to illustrating. We can't label and remove these bones until you're done."

While Leo removed Jennie's drawing materials from his pack, Mr. DeWeece slung his arm around Jennie's shoulders. "Make sure you get all the details exactly right on those chevron-looking bones on the tail." He lobbed a grin at Leo. "What have we got here, Leo?"

Leo stared at Mr. DeWeece, his mouth hanging open. He rasped, "Double beam."

"That's right. Double beam." Mr. DeWeece turned his smile on Jennie. "Title the drawing *Diplodocus*."

Twelve Months Later
Leo

Leo fiddled with his string tie, wishing he could remove it and stick it in his pocket. But as a guest of honor on this auspicious occasion, he needed to maintain a formal bearing. If he'd been told a year ago he'd have to sit on a raised platform with Mr. DeWeece and Jennie and be gawked at, he might not have admitted his part in locating the diplodocus spine. He hoped he didn't sweat through his suit before the evening was over.

At least a hundred people milled around the curtain-shielded display in the center of the room. Guests sipped punch from glass goblets, partook of ridiculously tiny sandwiches and pickled mushrooms, and visited in hushed tones while a half dozen stringed instruments serenaded them from the corner of the makeshift stage. Leo's college professors were there, as well as community leaders, curiosity seekers, and even the mayor. His and Jennie's parents were stationed near the front edge of the stage—all four of them, each beaming with pride. Last summer, he wouldn't have imagined Father and Mr. Ward being in attendance at such an event. Their presence proved God's amazing ability to heal.

On his right, Mr. DeWeece sat with his legs crossed, his linked hands resting on his knee, and his foot gently bobbing to the beat of the classical piece. Leo wished he could be as nonplussed as the Cañon City businessman appeared. But then, Mr. DeWeece was accustomed to pomp and circumstance. Leo couldn't help hoping it would be his last such event. He didn't mind digging in the dirt, but this kind of gathering was, as Daisy might put it, too much fuss and feathers.

Leo risked a peek at Jennie, who sat primly on his left. She, too, appeared calm on the surface. But a closer look revealed that her gloved hands quivered in her lap. He longed to place his hand over hers as a mute sign of support, but this was no place for a display of affection. He would save that for later, when the crowd had cleared and the two of them were alone.

Amazing how grown-up she looked with her light-brown hair piled in a pouf at the crown of her head. Her parents must have splurged on a new outfit for the evening, because he'd never seen her wear the ruffly cream-colored shirtwaist and dark-green skirt with— What did Myrtle call it? Oh, yes, a flounce at the hem. But her familiar pointy-toed shoes peeped from under the flounce. He swallowed a smile. She hated those shoes. But he liked them. They slowed her pace and gave him extra minutes to walk while holding her hand in the bend of his arm.

He loved walking with Jennie's hand in the bend of his arm.

Mr. Figgins emerged from the crowd and stepped up onto the stage. The musicians' conductor brought the music to a stop, and people all around the room ceased talking and aimed their faces to the stage. Mr. Figgins thanked everyone for coming, showering extra attention on the mayor and members of the press. The long-awaited reveal of the complete diplodocus spine at the Denver museum had brought newsmen from all over the state. Several cameras flashed while Mr. Figgins delivered a speech about the museum's new wing dedicated to Jurassic specimens.

Then he shared how the discovery of the latest and largest specimen to date came about, pacing back and forth at the front of the stage as he spoke. He drew to a stop and held his arms out in a sheepish gesture. "But I know you didn't come tonight to listen to me blather on." Soft laughter rolled through the crowd. "You came to see *Diplodocus*!" He said the name the way someone might announce the title of a Broadway play.

Applause and cheers rose from the gathered spectators.

"But first allow me to introduce the team who discovered this amazing artifact and, therefore, are responsible for tonight's celebration." He swung his arm toward the three of them. "Mr. William Dallas DeWeece . . ."

Mr. DeWeece stood, as they'd been instructed to do by the event coordinator, and gave a slight bow. The audience politely clapped.

"Mr. Leo Day . . ."

Leo managed to rise and make a stiff bow. More applause.

"And Miss Jennie Ward."

Jennie stood and curtsied, blushing a delightful shade of pink as people clapped.

Then, as planned, Mr. DeWeece, Leo, and Jennie walked forward and stood next to Mr. Figgins. Leo's nervousness increased with every inch he advanced. They'd waited long months for the bones to be transferred to Denver, reassembled, and positioned for display. During those months, Mr. Figgins laid the groundwork for revealing the find to the public on the same day *The Scientific Monthly* issue with Mr. DeWeece's article released. Jennie's drawing of the diplodocus skeleton filled the issue's cover, and sketches of individual bones peppered the article. This grand opening had stirred excitement and anticipation for weeks throughout the entire state, and it seemed he'd waited a lifetime as all the pieces came together. Now it was here. Would people expect more than what the excavation team had uncovered? Would they be disappointed?

Mr. Figgins snapped his fingers, and four men in black suits moved to assigned locations at both ends of the curtains. A hush fell, as reverent as the one Leo experienced the day he came upon the first exposed vertebrae. He held his breath, his gaze locked on the curtains. A small hand slipped into his—Jennie's. He gave it a gentle squeeze, grateful for the contact. Mr. Figgins made a downward sweep of his arm, and the men yanked the ropes.

The curtains fell in a puddled heap at the base of the skeleton. For three full seconds, no one made a sound, and then raucous applause exploded. Leo's breath whooshed out. From every corner of the room, camera bulbs flashed. Chatter erupted. Mr. DeWeece pounded Leo on the back with such exuberance that Leo lost his grip on Jennie's hand. The man stepped past him and swept Jennie into a hug. Then he hopped down from the stage and moved through the crowd, shaking hands and posing for photographs.

Jennie looked at Leo, her eyes wide. "Do we have to do that, too?"

He leaned close to her ear. "Would you rather get out of here?"

She nodded. He took her hand and led her along the back of the stage, behind the stringed orchestra, which had begun playing again, and out the doors into the museum's lobby. He closed the door behind them and heaved a sigh of relief.

"If I ever questioned if I should become a preacher, I now know without a doubt it's not for me. I don't ever want to be in front of a crowd like that again."

She released a trickling laugh. "I guess you're going to have to change your ambitions from being a famous paleontologist, then." She placed her palm against his suit front, directly over his heart. "I know it was overwhelming, but truly, Leo, I'm so proud of you. You followed the path God carved for you, and He honored your obedience."

"Thank you, Jennie." Leo lowered Jennie's hand from his chest lest she become alarmed by the rapid thud of his heartbeat. "I'd like to thoroughly examine the display, but not with everyone else in there. Do you mind waiting until the room clears? Then we can go back in."

She shrugged. "I don't mind. But what about our folks?"

The celebration organizers weren't the only ones who'd made arrangements for the evening's events. "I told them we might need to stay around afterward for photographs and for them to go on home. I'll hire a carriage to take us when we're done."

Her smile approved the plan.

They stood off to the side and visited in the easy way they'd developed over the past year. It would be wonderful to have her on the college campus with him when school started again in a week. Thanks to the payment from the magazine for her illustrations and the tuition discount bestowed on employees of the college, Jennie's freshman year was fully covered—a true gift from God.

People filed out of the exhibit room in pairs or small groups, and finally Mr. Figgins emerged. He scanned the area, and his gaze landed on Leo. He strode over.

"Mr. Day, I hope we did you and your dinosaur proud this evening."

"You did. Thank you." Leo shook the man's hand. "The event was a real success. But"—he scratched his cheek—"with so many people around the skeleton, Jennie and I didn't have a chance to really see the display. May we go in now?"

"Of course. I'll be in my office, working on reports for quite a while, so take your time."

Leo took Jennie's hand. "Ready?"

She nodded and they entered the exhibit room. Electric lights glowed, illuminating the entire sixty-six-foot-long spine with its single leg suspended by wire from the ceiling. Leo led her slowly across the room and stopped beneath the leg bone that had caught his attention his first day in Cañon City a little over a year ago.

With his eyes locked on the bone, he pulled in a big breath and sighed it out. "Think about it, Jennie . . . Even before this dinosaur walked the earth, God already knew that on June 4, 1915, Leo Day would look out a train window and see Jennie Ward standing on a pipeline formed of redwood staves, waving a bone . . ." He shifted his gaze to her sweetly upturned face. "And his life would never be the same."

Turning slightly, he lifted his hand and gently cupped her cheek. "There's something else He's known since the beginning of time . . . that I would fall in love with you." His lips twitched, a smile of remembrance tugging. "I think I've loved you since you gave me a sassy grin and called me 'college boy.' "

Tears swam in her eyes, highlighting tiny flecks of gold in her chocolate-colored irises. He stroked her cheekbone with his thumb, relishing the velvet softness of her skin. "I can't imagine going through the rest of my life without you. But you're still very young, and you'll be on a college campus soon, with lots of other boys who will no doubt also be captivated by your beauty and spunk. I don't want to presume upon you or rush you into something you're—"

"I love you, too."

His thumb stilled. He bent his knees slightly and peered directly into her eyes. "You do? You're sure?"

She slipped her fingers through his and drew his hand from her face. "I've never been more sure of anything in my life." She wrapped his hand between hers and held it beneath her chin. "And I can't imagine going through life without your prayers, your encouragement, your teasing grin . . ." She laughed, the most beautiful sound in the world. "I love everything about you, Leo. God designed you to be the other half to my whole."

He pulled her hands close and kissed tips of her gloved fingers. "Then, Miss Jennie Ward, would you consent to becoming my wife?"

The tears hovering on her lower lashes spilled with her exuberant nod.

He tipped his face as she rose up on tiptoe, and he placed his lips on hers, softly, tenderly, savoring the first physical expression of his love. Then he stepped back and began shrugging out of his jacket.

"You know, Jennie, I thought finding the complete spine of Mr. Diplodocus would be the highlight of my life."

She watched him, her face pursed in puzzlement.

"But I was wrong." He folded his jacket and handed it to her.

She draped it over her arm, still staring at him with confusion crinkling her brow.

"Your *yes* is my highlight, the fulfillment of the heartfelt hope I've harbored for the past year, and I have to celebrate." He moved a few feet away, braced himself, then turned three perfect cartwheels in a row. As he landed the final turn, he threw his arms wide and crowed, "Ta-da!" The sound hit the tin-tiled ceiling and echoed back at them.

Jennie burst into laughter. She tossed his coat aside and ran to him in her silly pointy-toed shoes. He caught her in an embrace and rocked side to side, laughing with her. Then he leaned back and took her hand, smiling into her precious face. "What do you want to do now?"

"I believe you promised me a carriage ride."

He silently vowed to never neglect a promise made to Jennie. "Indeed I did."

She slipped free of his light grasp and double stepped in reverse, the click of her heels loud on the marble floor.

He scooped up his discarded coat. "Hey, where're you going?"

"To summon a carriage, of course." An impish twinkle lit her eyes. "Try to keep up, college boy."

Laughing, Leo tossed the coat over his shoulder and caught up to her in two long strides. He deposited a kiss on her teasing smile, then slipped his arm around her waist. "Don't worry about me, Miss Mountain Goat. I'll always be by your side."

Readers Guide

1. When Jennie's prayers seemingly went unanswered, she stopped talking to God. How can we hold on to faith in seasons when God seems silent?

2. Despite her husband changing into someone far different from the man she married, Etta remained faithful and loving to Claude. Why do you think she didn't abandon the marriage? Was her choice the best one? Why do you feel that way?

3. Leo feels like a failure for breaking away from the family tradition of ministry. How were his feelings valid? Define ministry, then contemplate the following: Is ministry limited to ministers? Explain your reasoning.

4. Claude is trapped in depression. Although much more is known today about mental illness than was known in 1915, a stigma still exists with varied opinions about its causes and treatments. Etta sadly muses that people would be more sympathetic toward a broken-down wagon than toward a broken-down man. Why is it so hard for some people to be compassionate toward the mentally ill? How can we be supportive to those who suffer from depression and other mental illnesses?

5. When Jennie confesses to Leo that her hope is gone, he advises her to stand in the echo of her mother's hope. Have you ever been inspired by someone else's faith in the face of conflict? Share how their example affected your faith journey.

6. Claude is often unreasonable, which tempts Jennie to disobey him. Yet she believes she is to honor her father and mother. How do we honor a parent who is unreasonable or, in our opinion, unworthy of honor? When, if ever, would it be appropriate not to honor a parent?

7. Jennie frequently teases Leo that he sounds like a preacher. Leo ponders how childhood lessons subconsciously linger. What childhood lessons, whether positive or negative, linger with you? How do we know which childhood influences we should hold on to and which we should release?

8. Leo tells Jennie, "I suppose whatever we take in will also come out." How can we ascertain we're taking in things that are honorable and helpful as opposed to hurtful or harmful for us physically, emotionally, or spiritually?

9. Jennie complains that despite her many prayers, nothing is changing, and Leo disagrees. He says, "In you, Jennie. [God's] changing you. I've seen you exercise patience and kindness during trying times with your daddy. I've watched hope unfold in you." Have you ever observed someone's faith blossom in the midst of a heartbreaking challenge or experienced it for yourself? How can we let difficult times make us better rather than bitter?

Acknowledgments

Thanks first of all to my husband, *Don,* for surprising me with a belated thirty-fifth-anniversary trip to Cañon City at the tail end of a pandemic. When I spotted the remnants of that battered redwood pipeline from the window of our train, a story seed was planted. I've had great fun watching the seed grow to full bloom.

I have to give *Daddy* some major props, too. His knowledge about dinosaurs and his belief that science and the Bible align rather than conflict guided me as I crafted Leo's character. Thanks, Dad, for being my first teacher and for always encouraging your children's dreams. You're the best father a kid could ask for.

What would I do without my writing friend *Connie*'s willingness to read through a manuscript and offer suggestions for improvement? Writing is a solitary activity, but I don't have to feel alone thanks to her support. This Lucy appreciates her Ethel!

While I'm thanking people who help on this writing journey, heartfelt thanks to my agent, *Tamela Hancock Murray,* for twenty years of guidance. You're tops! And I so appreciate the *editorial team at WaterBrook,* who works with me to make the stories shine. I am blessed by some of the best in the industry, for sure.

Most important, deepest gratitude and awe to *God,* who guides my fingertips in crafting stories of the hope we can possess when we place our lives in His capable hands. I cannot imagine navigating this life without His Spirit's presence, His bolstering strength, and His endless grace. May any praise or glory be reflected to my heavenly Father.

About the Author

KIM VOGEL SAWYER is a highly acclaimed bestselling author with more than 1.5 million books in print in seven different languages. Her titles have earned numerous accolades, including the ACFW Carol Award, the Inspirational Reader's Choice Award, and the Gayle Wilson Award of Excellence. Kim and her retired military husband, Don, live in central Kansas, where she continues to write gentle stories of hope. She enjoys spending time with her three daughters and her grandchildren.

Also from bestselling, award-winning author
KIM VOGEL SAWYER

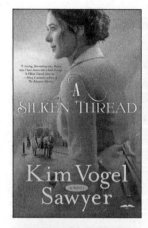
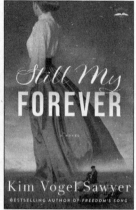
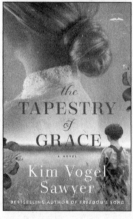
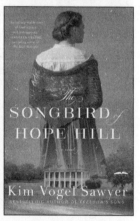

Kim Vogel Sawyer offers uplifting and inspiring fiction
that is grounded in biblical truth. With meticulous research,
vivid storytelling, and themes of hope, redemption, and
faith, these stories offer something for every reader.

Learn more about Kim's books at waterbrookmultnomah.com